THE REGENCY LORDS & LADIES COLLECTION

Glittering Regency Love Affairs from your favourite historical authors.

THE REGENCY LORDS & LADIES COLLECTION

Available from the
Regency Lords & Ladies Large Print Collection

The Larkswood Legacy by Nicola Cornick
My Lady's Prisoner by Elizabeth Ann Cree
Lady Clairval's Marriage by Paula Marshall
A Scandalous Lady by Francesca Shaw
A Poor Relation by Joanna Maitland
Mistress or Marriage? by Elizabeth Rolls
Rosalyn and the Scoundrel by Anne Herries
Nell by Elizabeth Bailey
Kitty by Elizabeth Bailey
Miss Verey's Proposal by Nicola Cornick
Prudence by Elizabeth Bailey
An Honourable Thief by Anne Gracie
Jewel of the Night by Helen Dickson
The Wedding Gamble by Julia Justiss
Ten Guineas on Love by Claire Thornton
Honour's Bride by Gayle Wilson
One Night with a Rake by Louise Allen
A Matter of Honour by Anne Herries
Tavern Wench by Anne Ashley
The Sweet Cheat by Meg Alexander
The Rebellious Bride by Francesca Shaw
Carnival of Love by Helen Dickson
The Reluctant Marchioness by Anne Ashley
Miranda's Masquerade by Meg Alexander
Dear Deceiver by Mary Nichols
Lady Sarah's Son by Gayle Wilson
One Night of Scandal by Nicola Cornick
The Rake's Mistress by Nicola Cornick
Lady Knightley's Secret by Anne Ashley
Lady Jane's Physician by Anne Ashley

ROSALYN AND THE SCOUNDREL

Anne Herries

M&B™

All the characters in this book have no existence outside the imagination of the author, and have no relation whatsoever to anyone bearing the same name or names. They are not even distantly inspired by any individual known or unknown to the author, and all the incidents are pure invention.

First published in Great Britain 2001
Large Print Edition 2009
Harlequin Mills & Boon Limited,
Eton House, 18-24 Paradise Road, Richmond, Surrey TW9 1SR

ISBN: 978 0 263 21035 4

Set in Times Roman 15¼ on 16½ pt.
083-0409-93908

Printed and bound in Great Britain
by CPI Antony Rowe, Chippenham, Wiltshire

Chapter One

Damn it! He must have been all kinds of a fool to come back to this country, thought Damian Wrexham. There was nothing for him here, except bitter memories. If he had the sense he had been born with, he would leave, return to India, or perhaps to a new life in Spain. At least it would be warm there. And yet he had undertaken the journey home for a particular reason. He had made a promise, and he did not break his word lightly.

He was standing with his back against a tree, brooding, staring at nothing in particular, when a flash of colour in the orchard caught his eye. His brow furrowed as he saw first the dog bounding towards him, and then, a little way behind, walking more slowly, the woman.

What a woman! She looked like a goddess of ancient myth, bestriding the Earth as her domain—Diana the huntress. Even in his misspent youth, Damian had not particularly admired the simpering

Society misses he had met in the drawing rooms of London. Indeed, one of the sins for which he had been banished was—in his father's opinion—his unfortunate penchant for the company of older women: married ladies, who found illicit pleasure in the bed of a young, rather wicked and handsome man.

'Miss Eastleigh?' he wondered aloud. Damian's eyebrows quirked in amusement. Surely not? This could not be the *old maid* he had been told was his nearest neighbour. Perhaps she had a young relative staying with her? His interest was stirred. 'It would seem that perhaps all is not quite lost…there may yet be some diversion in this place…'

Damian smiled to himself. He had begun to think he would have to go up to London to relieve the tedium, but now his mood of restlessness fell away like a second skin. Would the goddess have anything to do with him once she discovered his reputation? It would not be long before someone felt it their duty to tell her of his past—that he was, in fact, a scoundrel and that no decent woman should have anything to do with him. At least, if she valued her reputation, she would not. But until then it might be amusing to pursue her…a mild flirtation, nothing more.

What a wonderful morning! It made one feel so much better, thought Miss Rosalyn Eastleigh as she walked up through the orchard towards the back of her house. The buds had begun to burst, convincing her that spring had finally arrived after weeks of damp, miserable weather; the sun was warm on her head, for as usual she had discarded her bonnet and her glossy dark hair had been whipped into an artless tangle about her face.

It was a face that, though undeniably attractive, could not be called pretty—at least, it could not in Miss Eastleigh's own opinion. She knew her complexion was too dark to be generally admired: her grey eyes were wide and candid, expressing too openly her often controversial opinions, her mouth too big, her nose too long. She was also taller than most men of her acquaintance, and everyone knew that gentlemen preferred petite, pretty women who fluttered their eyelashes and looked helpless. Men did not spring to assist Miss Eastleigh to a chair when she walked into a room: she was only too capable of managing for herself.

Not that Rosalyn gave much consideration to either her appearance or what the gentlemen might think of her. At seven and twenty she had spent too long on the shelf to bother about marriage. It was years since she had given the idea more than a passing thought.

'Come, Sheba!'

She whistled to the madcap dog her brother Freddie had foisted on her during his last flying visit to the country. Sheba was a black and white mongrel who, Freddie had assured her, was the *sweetest* little thing and would cause no trouble. At the time, the puppy had been no more than a ball of fluff, undeniably pretty and very affectionate.

She was still affectionate some nine months later, but had grown into a great, long-legged, boisterous dog, who was forever into some mischief. Hearing her mistress call, Sheba bounded towards her, jumping up and scrabbling at Rosalyn's gown with muddy paws.

'Down, you wretch!' ordered Sheba's mistress, brushing at her skirt in a vain attempt to save it. 'How did you get into such a state? This is the third clean gown you have ruined this week. I think you do it to spite me. I've a good mind to sell you to the gypsies—and, believe me, I would if I thought Freddie would ever forgive me.'

Sheba gave an excited yelp, understanding perfectly that her mistress did not mean a word of what she was saying. She lolloped off in pursuit of one of the kitchen cats, barking noisily.

'Disgusting animal!' Rosalyn said, smiling in exasperation. 'Sheba! Come back here.'

Sheba paid not the slightest heed. As a puppy she had developed an annoying habit of disappearing into the surrounding countryside for hours at a time, though so far she had always found her own way home eventually—usually wet and always hungry!

'You should teach that dog to obey you, or you

may find she becomes impossible to control. Those half-breed collies can be a nuisance if they aren't properly trained.'

Rosalyn was startled by the man's voice. She had thought herself alone, failing until that very moment to notice him leaning against the trunk of an apple tree. Her eyes narrowed thoughtfully as she looked at him. This man was unknown to her—a stranger to the neighbourhood.

He was dressed plainly in a brown coat and cream riding breeches; his leather boots, though obviously well made, had seen considerable wear. Extremely attractive in a rugged, outdoor style, his skin looked tanned as if he had spent time in the sun, perhaps a much warmer climate than England's. Rosalyn noted that his raven black hair was cut short in a fashion she recognized as à la Brutus, which was a style much favoured by Freddie's friends; but, despite the haircut and the excellent fit of his coat, there was a carelessness about his attire that her brother would have frowned over.

'Forgive me…' Rosalyn realised she had been staring. 'I was startled. I had not expected to see anyone here. May I help you? Are you in some difficulty?'

Her neighbours usually visited at the front door. They came by carriage or on horseback, but never walked casually across fields and miles of open country, as this man must have, to reach her orchard.

Who was he—and what did he want here? She hesitated, a little wary, half-inclined to call Sheba to her.

'I have been watching you,' he said, a half-smile on his lips. 'Fair Diana, the huntress—come to earth in search of human souls.'

As compliments went, it was unusually apt. In all the illustrations Rosalyn had seen of the goddess, Diana was generously formed and looked capable of living up to her reputation. Which could just as easily be said of Rosalyn.

'I am sorry to disappoint you. No goddess, I am afraid, merely Miss Eastleigh taking her rather boisterous dog for a walk,' she replied, concealing her amusement with a wry look.

It was a long time since a man had paid her a compliment. Freddie's friends were too young to be interested in his spinster sister, and her neighbours were married, kind but incapable of paying such a tribute.

'Miss Rosalyn Eastleigh?' He seemed slightly taken aback as she affirmed it with a nod. He stood straight, bowing his head to her. 'I thought… Excuse my execrable manners. Miss Eastleigh, allow me to introduce myself. I am Damian Wrexham. Your new neighbour. At least, I expect to be residing here for the next few months.'

'Oh, yes, I remember now. Lady Orford told me her husband had let the Hall. I thought she said it was to an Indian gentleman, but I was obviously mistaken.'

'No, not at all,' Wrexham replied, a flicker of amusement in his eyes, which she had just noticed were very dark. 'My…pupil, Jared, is of Indian descent through his father, though his mother was an Englishwoman. A rather intrepid lady, I understand. Apparently, she went out to India with her own father, who was a missionary, and fell in love with…Jared's father. Despite all the difficulties and inevitable scandal, she married him and bore him a son.'

'How exciting.' Rosalyn's interest was fairly caught now. 'How brave of her to follow the calling of her heart and forget convention. I have often longed for adventure. India is very beautiful, I believe.'

'Yes. Very. Exotic, wild, dangerous—but undeniably beautiful.'

They had been walking as they spoke, he matching his steps to hers. Now, having reached the house, it seemed natural to invite him in. Rosalyn offered her invitation without hesitation, her manner exactly as it would have been with any other neighbour who chanced to call.

'I am about to have nuncheon, which for me is bread and butter, cold meat and tea. You are welcome to share it, Mr Wrexham, though it is but poor fare for a gentleman. I dare say we could find you some wine to make it more palatable.'

'Another day, perhaps.' He gave her an enigmatic look, which she found difficult to interpret. 'I came in the hope of persuading you to dine with us tomorrow evening, Miss Eastleigh. As I believe I mentioned earlier, Jared is my…pupil. His father wishes him to spend some time in England, and I am teaching him English ways and manners. However, I have no hostess and you…to be frank, I expected *you* to be older.'

The expression in his eyes was so full of wicked humour that she discovered the reserve she had first felt towards him had flown. Her brows rose and she gave him what could only be termed an *old-fashioned* stare.

'Indeed, sir. I wonder why?'

'No, do not look at me so,' he murmured wickedly. 'You cannot know what I have been told, ma'am.'

'Oh, I think I can guess.' Rosalyn was betrayed into a laugh. 'You were told I was an old maid. No, do not deny it, Mr Wrexham. It is quite true, you know. I am seven and twenty, and set in my ways. It would be a very brave—or foolish!—man who thought otherwise.'

'I am forewarned,' he replied, eyes gleaming. He raised one mobile brow. 'Forgive me, Miss Eastleigh, if I presume on your good nature. But you do see my problem? Ours is an all male-household, apart from the Orfords' excellent housekeeper, of course. Would it be quite proper, do you think, for a lady to dine with us? Even a lady of your advanced years…'

'Alone?' Rosalyn was amused. He was a shameless flirt, of course, but she liked his humour. 'Oh, no, not at all. Quite improper. That would not deter me, however—if it were not that to accept such an invitation would lacerate poor Maria's feelings.'

'Maria?' His brows arched. 'Tell me at once, I beg you! No, ma'am, do not laugh. It is of the utmost importance. I most ardently desire to know—who is *poor* Maria?'

'Miss Maria Bellows, my cousin, a very respectable lady in her middle years. She lives with me. Has done so since Papa died three years ago.' Her own expression was little short of wicked, which made Damian chuckle deep in his throat. 'You *must* understand, Maria felt it her duty to devote herself to me. I could not refuse, of course, since she would otherwise have had to find herself a position as a governess—or some other equally unpleasant post—and, of course, it would not be proper for me to live alone. Indeed, it would be quite shocking—do you not agree?'

'Even at your advanced age? One would have thought that quite acceptable.' His brows rose once more. 'Unless you have an unfortunate propensity for wild orgies if not strictly watched?'

'Wretch!' Once again Rosalyn was betrayed into laughter. She decided she rather liked her new neighbour. If he was always so entertaining, he would enliven many a dull dinner party that summer. 'You deserve to have your ears boxed, sir—but I shall forgive you, providing you extend your dinner invitation to Maria as well as myself.'

'You *will* come?' She saw warm approval in his eyes and felt herself blush, something she had not done since leaving the schoolroom. 'You are generosity itself, Miss Eastleigh. I believe you will like Jared—and I am certain he will adore you.' He smiled at her, a smile so charming and full of warmth that it took her breath away. 'Tomorrow at six-thirty, then. We dine at seven. Late hours for the country, perhaps, but in India we have been used to dining in the evenings, because it was always cooler then. It will not upset you?'

'Not at all. We shall look forward to it, Mr Wrexham.'

'Until tomorrow, Miss Eastleigh.'

He bowed, then turned and walked back towards the orchard, obviously intending to return the way he had come.

Rosalyn stood watching him for a few moments. The chance meeting had lifted her spirits—if only because it made a change to converse with a man who was actually taller than she. No, that wasn't her only reason for liking him. She had found him amusing and he intrigued her, blowing away the slight cloud of ennui that had been hanging over her.

She sensed a slight mystery about him. Twice he had spoken of Jared as his pupil. Somehow Mr Wrexham did not strike her as being the kind of man who became a tutor. His skin had a deep tan, as if he had spent much of his life outdoors. She thought he looked too active—too physical—to be a teacher. He would have been more at home as a soldier—or some kind of a bodyguard, perhaps?

Rosalyn laughed at herself. Now what had made her think of that? Perhaps because he had been living in an exotic environment, where such guards were often necessary. She recalled reading recently a report in a newspaper of an Indian prince having survived an assassination attempt; it had only been a few lines, but had interested her more than all the usual stories of society events.

Her new neighbour could of course have had nothing to do with that infamous affair. Mr Wrexham was unquestionably a gentleman—but very different from the gentlemen she was accustomed to meeting in society. It was not just the casual way he wore his clothes, or his very direct manner of speaking…but a certain vitality, and an alertness she had sensed rather than seen. There was something out of the ordinary…unorthodox about him. One sensed that he would never bow to convention; he was too large a character, too bold to concern himself with the rules which governed others.

He was, she felt sure, a man who had tasted life to the full, no longer young—perhaps in his late thirties. He had spoken of India as being exotic but dangerous, and he too was a little like that. A man with a past. Yes, that description suited him very well.

Rosalyn was smiling at her own thoughts as she went into the house, to be met in the hall by a small, plump lady, who was wearing a grey gown and a lace cap over hair which even her kindest friend could only describe as mousy.

'Ah, there you are, dearest,' she said, giving a nervous little laugh. 'Has your headache quite gone? You are looking much better.'

'I feel better. The walk did me good.'

Rosalyn had forgotten the headache, which was merely an excuse to get her away from the house and her cousin's chattering for a while. Maria meant well, and she was devoted to her, of course, but sometimes she could be just the tiniest bit irritating. Oh, no, that was unfair! Rosalyn scolded herself for the uncharitable thought. But Maria would fuss so!

'Who were you talking to just now, Rosalyn? I couldn't help seeing you when I looked out of the parlour window. I do not believe I know the gentleman?'

'No, you wouldn't,' Rosalyn said, amused by her curiosity. Maria was such a busybody, but she could not help her nature. 'I met him for the first time this morning. He is Mr Damian Wrexham, our new neighbour. Or one of them, at least. His pupil is an Indian gentleman.'

'Oh, dear…' Maria looked uncomfortable. 'So unfortunate that Lord Orford should have let to strangers for the summer. Dear Lady Orford always gives such splendid dinners.'

'Well, she left her cook behind for the benefit of her tenants, Maria. So I'm sure you will be pleased to hear we've been invited to dine tomorrow night.'

'To dine…' Maria reached for her lace kerchief, dabbing at her lips. She was clearly disturbed by the news. 'But, Rosalyn, my dear…an Indian gentleman…do you think we should?'

'Maria! I am ashamed of you,' said Rosalyn with a look of mild reproof. 'Do not be a snob, dearest. Mr Wrexham is a very agreeable gentleman, and I am sure Jared will also be perfectly acceptable. Besides, I promised Lady Orford I would help introduce her tenants to the neighbourhood.'

'Oh, well, if you think…' Maria gave a little sigh of resignation. She had learned long ago that it was useless to expect Rosalyn to abide by her own very strict code of the behaviour proper to a lady. And she was only too aware that she was here because Rosalyn was too generous to turn her out. 'Of course it is not for me to object. I am here only as your guest. You must do exactly as you wish.'

Rosalyn ignored the opening.

'I am sure you will enjoy yourself, Maria. Besides, I did promise Lady Orford. You would not want me to break my word?' Maria silently shook her head. 'I am sure they are very respectable people. Lord Orford would not otherwise have let them the house.'

'No, of course not. You do very right to chide me, Rosalyn. I fear I am a foolish woman and I dare say I wear your patience to the limit.'

'I know that you act always out of affection and concern for me.' Rosalyn bestowed a careless kiss on her cheek. Despite Maria's unfortunate ways, she was quite fond of her cousin and was at some pains not to hurt her by speaking too sharply. 'Shall we have nuncheon, Maria? The walk has given me an appetite.'

It was late, past eleven. Rosalyn heard the long-case clock in the hall strike the hour and yawned over her book. Maria had gone to bed nearly an hour earlier, but she had stayed on to finish the last chapter. However, the ending had proved only too predictable, and she laid the book aside with a sigh of disappointment.

Sometimes…just now and then…she found her life a little tedious. Rosalyn was very attached to her home, a rambling old house, often draughty in the winter and filled with the clutter of years, but she was occasionally lonely. It was her own fault, of course. Aunt Susan had asked her to live with her in Bath, and Freddie would have welcomed her if she had taken up his offer to visit him at his London house. However, neither of the two alternatives would have suited her independent nature.

At Lyston House, she was her own mistress, free to come and go much as she pleased—to ride about the countryside unaccompanied, to walk bareheaded and visit only with the friends she had known and liked all her life.

She found society as it was lived in London and Bath a little too confining, too narrow. Rosalyn had a quick wit and rebellious spirit, both of which had been shamelessly encouraged by her father. While Sir Robert Eastleigh lived, his daughter had never known a moment's boredom. They had been friends and constant companions, delighting in each other's presence.

Oh, she did miss him so!

Tears stung her eyes as she recalled the last few weeks of her father's life. After having been revoltingly healthy for as long as she could remember, he had succumbed suddenly to a debilitating illness, which had left him bedridden. He had hated every moment he was forced to spend lying there, a prisoner of his failing body, and lost his temper with everyone who came near him—everyone except Rosalyn. Only she had been able to placate him, to make him smile at his misfortunes.

During those final weeks, they had drawn even closer. Rosalyn had been devastated by his death, and was not truly over it even now. All her family had tried to persuade her to go into society more now that she was free to do so, but she knew that she would never find a replacement for her beloved father amongst the gentlemen who frequented the drawing rooms of Bath and London. Sir Robert had been essentially a countryman, a huge man in both form and character with a bluff, good-natured manner…more alive and honest than most others she had met.

It was odd, she thought, as she got up and wandered over to the window to look out at the moonlit night, but Mr Wrexham had reminded her a little of her father. No, that was wrong. She shook her head as she stood staring at the gardens, turned to silver now and more lovely than ever. They were not alike…except perhaps in their manner of speaking. Sir Robert had called himself a blunt man…too blunt for many, which was why he seldom went into society himself. Rosalyn had inherited many of her father's qualities, though perhaps plain speaking was not always considered a quality but rather a fault.

Her reverie came to an abrupt halt as she saw a shadowy figure lurking in the shrubbery. Someone was there! A man…at least, she was almost sure it was a man. Rosalyn felt a shiver of apprehension run down her spine. None of her own servants would be in the gardens so late. Besides, why would they need to hide in the bushes?

Suddenly, she heard a familiar barking. Sheba came running out of the shrubbery and a person followed...not a man's figure, much smaller...a youth of perhaps twelve or thirteen years. He ran after the dog, calling to her in a strange-sounding tongue. Because of the moonlight, Rosalyn was able to see the young man quite clearly. He was wearing a turban and his clothes were odd...Indian! Yes, of course, that was what they must be. He was the pupil Mr Wrexham had spoken of earlier.

He had caught up with Sheba. The dog stopped, its tongue hanging out, sitting back on its haunches and allowing the youth to stroke its fur. Rosalyn watched, smiling to herself as she saw the way her dog covered the youth's face in enthusiastic licks. She wondered whether she ought to go out to them. The young Indian lad was surely too young to be out at this late hour? What could Mr Wrexham be thinking of to allow it?

Her hand was reaching for the window latch when she saw another figure emerge from the shadows. A man this time, also dressed in those rather odd-looking clothes. He darted at the youth and had almost caught hold of him when he seemed to become aware of the intention. He gave a shrill scream, obviously startled by the sudden interruption of his play. Seeing the way he shrank back, Rosalyn unlocked the French windows, determined to investigate further.

At that moment two things happened simultaneously. The man glanced towards her and Sheba sprang at him. Rosalyn could never afterwards be sure whether the shock on his face was due to seeing her or to her dog's attack. He gave a cry of pain, clutching at his arm where Sheba had bitten him, then retreated a few steps. He was saying something in his own tongue, something addressed to the youth. Whatever it was made the lad shake his head and look fearful.

'Sheba, no!' Rosalyn called as she saw the fur rising on Sheba's back. The bitch clearly sensed menace towards her new-found friend and was prepared to defend him with her life. 'Who are you, sir? What are you doing in my garden at this hour?'

Her question was addressed to the man. He stared at her for a moment, clearly undecided what to do next. She believed he understood her. Something in his manner told her that, though he continued to speak to the boy in his own language.

Rosalyn had reached the boy and dog. She placed a restraining hand on Sheba's collar, standing so that she was between the youth and the man. She raised her head, defying him to attack the young man again.

'Please explain yourself, sir. What are you doing here—and why is this youth afraid of you?'

He stared at her in silence a moment more, then turned and pushed his way into the shrubbery. She could hear the sounds of his retreat, twigs snapping, leaves rustling. He had obviously been angered by her interference.

'He will not come back now,' the youth said behind

her as the sounds died away. He spoke in English, his voice cultured but with a slightly foreign accent. 'You and the dog have saved me, *mem-sahib.*'

Sheba was still growling low in her throat. Rosalyn could not recall her ever having attacked anyone before. She rubbed her fingers at the back of Sheba's ears, shushing her.

'Who was that man?' she asked of the youth. 'Why were you afraid of him?'

'I am not afraid of him,' the lad replied proudly. 'I was merely displeased that he had followed me. I am not afraid of anyone.'

'I see…' Rosalyn hid her smile. He was certainly a very proud young man. She glanced down as Sheba stiffened, then barked. 'Be quiet, Sheba. You will wake the household.'

'Is she your dog?' The youth looked eagerly at Rosalyn. 'She followed Sahib Wrexham home this morning. He said she belonged to Miss Eastleigh, our neighbour, and sent her away—but she came back and I saw her in the gardens when I could not sleep. She ran this way and I followed her. I am sorry if I disturbed you, but I wanted to be sure she found her way home.'

The youth's voice had a high, sing-song quality, but his command of the English language was perfect, which it would be, of course, if he had an English mother.

'You must be Jared, I think? Mr Wrexham told me you were his pupil.'

The youth seemed to hesitate, then nodded. 'Yes, *mem-sahib*. I am Jared and Sahib Wrexham is my…I am not sure how to say it. Is the word tutor or teacher?'

'In Mr Wrexham's case, I should think tutor would be best,' Rosalyn said with a faint smile, 'since I do not imagine he teaches you the usual lessons, does he?'

'What are the usual lessons?'

'Oh, reading, writing, arithmetic…'

'I can do all those,' Jared replied, a hint of pride in his face. 'Mama taught me to read when I was a small child.'

'How old are you now?'

'Fourteen and three months, *mem-sahib*.'

Older than she had thought, but slight for his age. Rosalyn hid her smile. Jared was clearly very conscious of his dignity. He certainly had exquisite manners—manners that would be acceptable in any society. She thought it unlikely he needed to be taught English ways, even if it was his father's intention to send him to a public school in England. So what was the real reason they had taken a house tucked away in the Cambridgeshire countryside?

Rosalyn remembered that she had thought Mr Wrexham a very unlikely teacher. What was his true function—was he meant to be guarding the youth? And why had the man with the dark, resentful eyes tried to grab hold of Jared?

She gave him a meaningful look. 'Does Mr

Wrexham know you are wandering about the countryside at this hour, Jared?'

'No, *mem-sahib*.' His expression became uneasy, anxious. 'Will you tell him tomorrow when you come to the house?'

'I do not think that will be necessary, do you?'

'He would be angry with me.'

'I think he would be very worried.' Rosalyn frowned. 'Who was that man just now? You were a little afraid of him, weren't you?'

'He would not harm me.' There was a scornful look in Jared's eyes. 'He would not dare. My father would punish him if he tried—but I do not like Rajib. Sometimes he looks at me so strangely…as if he hates me. I know he never liked my mother. So I do not like him, but I am not afraid.'

The boy lifted his head, a defiant air about him.

'You should speak to Mr Wrexham. Perhaps if he knew you do not like Rajib he would send him away.'

'Rajib is my servant.' Again there was a hint of hauteur in the youth's manner. '*I* may send him away if I choose—but then Nessa would have no one to share her duties. She is old and it would be too much for her.'

'Who is Nessa?'

'She is my ayah. She was also my mother's friend and looked after her before she died.'

Rosalyn saw a suspicion of tears in his eyes. He was clearly still grieving for his mother.

'When did your mother die, Jared?'

'Last year.' He blinked hard but did not let the tears fall. 'Everything was better when she was alive—now it has all changed. I am no longer wanted in my father's house.'

'What do you mean?' Rosalyn's compassion was aroused by the hurt tone of his voice. 'That is a very odd thing to say. What makes you think your father does not want you?'

The youth's expression changed, as if a shutter had closed on his thoughts and emotions. 'I am not allowed to talk about that,' he said. 'I should go back now.'

'Will you let me walk with you?'

'I can go alone. There is nothing to fear.'

He was so proud, so dignified. Rosalyn's heart went out to him.

'I am sure you are right,' she agreed. 'But why do you not take Sheba with you? You can hold her collar as I am now. She knows her way...and you might get lost alone. If you let her go when you reach the house, she will come back when she is ready.'

'You are kind, *mem-sahib*,' he said, smiling suddenly. His teeth were very white and even against the dusk of his skin. 'I like you. I am glad Sahib Wrexham asked you to visit us. I *shall* take Sheba with me—but only because I am not sure of the way.'

'Of course.'

Rosalyn hid her smile. She watched as the boy set off, a tight hold on Sheba's collar. He turned his head to look at her; she waved, then went back inside the house and locked the French windows.

Damian Wrexham watched from the shadows of the shrubbery, a frown on his face. He had not been close enough to hear what Jared had said to her. It was a deuced nuisance that they should have met in such unfortunate circumstances. He could only hope that nothing had been said or done to arouse her suspicions. Miss Eastleigh was an intelligent woman—an unusual woman.

If she took it on herself to interfere…it could ruin his plans. And that could prove dangerous for them all.

Rosalyn was yawning over her needlework when Maria came into the parlour the next morning. She had spent a restless night, dreaming of menacing men hiding in the bushes—and Mr Wrexham. She could not recall just what she had dreamt, but she knew it had caused her to start up in alarm.

'Two letters for you,' Maria said, handing them to her. 'From Freddie and Mrs Buckley.'

'Aunt Susan?' Rosalyn was surprised. 'She wrote only last week. I wonder what…' She gave a cry of surprise as she broke open the wax seal and began to read. 'Oh, the poor child!'

'Is something wrong, dearest?' asked Maria. She

seldom received letters of her own and looked forward eagerly to hearing Rosalyn's news. Rosalyn obliged her by giving her a resume of the letter.

'Cousin Celia's daughter has been ill with scarlet fever. She is over it now, according to Aunt Susan, but still poorly. Her doctor advises complete rest for at least several weeks. My aunt wonders if we could have her here for a while…' Rosalyn glanced at her cousin. 'You would not object to that, Maria?'

'I should hope I am not so heartless,' replied Maria, slightly wounded that Rosalyn should even think it. 'Write at once and say we should be happy to have the poor little lamb. You know how I love the dear children, not that I have met your Cousin Celia's little ones as yet.'

'I do not know what she is like now—her illness may have changed her—but when we last met, Sarah Jane was a horror,' said Rosalyn. 'All Celia's children are—to say the least of it!—over-exuberant.'

'Rosalyn!' Maria chided gently. 'What a thing to say about the little darlings. Of course, I know you are only teasing, the way you do sometimes—but you really ought not, my love.'

'I can assure you there is nothing amusing about being at the mercy of Celia's offspring. She has no notion of discipline—which is one of the reasons I do not choose to live with Aunt Susan. Celia and the monsters visit her far too frequently.' Rosalyn pulled a wry face. 'I cannot promise you it will be a pleasure to have Sarah Jane staying. Indeed, it may be quite the opposite, but I fear we must endure it. We can only brace ourselves for the ordeal and hope her stay will not last too long.'

'Rosalyn dearest!' Maria was truly shocked. She had never quite accustomed herself to her cousin's plain speaking, and could never be sure if Rosalyn was funning or not. 'I see what it is. You've worn yourself out with that mending. I've told you before, there is not the least need for you to trouble yourself. I can very well…'

Rosalyn slipped her brother's letter into her pocket. For some unaccountable reason she was restless, and her head ached.

'Are you going out?' asked Maria as she stood up.

'I have a little headache. I think I shall take a walk.'

'Yes, that is a very good idea,' said Maria. 'Leave that mending for me. It is always a pleasure for me to do those irritating little tasks for you.'

'You spoil me, cousin. I do not deserve it.' Rosalyn shook her head at Maria's protest. 'I may not be back for nuncheon. Do not wait for me, Maria.'

'Do not tire yourself, my love. Remember, we are invited out this evening—though to be sure, I should not mind if we did not go.'

Rosalyn was no longer listening. She took a warm shawl from the hall-stand, wrapping it about her shoulders as she went out into the back garden.

What on earth was the matter with her? She was surely not so selfish that she resented the idea of having her cousin's sick child to stay? No, no, it was not that; it would make little difference to her own life since Celia was sure to send the nursery maid. It was this strange restlessness that was making her have a fit of the sullens…the same feeling that had disturbed her sleep the previous night.

Her thoughts took an abrupt turn as Sheba suddenly jumped at her from behind, almost sending her flying.

'Heel! You stupid dog. Have you no sense?' The man's voice sent a shock of recognition through her. Rosalyn swung round to find herself face to face with her new neighbour. 'Forgive me, Miss Eastleigh,' he apologised. 'I was returning this wretched animal to you. She pulled at the leash when she saw you and I foolishly let her go. Are you hurt?'

'No, not really.' Rosalyn smiled, her spirits lifting insensibly. 'I am used to her ways. It was not your fault. She does this all the time.' She shook her head at the dog, who was playfully jumping about her, pulling at her shawl. 'Sheba! Bad girl. Sit!'

To her utter amazement, Sheba immediately sat, head up, tail wagging, alert and ready.

'Good gracious! She actually obeyed me. Did you teach her to do that, Mr Wrexham?'

He laughed at her astonishment. 'In this instance I cannot claim the credit. I believe it was Jared. I found them both curled up on the rug this morning, sound asleep. Jared does not like English beds. He told me you met last night, here in the gardens of your home.'

'Yes.' Rosalyn was surprised that boy had told him. 'I sent Sheba home with him. It seemed…unwise for a boy of his age to be wandering the countryside alone at night. Although I do not imagine he was in any real danger, I did not think you would approve. I believed Sheba would give him some protection, should he need it.'

'That was thoughtful of you, and I agree he should not have been out so late—but he is far more mature than you might imagine. Indeed, I believe he has been forced to grow up too soon. He needs to have some fun—to enjoy himself like other boys of his age.'

'Like other boys…' Rosalyn looked at him consideringly. 'Just who is he, Mr Wrexham? Last night I thought…I suspected…he might not be quite as you had described him. '

'Did you, Miss Eastleigh?' Damian nodded, his expression a mixture of vexation and amusement. 'Yes, I expected that. Rajib told me what happened. I came to explain—to set your mind at rest. Rajib was merely trying to watch over the boy, something which I am afraid Jared finds very irritating.'

'Yes, I imagined it must be something of the sort,' Rosalyn said. 'I would ask you in, but I have just escaped for a breath of air—and we can talk more freely if we walk for a while. If we went in, my cousin would be bound to join us, and then we should not be alone for a moment.'

'Poor Diana.' His eyes gleamed in appreciation. 'You were not meant for captivity, Miss Eastleigh. You should be free to live as you will…be it above in the heavens or here on earth. I fear domesticity irks you beyond bearing at times.'

How could he know that? He read her mind too well! Rosalyn gave him what was meant to be a quelling look, frowning as she saw the answering laughter in his face. Was he never serious?

'Tell me about your charge, Mr Wrexham. He is rather a special young man, is he not?'

'Very special. Forgive me if I do not give you precise details. There are reasons, believe me.'

'Yes, I see that. I imagine his father is a very wealthy man—perhaps an important man?'

'How clearly you see things. A virtue I have seldom found in your sex.' He gave her a wicked look as her eyes smouldered. 'No, do not defend them, Miss Eastleigh. I am a rogue and my opinion is of no account. I am sure all ladies have endless virtues, even if I am not quite sure what they are…'

She was amused by his outrageous statement, but shook her head severely to warn him that he was being frivolous.

'I shall not encourage you, sir. I am persuaded you

know your own faults. You were telling me about Jared. Pray continue.'

Damian laughed. 'Indeed I was and I shall. For reasons I may not divulge, Jared's father decided it might be safer for him to live in England for a few months. Since Ahmed and I have long been friends…'

'Ahmed?'

'A name permitted only to a privileged few.' Damian gave her a straight look. 'It is best for all concerned that his title is not known here. As I was saying, Ahmed asked me to bring the boy back to England with me.'

Rosalyn nodded. 'It was your intention to return home at this time?'

'Yes. I have business of my own here. It enabled me to remove Jared from an environment that is not exactly welcoming at the moment.'

'He told me he was no longer welcome in his father's house.'

'Did he?' Damian's eyes narrowed. 'Did he say why?'

'Only that things had changed since his mother's death last year.'

Was that a look of relief in Mr Wrexham's eyes? Rosalyn could not be certain.

'Yes, that is unfortunately true,' he said. 'Jared's father took another wife—a rather young and pretty girl. There was some jealousy—on both sides, I believe.'

'Ah, yes. I understand.'

'So, as Ahmed had always promised his first wife that Jared would spend some years at an English school…he thought now was the right time to send him.'

Rosalyn turned to her companion. Why did she suspect that he was not quite telling her the truth? He could have no reason to lie, surely? And yet she had the distinct impression that he was keeping something back from her. Why? Why not be completely frank now that he had begun? Perhaps he did not quite trust her.

'So…' His dark eyes dwelt intently on her face. 'I hope what you have learned today has not changed your mind about visiting us this evening, Miss Eastleigh?'

'No, certainly not,' she replied. 'Quite the opposite. I liked your pupil, sir. He is charming, and I hope that we shall all get to know each other well over the summer.'

'Thank you.' His smile was lazy, his manner relaxed, giving nothing away. 'It will mean a great deal to us to have your friendship, Miss Eastleigh. We are both strangers in this place—and I would have Jared make friends here, if that is possible.'

Something more lay behind that statement. Rosalyn was intrigued. Her first impression of this man had not changed. She liked him—but she sensed that he had been forged in the fires of experience, not all of them exactly pleasant. He was a man with a past…and it might be interesting to discover the secrets he had left undivulged.

'Do not search too hard for answers,' he said, a meaningful look in his eyes. 'It is merely that Jared misses his mother very much. I believe it will help him to spend a little time with you—you are in some ways a little like Anna. If you took an interest in him, it might help him to recover from his grief.'

'I should be delighted to help in any way I can,' Rosalyn replied. 'Though I am not sure what I can do…'

'Just be yourself,' he said and smiled. 'What else?'

As Rosalyn stared at him, her heart suddenly starting to beat wildly, he took a step towards her, then bent his head and kissed her very softly on the mouth.

'I should not have done that,' he admitted as she moved back, clearly startled. 'It was irresistible—but wrong of me.'

'It *was* rather forward of you,' Rosalyn said. She was conscious of her flushed cheeks and the tumultuous racing of her pulses. What was the matter with her? She ought to be angry, but she was merely confused. He had surprised her. 'I should prefer you to give me warning another time; a kiss is something to be anticipated, sir…and savoured.'

For a moment he stared at her with a kind of disbelief, then he threw back his head and laughed…

warm, natural laughter that made Rosalyn tingle deep down to her toes.

'When I was last in England, such an impertinence would have brought me a slap or a sharp setdown,' he said, entranced by her answer, which in its way was more outrageous than his own behaviour. 'I was right—you are a very unusual woman, Miss Eastleigh.'

'And you are unlike any gentleman of my acquaintance,' replied Rosalyn, her colour heightened. 'However, since you have been in India for some years, I dare say you might have forgotten the proper respect due to a lady?'

His laughter was so warm and infectious that she was unable to prevent a smile. Besides, she was rather flattered that he had been tempted to kiss her. It was a long, long time since anyone had shown her anything other than a rather tiresome respect. And she wasn't that old! Not so old that she could not be amused by a mild flirtation.

'That's done for me, hasn't it?' he said, eyes gleaming. He was enjoying their banter. 'How refreshing, Miss Eastleigh. You are even more like Anna than I first thought. I think a more intimate acquaintance with you will be good for me as well as my pupil.'

The reference to Anna was clearly meant as a compliment. Rosalyn was curious about the woman who had dared to marry an Indian gentleman—something that must have seemed beyond the pale to ladies of her own class.

'What was she like?'

'Jared's mother?' Damian looked thoughtful. 'Very beautiful...very determined to have her own way. She usually got what she wanted, though I never heard her raise her voice, nor did she nag. She simply seemed to assume that everyone would want to give her what she wanted—and they did. Her husband adored her and was devastated by her death: the reason for a rather hasty and unwise marriage was the grief he could not handle alone. You see, Anna was the strong one in that particular partnership.'

Rosalyn had never heard a man describe marriage in such terms. She was sure it was not the way most men would think of the marriage contract, but it sounded right to her: it should be a partnership but, in her experience, so often was not.

She smiled. 'Then I fear Anna and I are not so much alike, Mr Wrexham. I believe I do have a temper, which I try—not always successfully—to control.'

'I shall remember that.' His expression made her catch her breath. He was so very attractive! 'And now, Miss Eastleigh, I have business I must attend. I shall leave you—until this evening.'

'Until this evening...'

Rosalyn watched as he strode off across the fields. What a forceful personality he had! Despite his undeniable charm, there was something about him that made her wonder if it would be wise to become too friendly with Mr Wrexham.

Chapter Two

Rosalyn had forgotten her brother's letter, remembering it only when she was changing her gown for the evening. She read it quickly, with growing surprise. Freddie was coming down the next week and would stay for several days. He was bringing two guests. Female guests!

It was not often that Sir Frederick Eastleigh paid a visit to Cambridgeshire. He preferred his house in London or the estate in Devon. When he did come, his visit was usually unannounced and of uncertain duration. To write of his intention—and to bring female guests!—must surely point to something out of the ordinary.

Was Freddie thinking of marriage? The idea sprang to Rosalyn's mind immediately, though she wisely kept it to herself when she joined Maria downstairs in the hall a few minutes later.

'Freddie may bring some friends to stay next week,' was all she told her cousin as they left the house to set out on their visit to the new residents of Orford Hall, 'so we shall have a house full of guests.'

'How nice,' Maria replied, cheeks pink with excitement. 'We go on very comfortably, just the two of us, but I do so enjoy entertaining guests. Especially dear Sir Frederick. It must always be a pleasure to welcome him home, must it not?'

'Yes. I am always pleased to see Freddie.'

Rosalyn was engrossed by her own thoughts. Her brother was still only one and twenty, but having come into the title and his inheritance on his father's death three years earlier, had become quite the man about town. Freddie's sister had smiled to herself when he'd joined the 'Corinthian' set, a section of society much favoured by those gentlemen who enjoyed sporting pursuits. She knew Freddie spent his time indulging in the pleasures his not-inconsiderable fortune could provide—racing his specially made curricle, gambling, fencing, learning to box—but, since at heart he was a sensible young man, she had never worried too much.

She wondered that he should even think of marrying so young, but perhaps she was reading too much into his letter? Yet there must be a reason why he was bringing the Hon. Mrs P. Jenkins and Miss Beatrice Holland to meet her.

Rosalyn dismissed her vague worries as the carriage drew to a halt outside the rather grand façade of Orford Hall. It had been built in the previous century, was far more modern than Rosalyn's own home, and featured a rather splendid portico of white marble columns and long gracious windows.

She was helped from the carriage by a footman and welcomed into the house by Mrs Browne, the Orfords' housekeeper, who relieved both her and Maria of all the paraphernalia of cloaks, scarves, gloves and mufflers necessary for a cool spring evening.

'Mr Wrexham and Master Jared are in the drawing room, waiting for you, Miss Eastleigh—the vicar is also dining with us tonight.'

'Oh, is dear Mr Waller here?' Maria brightened. She was quite partial to the slightly deaf but agreeable Reverend Waller. 'That is nice. Thank you, Mrs Browne. I believe I shall keep my shawl. I feel the chill in the evenings still.'

'Very wise, ma'am. It doesn't do to invite problems at our age…'

Seeing that her cousin was content to indulge in a comfortable gossip with the Orfords' housekeeper, Rosalyn moved towards the drawing room. She had been a frequent visitor for years, and was almost as much at home in the Orfords' house as her own. On the threshold of the large salon, she stood for a moment taking in the scene of pleasant domesticity; the room was comfortable rather than fashionable, furnished in rich shades of crimson and gold, and had a welcoming atmosphere with a roaring fire, bowls of flowers and the faint smell of lavender.

Damian Wrexham was engaged in an amiable conversation with the vicar—wine glass in hand—but at her approach both gentlemen got to their feet and turned to her with a smile of welcome.

The Reverend Waller spoke first, 'Good evening, Miss Eastleigh. How nice to see you here this evening, m'dear. I have been meaning to call for a day or so now.'

'You are always so busy, sir.' Rosalyn smiled at the vicar, who had been a good friend to her at the time of her father's illness. 'But you know your visits are always welcome.'

'Oh, yes, yes, always a pleasure,' said the Reverend, nodding at her happily. 'The Orfords always set a good table.'

He seemed to have forgotten he was not dining with the Orfords, but, seeing the amused smile in her host's eyes, she did not believe any offence had been taken.

'Miss Eastleigh,' Damian Wrexham said, coming to greet her. He took the hand she offered, carrying it briefly to his lips. 'I am happy to welcome you to our—temporary home. Come, Jared, say hello to Miss Eastleigh.'

Rosalyn's heart fluttered as she saw how attractive her host looked in evening dress. She was sure that even Freddie could find no fault with the fit of his coat of blue superfine, or the extremely elegant neckcloth he had tied—and the high polish on his boots would make her brother envious.

'I am happy to be here,' she replied, smiling as Jared came to greet her. He too was dressed in formal English clothes—apart from a very splendid turban of gold cloth—and looked a little ill at ease. 'How are you, Jared?'

'Very well, *mem-sahib*.' His shyness was very different from his behaviour of the previous evening. 'You are welcome here.'

'Thank you.'

Rosalyn would have said more, but at that moment Maria came in and the youth retreated after introductions had been made. He stood by the window, looking out at the night, such a sad expression in his dark eyes that Rosalyn was moved to mention it to his tutor.

'Jared does not seem happy tonight, sir. Has something occurred to upset him?'

'I have for the moment been forced to curtail his freedom.' Damian glanced at his charge and frowned. 'He does not enjoy being kept a prisoner indoors.'

'A prisoner?' Rosalyn's brows arched. 'Surely not?' What could he mean?

'An unfortunate choice of words,' Damian said, his mouth twisting wryly. 'Do not imagine Jared is ill treated, Miss Eastleigh. Everything I am doing is for his own benefit.'

'Of course.'

Why would he speak of his pupil as a prisoner? Was there something sinister here, something Mr Wrexham was afraid to reveal? Her reflective gaze rested on the Indian youth, but she was not aware how much of her thoughts were betrayed by her expression.

'Sometimes circumstances dictate our actions, Miss Eastleigh. We are not always masters of our own fate.'

'I suppose not.' Rosalyn's attention returned to her host. She gave him a speaking look from her fine eyes. 'You will naturally make it your business to see that your pupil has regular exercise in the fresh air?'

'Naturally.' Damian's eyes gleamed with a secret amusement. 'Unfortunately, Jared does not always appreciate company—unless it is your wretched dog. She followed me home again and has been here for most of the day.'

'So that's where she went.' Rosalyn nodded. 'It seems she has attached herself to your household, sir. But I can assure you that Sheba will not harm Jared. Indeed, I believe she would protect him with her life if need be.'

'And you have no objection to her desertion?' His eyes quizzed her, bringing a faint flush to her cheeks.

'None at all. If having her here gives Jared pleasure, she is welcome to stay. Besides, Sheba has always had a mind of her own. As you may have observed, she takes very little notice of anything I say to her.'

A delightful little twitch of mirth touched her mouth, bringing an immediate response from the man.

'Then I shall not waste my breath in sending her home.'

'I fear Sheba is too independent to obey. Unless it suits her, of course.'

'As is her mistress, perhaps?'

'Touché!'

Rosalyn's laugh rang out joyfully. She gave him a look of playful reproach. This man read her mind far too well for comfort. She would have to watch herself in his company.

Her laughter caused both the vicar and Maria—who had been happily chatting to one another—to stare at her in some surprise. Although always good-natured, it was seldom that Rosalyn had been heard to laugh in just that way. Their curiosity, combined with the wicked look in Mr Wrexham's eyes, made her blush once more.

'Excuse me,' she whispered, feeling slightly flustered but unsure why. 'I believe I shall talk to Jared for a few minutes.'

She left her host to stare after her as she crossed the room, unaware of the whimsical expression her banter had brought to his eyes.

Jared looked at her uncertainly as she approached but, seeing her expression of warmth and approval, seemed to relax his guard.

'Sheba is in my room,' he confided in a low voice.

'I fed her before I came down. You need not fear she will go hungry while she is here, *mem-sahib.*'

'I had no such fear. I am perfectly certain she will be well cared for in your house, Jared.'

He grinned at her, his dark eyes glowing like wet coals. 'You do not mind her being here?'

'I have just told Mr Wrexham she may stay—if it pleases you?'

The youth nodded vigorously. Rosalyn noticed the huge emerald in his turban. It must surely be very valuable?

'You are generous, *mem-sahib.*'

'I see no reason why we should not be friends, do you? If you and Mr Wrexham would like to walk over to visit me, you will always be welcome.'

'Perhaps you would care to ride with us tomorrow?'

Rosalyn was startled, glancing swiftly over her shoulder as Damian joined them. He was bearing a crystal glass filled with champagne, which he handed to her.

'I hope you like champagne—or would you have preferred sherry?'

'This is wonderful. Thank you—for the champagne and the invitation.' She met the quizzing look in his eyes this time. 'Both are equally welcome to me. I ride most days before breakfast—alone, because my cousin does not care for it.'

'Our horses have just arrived,' Damian informed her. 'Jared is an excellent horseman and the exercise will do us both good. Would you not agree, Miss Eastleigh? Regular exercise in the fresh air, was that not what you recommended?'

'Oh, certainly!' She responded to his mocking look with an answering one of reproof. 'At what time shall we meet—and where?'

A time and place was agreed and almost immediately afterwards, Mrs Browne came in to announce that dinner was ready.

Placed between Jared and the vicar at table, Rosalyn was able to observe the way her host set himself to charming Maria. It was not by any means an easy task but, little by little, Maria thawed towards him. His gentle manner reassured her so that her smiles became warmer, reflecting approval.

Once, her host caught Rosalyn watching him and the expression in his eyes almost overset her. He knew she realised what he was doing and was sharing his amusement with her. His sense of humour was positively wicked! She had not been able to share a private joke like this with anyone since her father died. She raised her fine brows at him, but he merely smiled and renewed his assault on Maria's defences.

Maria responded by repeating most of the local gossip, telling him whom he ought to meet and offering to introduce him to everyone when he attended church on Sunday. By the end of the evening, she was positively glowing as she assured Damian that she would be delighted to welcome both him and the 'dear child' at any time.

'We are to have visitors soon, you know.' She gave Damian an arch look as they took their leave later. 'Sarah Jane is very much Jared's age. They will be company for each other.'

'You are very kind to take pity on us, ma'am.' He bowed over her hand, kissing it respectfully. 'I should be delighted to bring Jared for tea one day.'

'I am sure you will always be welcome.' Maria blushed as she saw Rosalyn looking at her, and recalled it was more properly her cousin's place to issue invitations. 'Would they not, Rosalyn dear?'

'Yes, of course.'

Rosalyn wondered why Mr Wrexham had gone to such lengths to win her cousin's good will. Her gaze was drawn irresistibly to his face, and the wicked, quizzing look she discovered there made her want to laugh. She frowned, suppressing the desire. Just what was in his mind? She felt his care with Maria was more than just kindness. Once again, she suspected there was something hidden here—some motive that was not immediately apparent.

The long-case clock was striking ten when Jared accompanied them into the hall to say goodbye. He had been allowed to stay up late as it was a special occasion, but, hearing his name called, Rosalyn turned to discover he was being urgently beckoned by a woman, quite an elderly woman with greying hair and dark eyes.

Rosalyn realised she must be Jared's ayah, and she was aware of curiosity in the other woman's gaze, curiosity and perhaps a slight hostility. But no, she believed that hostility was directed at Mr Wrexham, for it was when he touched Jared on the shoulder that her eyes flashed with jealousy.

'Come,' Nessa said in English. 'Time for you to sleep now, my lord.'

'Goodnight, *mem-sahib*,' Jared said, giving Rosalyn a formal bow. 'Nessa calls me. I must go to her.'

'I shall see you tomorrow.'

Rosalyn watched as the youth ran to his ayah, and as she saw the loving way the woman greeted him, she realised that Nessa was merely possessive of her charge. No doubt she was feeling out of place, and uneasy in a strange country. But why had she called him *my lord*? Could it be that the young Indian boy was even more important than Rosalyn had thought?

There was some mystery here!

'Until tomorrow, Miss Eastleigh. I shall look forward to our ride.'

Rosalyn turned to her host. She offered her hand. He kissed it briefly as he had Maria's, but his eyes swept up to meet hers in such a wicked, teasing look that she was caught off balance and her heart did a rapid somersault.

'Thank you for this evening,' she replied with a prim nod of her head to hide the flood of emotion. 'It was kind of you to invite us, and I shall look forward to seeing both you and Jared tomorrow.'

His mouth twitched at the corners. He was amused by her formal society manners. Good gracious! Had he read her mind? Did he know she found him attractive? Or was he laughing at her, hiding something from her? There was certainly more to this rather odd household than met the eye!

Rosalyn felt her cheeks flush as she followed her cousin out to the waiting carriage. It was cooler now and she hugged her cloak about her, feeling a shiver run through her. The English climate could be so treacherous, promising spring one moment and reverting to winter the next.

'What a truly charming man Mr Wrexham is,' sighed Maria contentedly as their carriage began to move off. 'As you know, Rosalyn dear, I was not sure about the wisdom of dining with a single gentleman—but with the dear vicar there, it was perfectly respectable. Besides, Mr Wrexham has such exquisite manners. He is such a pleasant gentleman, did you not think so, my love?'

Rosalyn made no comment. Perfect manners perhaps—but what kind of a man was he really? Why had he come here to this quiet corner of England? She sensed something secretive, something perhaps not quite as it ought to be.

Was there something sinister going on? Why was Jared being kept almost a prisoner? She had thought there was apprehension in the youth's manner once or twice when his tutor spoke to him...and yet she could not think him in any danger from Mr Wrexham. No, surely not! The memory of his smile made her pulses flutter—but she was not such a fool as to be taken in by his charm. Or was she?

Maria continued to chatter for the remainder of their journey home. Since she required no more than a murmured yes or no at appropriate moments, Rosalyn was able to let her thoughts wander at will.

Rosalyn had seen the challenge in Mr Wrexham's eyes. She was sure he had sensed the doubts filling her mind. He was a man she could like, she had known that from the beginning—but was he a man she could trust? Her instincts told her to be wary, even as her heart urged her to throw caution to the winds and accept what fate was offering.

But what was she being offered? A mild flirtation perhaps...with a man she knew nothing of—except that his smile could make her heart beat very fast, which perhaps made him a dangerous man to know.

Rosalyn's thoughts went round and round like fallen leaves in a storm.

Just who was Mr Wrexham? She had sensed from the start that he was a man with a past...but what kind of secrets was he hiding? He was definitely hiding something!

'I have seldom enjoyed an evening more,' Maria said happily as they went into the house. 'You must give a dinner party next week, Rosalyn—and invite Mr Wrexham.'

Rosalyn made no reply. She was not sure she would be wise to continue the acquaintance, and yet already her mind had begun to race on, to their next meeting. There might be something a little dangerous about her new neighbour, but of one thing she was quite certain...he was the most interesting person to come into her little world for an age.

Damian was thoughtful as he took his customary turn about the garden before retiring. It was a damned nuisance that Nessa had disobeyed his orders not to come down until the visitors had left. She had been warned not to address Jared by his title, but she could not bring herself to abandon the habits of a lifetime. Devoted as she undoubtedly was to the boy she had nursed since he was a baby, she could, if she were not careful, ruin all Damian's carefully laid plans. And then all their lives might be in danger.

Miss Eastleigh's expression had left him in no doubt of her suspicions—and if she were to voice them aloud, they could force him to look elsewhere for a safe place to keep Jared hidden.

Would it be better to look for a different house immediately, somewhere nearer London, perhaps—somewhere he would find plentiful opportunities to accomplish his rehabilitation into the society that had rejected him years ago?

Damian sighed inwardly, cursing the need for his return to this damned country. Left to himself, he would have been happy to continue his life in India. He'd had everything he wanted or needed there—but the tenuous ties of his past had drawn him home. He had come because he needed to put things straight, and because he was needed here.

And there was Jared, of course. He had given his word to the youth's father, and he would not break it. He was aware of Nessa's resentment at his authority, over her and Jared. It was a nuisance, but it could not be helped.

Hearing something behind him, Damian turned sharply. Someone was behind him, in the bushes. His hand instinctively reached towards the pistol in his pocket.

'Who is there?' he demanded. 'Come out, damn you! Or I'll break your scurvy neck.'

'It is I, *sahib*,' said Rajib, emerging from the shrubbery. 'Jared has run off again with the dog. I came out to look for him.'

'Damn!' Damian frowned. 'That stupid animal. It is a pity the bitch ever followed me here. I dare say Jared would not have wandered so far without it.'

'I could get rid of it,' Rajib suggested. 'No one need ever know.'

'You harm that dog and I'll send you back to India

quicker than you can blink! Do you hear me? The animal is a nuisance, but it belongs to Miss Eastleigh. She has allowed Jared to share it—and I have no intention of paying her back by killing her dog.'

'Perhaps you should lock Jared in his room at night?' Rajib gave him a look that made Damian's blood run cold. 'Unless you want him to wander the countryside?'

The meaning behind Rajib's words made him angry. He took a step towards him, eyes glittering in the moonlight.

'Perhaps you should mind your own business and leave me to mine?' he muttered. 'While Jared is in my care he will not be locked in during either the day or the night. It would disturb and frighten him—more than he is already. I shall talk to him, make him see he must stop this wandering at night.'

'If anything should happen…'

'Why should anything happen here?' Damian's eyes narrowed. 'At home he was not safe, we both know why. Here there is no reason to fear another attack on his life—is there?'

The Indian's dark eyes fell before his burning gaze. 'No, *sahib*. Jared should be safe here—but still it is wrong that my master's son should wander alone at night.'

'I shall look for him,' Damian replied. 'Go to bed, Rajib. You may safely leave this to me.'

Rajib put his hands together and bowed his head, but not before Damian had seen the resentment in his eyes.

He watched the Indian walk back to the house, then sighed. If only he had been sure enough of his suspicions to speak out before they left India. And yet was it not always best to have the enemy where you could see them? Besides, he could not be sure if Rajib was Jared's enemy or only his; it might just be that he was merely jealous of the trust Ahmed had placed in him. He and Nessa considered the boy their property, and resented the fact that Ahmed had placed so much trust in him.

Turning away, Damian went off to search for his charge. It was unlikely that Jared would come to much harm with that great dog in tow. As Miss Eastleigh had said earlier, Sheba would probably defend the boy with her life if need be.

A smile touched Damian's mouth as his thoughts returned to that particular lady. He had been misled by Lord Orford's agent's information. She was certainly not young, but neither was she a dried-up old maid. Her cousin had proved easy enough to win over, but what did Miss Rosalyn Eastleigh think of him?

He believed she did not quite know whether to trust him or not. She had shown plainly that she felt the restrictions placed on Jared were not quite fair. And Jared's own manner towards him was, to say the least, prickly, which might make anyone suspect him of being unkind. Yet Miss Eastleigh could not think him capable of harming the boy?

He was annoyed to discover it mattered to him. He would not like to have her think him too stern a guardian, that he might actually abuse the youth.

What a fool he was to let such considerations weigh with him! His duty was to keep Jared safe, no matter what. If the boy was unhappy with his situation, that was not his fault. Besides, what should he care for the opinions of a woman who could mean nothing to him?

There could never be anything between him and Miss Eastleigh—he would be foolish to let himself think otherwise.

Damian had no time for flirtations, and certainly no intention of a deeper relationship. Marriage was not on his agenda. He had far too many problems as it was! And yet she intrigued him. She was a most unusual woman.

He chuckled softly to himself as his mood changed and he imagined suggesting a more intimate relationship to Miss Eastleigh. In other circumstances, he would have enjoyed pursuing her…tempting her into his bed.

What a delight she would be! He had already caught glimpses of a passionate nature, though she did her best to hide it. It must irk her no end to be forced to live the restricted life of a maiden lady. She was an Amazon, fearless and brave, and more rightly belonged in another age.

Catching sight of Jared playing with Sheba in the bushes, he called to them. The dog responded at once, and Jared followed reluctantly. Damian studied his rebellious face. The trust Ahmed had placed in him was proving more of a burden than he had first thought; nevertheless, he was determined to carry out his promise.

'Have I not told you to stay in the house unless I am with you?'

'Yes, *sahib*.' Jared kicked at the grass stubbornly. He had taken off his English clothes and was dressed in the loose Indian trousers and tunic he preferred. 'I was only in the garden—and Sheba was with me.'

'I know that.' Damian frowned. 'Do not force me to be stricter with you, Jared. I do not want to restrict your freedom completely—but if I have to, I shall. Do you understand me?'

'Yes, *sahib*.' The dark eyes looked up at him. 'You won't send Sheba away?'

'No—but you must obey my instructions, Jared. You know why.'

'Yes…' For a moment anger, rebellion and fear showed in his face, then the shutter came down. 'Yes, *sahib*. I know.'

Damian watched as he went up to the house, the huge dog lolloping about, barking and leaping at him.

It would be no better anywhere else, Damian decided. He would just have to pray that Miss Eastleigh was discreet enough not to voice her doubts to others. If gossip became rife, he would simply have to move on.

Rosalyn's heart leaped as she saw them riding towards her, the man and the youth, both so at home in the saddle…both riding horses she recognized as being pure Arab and mettlesome creatures.

'Miss Eastleigh.' Damian reined in, sweeping off his hat in greeting. 'I am delighted you managed to keep our appointment.'

'Did you imagine I would cry off?' Rosalyn gave him a direct look. 'I am not such poor stuff, sir. Besides, I wanted to invite Jared to tea this afternoon. My cousin is to bring her daughter to stay with us next week. You will both be invited to take tea with us then, of course—but I should like to have Jared to myself first.'

Jared was looking at her oddly.

'That is if you would like to come, Jared?'

'Very much, *mem-sahib*.'

'Good—that is settled, then.' She smiled at Damian. 'Shall we ride towards the river? It is the boundary between Lord Orford's estate and that of our other neighbours—the Sheldons. Have you met Sir Matthew yet?'

'No, we have not been so fortunate as yet.'

'You must attend church on Sunday morning. That is the best way to meet everyone,' Rosalyn said. 'Either I or the vicar will be pleased to introduce you to your neighbours.'

Damian brought his horse to a gentle trot beside her while Jared raced on ahead. It was obvious the youth had an excellent command of his mount, so Rosalyn was surprised when her companion shouted to warn him not to venture too far ahead.

'He seems quite capable of managing his horse,' she remarked. 'And we shall not be far behind him. Jared seems to resent restrictions. Do you not think it may make him more rebellious still if you hold the leading strings too tight?'

'Jared is my charge,' Damian replied seriously, his eyes meeting hers without flinching. 'I have no wish to hold him on too tight a rein. Perhaps we could increase our pace so that I do not lose sight of him?'

Rosalyn agreed to it, spurring her own mare to a canter. It meant they were no longer able to converse, but she gave herself up to the pleasures of the countryside, gradually increasing her speed until she was able to reach Jared's own horse and even race him for a while. She glanced over her shoulder, realising that Mr Wrexham was holding his own mount in check and seemed content to watch over them.

Once again, she was aware of a mystery, of something slightly sinister hidden beneath the surface.

Surely he could not imagine any harm could come to Jared in this peaceful corner of England?

Once again, she was intrigued by the situation at Orford Hall. Just who was Jared—and why did Mr Wrexham need to keep such a careful eye on him?

It was often necessary to guard the children of wealthy or important men—but Mr Wrexham seemed particularly vigilant.

They rode for almost an hour, alternating between a thrilling gallop and a brisk trot, before Damian insisted on accompanying to her own stables. She invited them to stay for some breakfast, but Damian refused, dismounting and coming to help her down.

He stood for a moment longer than necessary with his hands about her waist. It was a rather pleasant sensation to be held thus, Rosalyn discovered. So pleasant that she allowed it to continue until she suddenly realised that he was staring at her very oddly. She drew away at once and he let her go, immediately catching the reins of his own horse.

'Jared will be here at three this afternoon,' he said as he looked down at her. 'Rajib will accompany him, but he will not come into the house.'

'Will you not take tea with us yourself?' Rosalyn frowned as he shook his head. 'Perhaps I did not make myself clear? The invitation was to both of you, of course.'

'Thank you, Miss Eastleigh. Perhaps I shall avail myself of your kindness another day—but today I have other business, so I must ask you to forgive me.'

'Very well.' She smiled at Jared. 'I shall look forward to your visit, sir.'

'I shall bring Sheba with me,' the youth promised. 'Then Rajib need not wait for me.'

'There is not the least need for him to wait,' agreed Rosalyn. 'I shall be very pleased to walk home with you myself.'

The satisfied expression on the youth's face told her that her suggestion had found favour.

'Until later, Jared.'

'We must leave,' Damian said, frowning slightly. He tipped his hat to her. 'Your company this morning was much appreciated, Miss Eastleigh.'

'I enjoyed myself.'

She stood watching as they turned their horses and rode away, Jared leading at first but gradually caught by the man as they disappeared over the rise.

Rosalyn discovered she was a little disappointed that Mr Wrexham had business elsewhere that afternoon, though she scolded herself for allowing it to matter. During a restless night, she had decided that she would not cut the connection, even though she suspected that everything was not quite what it seemed up at the Hall.

Mr Wrexham could never be more than a slight acquaintance, of course. Just a stranger who had come to stay for a few months and would move on when summer was gone.

Like a migrant swallow, she thought, watching a bird swoop beneath the eaves of the stables to a neat mud nest which seemed to be defying the laws of gravity and looked terribly vulnerable.

In the autumn the swallows would be gone and so would Mr Wrexham.

* * *

As she went into the house, Rosalyn heard voices. Good gracious! Could that be Aunt Susan? She had written to invite her aunt to bring her granddaughter Sarah Jane to stay, but she could not possibly have received the letter so soon.

Going quickly into the parlour, she discovered that it was indeed her aunt. Maria was still wearing her dressing robe and looked flustered, though she had had enough presence of mind to ask for tea to be brought to the small parlour.

'How lovely to see you,' Rosalyn said and went to kiss her aunt's cheek. 'I wrote yesterday to tell you to bring Sarah Jane, but did not expect you for several days.'

'Forgive me for descending on you like this,' said Susan Buckley, pulling a wry face. 'I was sure you would not mind my bringing Sarah Jane, so I did not wait for your reply. Tommy has gone down with the measles and Celia was at her wit's end to know what to do. She was terrified that, even though we kept them apart, Sarah Jane would take it from him—and on top of her last illness, that might be too much for the poor child. She really was very poorly with the scarlet fever, you know. It quite pulled her down.'

'Oh, I am so sorry,' Rosalyn said, immediately sympathetic. 'You did very right to bring her straight to us. Where is she?'

'Maria took her to rest upstairs, because she complained of a headache,' Aunt Susan replied. 'Sarah has always been so full of life. It upsets me terribly to see her like this.'

'Yes, of course. It must—and you must be worried about poor dear Celia and little Tommy,' said Maria. 'You mustn't worry, we shall take very good care of Sarah Jane—shan't we, Rosalyn?'

'Yes, certainly we shall.' Rosalyn smothered a sigh. She remembered Sarah Jane as being a very dominant personality, and thought she would not be an easy guest, especially if she was feeling unwell. 'How long can you stay, Aunt?'

'I must leave again tomorrow,' Mrs Buckley said regretfully. 'Celia cannot cope without me. Besides, she is increasing again and ought not to go near Tommy while he has the measles. He cried so when I left, the poor darling. I would not have left him at all if it had not been so urgent.'

'Must you leave so soon?' Maria was horrified. 'You will wear yourself out with all that travelling.'

'I have no choice,' replied Mrs Buckley. 'Besides, I shall not rest until I know how Celia and Tommy go on.'

'You must take the journey steadily, Aunt,' Rosalyn said, agreeing with Maria for once. 'It will not help either Celia or Tommy if you are ill yourself.'

'Good gracious, my dear,' her aunt said. 'I am as fit as a fiddle. Travelling is nothing to me. When I was first married I did the Grand Tour, you know. I sometimes think I should like to travel now—but not until Celia's children have grown up a little.'

She put down her teacup and patted the sofa beside her, encouraging Rosalyn to sit with her.

'I have done nothing but rattle on about my own affairs since you came in, my love. Maria tells me you have a new neighbour—and his pupil is an Indian boy. It sounds very exciting.'

'Mr Wrexham and Jared have taken the Orfords' house for some weeks,' Rosalyn said with a smile. Goodness, Maria had been busy! 'If you could stay longer you might have met them both. Jared is coming to tea this afternoon, but Mr Wrexham has business elsewhere.'

'Wrexham…' Susan Buckley wrinkled her brow in concentration. 'Now where have I heard that name? I suppose he is no relation to the Oxfordshire family? Sir Robert Wrexham was a cousin of Earl Marlowe. I almost became engaged to Sir Robert when I was a gel…but the Earl did not approve of me. Neither my fortune or consequence was large enough to satisfy his pride—and naturally his word was law.' An odd expression came to her eyes. 'I always thought it served him right a little when his eldest grandson was sent away in disgrace. Now, what was the boy's name? I cannot recall it…something odd, I believe.'

A tingling sensation started in the nape of Rosalyn's neck. 'Why was he sent away?'

'Oh, I never did know that,' replied Mrs Buckley. 'I was married and had a child of twelve years by then; my husband would not have sullied my ears with scandal—he was always so protective of me. Dear George.' She sighed and looked sad for a moment as she thought of her dead husband. 'But I do know it was thought very bad. Marlowe's grandson could not have been more than seventeen or eighteen at the time. Oh, it must be all of twenty years ago.'

'So he would be about seven and thirty now?'

'Yes, I should imagine he must be.' Rosalyn's aunt looked at her. 'How old is your Mr Wrexham?'

'About that age, I would suppose.'

'Has he spent the last few years in some outlandish place abroad?'

'In India…' Rosalyn shook her head as her aunt's eyes lit from within. She had clearly scented an intrigue. 'No, you are wrong, Aunt. I very much doubt if it is the same man.'

'What is his first name—is it Damon or something similar?'

'Damian, I believe.'

'Yes! Yes, of course. Damian.' Her aunt was clearly intrigued. 'The scandal was over a woman, of course. There was more to it—but I cannot quite remember the details. I think someone may have been killed. No, I am not sure of that. I do know that his father disowned him, said he would never allow him to return home while he lived, which he isn't—living, I mean. Poor Lord Edward died soon after from a fall while out hunting. Not that I ever liked him. He was much like the Earl, a cold proud man as far as I can remember. Lord Jacob, his brother, was so much kinder—and their cousin, of course. I was quite attached to Sir Robert, I recall.'

Rosalyn felt a little shiver down her spine. What could Mr Wrexham have done to make his father disown him? She carefully kept her voice level as she asked, 'Do you still keep in touch with the family?'

Susan Buckley stared at her. 'Sir Robert died some years back. I haven't spoken to Lord Jacob in years—but I know his wife. We speak when we happen to meet, which is once or twice a year, when Lady Ruth comes to Bath to take the waters. She has been an invalid for years.' She hesitated, observing Rosalyn's heightened colour. 'Would you like me to ask her about her nephew Damian?'

'Oh, no, of course not,' Rosalyn cried. Suddenly, she did not want to learn that Mr Wrexham was a man she ought not to know. 'It would be embarrassing if he heard…no, it is nothing to do with me. Besides, it all happened so long ago. If he has come back to England, the scandal must surely have been forgotten?'

'I am not so sure about that,' her aunt replied, frowning. 'Some things are never forgotten or forgiven. If the tale was remembered…well, it might be awkward for you to know him.'

'Mr Wrexham could not possibly be the man you are thinking off.' Rosalyn was surprised to hear Maria's instant defence of their neighbour. 'He is a perfect gentleman. There must be some mistake.'

Rosalyn hid her smile as her aunt's brows rose.

'Yes, Aunt Susan,' she said. 'I am sure there is a mistake. And if there is not…it is a very long time ago. I do not think we should stir up trouble where none exists, do you?'

'No, perhaps not,' Mrs Buckley agreed, making a mental note to do a little research on the mysterious Mr Wrexham when she returned to Bath. 'Besides, as you say, it is not really our business.'

It was not their affair. Rosalyn was determined not to let the old rumour disturb her peace of mind. Whatever Mr Wrexham had done in the past, it could not affect her or her way of life.

She would put it from her mind. She would not give it another thought.

Damian Wrexham looked about him as he paused outside the inn on the outskirts of Cambridge. He was tempted to walk away, wishing now that he had never agreed to meet his uncle—that the letter had never reached him in India. Or that he had not been fool enough to respond to the desperate appeal it contained.

He sighed and pushed open the door of the sixteenth-century inn. His memory of Jacob Wrexham was one that could not be denied. Of all the family, Jacob was the only one who had lifted a finger to help him. If it had not been for his uncle, he would have been forced to leave England without a guinea to his name. How could he refuse a request for help from the man who had stood by him all those years ago?

A musty smell of stale ale and neglect met him as he went inside. Surely they could have met somewhere decent? Damian glanced round, searching for the man he remembered. There was no one…no one but a rather tired-looking man in the corner. Surely that could not be his uncle?

The man was standing up, smiling, walking towards him.

'Damian?' he said, a look of relief spreading over his face. 'I was afraid you wouldn't come.'

'I gave you my word, sir. Whatever you may believe of me, I do not break a promise.'

'No, Damian,' Lord Jacob said. 'I never believed a half of what was said at the time. I knew you were not capable of murder. Reckless, headstrong—but not a villain.'

A wry smile flickered over Damian's mouth. 'Then you are the only one, sir. My father and grandfather both died believing it.'

'No, Damian. Not the old man. Your father…' Lord Jacob sighed. 'He never forgave you, but Henry did… towards the end. He wanted you to come home. We tried to find you but, by the time we discovered your whereabouts, it was too late. He died with your name on his lips. He wanted your forgiveness, Damian.'

'He had nothing to be forgiven for—except his stubborn nature.' Damian's mouth set hard. 'He believed what he was told and acted on it, nothing more. My father always hated me…as you know. The old man seemed fond of me when I was a boy, but he refused to listen when I tried to explain. The fight was forced on me, Jacob. I killed Roderick Harrington, but it was a duel. I had to face him…' He shuddered at the memory. 'Well, you know. I told you in confidence, though you do not know the whole—no one knows the extent of it.'

'I know that you did not deserve what happened to you.' Lord Jacob took his arm. 'Come and sit down, Damian. We have much to talk about.'

'Could it not have been left to the lawyers?' Damian was more disturbed than he cared to admit by this meeting. Cast out by his family, he had put his memories aside, throwing himself into the life of exile that had been forced on him. 'I never expected to inherit anything. Why can I not simply sign the estate over to you?'

'Can't afford to take it off you,' replied his uncle with a rueful smile. 'Your father gambled away a fortune before he died—and the old man let the place go to rack and ruin. He seemed not to care after you left. I tried to help, but he would never listen to me.'

'No…I remember.' Damian smiled wryly. 'What do you want me to do—pay the debts?'

'Could you?'

'Perhaps—if I thought it was worth it.'

'I'd heard you'd made money.' His uncle looked uncertain, awkward. 'Is it any use appealing to your feelings for the family name?'

'Good God, no!' Damian laughed. '*That* means nothing to me. When I was younger perhaps…but now, nothing. I came because I owed *you* something—if you are in trouble yourself?'

'I had expected the old man might leave what was left of it all to me. But his will is quite clear. I can only inherit if you are dead. Besides, there is only that old barn of a house—and debts. The land was sold or mortgaged long since.'

'If I paid the debts, what would you do with the house?'

'Sell it,' his uncle replied promptly. 'Without the land it is nothing more than a millstone around anyone's neck. I wouldn't want to live there—and nor would my son.'

'So what do you want me to do?'

'I can't sell without your signature,' his uncle said. 'And the debts will have to be paid eventually. If I have to find the money it will put a great strain on my personal finances—and I do not care to leave such a burden for my own son.'

'And I am the heir, so I am responsible.'

His uncle made no reply, but his expression showed that he did feel it was Damian's responsibility.

'Yes, of course,' Damian murmured, nodding to himself. 'Leave it to me, Uncle. I'll have a look at the house one of these days, and in the meantime I'll arrange for the debts to be settled—providing a proper accounting can be made.'

'What do you mean?' Jacob looked startled. 'I have already agreed them with the lawyers. You can't want to be bothered with all that?'

'I most certainly do,' replied Damian. 'I am aware that it is not quite the thing to take a healthy interest in money in your world—but my fortune was not easily earned and I do not intend to throw it away. I shall not pay anything that cannot be proven.'

'You must do as you think best, of course.'

'I intend to, sir.' He saw the shocked expression on his uncle's face and laughed. 'If that is all, I believe our business is finished.'

'Damian…won't you even consider setting up a home in England? You could restore the house, buy back the land, take your rightful place in society.' Lord Jacob looked at him oddly. 'Won't you visit us…discuss the situation?'

'There is nothing to discuss,' Damian replied. 'I came back for a purpose. When that is done, there will be nothing more to keep me here.'

Yet even as he spoke, he knew that he was not

speaking the whole truth. He had believed that he would never wish to live in England again, but now he was not so sure.

Chapter Three

Rosalyn had hoped to have Jared to herself when he came to tea. She had guessed that he was feeling lonely, missing the warmth and colour of India, and the people he loved—perhaps his family most of all. Now that her aunt had arrived, she accepted her hopes of a tête-à-tête were at an end.

To her credit, Aunt Susan behaved exactly as she would with any other youth of her acquaintance. She pressed a dish of little, sweet almond cakes on Jared, together with the lemon barley water Rosalyn had herself prepared, as she began to quiz him.

'How do you like England?' she asked. 'Are you going to school here?'

Jared's manner was polite but formal as he fended off her questions, though clearly uncomfortable to be the object of her curiosity. Rosalyn cursed the misfortune which had brought her aunt's visit forward. Especially when Sarah Jane decided to put in a belated appearance.

The girl was pretty in a fair, insipid way, her pink dress too frilly and ornate for Rosalyn's taste. Sarah looked like a dressmaker's mannequin—delicate, precious and unnaturally tidy.

'Ah, there you are, dearest!' her loving grandmother said, smiling on her indulgently. 'I am glad you have decided to come down for tea. Are you feeling better?'

'A little…' Sarah Jane's large blue eyes regarded Jared with a mixture of curiosity and hostility. 'Who is he? His skin looks a funny colour.'

'Sarah!' Rosalyn admonished sharply. 'Jared's skin is a very nice colour. He comes from India, where the sun is extremely hot.'

'Hasn't he got a parasol?'

Rosalyn was about to answer her, but Jared got there first.

'My father has a thousand parasols,' he replied scornfully. 'Some of them are bigger than this room. You are an ignorant little girl. My father's people are all dark-skinned. It is your people who are strange with their red and white skins that burn quickly in the sun.'

Sarah Jane's mouth opened and closed like a fish out of water. No one had ever spoken to her in that way in the whole of her life. She was not sure how to reply; however, there was something about him that seemed to command her respect, so she reached for a cake and ate it in silence.

Mrs Buckley and Rosalyn stared at each other, both

struggling against a desire to laugh, though Maria was clearly horrified, but wise enough on this occasion to keep silent. Before anyone could think of the right words to ease the situation, the door was thrust open and Sheba came bouncing in. Sarah eyed the dog uncertainly, but Jared called to her and she obliged him by jumping all over him and licking his face thoroughly. It was then that Rosalyn had an inspiration.

'Jared,' she suggested. 'Why don't you and Sheba take Sarah Jane into the gardens? She has never been here before so you could show her around the grounds.'

'I'm not sure—' began Mrs Buckley, but before she could finish, Sarah Jane was out of her chair, obviously eager to take up the suggestion. 'Well, if you feel up to it, dear. I dare say a little air will not hurt you.'

Sarah Jane ignored her grandmother, her eyes firmly fixed on Jared. 'Come on, then,' she said with an imperious lift of her head. 'I want to see the gardens.'

For a moment mutiny flared in Jared's dark eyes, then he turned to Rosalyn, his manner clearly that of someone struggling to maintain his dignity in the face of severe provocation.

He inclined his head to her. 'Since it is your wish, Miss Eastleigh, I shall take the…child into the gardens.'

He was fourteen, Sarah Jane thirteen and a half—but of course he was male and therefore superior.

Neither Rosalyn nor her aunt dared to so much as breathe until the pair had departed, Sheba enthusiastically following at their heels. Once the children were safely out of range, their eyes met in shared amusement.

'Oh, dear,' Mrs Buckley said, dabbing at her wet cheeks when she had stopped laughing a little later. 'I just hope she will not suffer a relapse. But indeed, I think the fresh air may do her good. Celia does tend to be a little…over-protective of her children at times.'

It was the closest Aunt Susan had ever come to admitting that her beloved grandchildren might possibly be spoiled.

Rosalyn nodded but refrained from comment. The French windows were open and occasionally they heard the sounds of laughter—both Jared's and Sarah Jane's—mingling with Sheba's barking.

Rosalyn, her aunt and Maria enjoyed a comfortable half an hour over the teacups, and when a slightly less immaculate Sarah Jane came rushing in with Sheba and Jared following behind, it was immediately apparent they had come to no harm.

'Can I go to tea with Jared tomorrow?' Sarah demanded impetuously. 'May I? Please say yes, Grandmama!'

'It is Rosalyn you should ask,' replied Mrs Buckley. 'I must return home in the morning. Your mother needs me.'

Sarah Jane turned her large, very bright eyes on Rosalyn. 'Please may I? Jared has promised to show me all sorts of things. Please do say I might!'

'If Jared has invited you…' Rosalyn glanced at him. He had assumed his rather haughty expression, but the gleam of anticipation in his eyes betrayed him. 'Then I see no reason why not. And now I must walk home with Jared as I promised his tutor.'

Sarah Jane's instant demand to be allowed to accompany them was firmly denied by her grandmother. She *was* still recovering from a severe illness, and too much exercise might undo all the good playing in the garden had obviously done.

The afternoon was pleasant as they began their walk, a cloudless sky and a bright sun warming the air. Rosalyn was pleased to have the opportunity of some time alone with Jared.

'You were very good with Sarah Jane,' she told him as they left the orchard behind and started to climb a grassy bank. To the right was a small copse, to the left open fields in which horses grazed. 'She can be thoughtless at times—but she has been ill. It will be nice for her to have someone of her own age to talk to now and then.'

Jared's teeth were very white, gleaming against the dusk of his skin as he grinned at her. 'She is not bad for a girl,' he said. 'At home the other children would not dare to talk to me as she does. But I do not mind it.'

Something in his eyes touched Rosalyn's heart. She suspected he had been very lonely. She did not pursue the subject he had raised, understanding that anything he wished to confide must come naturally, without prompting.

'I am sure Sarah Jane will be safe with you, Jared. Perhaps you could teach her some manners? I fear she has been indulged more than is good for her.'

They had almost reached the Orfords' house now. Rosalyn's heart took a flying leap as she saw the man coming to meet them. He was wearing riding clothes, but his coat was dark blue and he had taken more care with his appearance than on the first time they had met.

'Miss Eastleigh,' he said. 'I returned earlier than I expected. Will you come in and take a glass of wine?'

'Thank you, Mr Wrexham, but I must not stay. My aunt arrived sooner than we thought, but she is to leave again in the morning. I should go back now or she will think I am neglecting her.'

'Then allow me to walk part of the way with you?' Damian glanced at Jared. 'I shall see you later. We have neglected our studies today and must make up for it.'

'Yes, *sahib*.'

Rosalyn wondered at the change in Jared's manner. Did he resent his tutor? He seemed subdued—but not frightened. Surely not frightened?

Sheba seemed uncertain when Rosalyn turned back, whining a little as if torn between two loyalties. Rosalyn ignored her and she ran after the boy.

'You have lost your dog,' Damian said. 'Shall I purchase a similar animal for Jared and send Sheba back to you?'

'No,' she replied, glancing thoughtfully at him as they began to walk back the way she had come. Could he really be the man Aunt Susan had mentioned earlier? What was the truth of the scandal which had caused his exile? 'I do not think that would serve. Jared has become attached to Sheba. Another dog would not be the same. Let him keep her for the moment.'

'You are generous, Miss Eastleigh.'

She shook her head. 'You must not imagine it to be a great sacrifice on my part. I am fond of Sheba, but she was foisted on me by my brother and has always been prone to roaming at will. I can spare her for a while. Besides, I have an ulterior motive…'

Rosalyn gave him a wicked look and went on to explain about her cousin's daughter, particularly the way she had suddenly thrown off her sickly air after being with Jared in the garden.

'I believe it may do them both good,' she confided, raising her candid gaze to Damian's face. 'Jared has not led an exactly normal life, I think?'

'It was not so bad while his mother lived,' Damian replied. 'His mother—Anna—did her best to give him some freedom, but when she died…circumstances changed.'

'Yes, I see.' Rosalyn sensed there was much more he was not telling her. She did not look at him as she asked, 'Is it your intention to stay in England beyond the summer, Mr Wrexham—or shall you return to India?'

'I have not yet decided.' Damian frowned. 'My business may take longer than I had imagined. Why do you ask?'

'Oh…no particular reason.' They had reached the orchard. Rosalyn stopped walking. She raised her head, giving him a challenging stare. 'You need come no further, Mr Wrexham. I shall be perfectly safe—and I am sure you must be wanting your dinner after having been out for most of the day.'

He caught her arm, detaining her as she would have walked away, swinging her back to face him. His expression was harsher than she had previously seen it, his eyes angry.

'What is it, Miss Eastleigh? What have you heard?'

Rosalyn hesitated, then breathed deeply. She supposed it was best to have it out in the open. 'Nothing certain, sir—merely some gossip concerning an old scandal.'

'Damn!' Damian cursed aloud. 'I had hoped to avoid this—it was so long ago. It seems I should have told you at once. I was sent away in disgrace by my own family.'

So her aunt had been right!

'There is no need to explain. It is entirely your own affair.'

'Is it? Are you not angry with me for concealing it from you?'

'No, not at all.'

'Indeed?' His brows rose in disbelief, but as he gazed down into her eyes he saw that she meant every word. 'You are indeed a remarkable woman, Miss Eastleigh. Are you not outraged?'

'By something that happened twenty years ago?' She shook her head. 'I think not, sir. Besides, I do not truly know what happened—only that there was a scandal and you were cast out by your family.'

'It was nineteen years and three months to be exact,' he replied, his face reflecting bitterness, anger and, she thought, regret. 'I killed a man, Miss Eastleigh. I have never tried to deny that—but it was a duel, and fairly conducted with witnesses to testify that I behaved properly. However, the circumstances…there were reasons why my family decided to disown me. Reasons I do not wish to discuss, even with you.'

'You have no obligation to do so.'

'Not yet…but under certain circumstances…'

He was going to kiss her again! Rosalyn felt suddenly breathless, her heart beating madly. She realised that she wanted him to kiss her, to hold her close to his chest, to make love to her. Her body was melting in the warmth of the wonderful new sensation flooding through her.

So this was desire! She had often wondered, but had never before come close to experiencing passion. It shocked and yet excited her to discover that she was capable of such strong feelings, for until this moment she had not thought it possible. She had never felt in the least inclined to welcome a man's kisses before. Without her being aware of it, her mouth softened, parting invitingly as she gazed up at him.

'Do not look at me like that,' Damian said harshly. Her response had surprised him, even though he had guessed her capable of passion. 'You can have no idea of the danger you risk at this moment, Miss Eastleigh. Remember! I have lived abroad too long to respect English customs. In India when a woman looks at a man that way…he knows how to react.'

Rosalyn felt the hot colour flood her cheeks. Goodness! She was inviting his embrace. What must he think of her? Indeed, what was she thinking of to allow it?

'You do not need to remind me of your lack of English manners,' she replied crossly. 'If you will let go my arm, sir, I shall cease to look at you at all.'

Her obvious annoyance at being reminded of the impropriety of her own behaviour—and the fact that she had not denied it—broke the tension in him. He laughed and released her.

'Forgive me, Miss Eastleigh. I am not usually such a brute—but you tempted me. I did want to kiss you. In fact, I wanted to do very much more. So you have no need to be embarrassed or to imagine yourself at fault. It was entirely my own decision. I beg you to show mercy. I fear I am a barbarian and do not deserve all the kindness you have already offered me.'

'There is nothing to forgive. I was as much to blame as you—though it was very wrong of me. You must be thinking me shameless?'

When he smiled at her as he was doing now, Rosalyn was unable to maintain her anger against him. Something warned her she would be wise to cut the connection now while she could, that she was skating on thin ice and would pay the penalty for her foolishness—but deep inside her there was a feeling which would not be denied. It was almost as if she had been waiting for this moment, for this man, all her life.

'Sarah Jane has been invited to tea with Jared tomorrow,' she said. 'I shall send her in the carriage at about three. You will permit Coachman and Nanny to wait for her?'

'Will you not come with her yourself?'

Rosalyn shook her head. 'Not this time, but we shall meet again soon, Mr Wrexham. At church tomorrow, perhaps—and you must come to dine with us when my brother arrives.'

She walked away then and he let her go.

She was a remarkable woman. She deserved much more than he could give her. He had thought to while away a few weeks by a mild flirtation, but he had suddenly discovered that his feelings toward Miss Eastleigh were anything but mild.

Rosalyn sat gazing out at the moonlit gardens. She had tried sleeping but was restless and found it impossible. Her strange thoughts had forced her to rise, but she was still unable to resolve them.

Why had she let Damian Wrexham turn her calm, pleasant world upside down?

Surely she had not fallen in love with him? No, of course not! They had only met three or four times. People did not fall in love just like that—did they?

Rosalyn sighed, twisting a strand of her long hair about her finger. She suspected that was exactly the way it happened. Oh, what an idiot she was! She had rejected so many offers of marriage when she was younger—all of them from very respectable gentlemen. Men of consequence, who had offered her a life of ease and luxury. Never once had she been tempted to accept—so why was she in such turmoil now? To fall for someone like Damian Wrexham was madness—foolish beyond belief!

Nothing could come of it, of course. Marriage was unlikely—even if it was possible. He might have a wife in India. No, no, she did not believe so ill of him. He must have mentioned it if he were married.

He would have had a mistress, of course. That was only natural. She would not expect him to have lived like a monk.

Rosalyn got up to return to her bed. It was wrong of her to allow her thoughts to take this route. If Mr Wrexham wanted a wife he would have married years ago. Besides, the very idea was out of the question. Not to be considered in the circumstances! Her family would all be against it. And anything else was impossible, of course.

Yet there had been a moment when she might have been willing to surrender all she held dear for love.

Rosalyn's cheeks burned in the darkness. Mr Wrexham had sensed how near she was to capitulation. That was why he had drawn back, of course—acting the part of the gentleman he claimed he was not—but why? Why would he do that? Because he respected her, or because he did not wish to become involved?

Did he think her an old maid? He had laughed at the idea when they met, but it was not so very far from the truth. Rosalyn had given up all idea of marriage when her father died. Her grief had left her feeling empty, drained, willing to settle for the comfort of her home and the friends she had gathered around her. But now…now she was aware that the dissatisfaction with her life had been growing for a while.

Even so, she had not considered marriage as a way out of her situation. Until now… Oh, dear! Rosalyn laughed at her own thoughts. She really must not let her dreams run away with her.

Mr Wrexham was not here to find a wife.

Just why was he here? Rosalyn pondered the mystery as she lay watching the dawn slowly creep over her windowsill, quite unaware that, as the light strengthened and he rose from his bed, Damian's thoughts were also far from easy. He too had spent a restless night chasing unwanted dreams—dreams he had imagined long dead.

Rosalyn saw him as soon as she entered the church the next morning. He was standing looking about him as though he wondered where he ought to sit. She hesitated, then touched his arm, smiling up at him as she whispered, 'You may sit with us if you wish. I am sure Maria will not mind.'

'Thank you. I did not wish to take anyone's special place.'

Rosalyn went into the pew reserved for her family, Maria following behind. Mr Wrexham came after her. From the corner of her eye, Rosalyn saw him bend his head, his lips moving in silent prayer. She had not been sure he would come. Or that he had retained the faith he had been born to—but it seemed he had despite the years spent in a foreign land.

Rosalyn said the usual prayers for her family and sat down. She carried her own Bible, which was covered in white leather. Mr Wrexham had none of his own, but Maria offered him hers and recited the prayers she knew by heart.

The Reverend Waller's sermon was as usual long and slightly muddled, but Rosalyn felt uplifted by it in a way she had not for some time. Perhaps it was the very pleasant tenor voice of Mr Wrexham which seemed to bring the familiar hymns alive for her?

Afterwards, she filed out of church, pausing to speak to the vicar for a few minutes. Several of her neighbours were looking at Mr Wrexham curiously. She introduced him to Sir Matthew and Lady Sheldon, and their two rather pretty daughters, smiling to herself as an instant invitation to dine that day was issued. The Sheldons had three more daughters at home to see settled, and Mr Wrexham was looking very presentable that morning.

Rosalyn had been thinking of issuing a casual invitation herself, but reserved it for another time.

She nodded farewell to Mr Wrexham, then began to thread her way through the small group who still lingered, leaving him to make the acquaintance of his neighbours in his own manner. By taking him into her family's pew that morning, she had given him all the credit he needed and she had no doubt he would soon be in great demand.

Rosalyn stood at the open landing window, gazing out. She could hear Sarah Jane's squeals of laughter and wondered at the extraordinary change in the girl. In just six days she and Jared had become almost inseparable. They visited each other every day, not just for tea but for hours at a time. There was no doubt that it was doing the girl a great deal of good. One had only to look at Sarah Jane to see that she was happy, thought Rosalyn.

She, on the other hand had not seen Mr Wrexham since their meeting after church. Rosalyn sighed. How fortunate the children were! They had no need to consider anything but their own amusement. While *she*…was being very foolish again!

She looked up at the sky, noticing that it was becoming overcast. The weather had been kind these past few days, but it looked as if they might be in for a storm. If it threatened to rain, she would send Jared home in the carriage. In the meantime, she must not dawdle here.

Freddie was due to arrive at any moment. He had sent a groom ahead to warn them, which was so unlike him that his sister had begun to suspect that his guests were even more important than she had imagined.

Rosalyn glanced at herself in a heavy, gilt-framed mirror on the wall, patting a stray hair into place. She had drawn her thick hair back into a neat chignon, allowing a few tendrils to fall about her face. It was perhaps a rather severe style, but it suited her as curls and ringlets would not, framing a face that had its own special beauty but was not pretty in the accepted sense. Her pale grey gown clung lovingly to her statuesque figure in a way that, had her likeness been taken at that moment, would have made her a perfect model for Queen Boadicea at the reins of her war chariot. There was something bold and fine about Rosalyn, something that was at odds with her status as a spinster.

Of course, none of this was apparent to Rosalyn herself. She saw a woman who was dressed plainly, not in the first stare of fashion, but certainly respectable, which was all she required. She turned her head as she heard running footsteps and Maria came rushing up the stairs.

'They have just arrived,' Maria said, a little breathlessly. 'I saw them from the parlour window and thought you would want to know.'

'Yes, thank you,' Rosalyn said. For some reason her heart had started to beat rapidly and she was nervous. 'I was about to come down. Take your time, Maria, get your breath back.'

'I shall follow you at once,' said Maria. 'I should not want to be backward in any attention to dear Sir Frederick. Besides, I dare say you have not thought, dearest—but he may have a special reason for bringing guests. Two ladies, you know.'

She gave Rosalyn such an arch look that it was all she could do not to make a cutting remark. A mere irritation of the nerves, of course. It could make no difference to Rosalyn if her brother married. After their father's death, Freddie had agreed that the Cambridgeshire estate would always be his sister's home.

'I've never particularly liked the place, as you know,' he had said, grinning at her. 'It suits me to have you live here, Ros—and it is what Father would have wanted.'

Her father ought, of course, to have made some provision in his will, other than the trust fund he had set up years earlier to give her financial independence. If he had expected to die he would no doubt have made it plain that he wanted Rosalyn to have a life tenancy of her home, but his illness had struck so suddenly, and he had been in such distress, that he must have forgotten that everything would to go to his son.

Such arrangements were quite normal. Daughters were expected to marry and leave home—or live as dependents in the house of a brother or close relative.

Rosalyn could not imagine having to live as the dependent relative of anyone, even her brother, whom she loved very much. She was used to running her household to suit herself, for she had done much as she liked even before her father's death.

But Freddie would not want to bring his wife here! Rosalyn reassured herself. Of course he wouldn't. If he was thinking of marriage—and that wasn't sure yet—he would continue to live in London and Devon as he did now. He did not particularly care for the country, except during the hunting season.

Rosalyn shook off her vague doubts. She was

halfway down the stairs when Freddie and his guests entered the house, which gave her a moment to study the ladies before they noticed her.

The younger of the two was a tiny little thing, very delicate and fragile in appearance, with golden ringlets and a perfect rose complexion. She was, Rosalyn thought, the prettiest young lady she had ever seen. Her companion, however, was a rather stout, cross-looking woman with a fussy hairstyle more suited to a young girl and frosty grey eyes.

Those eyes were staring up at her, Rosalyn realised, and they were distinctly hostile.

'Freddie!' she cried and hurried down the last few stairs. 'How lovely to see you, dearest.'

'Ros!' Her brother took two huge strides towards her, embracing her in a bear hug. 'It's been too long, I know. Forgive me?' His grey eyes looked into hers. 'I shouldn't have neglected you.'

'You haven't,' she replied, smiling at him. 'But you *are* neglecting your guests. Pray introduce me.'

'What an idiot I am!' Sir Frederick turned to the older woman, a flicker of something in his eyes…something his sister thought might be a mixture of both respect and dislike. 'This is Mrs Jenkins, Ros—ma'am, my sister, Miss Rosalyn Eastleigh.'

'We have heard so much about you,' the woman said in a high, false tone. 'We have been longing to meet you—isn't that so, Beatrice?'

'And this…' said Freddie, ignoring her as he took the young lady's hand and drew her forward. 'This is Miss Beatrice Holland. Say hello to Ros, dearest.'

'Miss Eastleigh.' Miss Holland blushed and curtsied, giving Rosalyn a shy smile. 'We are so very happy to be here. I do hope we have not caused a great deal of trouble for you?'

'Of course not—' Rosalyn began but was interrupted by Mrs Jenkins.

'Of course it is no trouble, Beatrice,' she said. 'Miss Eastleigh must always be happy to entertain her brother's guests in his house.'

'Aunt Patricia…' Beatrice said, her colour deepening in acute embarrassment. 'Please…'

'Mrs Jenkins is perfectly right,' Rosalyn said easily. 'I am always happy to entertain Freddie's guests.' She turned her steady gaze on her brother. 'Freddie, I think perhaps you have something important to tell me? But we should go into the parlour.' She frowned, then looked back at the older woman. 'Mrs Jenkins, you must be tired from your journey. My cousin will take you up to your room at once. Maria, please look after Mrs Jenkins for me! We shall all meet again very soon.' She smiled at her brother and the pretty but nervous child, whose hand he was clutching with such determination. 'Freddie, won't you bring Miss Holland into my parlour *now*?'

From the indignant expression in Mrs Jenkins' eyes it was clear that she thought Rosalyn's behaviour high-handed, but Freddie was quick to respond, giving his undivided attention to Beatrice as the housekeeper helped her off with her pelisse and bonnet. Seeing that she could not count on his support, Mrs Jenkins went away with Maria, who was fluttering around her and trying very hard to soothe the feathers Rosalyn had so clearly ruffled.

'So you guessed at once,' Freddie said, looking at his sister in some apprehension. He had always been slightly in awe of his elder sister, who was his equal in height and, he sometimes thought, his superior in everything else. 'I suspected you might. I suppose I should have told you, but—'

'There was no need,' Rosalyn cut short his apology. 'I am delighted to welcome Miss Holland here—and though you still have not told me, I suspect you mean to marry her?'

'Oh, Freddie.' Beatrice looked at him with big, reproachful eyes. 'You did promise to tell Miss Eastleigh before we came down. I am so sorry…he did promise, honestly.'

'Well, now he has done so,' Rosalyn said giving her a warm smile. 'And I am delighted, of course. You are very welcome here, my dear Beatrice. I may call you that, I hope?'

'Yes, of course.' Beatrice dimpled, looking shy. 'You really don't mind, Miss Eastleigh?'

'Only that you call me Miss Eastleigh, when I would prefer us to be friends…Rosalyn, please.'

Rosalyn moved towards her, taking her hands and kissing her cheek. 'So pretty. You are very lucky, Freddie. I hope you appreciate your good fortune?'

'Rather,' Freddie replied with such a besotted look at his fiancée that Rosalyn knew he was head over heels in love with her. 'They were all after Bea—all the fellows in town—but she preferred me. I can't imagine why. I'm not much of a catch compared to Lord Hamilton or Devonshire.'

'You silly thing!' cried Beatrice and immediately endeared herself to Rosalyn. 'I wasn't in love with either of them. Aunt Patricia did think I ought to have accepted the Duke…but I really couldn't. Not once you had shown a preference for me.' She gave Rosalyn a shy smile. 'I wasn't sure Freddie even liked me at first.'

'You must have known?' Freddie said, looking incredulous.

She shook her head. 'No, not at first…not until the masked ball when we went on to the balcony and…' She blushed and looked uncertainly at Rosalyn. 'You will think me very forward to have let Freddie kiss me before we were engaged, but I had been wishing he would give me some sort of a sign and—'

She broke off as her aunt came bustling into the room, Maria trailing unhappily behind her. It was clear that Mrs Jenkins was not willing to be denied any longer.

'So, my dear?' She turned her baleful eyes on Beatrice. 'Is it all settled then? Miss Eastleigh knows you are to marry Sir Frederick?'

'Yes, Aunt.'

'Good…' Mrs Jenkins gave Rosalyn what could hardly be called anything other than a glare. 'I wanted to announce it before we left London, but Sir Frederick insisted you must be told first.'

A cold dislike for the woman settled in Rosalyn's breast. There was surely no need for her belligerent attitude?

'There was no hurry for that, surely? You do not imagine that my brother would cry off at the last moment, I hope?' She had the satisfaction of seeing Mrs Jenkins turn pale. 'I am very glad Beatrice and Freddie came to tell me themselves. I admit I should have been distressed to read of it in *The Times*. And I fear Freddie has never been much of a letter writer.'

'I thought we could give a few parties, Ros?' Freddie was looking at her gratefully. 'Introduce Beatrice to the neighbours—'

'An excellent idea,' Mrs Jenkins put in before Rosalyn could answer. 'Since Beatrice will be living here after you return from your honeymoon, it will be much better if she makes a few friends first.'

Rosalyn saw the look of discomfort in her brother's face. He was clearly angry with Mrs Jenkins for coming out with the news in such a way, but his guilty expression told her that it was indeed his intention to bring his bride here. Rosalyn's heart sank, though she tried not to show she was disturbed.

'Then it will obviously be best for us to give some dinner parties and perhaps a dance,' she said, keeping her voice light and unconcerned. She would speak to her brother later—alone! 'As it happens, I have already sent out some invitations for a dinner tomorrow evening, just a few of my closest friends—but I shall make immediate preparations for something more elaborate. An engagement dance, I think.' She glanced at Freddie, who had been frantically trying to catch her eye. 'When is the wedding? Have you decided on a date yet?'

'We thought the end of next month,' Freddie said. 'I shall take Bea to Paris for three weeks afterwards and—'

Rosalyn gave him a warning frown. 'We do not need to discuss this just yet, Freddie. Later, perhaps…' She welcomed the arrival of a maid with the tea tray. 'Ah, here we are. I am sure we can all do with some refreshment. Maria, please pour if you will. I must just speak to Mrs Simmons. Excuse me, please. I shall not be a moment. Do not wait for me, I beg you.'

'Yes, of course, Rosalyn dear.'

Maria gave her a nervous look as she got up and went from the room. Of course, Rosalyn thought, she must be worrying about *her* future. If Freddie and his new wife were to live here, Maria would not be needed as Rosalyn's companion.

Rosalyn felt a flush of anger. What had Freddie been thinking of to let all this come as such a surprise? But of course he had not thought at all! He had merely carried on as he always did, expecting everyone to fall in with his plans. It was so like him that his sister could not feel as angry with him as he deserved.

'Ros—wait a moment!' Freddie had come out into the hall after her. 'Please, let me explain…'

Rosalyn turned to look at him. 'Later,' she said. 'You have no need to explain anything: this is your house. You are perfectly entitled to do as you wish with it.'

'I could strangle that woman!' Freddie said wrathfully. 'I had hoped to talk to you about this in private—to explain why Beatrice would like to live here.'

'Can it not wait until later?' Rosalyn asked. 'I have to make arrangements to send Jared home in the carriage. It has just started to rain and I do not want him to get a soaking.'

'Jared?'

Freddie looked puzzled, so she gave him a brief explanation.

'Jared and his tutor are renting Lady Orford's house. We have Celia's daughter staying. They are much the same age, and Jared and Sarah have become friends.' Her smile was a little strained. 'I'll tell you more when the others have gone up to change for dinner. Excuse me, Freddie, this will not wait.'

She walked off and this time her brother did not try to delay her, merely standing in the hall and staring after her with a look of frustration on his handsome face.

'Of course I have no objection to your bringing Beatrice here,' Rosalyn said when she and Freddie were alone an hour or so later. 'It *is* your house and you have a perfect right to do as you wish.'

'I don't want us to quarrel over this,' Freddie said, his expression a mixture of shame and determination. 'I promised this would be your home for as long as you required it, and I haven't changed my mind. Beatrice won't mind at all—and she is such an adorable goose that she will be glad to have your help with running the house. You need not fear that she will want to be interfering in your arrangements—and of course we shall still spend much of our time in London. At least until we have a family. Bea wants a large family, that's one of the reasons she would prefer to live here—for the children's sake. I told her this house was much larger than the one in Devon and she said she would like to see it—to share it with you.'

'Any woman would prefer this house,' Rosalyn said, frowning slightly. 'The one in Devon was meant only as a summer retreat—and is much further from a decent-sized town. Here, she would be near enough to Cambridge to go shopping when she pleases. I have always found it a perfect combination, living in the country but with a town nearby.'

'I'm sorry, Ros,' her brother said again. 'I know this must have been a shock for you.'

'I should certainly have preferred to have been told sooner,' Rosalyn said. 'It would have given me more time to think about the future.'

'I've told you, there is no need for you to move away.'

'What about Mrs Jenkins?' Rosalyn lifted her gaze to meet his. 'Are you planning to include her in your household?'

'Good God, no!' said Freddie, looking horrified. 'I would not stand for it even if Bea wanted it—and she certainly doesn't. That woman has made Bea's life a misery for months on end, hounding her to make a good marriage. It is because Bea wants to get away from her that we've arranged the wedding so quickly.'

'I can understand that,' Rosalyn said, giving him a rueful look. 'Is she Beatrice's only relative?'

'Yes—since her mother died.' Freddie frowned. 'Bea is an heiress—or she will be when Mrs Jenkins dies. She made quite sure I knew how much Bea will inherit. If it weren't for Bea's sake, I would tell her to take herself off—but I cannot be the cause of Bea's losing twenty thousand pounds, can I? She would not thank me for it, you know.'

'You don't care about the money?'

'I would have married her without a penny—but it's Bea's inheritance. I cannot deprive her of that, even if I don't like the old battleaxe.'

'Freddie dearest!' Rosalyn pulled a face at him. 'You must not speak so disrespectfully of your fiancée's aunt. Let us hope she won't visit too often when you are married.'

'Unfortunately, her own estate is in Huntingdon,' Freddie said with a gloomy look. 'Too close for comfort. I dare say she will descend on us several times a year.'

Rosalyn laughed at his expression. His words had made it plain to her that she would have to think very hard about the future. She might just have managed to live for a while with Beatrice—who was a sweet girl and would need help if she was to run this huge house efficiently—but not if Mrs Jenkins were to become a frequent visitor.

'Well, you must try to keep on terms with her if you can for Beatrice's sake,' she said. 'And now, Freddie, we should both go and change or we shall keep our guests waiting for their dinner.'

'Are you very upset, Ros?'

Freddie looked so anxious that the last remnants of Rosalyn's anger melted away. 'No, of course not,' she said and went to kiss his cheek. 'I think I shall like Beatrice very much—and I am naturally happy for you.'

'And you won't run off and leave us?'

'Not immediately,' Rosalyn promised. 'In time I shall probably want my own house, but not just at once—and of course I shall visit you several times a year. I do hope my visits will not cause either of you to quake in your shoes?'

'As if they would!' Freddie looked relieved. 'But I really do wish you would continue to think of this house as your home. There is no need for you to leave. Unless you marry, of course.'

Rosalyn shook her head at him, but would not be drawn further. As they parted, each going up to their own rooms, she allowed herself a moment of regret. She *had* been happy here, and there were so many memories. She would miss the life she had known here when she was forced to leave.

But leave she would, that was beyond question. It would not be fair to Beatrice if she remained here, because she would always be the mistress. At least until the girl became more assertive, and that might eventually lead to tension and quarrels.

No, it would not do, Rosalyn decided. She could not consider it. She must find herself a new home.

At least she was financially independent—her father had seen to that years ago. She would not be able to afford a house like this, of course—but she might buy a medium-sized cottage or even a house in Bath.

Either would be preferable to living with Aunt Susan or her brother. The trouble was, of course, that she was far too independent. Perhaps that was why she had never married.

A picture of a man's face flashed into her mind and she sighed. There was no point in thinking of Mr Wrexham. She had not met him on any of her walks or rides these past days, which seemed to indicate that he might be avoiding her.

She had sent him an invitation to her dinner for the following night, but so far he had not answered. It was her own fault. She must have shown her feelings too plainly the last time they met. Since he did not wish to become more involved with a woman who was too old to be thinking of marriage, Mr Wrexham had clearly decided to stay away from her as much as possible.

Chapter Four

Damian threw off his capped travelling cloak as he entered the hall. He greeted the housekeeper with a nod, answering her kind inquiry about his journey pleasantly, before striding into the study where a cold meal and wine awaited his coming. There was also a roaring fire in the large open hearth, which was welcome after a long, hard ride.

He had made a brief, angry inspection of the property left to him by his grandfather, and returned to the Hall almost immediately. He was tired and frustrated by what he had seen—the neglect of a once great estate—and did not immediately bother with the small pile of invitations awaiting him on his desk. When he did, he discovered the invitation from Rosalyn and a smile came to his lips.

Damian relaxed as he sat before the fire with a glass of wine, letting the tiredness and the frustration seep out of him. He glanced at the invitation again; it was very formal. Miss Eastleigh was simply repaying his hospitality.

He had hoped for this when he had first invited her to the Hall. If two respectable ladies like Miss Eastleigh and her cousin showed they were willing to be his friends, he would soon be accepted by the whole county. That had, of course, been his aim when he'd first heard of the spinster living nearby…but that had been before he met Miss Eastleigh. Now his feelings were very different.

He recalled the way Miss Eastleigh had looked into his eyes the last time they had talked. He had known she wanted him…really wanted him, as he wanted her. There was nothing of the milk-and-water English miss about Miss Eastleigh! No, indeed there was not! She was a goddess come to Earth, Diana the huntress, beautiful, brave and passionate. He felt desire stir inside him, burning its way to the centre of his manhood as he thought of her—and the resolution it had taken to let her walk away the afternoon he had accompanied her to her home.

She would have come to him in love if he had asked it of her, though, having heard the old scandal, she must surely be aware that a marriage between them was impossible. He could never ask her to share the shame attached to his name. He had hoped it might be possible to rehabilitate himself into English society, to make a new life here in England—but now he had begun to think it would never work. There would always be someone to point the finger and whisper behind his back. He could not ask Rosalyn to share that, even if she would. He would be a fool to let himself hope—to wish for the moon. He had learned long ago that to hope for too much brought only despair.

Besides, his business was unfinished. He had come back to England unaware of the true situation. Now, after his shocking discovery, he knew that he must settle an outstanding debt. Something that should have been done long ago. As yet he was not quite sure how his objective was to be achieved, but he would discover a way—and when he did, his disgrace would be complete.

Rosalyn had asked if he meant to return to India, and he had told her he was not sure. But things had changed. He had a score to settle, and when he had, there would be no question of his remaining in England.

She had been tossing and turning for ages! Rosalyn could not understand why she was so restless. She sat up and yawned, then reached for her dressing robe and slipped it on. It was impossible to sleep! Her thoughts were chasing themselves round and round in her head like fallen leaves swept up in a gale. Yet surely she was not letting her brother's imminent marriage distress her? Why should it? She could put up with Mrs Jenkins for as long as necessary, even if it meant biting back the angry words that sometimes leapt to her tongue.

The woman was both rude and careless of the feelings of others, but Rosalyn could cope with her. She would find the strength from somewhere. Not like poor Maria, who had been almost in tears when she went to her room before retiring for the night.

'I am sure I don't know what I shall do when Sir Frederick marries,' she had told Rosalyn, sniffing mistily into her kerchief. 'Mrs Jenkins has made it clear I shall not be welcome here.'

'It really has nothing to do with her,' Rosalyn said gently. 'Cheer up, Maria. I shall not stay here for ever, and I do assure you—you will always have a home with me. Indeed, if I decide to set up a house of my own I shall need you more than ever. You must know that I would not allow you to be turned out without a feather to fly?'

Maria had brightened a little at that, though it was obvious she was greatly distressed at the way their lives were about to change.

Of course she could not desert her cousin, Rosalyn told herself as she walked over to the window to gaze out at the night. Yet the idea of them both settled in a country cottage was somehow very lowering. The purchase of a house would naturally eat into her capital, and that meant she might not be able to live in quite the same style as she had here…but, she scolded herself, if all she had cared for was consequence she might have married long ago and none of this would have arisen.

Rosalyn took a branch of lighted candles and went down to the parlour she had always thought of as her own. She had left a favourite book of poems lying on the sideboard and thought perhaps it might help to lift her spirits. However, when she reached the parlour, the book had mysteriously disappeared and, having set down the candlestick, she wandered towards the French windows, unlocking them and venturing out into the gardens.

Perhaps a little fresh air might help to ease the headache that had begun soon after dinner. Mrs Jenkins had such a loud, harsh voice. Rosalyn truly pitied her brother if he was forced to play host to her too often, and wondered if even the considerable fortune she was intending to leave to her niece was worth having to put up with her company.

Money had never meant a great deal to Rosalyn, but she was beginning to realise she *had* taken it for granted. Her father had never questioned what she spent, never allowing her to use one penny of her own money for household expenses. All that would change now. She would not be poor, but she would have to learn economy.

A shadow moved from out of the shrubbery, making her start with fright. For a moment her heart beat so madly that she could scarcely breathe, then, as the clouds obligingly moved away, she was able to see him clearly in the resulting moonlight.

'Did I startle you, Miss Eastleigh?'

'Mr Wrexham,' she said, a note of welcome in her voice. Her spirits leapt gladly. It seemed such an age since she had seen him, but she tried not to show how pleased she really was by this surprise meeting. 'I was startled for a moment. What are you doing here?'

'I brought Sheba for a walk,' he replied. 'She ran into your gardens and I was forced to follow. I'm afraid I seem to have lost her for the moment. I was looking for her when I saw you.'

'She will find you when she is ready,' Rosalyn said, smiling in understanding. 'It is such a lovely night, do you not think so? I came out because I could not sleep. I thought the fresh air might do me good—take away my headache.'

'I am sorry you are unwell.'

'More like out of temper,' Rosalyn said with perfect truth. 'Perhaps we could walk together for a little, sir? You must take Sheba back with you, or Jared will wake and miss her. I believe she usually sleeps at the bottom of his bed. Or so he has told us.'

'Yes.' A smile lifted Damian's mouth at the corners. 'I know. She was there when I looked in on him on my return this evening. She must have followed me downstairs, and when I went out for my walk, she decided to come with me.'

'Do you often walk at night?' Rosalyn glanced at him as he fell into step beside her. 'I have not seen you for some days…' She blushed at what she had said but did not apologise for it: it was, after all, only the truth. 'Have you been away?'

'Did Jared not tell you?'

She shook her head, her eyes dwelling intently on his face. He had such strong features and, she suspected, a character to match. Those broad shoulders would be such a comfort to lay one's head against in times of stress, even for someone as independent as she. An inquiring look came into his eyes as she continued to gaze at him, and, blushing, Rosalyn looked away. He seemed always to read her mind, and that might be embarrassing when her thoughts were so confusing.

'No, he did not mention it.'

'I dare say he was relieved to have no lessons for a while. Yes, I was obliged to leave him for a few days…on business.'

So that was why she had not met him out walking! He had not been avoiding her after all. Insensibly, her spirits lifted, banishing the cloud that had shadowed her for days.

'I see. So he will not be so free to spend all his time with Sarah Jane now you are back? They have fallen into the habit of visiting each other every day—not just for tea, but for most of the day. I think they have become great friends. She will miss him if he does not come so often to the house.'

'She will be welcome to share his lessons,' Damian replied. 'She may find it boring, of course. Jared studies world affairs, fencing, shooting—and politics.'

'Does he? Good gracious!' Rosalyn was surprised. 'That is rather a demanding schedule for a youth of his age. I had no idea. I imagined you might teach him some manly sports for when he goes to school here—but not world affairs.'

'It is important for him to know these things. It is very possible that he will have an important role to play one day.'

'Who is Jared's father? Or should I not ask?'

Damian hesitated for a moment, then sighed. If he could not trust his instincts now, he was lost. Besides, his inclination was to share his thoughts with her—to open his heart to her—as he had not to another person since he was sent into exile.

'Ahmed is a prince. One day, when his own father dies, he will be the ruler of a mountain state in India. Jared is Prince Ahmed's oldest son—but there has been dissent over his right to step into his father's shoes, because his mother was not Indian.'

'I see…that might pose problems with religion and other things, I suppose.' Rosalyn began to understand the need to keep a close watch on the youth. 'It could well cause unrest amongst fanatics, I think?'

'Particularly in the matter of religion, though Prince Ahmed always insisted his son should be brought up in his own faith. Anna did explain to Jared that there were other religions, but she was not allowed to take him to her church.'

'Did her husband allow her to keep her own religion?'

'In private, yes.' Damian frowned. 'I hesitated to tell you the truth at first, Miss Eastleigh, because it may shock and disturb you. We came to England because there was an attempt on Jared's life.'

He did not add that it was only his own prompt action that had saved the boy, that in doing so he had been wounded and come close to losing his own life.

'It was merely chance that saved him. Ahmed was terrified the next attempt would succeed and begged me to bring the boy to England with me.'

'Oh, no! That is terrible.' This was much worse than she could ever have imagined. 'The poor child—no wonder he seemed so sad and frightened when I first saw him. But who could want to kill Jared?'

'Enemies of his father,' Damian replied, looking grim. 'Many people—including Ahmed's own father—think the prince should disinherit his eldest son in favour of the son his new wife has recently given him. So far he has stubbornly refused to consider it. His obstinacy was the cause of much unrest, which is why Ahmed desired me to bring his son to safety in this country.'

'And why you have been forced to stop him wandering all over the countryside alone—to keep such a strict watch over him.' She understood perfectly now what had seemed harsh before. Her intuition had been right, and she had been wrong to allow herself to doubt this man's integrity even for a moment.

'Yes, that is exactly my dilemma.' Damian smiled at her. 'Jared would be quite safe with Rajib, of course—but he does not like him. Neither do I, as it happens. I have begun to think I would have done better to leave both Rajib and Nessa in India.'

'Oh…' Rosalyn looked at him curiously. 'Surely Jared is fond of Nessa, and she of him?'

'Yes, he is,' Damian said. 'I was thinking of my own comfort. Unfortunately, both Rajib and Nessa resent my authority. They disobey my orders whenever they dare—and their influence on Jared makes him disinclined to listen to me.'

'That must make things difficult?' Rosalyn remembered Jared's sulky looks the evening she had dined at the Hall, and that it had made her wonder if Mr Wrexham was treating his pupil as he ought. 'Perhaps you should send them back to India?'

'Only if Jared wishes them to go. If things change, settle down, his father may send for him.'

'And will you go with him?' Rosalyn could not quite prevent the catch in her voice. 'You must have so many ties in that country…it must seem more your home than England after so many years.'

Damian looked at her, seeing the faint flush in her cheeks.

'What exactly is it you are asking?' he said. 'What do you want to know, Miss Eastleigh...whether I have a wife or a sweetheart waiting for me in India, is that it?'

'No...of course not,' Rosalyn replied quickly, but she could not look at him. 'It would be impertinent of me to ask such questions. I have no right...'

Damian caught her arm, swinging her round to face him. He seemed very intense, almost angry. His reaction was unlike the behaviour she had come to expect of him, and startled her.

'No right?' he said. 'Why are you lying, Miss Eastleigh—to yourself and me?'

'I am not lying.'

'I think you are,' he replied, an odd, machiavellian light in his eyes. 'Well, have you no comment to make? Will you not ask why I think you are lying?'

Rosalyn's mouth was dry. She swallowed hard, her heart beating madly as she looked up at him.

'It doesn't matter,' she whispered. 'I...Damian...'

Before she could say anything more she was in his arms; his lips were on hers, soft, persuading...demanding. Rosalyn melted into his body, yielding her mouth and her whole self as the kiss sent her senses spinning into space. It was the most wonderful feeling of her life, so wonderful that she wanted it to last forever and she sighed with regret when he let her go.

'There, my sweet girl,' Damian said and stroked her cheek with his fingers. 'That is why you have the right to ask any questions you like—and the answer to them all is no. There is no one else.'

'Oh, Damian,' she murmured. 'I don't know what has happened to me. I have never felt this way in my life…never wanted to…' She stopped and dropped her gaze in confusion. What had she been about to say? That she wanted him to make love to her? Surely she could not have been on the verge of saying anything so scandalous!

'Wanted to what?' he asked teasingly. 'Are you telling me you want me to make love to you?'

'No—yes!' Rosalyn could not deny the urgings of her own body. She laughed as she saw the wicked gleam in his eyes, her natural honesty making her say, 'Of course I want you, Damian. I should hardly have allowed you to kiss me like that if I did not.'

'Was it your first real kiss?'

'There have been others,' she confessed, a mischievous smile tweaking the corners of her mouth. 'But none that I truly wanted—none that made me feel the way you did just now.'

'But what?' He gazed deep into her eyes. Her naughty, teasing look enchanted him. 'There is a but, isn't there, my dearest Rosalyn? You are not sure that you can give yourself to such a wicked man as I—is that it?'

'You are not wicked,' she replied, laughing. 'No,

it is not that, Damian. I have never thought myself missish, but...'

'But you are not quite ready to cast the world off for love?' His eyes teased her gently. 'To become a fallen woman in the eyes of your contemporaries?'

'I am not sure,' Rosalyn said. Her heart and body clamoured for him, knowing no caution, yet her head told her to wait, to take care. What did she really know of this man who had shot into her life like a comet passing across the sky? 'I know it is foolish of me to hesitate. At my age I ought to be grateful for the chance of knowing love, for however brief a time—and I am not making demands, not asking you to marry me. I know you have no thought of taking a wife.'

'Do you, indeed?' Damian's mouth quivered. He struggled to contain his amusement as he realised she was giving serious consideration to becoming his mistress. Something that for her would be a huge step. She was unique, beyond price. More than anything, he wanted to sweep her up in his arms and run off with her—but he too was aware of the need for caution. 'I admit I have no right to ask you or any other woman to share my disgrace—but that does not mean I have not thought of it.'

'Your disgrace?' Rosalyn gazed up at him in surprise. 'You mean the old scandal?'

'There is—or will be more,' he said. 'I cannot tell yet how much, or what will happen in a few weeks' time. Until I am sure, I could not offer you marriage, Rosalyn. Any intimate relationship between us would be of uncertain duration.'

'Yes, I see.' She had known it instinctively, but it still hurt her to hear it from his lips. She blinked back her tears, looking bravely up at him. 'Give me a little time, Damian. I must be certain.'

For answer, he kissed her again. Such a tender, loving kiss that her resolve was almost broken, her body racked with a sharp longing for the pleasure she had never known but sensed she would find in this man's arms. Why wait? For what? She was seven and twenty, unlikely to meet another man she could love. She would be a fool not to take her one chance of happiness while it was offered, regardless of how long it might last.

'Damian,' she began breathless. 'I think—'

'No, do not say it.' He placed his fingertips to her lips, halting the reckless words she would have spoken. 'Not tonight,' he said, smiling at her puzzled look. 'To take such an advantage would be unfair of me. You must have time to consider, my love. I shall be at your dinner party tomorrow evening. You can give me your answer then.'

As if to underline what he had said, Sheba came bounding up to them, barking and leaping around them as if she had made some miraculous discovery at finding them together.

'I must go in before that wretch wakes the household,' Rosalyn said and reached up to kiss his cheek. 'Goodnight, Damian. I want you to know that I do care for you and always shall…whatever happens between us.'

He seized her, holding her pressed hard against him as he kissed her once more. He felt her surrender, felt the way her body moulded to his, the need and vulnerability in her—and he let her go, giving her a little push to send her on her way before it was too late.

'Go, my Amazon,' he murmured huskily. 'While I still have the strength to let you.'

He watched as she walked away from him, fighting the fierce desire leaping in his blood and cursing the sense of fair play that was forcing him to let her leave. If she came to him…if she gave herself to him…it must be right for them both. He wanted her so desperately tonight, but cared for her too much to take her when she was so vulnerable.

As he turned, he caught sight of a face at an upper window of the house. Rosalyn had only just gone inside the parlour so it could not be her. Someone must have been watching them—but who?

Damian cursed his own carelessness as he called the dog and began to retrace his steps through the shrubbery. He and not Sheba had determined their course tonight. Something had drawn him here, tugging at that inner core…the part of him he had thought dead long ago.

He had hardly believed his eyes when he saw Rosalyn come out into the garden wearing only a flimsy dressing robe, almost as though his spirit had called to hers. He doubted she had even been aware of the way the lovely shape of her body was revealed by the silky material, of the sensuous perfume of her warm skin…of what it had done to him. The temptation to hold her, to kiss her, had been overwhelming—but if someone had seen them together? Had jumped to the wrong conclusions!

He knew only too well what certain minds—and tongues!—could make of an innocent kiss, how cruel gossip could destroy a tender soul. It was in defence of a woman's honour that he had called out Roderick Harrington. Only after the man was dead had he discovered that another man had been most to blame.

Roderick Harrington had enticed the girl, snatching her as she walked alone down a country lane and bundling her, screaming and terrified, into his carriage—but it was his brother who had raped and shamed her. It was Mr Bernard Harrington who had broken her heart, causing her to take her own life because she could not face the scandal she feared would shame her family.

And it was also Mr Bernard Harrington who had ruined Damian's father at the card table, and hastened his death. It was because of him that an old man had died alone, lonely, regretting the loss of his eldest grandson. It was Bernard Harrington he was determined to bring to justice...by challenging him to a duel, if he could find no other way.

Rosalyn did not expect to sleep after her chance encounter with Damian in the gardens, but once her head touched the pillow, she fell into the sweetest dream. Although she could not recall the details on waking, she knew she had dreamed of being with Damian—and that it had made her feel very secure and happy.

She was relaxed as she took her mare out for a brief gallop across the fields, before returning to the breakfast room to find Maria and Mrs Jenkins already there.

'Has Freddie come down yet?' she asked, then turned to Mrs Jenkins. 'I gave instructions that Beatrice should have breakfast carried up to her room. You need not have come down, ma'am. Maria and I prefer it, but you are welcome to have your tray upstairs if you so choose.'

'I do not care for the habit of sleeping in late,' Mrs Jenkins said, giving her an odd look. 'As it happens, I sleep very little. I always keep a book at my bedside. Last night I borrowed a book of poems, though I do not approve of Lord Byron's work. I believe he shows a lack of propriety, both in his work and his morals. Scandalous!'

Such a forbidding stare accompanied her words, that Rosalyn was at a loss to understand her meaning.

'I am sorry you do not care for Lord Byron's poems, ma'am. However, I am sure my father's library contains much that will please you.' Rosalyn turned to her cousin, who was looking decidedly dejected. 'Will you walk down to the greenhouses and beg a few flowers for the house from Tom, Maria? I am not sure what he has, but I am certain he will find us something—and you always arrange them so beautifully.'

'Yes, of course.' Maria glowed at her praise. 'I shall go at once.'

'Only if you have finished your breakfast.'

Maria assured her she had, and seemed in a hurry to leave. She had clearly been upset. What could the odious Mrs Jenkins have been saying to her earlier?'

'Maria is always so obliging,' Rosalyn remarked after her cousin had gone. 'She has been such a help to me since my father died.'

'I imagine you could not have continued to live here alone,' Mrs Jenkins remarked sourly. 'Though whether it was wise for you to have done so, with only Miss Bellows as your companion, remains to be seen. You might have protected your reputation more securely had you lived with a married lady—someone with a little more standing in society.'

'Protected my reputation more securely?' Rosalyn stared at her, too astonished to think what she could mean. 'I really do not understand you, ma'am.'

'Do you not?' Mrs Jenkins gave her a false smile.

'I shall say no more for the moment, but you would be unwise to think me a fool. You may not care what others think of *you*, Miss Eastleigh—but my concern is for Beatrice. I shall do all I think necessary to protect her good name.'

Rosalyn was struck dumb. What on earth was she hinting at? Unless she had seen…? A horrid thought struck her. Mrs Jenkins's bedchamber overlooked that part of the garden in which she had chanced to meet Damian the previous night! Had she seen them together? Had she seen them embracing? If she had been unable to sleep…it was quite possible that she had been at the window.

Recalling that she had been wearing a flimsy wrapping gown over her night-chemise, Rosalyn could not help blushing. It must have seemed to a casual observer that she had gone out on purpose to meet her lover.

'You have no need to be concerned either for Beatrice's or my own good name,' she replied with as much dignity as she could muster. She stood up, knowing that she must escape before she lost her temper and said something rude. 'If you will excuse me, ma'am, I have guests coming this evening and must speak to Mrs Simmons urgently.'

Rosalyn walked from the room with dignity, head high, back straight. Of all the unfortunate things! Naturally a woman of Mrs Jenkins's order would assume the worst. She would think that Rosalyn had gone out deliberately to meet a lover—and in her night-clothes!

She felt very angry at having morality preached at her in her own home, but knew she was to blame. Living alone for years, she had become accustomed to wandering about the house in her night-attire. And she *had* given into temptation the previous night. Indeed, if Damian had not shown restraint, she might have given herself to him there and then.

Last night in the moonlight, her reputation had not seemed to matter very much. Now she realised that any relationship between her and Damian would have to be discreet. She would not want to cause a scandal that might reflect badly on Freddie and his young wife.

How unfair it was! If Rosalyn had been born male she could have taken as many lovers as she chose without causing a ripple of scandal—and as the first-born she would have inherited this house!

A little worm of resentment worked inside her. She did not care about the title or the money, but it was upsetting that she could no longer call this house her own—that she must think of leaving her home.

Rosalyn's thoughts went round and round in her head, chasing each other like a puppy dog after his tail. She longed to be in Damian's arms again, yet knew how much she risked. If she gave herself even once without marriage, she would have no chance of making a decent match—and if the affair became public knowledge, she would be finished in the first rank of Society, despised by all decent women.

Yet what did she care for any of these things? She had never needed more than a few close friends, nor had she met anyone else whom she would wish to marry—so what would she really be giving up?

She felt frustrated and uncertain, unlike her usual positive self, perhaps because she had never been faced with such a conundrum before. Oh, bother! She had too much to do to think of this now. Once her brother was married, she would be in a better position to decide.

She would in any case be leaving this house. If she were to leave England, perhaps the scandal would not be so terrible. Rosalyn had always longed for travel and adventure—and since she must leave her home, why should she not follow her heart?

Would Damian be prepared to take her with him when he left the country—to share his life with her?

She would be his mistress, something she had been taught was beneath contempt for a respectable, unmarried lady—but if he loved her she might find something precious, something that made the sacrifice of her reputation worthwhile.

It was a frightening proposition, because she would be cut off from all that she had ever known and loved—and yet, what was the alternative? To sink into a lonely and disappointed old age? No!

No, her rebellious heart cried. She wanted so much more. She wanted Damian Wrexham.

Rosalyn's pulses raced wildly. Suddenly the future held many possibilities. She felt recklessly alive. She would tell Damian they must be patient for a while—and then, if he still wanted her, she would go away with him.

Rosalyn's dinner guests were surprised but pleased to learn of Sir Frederick's betrothal. His bride-to-be was such a shy, pretty child that her arrival in the neighbourhood was thought to be a definite asset. She and Sir Frederick would naturally entertain more frequently and more lavishly than a spinster lady, and that was generally welcomed.

Rosalyn was aware of Damian's dark eyes watching her from across the table. She smiled at him, ignoring the narrowed, hostile stare of Mrs Jenkins. She could not possibly have seen Damian clearly enough the previous night to be certain of his identity, though she might suspect it.

Rosalyn hardly cared. Mrs Jenkins would surely say nothing of what she suspected outside this house, if only for her niece's sake. And once the wedding was over, it would not matter. Besides, she had gone beyond caring. It was an age since she had felt so excited…so alive!

Rosalyn's wide, clear eyes shone as she met Damian's quizzing gaze. She was sure that he had read her mind—that he could guess her thoughts. Now that her decision was made, she felt as light as air, floating on warm currents like a bird.

In a month she would be free to go to him!

'You look extremely well this evening, m'dear.'

Rosalyn turned to the vicar, who was placed at her left. She smiled at him, seeing the kindness in his eyes. He was a good man, genuinely caring but not overly critical of his parishioners' failings, being all too human himself.

'Thank you, sir. I am feeling very well.'

'It is good news about Sir Frederick, is it not?'

'Yes, certainly.'

The vicar looked thoughtful. 'I hope you and Miss Bellows will not be leaving us?'

'Not immediately,' Rosalyn replied. 'Lady Eastleigh will want to be mistress of her own house in time, of course. I have assured Maria she may be sure of a home with me—wherever I go.'

'Oh…' He seemed concerned at this. 'So you might not be living near by. I see… Dear, dear me, that would be a sad loss. Miss Bellows has always been a tireless worker for the church. We shall miss her very much—and you too, Miss Eastleigh, of course.'

Clearly he was most distressed by the thought of losing Maria's help. Rosalyn was struck by his expression. She had known Maria often helped at the church bazaars, of course, but until now she had not believed it was anything other than a way of passing the time. Now she wondered if there was more to her cousin's devotion to church matters than a desire to be of service to the community.

Later that evening, when she saw the two of them talking earnestly together, her suspicions began to harden into certainty. How blind she had been! Why had she never noticed how much more animated Maria became when she was with the vicar?

'A penny for your thoughts?'

Rosalyn felt the warmth of Damian's breath on her bare shoulder as he leant across the arm of the sofa to whisper in her ear. She glanced back at him, pulses racing as she met his challenging gaze and the message he was sending her. How she wished they were alone! Her eyes sparked with mischief and her lips parted slightly, revealing far more of her feelings for this man than she knew.

'I was thinking it would be nice if I could push Maria and the vicar into declaring their affection for each other before I leave here.'

'Are you thinking of leaving?' Damian looked at her intently.

'Yes, I believe I shall—after the wedding. I could do nothing before then, of course.' She smiled as she saw understanding in his eyes. 'I had thought of finding a country cottage, or perhaps a small house in Bath—but now I think it might suit me better to live abroad. I have often wished to travel, you know. And after the wedding, I shall be free to live my own life.'

'Ah!' Damian's eyes seemed to smoulder with heat: the heat of desire. She could almost feel his lips on hers, almost taste them. If he continued to look at her that way she would grow faint with longing. 'Yes, I understand. After your brother's wedding? Many things may have happened by then. I too may be thinking of leaving England.'

They understood each other perfectly. Rosalyn's heart fluttered. She had given her promise. There was no going back now. Indeed, she had no wish to retract. She yearned for the moment they would be together as one.

'Mr Wrexham?' She was jerked rudely back to the present by the strident voice of Mrs Jenkins. 'Are you by any chance a relative of Lord Edward Wrexham?'

Damian looked at her, and by instinct moved away from Rosalyn. Something in the older woman's manner alerted him to danger. He had met her type in the past, and knew what to expect.

'Yes, ma'am,' he replied in a cool, steady tone. 'He was my father.'

'Your father?' Mrs Jenkins gave a shriek of outrage. 'Then you are Damian Wrexham—the devil who murdered my youngest brother! Deny it if you dare! You killed Roderick! You are a murderer!'

The accusation was made in such a shrill tone that it attracted the attention of every person in the room. Damian was silent, his eyes flicking to

Rosalyn as if in apology, but his expression did not change, nor did he give any sign of being disturbed by Mrs Jenkins's charge.

'Do you deny that you murdered Roderick Harrington, sir?'

'I do not deny that he died from a wound I inflicted,' Damian replied, not a flicker of emotion in his face. His body was stiff with pride, his eyes colder than the northern sea in winter. 'It was, however, a fair fight.'

'A fight you forced on him,' Mrs Jenkins accused. Her large bosom swelled with indignation, her face going puce with temper so that she resembled a large, purple-clad toad with popping eyes. 'I do not know how you have the effrontery to force yourself on decent people. Had I known you were a welcome visitor in this house, I should not have brought Beatrice here.' She turned her baleful gaze on Rosalyn. 'I can only think that you were not aware of this man's shameful past, Miss Eastleigh.'

Silence had fallen over the room. Rosalyn was so angry she could have struck the woman's spiteful face. How dare she? Oh, how could she create such a scene? The malicious expression on Mrs Jenkins's face sent a shiver down her spine. What a truly unpleasant woman she was!

'Well, have you nothing to say?' demanded Mrs Jenkins as Rosalyn remained silent. 'Will you kindly request this person to leave—or must I take Beatrice and return to Huntingdon?'

'Take Bea—' Freddie was stung into life. He took a protective step towards his fiancée, a look of alarm in his eyes. 'What's all this? I don't understand. Rosalyn...Wrexham, is this true?'

'Damian...' Rosalyn whispered, her face pale with shock. She felt unable to do or say anything, torn between her love for him and loyalty to her brother. 'I...' Words failed her—only her eyes conveyed her distress.

'It is true that I killed Roderick Harrington in a duel,' Damian said, his eyes narrowing to contemptuous slits as he recognized the weakness in Freddie's character. It was clear that he would not stand up to his fiancée's aunt, would not defend his sister. 'There were, however, reasons—which I shall not go into at this moment.'

'It was murder,' insisted Mrs Jenkins, addressing the room at large. 'The charge was quashed, of course. He got away with it because his grandfather was the Earl of Marlowe, but it was murder. Either he leaves this house now or I shall take Beatrice—and the wedding will be cancelled!'

'Freddie!' Beatrice looked at him with frightened eyes. 'Oh, please do not let her...' She lapsed into silence as her aunt glared at her, clearly terrified that she would carry out her threat. As indeed she would, Rosalyn saw that at once.

'Do not distress yourself, Miss Holland.' Damian bowed stiffly in her direction. 'I shall, of course, leave at once. Had I known, I should not have burdened you with my presence. There will be no need for further communication between us. Rosalyn, forgive me. I must leave.'

'Damian!' Rosalyn could not be certain whether she said the words aloud or merely in her heart. 'Please do not go…'

She watched as he walked from the room, head up, back straight and stiff, and she longed to run after him but knew she must not. If she gave the odious Mrs Jenkins any reason to destroy the happiness of Beatrice and Freddie, she would never forgive herself. She must let him go, though her own heart felt as if it had shattered into a hundred tiny pieces.

'Aunt Patricia,' Beatrice said, breaking the awkward silence after he had left. 'Surely you cannot think Rosalyn knew who that man was? He has but recently come to the district—is that not so, Freddie?'

'Yes. Of course Ros did not know what he had done,' he said, giving his sister an odd, defensive look. 'No one did. Good grief! He would not have been invited if any of us had guessed…'

Maria opened her mouth and closed it, clearly thinking now was not the time to defend Mr Wrexham. Rosalyn was silent, her stomach churning with both nerves and anger. She had been forced into an impossible situation. For the moment she was unable to speak her mind as she would have liked—for Freddie's sake. Yet not to do so was unbearable.

'Mr Wrexham's past has never been of any concern to me,' she said at last. 'Naturally I should not have invited him this evening had I known…of the unfortunate tragedy in your family, Mrs Jenkins.'

The glitter in the older woman's eyes told Rosalyn that she was neither convinced nor satisfied, but for the moment she seemed prepared to let it go.

'I was sure you could not have known,' she said with a cold smile. She fluttered her fan, glancing about her as if to apologise. 'You must all forgive me for causing a scene—but I really could not bear to stay under the same roof as that wicked man. Not once I was certain it was indeed he.'

There were embarrassed murmurs from the guests, several of whom had rather liked Mr Wrexham and, though shocked by what they had learned that evening, were not certain of their own feelings on the matter. Mrs Jenkins had found herself in an unfortunate position, of course, and there was a great deal of sympathy for her; but a duel was not necessarily murder—in the eyes of the gentlemen at least.

Rosalyn turned away. How could she bear to stay in the same room as Mrs Jenkins? Her nerves were stretched to breaking point and she felt like screaming aloud in her rage, yet she knew she must remain calm—she must pretend to accept the woman's apology, for Freddie's sake. She curled her nails into the palms of her hands, willing herself not to speak, not to say something that would ruin everything. She must do nothing that would harm her brother or Beatrice.

'Rosalyn dearest.' Maria was at her side as the tension eased and people began to talk and laugh in an effort to cover their embarrassment. 'That dreadful woman! Really, I cannot think what she was about. It is bad enough that she thinks she owns the house…'

Rosalyn's chin went up, anger and pride warring for supremacy. 'Do not let her upset you, Maria. We must think of Freddie and Beatrice. It is only for a few weeks, after all.'

'How brave you are,' Maria replied, with a warm look of approval. 'If I had been you, I should have said something extremely rude—and not simply because of what she did this evening. I tell you frankly that I cannot like her. Nothing would persuade me to remain in the same house as Mrs Jenkins—if it were not that I know you need my support, I should leave immediately.'

Maria's fighting words conjured up such a comical picture in her mind that Rosalyn suddenly found herself smiling.

'You know my wretched tongue,' she said. 'It was with the greatest difficulty that I held back this evening. Under any other circumstances, I should have been delighted to show her the door.'

'And I should have locked it after her,' declared Maria stoutly. 'The dear vicar was horrified. He likes

Mr Wrexham—says he is a true gentleman in every sense of the word. Indeed, we both felt he behaved very creditably throughout it all.'

'The vicar is very right,' Rosalyn replied. 'I have always respected his judgement. I believe him to be a good man. Kind, considerate and sensible. A man to be relied upon in times of anxiety.'

'Yes. He is all that and more.' Maria looked thoughtful. 'Oh, our guests are leaving, dearest. You should say goodbye to them.'

'Yes, of course.'

Rosalyn had recovered her composure by now and was able to accompany her friends to the door, where they took an affectionate leave of her. She could see concern in several of their faces, but none of them were willing to speak of the embarrassing incident openly. It was best brushed under the mat and forgotten.

When they had all gone, Rosalyn went immediately to her own room without returning to the parlour to wish her family goodnight. She did not feel like talking to either her brother or Mrs Jenkins, so when someone knocked at her door just as she was about to undress, she sighed in resignation.

'Yes. Come in.'

It was Freddie. He looked at her awkwardly, his colour heightened. She sensed that he was feeling both ashamed and ill at ease—as indeed he ought!

'Ros…' he began, dropping his gaze as she met his eyes. 'I'm not sure what to say.'

'Then say nothing. I understand your position.'

'You could not expect her to welcome the presence of a man who…killed her brother?'

'No, of course not. It was unfortunate that neither of us were aware of it. However, she might have spoken to you privately. There was surely no need to make a scene in front of our guests—to force Mr Wrexham to leave like that?'

'Good grief, no!' Freddie said. 'It was a wretched thing to do. Most embarrassing for everyone.'

'She is an unpleasant woman,' Rosalyn said quietly. She gave him a direct look. 'I am sorry but I cannot like her, even for your sake. I hope she will not ruin your marriage, Freddie. You will have to be careful or she will make your lives miserable.'

'You know how I feel. If it were not for Bea—I would have liked to throw her out.' He relaxed a little as his sister was betrayed into a smile. 'I am sorry. Truly, I am. I would not have had you placed in such an abominable position for the world. Do you…do you like Mr Wrexham, Ros?'

'Yes. Very much, as it happens.'

'I thought you might.' Freddie played with his watch chain, clearly feeling both guilty and awkward. 'You weren't thinking of marrying him, were you?'

'Would it matter to you if I was?'

'Not personally. Seemed a decent enough chap to me—but you know how things stand at the moment.'

'Yes, of course.' For a moment Rosalyn was angry.

Did he not realise how selfish he was being? 'If it will set your mind at rest, Freddie—I have no plans to marry Mr Wrexham, and I shall not invite him to this house again while Mrs Jenkins is here.'

'Ros…I know I have no right to ask, but will you promise not to see him until after the wedding? She's such an awful woman. She might refuse her permission if she heard gossip about…the two of you.'

'Oh? What kind of gossip?' She gave him a frank, direct stare. Freddie could not meet her eyes. Obviously, Mrs Jenkins had reported what she'd seen the night Rosalyn had met Damian in the garden! 'There is nothing for anyone to gossip about, Freddie. No matter what anyone has told you. Believe me—there has been nothing more than a kiss.'

'Good grief! I didn't think there had,' Freddie said at once. 'I know you, Ros—but people always like to believe the worst. And you have been living here practically alone—' He quailed at the look in his sister's eyes. 'Forgive me. That was very bad of me. I should not have said it.'

'No, you should not.' Rosalyn glared at him. She was very angry now. 'I am my own mistress. My behaviour is my own affair. I believe I am capable of deciding what is or is not proper for me to do. You should leave now, Freddie, before I lose my temper and say something we shall both regret. I promise not to shame you—at least until after you are married!'

'Ros...' He realised she was very angry and stopped. 'Sorry...I've made a mess of this. I did not mean to upset you. '

Rosalyn did not answer. She waited until the door closed behind him before throwing a cushion at it. The action did little to relieve her feelings. Losing one's temper was never an answer in itself. But she was very angry. How could her own brother say such things to her? It was all the fault of that wretched woman!

Oh, why did she have to come here? Why was the situation so awkward?

Rosalyn was restless, so frustrated and incensed that she longed to scream. Why did everything have to be so complicated? Why could she not simply follow her heart? Do as she wished? Yet her own good sense told her that she would have to be very careful. She must do nothing to cause a split between her brother and the girl he loved.

Yet she had to see Damian! She had to see him alone, to explain to him that Mrs Jenkins's revelations had made no difference to her feelings—or her intention of going away with him once the wedding was over.

She must and would see Damian, but she must contrive to keep it a secret from everyone in this house. Particularly the odious Mrs Jenkins!

Chapter Five

'Why may I not visit Sarah Jane?' Jared demanded. Mutiny flared in his dark eyes as he faced his tutor across the room. He looked every inch a prince, his manner haughty and proud. 'Why can she not come here any more?'

'Because I say so.' Damian sighed inwardly as he saw the stubborn set of Jared's jaw; he recognised the all-too-familiar signs of rebellion and knew he must explain more fully. 'Your father would not approve of your becoming too attached to the girl—and there are other reasons. Neither of us will be visiting that house again, nor any other in the area, I dare say.'

'Why? Are you ashamed of me? Ashamed of the colour of my skin?'

Anger flashed in Damian's eyes. 'Where the devil did you get that idea? You know I have never cared for such things. You have always been as a younger brother to me, Jared. I was your mother's friend as well as the prince's. I care only for your safety and well being. You must know that? Surely you cannot believe me capable of such prejudice?'

Jared looked uncertain. 'Nessa said you would turn against me now you are amongst your own people—that you would find me a nuisance.'

'If Nessa told you that she is either lying deliberately or mistakes the matter,' Damian said, his mouth thinning in annoyance. 'Believe me, Jared. I shall always care for you. The only thing I find a nuisance is that I am forced to curtail your freedom all too often. I do not enjoy making you stay within the grounds—nor do I wish to stop you making friends, believe me.'

'My father has cast me out.'

'Only for your own safety.'

'He will never allow me to return to India. I am the cause of too much trouble amongst the people. I do not belong there—or here.'

There was both pain and anger in the youth's face, reminding Damian of the feelings he had experienced years before, when he too had been forced to seek a new life in exile.

'You belong with me, Jared.' Damian pulled a wry face. 'I too am a social outcast—so we are two of a kind. Where I go, you go; I'm afraid you're stuck with me until your majority. Then you will be free to tell me to go to hell if you so choose.'

His words brought a smile to Jared's face. 'Do you mean it? Shall I always belong with you, *sahib*?'

'Have I not said it? You have reason to know I do not say things lightly, have you not?' Damian grinned as Jared looked rueful. 'Come, there is no need for anger between us. You are no longer a child, Jared.'

'Some treat me as if I am,' Jared replied, a flash of hauteur in his eyes.

'Then I shall not be one of them, unless you force me to it. Act like a man, Jared, and I shall respect you as one.' Damian moved towards him, laying a hand on his shoulder. 'My name is Damian. Why do you not begin to use it? We are not in India now. It may be that neither of us will ever return. Perhaps it would be best if you left the old ways behind now, Jared. Your mother was English—a very intelligent, lovely lady. You have no reason to be ashamed of carrying her blood, though I know some of your father's people would have you think so. In certain cosmopolitan societies people of mixed race adopt European ways and are accepted, even admired for their differences—and their talents. You are intelligent and knowledgeable. You could find a place for yourself in such a society, Jared. You are very like your mother, more like her than your father, perhaps. If it had been otherwise, you might have been more accepted at home.'

'My mother loved me.' Jared's eyes were shiny with the tears he was too proud to let fall. 'You do believe she loved me?'

'Always.' Damian offered his hand and after a moment the youth took it. 'If I thought it best that we should go away—disappear, perhaps even change our names—would you trust me?'

Jared was silent for a few seconds, considering, then he smiled. 'Yes, Damian,' he said. 'I shall trust you—but I would like to see Sarah Jane once more. She is my friend, perhaps the only true friend I have apart from you. I want to give her a present…so that she will not forget me.'

'I'll do what I can,' Damian promised. 'Be patient, Jared. It will not be easy. I cannot risk going to the house at the present, for Miss Eastleigh's sake. Nor can I let you go. But I shall find a way. I promise.'

'Why can I not see Jared?' Sarah Jane stamped her foot, her face pink with temper. 'He is my friend. I hate you. You are mean to stop me seeing him. I shall see him, I shall!'

Rosalyn sighed. She could not approve of Sarah Jane's tantrum, but she understood completely how the girl felt. It *was* unfair. No one was more aware of that than she.

'I'm sorry,' she said. 'Please do not be cross with me, Sarah Jane. Believe me, I really do not want to stop you seeing Jared. I have no choice for the moment. It is just as difficult for me. I would like to see Mr Wrexham but I may not—not just yet.'

'It's because of that horrid woman, isn't it?' Sarah

Jane said, her face sulky. 'I heard her saying things to Beatrice this morning—about you and Mr Wrexham. Beatrice tried to defend you from her insinuations and she made her cry.'

'Mrs Jenkins does not like Mr Wrexham because of something that happened a long time ago.' Rosalyn explained without going into precise details. 'She has threatened to stop Freddie marrying Beatrice if Mr Wrexham comes here again…and that would make both her and Freddie very unhappy. You must see that we have to consider their feelings as well as our own? At least for the time being.'

'I like Beatrice. I do not want her to be unhappy—but Jared could come,' Sarah said, her face mutinous. 'Or I could go there. That horrid woman need not know where I've gone.'

'That would be deceitful,' Rosalyn said, crossing her fingers behind her back. It was wrong of her to deny Sarah Jane the very thing she was planning for herself. 'Besides, your mother will be wanting you home soon. Her letter says your brother is on the mend.'

'I must see Jared before I go home,' Sarah Jane pleaded, her large eyes filling with tears. 'I want to give him something…something to keep so that he will always remember me.'

Rosalyn nodded. Sarah Jane had made a friend. She did not want to forget him, nor was it right that she should be forced to give him up when her own grandmother had approved the friendship.

'I might be able to arrange a meeting,' she said. 'Be patient, Sarah. I'll try my best. I promise. Now go downstairs and find Maria, there's a good girl.'

Sarah Jane went reluctantly, clearly still feeling the injustice of what had been imposed on her. Rosalyn crossed over to the window and looked out at the view. It was drizzling with rain. She could hardly pretend she was going for a walk in this weather. And if she ordered the carriage, everyone would want to know where she was going. Mrs Jenkins would probably ask to go with her in order to spoil any plans she might have for meeting Damian.

It was no use. She would have to wait until it was fine—until she could be sure that Mrs Jenkins was safely out of the way.

The opportunity to escape did not present itself for three days. Three long, wet and gloomy days in which Sarah Jane grew ever more obstinate and Rosalyn found it almost impossible to sleep at night. During this time her resolution hardened. Why should Mrs Jenkins dictate who she and Sarah might know? She was determined to find a way for them both to see their friends, but without causing harm to Beatrice and Freddie. When at last the chance came, however, the weather could not have been kinder. It was a warm, dry day with scarcely a cloud in the sky.

A luncheon party had been arranged at the

vicarage. Mrs Jenkins had asked to look at the church before deciding finally whether the wedding should be held there or in London.

'There will be nearly two hundred guests,' she announced grandly. 'I am not sure a village church will be large enough. Our own in Huntingdon is certainly not suitable.'

Beatrice had looked anxious, having previously declared that she would prefer a smaller wedding if it could be held here. She was obviously a country girl at heart, and did not care for all the fuss and consequence of a large society wedding.

So the visit to the church had been arranged for the Friday morning, followed by a cold collation to be prepared by the vicar's housekeeper. When Rosalyn announced that Sarah Jane had been sick and she must stay behind to care for her, there were cries of disappointment from Beatrice and a suspicious glare from her aunt.

'Let me stay with her, Rosalyn,' begged Maria. 'I should be the one to remain behind and nurse poor Sarah.'

'You are needed at the church,' Rosalyn replied. 'You know more about the flowers and the music—besides, I have a little headache. I shall sit quietly with Sarah and have a nice rest. No one is to worry about me, I shall be quite content to stay home.'

'You do look a bit pale,' Freddie said, settling the matter. 'Poor Ros. You do look tired. I dare say we have worn you out these past few days. You are not used to so many people visiting at once. Stay here and read a book or something.'

Did her brother imagine she was at her last prayers? Rosalyn murmured her thanks, hiding a wry smile. She did not feel in the least guilty at deceiving them all. If her brother had supported her—if he had stood up to Mrs Jenkins in the first place—there would have been no need for deceit.

She waited until the carriage had rumbled out of sight, then called to Sarah to come down.

'We have to be quick,' she said, catching the girl's hand. 'No one must realise where we've been. If anyone asks you later, we just went for a little walk in the orchard.'

Sarah Jane nodded, her cheeks pink with excitement. It was a real adventure, made all the more thrilling because she was being asked to tell white lies by an adult. Sarah knew the difference between real lies and fibs—and this was on the borderline. They were being very wicked, but she liked her cousin Rosalyn all the more because of it.

They slipped out of the house by a side door, making their way casually towards the orchard. Once out of sight of the house windows, they increased their pace. It was when they began to cross the pasture land behind the orchard that they saw the two horsemen coming towards them.

Rosalyn knew at once who the riders were, as did

Sarah Jane. The girl gave a cry of pleasure and started to run to meet them. Only a great effort of will on Rosalyn's part prevented her from doing likewise.

'Jared!' Sarah Jane cried, her face lighting up with pleasure. 'We were coming to see if you were at home. Oh, I have missed you so! It seems ages since I saw you last.'

He leapt from his horse's back and caught her hands as she reached him, so obviously thrilled to see her that any doubts Rosalyn might have had about the wisdom of this meeting were forgotten. She watched as the two walked a little way off, the horse following behind, then stopping to graze the rich pasture. The young people's pleasure in each other was plain to see, and made her feel a little sad that they must part again so soon.

Damian had not dismounted. She glanced up at him, her heart catching as she saw his stern expression. Was he angry with her? Had she offended him by seeming to take her brother's part the other evening?

'I shall not get down,' he said. 'We may be seen even here. We have ridden this way every day in the hope that you might choose to walk in this direction.'

'I could not come sooner. Sarah Jane wanted to see Jared, but it was difficult.'

'So I might imagine.' His dark eyes studied her intently, reading so much that she had not been able to say. 'And you? Have I placed you in an impossible position, my love? Do you wish we had never met?'

'No, of course not!' She gazed up at him, willing him to see the need in her, the longing her upbringing forbade her to express in words. 'I wish I could come away with you now. If I were free…' She blushed hotly as she saw the sudden blaze of desire in his eyes. 'Damian…you know. You *must* know how I feel?'

His look seemed to embrace her, holding her as closely as his arms ached to do, caressing her so that she could almost feel the softness of his lips on her.

'Will you really come with me? Follow me to some strange, foreign land—knowing you can never return to your family? That you are forever lost in their eyes? A scarlet woman…forbidden your own kind for as long as you live.'

'Yes. Yes, I shall. Only duty holds me here now. I do love Freddie—but he doesn't deserve it. I was so upset that you were forced to leave the other night, that Freddie did nothing to make things easier. He should have refused to be bullied by that woman.'

Damian's eyes lit with laughter. 'You are too severe on him, my Amazon. Beside you, most men would fare no better than Sir Frederick. He has not your courage, my love. And it was better that I left immediately. I might otherwise have said things I ought not—revealed a secret that is not mine to share, even with you.'

'The reason why you fought that duel?' Rosalyn asked. She gazed up at him, sensing a long-remembered grief and wondering what it was that still held the power to hurt him after all this time. 'You had good reason to kill him, didn't you?'

'I believed so.' His expression was grave, eyes darkly reflecting his inner turmoil. 'Perhaps I shall tell you one day, but not unless there is need—and not in front of that woman.' He glanced towards Jared and Sarah, calling out a reminder. 'We must go soon, Jared!'

'Must you go?' Rosalyn wanted to beg him to stay. She could not bear to be parted from him again so soon, knowing it might be for some weeks. 'It seems an age since… since we were in the garden together.'

Damian smiled, reaching down to touch her hand briefly. 'We ought not to risk being seen together just yet, for your sake—and Miss Holland's. I must go to London for a few days. When I return, perhaps we can meet again? '

'I will send a message when it is safe,' Rosalyn promised. 'There is a groom I think we can trust. How long will you be away?'

'A week…two at most.' Damian frowned. 'There is something I must settle. Afterwards…I must take Jared somewhere else, but I shall see you again first. And when your brother is married…'

'I shall come to you,' Rosalyn said without hesitation. 'We shall go abroad somewhere, Damian.

The scandal will not touch us there, nor shall we harm others by what we do.'

'I love you,' he said, his dark, expressive eyes seeming to caress her. 'Remember that, whatever else you may hear.'

'What do you mean?'

'I am not certain...perhaps nothing.' He looked at the boy and girl once more. 'Jared!'

Jared pressed something into Sarah Jane's hand, then turned to his horse, put a foot in the stirrup and mounted. The girl stood staring after him as he and Damian rode away, then turned to smile when Rosalyn came to stand beside her.

'He said we shall always be friends, no matter where we are,' she said, looking a little dazed as she showed Rosalyn what he had given her. 'I gave him a smooth pebble I liked—but he gave me this. He said I should keep it and one day we would meet again.'

'That is a beautiful pearl,' Rosalyn said as she saw Jared's gift. It was as large as a pigeon's egg and slightly pink. 'It is very valuable. You must take great care of it, Sarah.'

'Yes, I shall,' she replied. 'One day I may have it set as a pendant. I shall wear it when I meet Jared again—when we are both older.'

Rosalyn said nothing. She thought it unlikely the two would meet again. Jared would return to India, to his own people—and Sarah Jane would find new friends. Yet perhaps she would never quite forget the sunny days of an English summer when she had made friends with a young Indian gentleman.

'We should go back, now,' she reminded the girl gently. 'I'm sorry we could not stay out longer.'

'Oh, it does not matter,' Sarah Jane replied, hiding a little smile as she turned away.

There was no point in telling Rosalyn that she and Jared had devised a way of sending each other messages—that they planned to meet as often as they could—because it would mean a disagreement between them. Sarah did not want to quarrel with Rosalyn, she liked and admired her—but nothing was going to stop her seeing Jared, at least until his tutor took him away or she herself was sent home.

When the others returned from their luncheon party, Sarah Jane was sitting on the sofa in Rosalyn's parlour, reclining against a pile of pillows, and looking for all the world like an invalid. She managed a wan smile for Maria in reply to her tender inquiry, replying that she was feeling a little better and might even attempt to eat something later.

Sarah Jane was a consummate actress, Rosalyn decided, feeling slightly guilty that she had encouraged it, and even worse because she was forced to continue the lies.

'And you, Miss Eastleigh,' asked Mrs Jenkins with

a hard stare in her direction. 'I trust you have recovered from your headache?'

'It was only a little one,' Rosalyn replied. 'I feel entirely well again now, thank you.'

The look Mrs Jenkins gave her would have curdled milk straight from the cow, but Rosalyn was able to smile. Now that she had seen Damian, had settled things between them, nothing could hurt her.

Beatrice began to chatter and the atmosphere lightened as she declared she adored the village church, that she wished with all her heart to be married there and nowhere else would do.

'I have told Aunt Patricia that it is quite large enough to invite all those friends I really wish to have at my wedding,' she said with a sweet smile that embraced them all. 'And she has agreed to have the wedding here. We have arranged it with the vicar for three weeks on Sunday.'

'So we shall have the reception at the house,' Rosalyn said. 'Do you wish me to engage more staff for the reception, Freddie? Or will you bring in outside help?'

Her brother was considered to be something of a gourmet amongst his acquaintances, and she knew he would have preferred a London wedding with all the trimmings, but he had given Beatrice her wish without a murmur of protest, as he would probably do for the rest of his life.

The arrangements were discussed at length.

Freddie decided he would bring his own Monsieur Maurice down from London ten days before the wedding and that they would hire as many women from the village as were needed to help in the house.

'We shall also need refreshments for the dance,' Rosalyn reminded her brother. 'And that is arranged for two weeks before the wedding itself.'

'Then I shall return to London tomorrow and beg Maurice to come at once,' Freddie declared. 'He hates the country, but I dare say he will make an exception to oblige me this once.'

Freddie's chef was very temperamental and inclined to throw tantrums if everything was not to his liking. Rosalyn shuddered to think of the chaos he was bound to bring to her household, but there was no denying he was an artist in the kitchen. His sauces had to be tasted to be believed, and even Rosalyn admitted that his wonderful food seemed to melt on the tongue.

'And I need another fitting for my wedding gown,' Beatrice said, turning to Rosalyn with a pleading look. 'Why don't we all go up to town for a few days?'

'I really ought to stay here,' Rosalyn said doubtfully. 'There is a great deal to do—and Sarah Jane to think of; she cannot be left alone for several days, that would be too unkind.'

'Surely Maria can see to anything that needs be done in the house?' Freddie said, frowning at her. 'I should like you to come with us, Ros. And you will want to purchase a new gown yourself for the wedding—and the dance also, will you not?'

'Please do go,' Maria added her voice to the others. 'Give me a list of all you want done and I shall be pleased to attend to everything. It will give me pleasure to think of you having a little trip to town, dearest. It is an age since you went anywhere. And Sarah and I will be quite comfortable together, shall we not my dear?'

'Yes, of course.'

Rosalyn was outnumbered. She could not refuse when Beatrice's soft eyes pleaded with her. Besides, why should she? It would be quite pleasant to stay in town for a day or so, and she did need some new clothes. She had not bothered with anything stylish since the summer before her father's death, making do with the services of a local seamstress.

Mrs Jenkins had a hard suspicious look in her eyes. No doubt she thought Rosalyn had a reason for wanting to stay behind.

'Very well, if it will please you, Beatrice. I shall come,' she said, giving in with a good grace. 'It is very true that Maria can look after things here.' She glanced at Sarah Jane, who was taking an interest in the conversation though remaining silent. 'I hope you will not be too lonely?'

'No, of course not,' Sarah replied. It would be much easier to slip away from the house with only Maria around, she thought with satisfaction. 'Will you bring me a present from town, Cousin Rosalyn?'

'Yes, of course. What would you like?'

'A riding habit,' Sarah replied without hesitation. 'I want to learn to ride. Papa always said I ought, but I did not want to—until now.'

'If that is what you would like, of course you shall have it.'

Rosalyn thought she knew why Sarah had changed her mind about riding. She could still hardly believe the change in her cousin's daughter. Sarah Jane had grown up tremendously these past two weeks, and was much the better for it.

'Now if you will all excuse me...' Rosalyn glanced at her brother. 'If we are to leave in the morning, I think I had better speak to Mrs Simmons immediately.'

The wedding was going to make a great deal of extra work for their housekeeper and her staff, and the sooner Mrs Simmons was prepared for it the better.

Rosalyn could not help smiling to herself as she left the room. She did not really mind going to London at all. Damian would be there. It was just possible that she might meet him somewhere—that she might be able to contrive to see him alone. Her heart lifted at the thought and she began to think that a shopping trip in town would suit her very well. Very well indeed!

'It is lovely to be alone with you like this,' Beatrice said, her arm tucked through Rosalyn's as they strolled together in Regent's Park. They had spent the morning at the dressmaker's and were enjoying the warm sunshine rather than returning home immediately. The lovely weather had brought a great many people to the park, and they were able to watch and admire the sight of several smart carriages bowling along the roadways. 'Aunt Patricia scarcely ever lets me go anywhere without her.'

Surprisingly, Mrs Jenkins had cried off from accompanying them at the last moment, saying she would remain behind and write her letters—a circumstance that both of them had found agreeable.

Rosalyn gave the younger girl a sympathetic look. 'It cannot have been easy for you since your mama died, to be tied so to your aunt. That will all change soon,' she said. 'When you are married you need not see her too often—indeed, Beatrice, I think you should begin to stand up to her. If you do not, she may make your life intolerable.'

'You cannot know how I have longed to escape from her,' Beatrice said on a sigh. 'My aunt—and her odious brother Bernard.' Her cheeks flushed as Rosalyn looked at her in surprise. 'I dislike Bernard Harrington so very much. He frightens me sometimes. Indeed, I have thought—' She stopped as if what she had been about to say was too shocking to be spoken aloud. 'No, I cannot say it! But I take good care never to be alone with him.'

'Beatrice!' Rosalyn was startled. 'Has he ever done anything…touched you in a familiar way?'

'Only once and then it was done when he was in his cups, but I confess I have been afraid of him since,' Beatrice confided, her cheeks pink. 'I dare not tell my aunt. She dotes on Bernard and will not hear a word against him. I suppose it is because of what happened to Roderick, because he died young…' Beatrice looked awkward. 'I rather liked Mr Wrexham. I do not believe he would murder anyone.'

'Nor do I,' Rosalyn replied and smiled at her earnest look. 'But you had better not let your aunt hear you say that, my dear. I fear that your hopes of an inheritance would then be at an end.'

'I have Mama's money in trust—some five thousand pounds, I think. Aunt Patricia's money means nothing to me. Indeed, I wish I need never see her again once Freddie and I are married.'

'Have you told Freddie that?'

'No…no, I have not.'

'Then I think perhaps you should mention it.'

Beatrice looked struck by this. 'Do you think I should? Yes, perhaps I shall. I certainly do not care for the money if he does not.'

'I think you will find that Freddie cares only for you.'

Rosalyn squeezed her arm affectionately. Beatrice had a lovely nature. She was already very fond of the girl and, despite all the problems her engagement to Freddie had caused, she was very glad they were to marry. She suspected that there was far more to Beatrice than her brother yet dreamed, and that she would be very good for him when she had had time to grow up herself.

Turning to glance to her right, Rosalyn caught sight of two men standing together a short distance away. Her heart began to beat very fast. As the path they were following wound in that direction they would have to pass them. The men were talking earnestly and had not noticed them—but one of them was Damian, and he was bound to see her if they continued in the same direction.

'Oh…' Rosalyn did not realise she had spoken aloud. Her pulses were racing wildly. She wanted to speak to Damian, but believed it would embarrass her companion. What ought she to do? To turn away might cause him to think she wished to avoid meeting him.

'Is that not Mr Wrexham?' asked Beatrice, her cheeks a little pink as she too noticed the men.

'Yes. Shall we turn away?'

'Why? I should like to have the opportunity to apologise,' Beatrice replied. 'In any case, it is too late. He has seen us. He is looking this way.'

'Yes, so he is.'

Damian's companion was walking away. He hesitated, seeming uncertain of what to do, then came towards them.

'Mr Wrexham,' Beatrice said, before he could

speak. 'I have not had the chance to apologise to you, sir. I was most distressed by what happened that evening.'

He swept his hat off, bowing to her. '*You* have nothing to apologise for, Miss Holland. I was sorry to spoil your evening.'

'*You* did not,' she replied and smiled at him.

'You are very gracious.' His dark eyes met Rosalyn's. 'I was not expecting to see you here, Miss Eastleigh.'

'We came up for a last fitting for Beatrice's wedding gown and a little shopping. We have been here two days and return home at the end of the week.'

'Ah…' Damian nodded. 'I myself expect to be here several more days. My business is taking longer than I had hoped.'

'Then we shall be back in Cambridgeshire before you,' Rosalyn said and glanced at the pretty silver watch pinned to the lapel of her gown. 'I see it is past noon. I suppose we ought to be thinking of returning home. Beatrice and I have been out all morning. Besides, we have an important engagement this evening. Lord Renshaw's ball…'

'Renshaw's ball?' Damian nodded, his eyes intent on her face. 'I believe it will be a sad crush.'

'But that means it will be a success, you know,' said Beatrice, laughing at him. 'If there was actually room to move freely, it would be counted a failure.'

'Yes, I believe you are right. It is years since

I attended such a function,' Damian admitted. 'However, I do seem to recall something of the sort. I wish you both a pleasant evening.'

Rosalyn sighed inwardly, as he tipped his hat once more and walked on. She had hoped Damian might have said he too would be attending the ball, but it had been a forlorn hope. It was to be a sparkling society affair, one of the most important balls of the new season. She could hardly expect Damian to be on the guest list. He had spoken of himself as a social outcast, though she imagined most people would have long forgotten the old scandal. Even so, it was unlikely he had been invited.

It had not been possible to arrange another meeting with Beatrice there, but perhaps it was for the best. She would be returning to the country soon enough.

Damian walked into the select gaming club. He had not bothered to put his name forward for membership, but was able to come and go at will as his uncle's guest. It was just one of the several clubs he had visited in the hope of finding Bernard Harrington. So far, that particular gentleman was proving difficult to track down. It seemed he must have reformed his old habits, for Damian had been told he was definitely in town.

He must seek him elsewhere. Perhaps Harrington's degenerate ways had given him a taste for low dives and gaming hells. Since he had not visited any of the exclusive clubs he had been used to frequent, he must be gambling at less respectable haunts. Damian was about to leave in search of him when someone laid a hand on his shoulder.

'Good lord!' a cheerful voice exclaimed as he turned to find himself staring at a man he had not met for years. 'Is it really you, Damian? I had heard you were in the country—why didn't you call on me?'

A slow smile spread over Damian's mouth, bringing genuine warmth to his dark eyes. His friend had put on weight over the years, but he was still the same honest, decent fellow he had always been—and there was real pleasure in his greeting.

'Renshaw,' he said and laughed as he found himself heartily embraced in a bear hug. 'I meant to call, but you know how things stand…' He shrugged expressively. 'I wasn't sure…'

'You must have known you would be welcome?' Lord Hugh Renshaw's brows rose. 'My house is always open to you. No matter what anyone else thinks, Damian! After what you did for Helen. You must know I would never turn my back on you.' He frowned at the memory. 'It should have been me. I should have been the one to call that devil out!'

'With your reputation as the worst shot in England? You could never hit a barn door from ten paces,' Damian replied, chuckling at his friend's affronted look. Then his smile faded, his expression becoming serious. 'Besides, we both loved her, Hugh. It only mattered that she should be avenged.'

'You did that,' Renshaw said grimly, and there was anger now in his gentle eyes. 'But suffered for it. It was a terrible price you paid—exile from your home and everything you loved.'

'If you think that, your wits must be addled,' Damian replied with a wicked grin. 'It was the best thing my father ever did for me, sending me to India.'

'You ain't a nabob?' Renshaw's eyes widened. 'Made your fortune, did you?' Damian nodded and he laughed, the old grief returned to its habitual place in a tiny corner of his heart. His friend slapped his thigh in high humour. 'Well, if that ain't the best thing I've heard in a month of Sundays. Have you come home to rub their noses in it? All those damned idiots who cast you out? Serve 'em right if you have!'

'Grandfather left everything to me. I had to come back, to sort out the mess. It seems there are quite a few debts. Jacob can do nothing without my help.'

'Leave 'em to sink in it, I would,' said his friend robustly. 'Pack of rascals, the lot of them! Begging your pardon, Damian, but there ain't one of your family worth the saving. Not one of them lifted a finger to set the record straight. It was my father who did that—and was glad to do it. Can't thank you enough for keeping quiet all these years. No one outside our family has ever known that my sister was…' He stopped, choked with emotion.

Damian saw the pain, still so raw after all this time, and gripped his shoulder. 'She was as dear to me as she was to you,' he said gruffly. 'The sister I never had.'

'I always hoped she would be more to you one day,' Hugh said and sighed as he remembered the lovely, innocent girl, hardly more than a child, who had died of shame.

'I must tell you something,' Damian said. 'Something I discovered too late…'

'Something to do with Helen?'

'Yes.' Damian looked grim. 'It seems we have some unfinished business, Hugh—and perhaps you can help me?'

'Yes, of course. Whatever you need,' Hugh assured him. 'Come and lunch with me. Tell you what, Lady Renshaw is giving a small affair this evening—why don't you join us?'

'A small affair?' Damian's knowing eyes mocked him. 'I have it on the highest authority that it is bound to be a sad crush and therefore a success.'

'Lady Renshaw's ball always is,' murmured Hugh and sighed in a melancholy way that did not deceive his friend for a moment. Hugh was proud of his lovely wife, and her extravagance. 'Between us, old fellow, I sometimes think Jane is set on beggaring me—but think of it like this, amongst so many, one more cannot make the slightest difference.'

Damian chuckled and promised to consider his

friend's invitation. He was not particularly interested in attending a society ball—and yet Rosalyn would be there. Perhaps he might be able to snatch a few moments alone with her.

Chapter Six

'You look lovely,' Rosalyn said and kissed the younger girl's cheek. It was early evening; they were in Rosalyn's bedchamber and Beatrice had come to show her her gown before they went downstairs. 'That shade of blue particularly becomes you, dearest.' She held up a choker of pearls to show the girl. 'Could you please fasten these for me? The clasp is a little awkward at times.'

'Of course.'

'Thank you,' Rosalyn said, patting the necklace on her neck as Beatrice fastened the tiny diamond clasp. 'Papa gave me these. I am very fond of them and do not wish to change the fastening, because I think it particularly pretty, though difficult to secure.'

'It is pretty—and you are beautiful,' responded Beatrice. 'I could never wear such a rich shade of green. On you, it is magnificent.'

'Thank you. Emerald has always been a favourite shade of mine, though I would not call myself beautiful.' Rosalyn glanced at the small gilt-and-bronze clock on her dressing chest. 'Perhaps we should go down? Unless you—' She had been about to ask if Beatrice thought she ought to go to inquire if her aunt was ready, but turned her head as someone knocked at her bedroom door. 'Yes, come in.'

A maid entered, giving her a rather flustered curtsy. 'Miss Eastleigh…Mrs Jenkins bade me tell you she is laid on her bed and too sick to leave it this night.'

'Aunt Patricia is ill?' Beatrice cried, looking anxiously at Rosalyn. 'Does that mean we may not go to the ball?'

'Wait here,' Rosalyn said, frowning. 'I shall speak to her. I see no reason why we should not go—unless she is very ill, of course.'

It was the second time Mrs Jenkins had cried off that day. Rosalyn hurried along the landing to her room, knocked and, being invited to enter, did so. Mrs Jenkins was lying against a pile of pillows and looking quite unwell, her complexion slightly yellow.

'I am sorry you are feeling poorly,' Rosalyn said. 'Shall I send for a doctor?'

'No, thank you. I am occasionally prone to these bouts of nausea. I shall be well enough soon. All I need is rest and quiet.' Mrs Jenkins sighed and held a lavender scented kerchief to her nose.

'Then I shall leave you in peace,' Rosalyn replied. 'If you need anything, you have only to ring and someone will come.'

'You mean to attend Renshaw's ball, then?'

'You would hardly wish Beatrice to miss such a prestigious affair?'

'No—no, I suppose not,' Mrs Jenkins said, reaching for her little silver vinaigrette, which was rather pretty and engraved with leaves and vines. 'I dare say she will be safe with Sir Frederick—and you.'

Rosalyn allowed herself a smile. 'Yes. I am convinced she will always be safe in my brother's care. Do not hesitate to ring if you need anything, ma'am. Forgive me if I leave you now: Beatrice is waiting.'

Mrs Jenkins waved her away. Rosalyn scolded herself for feeling as if a weight had been lifted from her shoulders as she returned to Beatrice. It was very unkind in her, but she could not help thinking the evening would be so much more enjoyable without Beatrice's disagreeable aunt watching every move she made!

Beatrice's prediction was proved correct the moment they entered Lord Renshaw's large and impressive house in Mayfair. The very handsome rooms were overflowing with richly dressed ladies and gentlemen, their jewels flashing beneath the light of brilliant crystal chandeliers. Despite the size of the rooms and the high ceilings, it was extremely hot and the ballroom windows had been opened to let in some air.

Rosalyn accepted a glass of cold champagne and made her way unhurriedly towards the windows.

She was in some part Beatrice's chaperon that evening and imagined she would not dance very much, if at all—though she had already noticed several gentlemen she knew: friends of Freddie and some older men who had occasionally called on her father before his illness.

She stood watching for a few moments, her foot tapping in time to the music, absorbing the atmosphere. It was a long time since she had attended such an affair and she found she was enjoying the experience.

'Are you not dancing this evening, Miss Eastleigh?'

Rosalyn's heart jerked as she heard the familiar voice behind her. She turned, her expressive face reflecting her great surprise and pleasure at seeing him.

'Damian!' she cried. 'I hoped—but you said nothing earlier and I supposed you would not be here.'

'Renshaw insisted on it,' Damian replied, a gleam of mischief in his eyes. 'I am not quite without friends—even though I do not choose to impose myself on them.'

'You cannot imagine a true friend would consider it an imposition to have you as a guest? If it were not for Freddie's situation, I should have requested Mrs Jenkins to leave the other evening.'

'Would you, my dearest Miss Eastleigh? How very brave you are.'

Rosalyn flushed. 'Do not mock me. I have no intention of allowing Mrs Jenkins to dictate to me once the wedding is over.'

'A veritable Amazon,' Damian murmured wickedly. How lovely she looked tonight! Especially with that faint flush of pride in her cheeks. 'Brave enough to dance with me? I wonder.'

'Yes, though I must confess Mrs Jenkins is not here to censure me.' Rosalyn caught his mood. Her eyes sparkled with a naughty sense of humour. 'No, no, you must not look so! It is unkind of you. She suffered a most unfortunate bilious attack and was unable to accompany us. However, in the circumstances, I see no reason why we should not dance, sir.'

'Then I am rewarded for having allowed Hugh to persuade me into coming this evening.' He bowed to her. 'Shall we see if I can remember how to dance, Miss Eastleigh?'

She laughed, taking his hand as the musicians struck up a popular melody and groups began to form on the dance floor. It was a country dance, which meant that Rosalyn passed from her own partner to others, returning after certain moves had been executed. She clasped his hand, smiling up at him for a moment before being claimed by the next gentleman.

'It is nice to see you in town, Miss Eastleigh,' the young man said. 'I do not suppose you remember me?'

'Of course I do, Mr Carlton. Freddie brought you

down to stay with us two years ago. I remember very well.'

'Grown up a bit since,' he said. 'I was still a bit wet behind the ears then. Dare say you thought me an idiot? Must have done—Freddie and me both, larking about when you were wishing to be quiet.'

'Not at all,' she replied and smiled at him. 'You gave me a copy of Lord Byron's poems. I often read something from it before I retire. It is quite a favourite with me.'

'Really?' Philip Carlton went pink with pleasure. 'Perhaps you would stand up with me later?' he asked as they were obliged to part company.

'Yes, of course.' She smiled again and passed on.

'One of your admirers?' Damian asked, mouth quirking at the corners as she took his hand once more. 'Tell me—do I have a rival for your affections?'

'Foolish man,' chided Rosalyn. 'He cannot be older than Freddie.'

'A case of calf love, then,' Damian murmured. 'Do you know how lovely you look this evening? I should like to kiss you.'

Rosalyn gave him a speaking look. He was wicked to tease her. Surely he knew how much she longed to be in his arms?

'We should spoil the formation if we left now,' she said softly. 'But I declare it is so hot in here I can scarcely breathe.'

They parted again, but his eyes relayed a message of understanding. She knew that sooner or later he would find a way of being alone with her.

It was not to be immediately, however. Rosalyn thanked him when their dance was over; she turned, intending to go out on to the balcony for some air, but was not allowed to leave the dance floor.

Her willingness to dance had been noted and she was besieged by gentlemen wishing to enter their names on her card, which she was obliged to allow or be thought churlish.

Rosalyn was a little surprised at her own popularity. She had not taken particularly well in her come-out season, and, not being in the least inclined to vanity, could not be aware that she had come later to her full potential. As a girl, her height had made her awkward and tongue-tied; but now her beauty shone out like a beacon, drawing old and young alike to her side, her ready wit finding her many admirers.

Damian watched with a wry smile on his lips. It was not to be expected that others would not see what had struck him so forcibly at their first meeting. Rosalyn exuded sensuality and charm. She outshone all the pretty young ladies at the ball, promising so much that any red-bloodied male would wish for in a woman. Such promise was not often met with amongst the young ladies on the marriage mart; it was more usually found in a mistress—a lady who had been married for some years to a man she did not love.

Rosalyn's life had been odd for a woman of her class. She had poise, beauty, intelligence—and a high degree of independence. This evening the various ingredients had blended into an irresistible whole, making her a target for every unattached male in the room.

Damian frowned as he recognised some of the men being drawn into her net. The young fools he dismissed as irrelevant, but there were others…at least three with old titles and spotless (comparatively speaking) reputations.

He reviewed them in his mind. Davenport had been a bit of a rake in his time, but was nearly forty and looking to settle. Marksby had recently become the Earl of Salter and was reputedly on the catch for a second wife, his first having died without giving him an heir—and Sir Edward Forster was quite simply a decent man, though slightly pompous in his manner. Any one of them could offer Rosalyn a secure future and an enviable position in Society. Far more than Damian could offer!

He was suddenly assailed with doubts. What was he doing here? Why on earth had he imagined he had the right to claim such a woman for his own? He was a fool and should have remembered he had other business to settle. He turned away. It was time he was leaving—time he followed the various leads Renshaw had given him earlier and sought out his quarry.

'Not going already?' Renshaw stopped him at the

ballroom door. 'I quite thought you were enjoying yourself with Miss Eastleigh. She's a beauty, ain't she? Can't think where she has been hiding herself all these years. If I wasn't madly in love with Lady Renshaw, I'd have joined the hunt myself.'

'She is certainly very lovely,' Damian said, cursing himself for a fool as the pain tore at his insides. 'Any one of them would be better for her than me, Hugh. What right have I to drag her down to my level?'

'Rise to hers,' advised his friend with a lift of his thick brows. 'If you are thinking of this other business…it was a long time ago, Damian. You cannot bring Helen back. Forget your plans for revenge and marry the lovely Amazon.'

'Take my rightful place in Society, you mean?' Damian laughed harshly. 'Yours is the only invitation I've received since I've been in town, Hugh. What kind of a life would that be for a woman like her? Look at her—she deserves her chance to shine. She deserves someone like Forster or Davenport.'

'You would condemn her to choose between a rake and a bore?' Hugh scowled at him. 'Shame on you, sir! You are a better catch than either of them. At least allow her to make her own choice. I am sure she is perfectly capable of doing so.'

'Perhaps you are right.' Damian relaxed and smiled wryly. 'I'm a stiff-necked fool at times. Too much pride, I dare say.'

'Miss Eastleigh looks warm,' his friend said. 'She

looks as if she needs a breath of air. If you do not offer her the chance to escape, someone else certainly will.'

Damian laughed. 'You are too persuasive, Hugh. However, I shall take your advice.'

He returned to the crowded ballroom. Rosalyn had ceased to dance and was clearly headed towards the balcony. He waited, following discreetly.

Her back was towards him and she did not immediately notice he had come after her. She had moved away to the shadows and was fanning herself, staring out into the gardens. He watched her for a moment, thinking she looked sad. He had sensed it before, understood that she too had known loneliness—that her life was not all it might have been. It was this that had first made him think she might be willing to step out of her world into a very different one.

'Rosalyn…'

She spun round at once, her lovely face suddenly alight with pleasure. 'Damian! I thought you were leaving?'

'I was—but Hugh stopped me.' He moved towards her, his eyes dwelling on her face so intently that her heart caught with fear. 'It might have been better if I had left. Better for your sake.'

'Why? Why do you say that? You know I love you… want you.' She spoke from the heart, bravely, with such a devastating honesty that he felt humbled, unworthy of so fine a woman. 'I have loved you almost from the first moment you came into my life. You challenged me, Damian, brought me to life—made me want to feel again.'

'Did I, my love? I am not sure it was well done of me. In the country I thought perhaps we had a chance of finding happiness…but tonight I have seen you as you ought to be. You shine like one of those stars above us, too bright to have your light dimmed by such as me.' He stepped closer, reaching out to touch her shoulder, his fingers straying up to caress her neck; his touch sent little shivers winging their way down her spine. 'You deserve so much more, my darling—so much that I can never give you.'

'This?' Rosalyn glanced back towards the ballroom, a look of dismissal on her face. 'Do you think I care for such things? You misjudge me, sir. Had I wished for a life spent in Society, I might have married a duke when I was eighteen. I have remained a spinster from choice, not necessity.' She raised her head, her face proud, angry. 'I may be seven and twenty—but I am not at my last prayers!'

'Indeed you are not.' Damian laughed. 'Tonight you are magnificent. I dare swear there are at least a dozen gentlemen in there willing to offer their hearts and fortunes to win you. And I did not mean to insult you. I just wanted you to be quite sure—to understand what you would be giving up if you came to me.'

'Foolish, foolish man! As if I was not already

aware of what I shall lose—and what I may gain.' Her eyes glittered with the sheen of tears she would never let fall. 'Do you think me a vain, silly creature—that my head would be turned by a few compliments?'

He saw that she was not quite won over by his apology. Smothering his conscience, he reached out to draw her into his arms. For a moment he gazed down at her, letting her nearness and the musk of her perfume seep into his senses, filling him with sweet desire; then he lowered his head, his mouth taking hers in such a gentle, tender kiss that she swayed into his body, surrendering herself in a way that almost made him lose control.

'Do you not know how much I want you—need you?' he breathed huskily. 'The thought of you torments my dreams. I have struggled against this feeling for your sake, Rosalyn—but I cannot fight you. You are too strong for me, my love.'

'I have given my promise,' she said, a hint of reproach in her eyes. 'I shall come away with you after my brother's wedding—if you still want me.'

'I shall never cease wanting you,' he murmured against her throat. 'I adore you, Rosalyn. I shall try to deserve your trust. Believe me, my love, I shall never hurt you…though I know I am not fit to worship at your feet.'

There was such an odd look in his eyes then that she wondered at it. Just what mystery lay in this man's past? Why did he look so bleak at times? What inner torment drove him?

'Oh, Damian—'

Rosalyn broke off as she saw her brother come out on to the balcony. She moved away from Damian, into the light.

'So there you are,' Freddie said. 'Beatrice thought… Oh, Wrexham! Didn't realise you were here.' He looked awkward, embarrassed. 'Should it be Marlowe? I heard you'd inherited your grandfather's title…'

'Wrexham will do,' said Damian. 'I've no use for titles or any of that nonsense.'

'No, I suppose you wouldn't have after…' Freddie cleared his throat. 'Sorry about the other evening. Bit difficult…hands tied, if you see what I mean?'

'It was unfortunate for everyone,' Damian said. 'I am sorry, but you will excuse me, I have an appointment I must keep.' He glanced at Rosalyn. 'Forgive me. I really must go.'

'Damian…when?'

'Soon,' he promised. 'Soon now, my love. Eastleigh, I must bid you goodnight.'

There was a strained silence after he had left. Freddie looked at his sister, eyes narrowed, searching.

'So you are determined to have him, then?'

'You need not worry that we shall make things uncomfortable for you, Freddie. Nothing will happen until after your wedding.'

'Bea tells me she doesn't care about her aunt's money.' Freddie sounded ashamed. 'Once we're married—I don't give a damn. At least, you know what I mean. Best to keep things discreet—but if it's Wrexham you want, you will have my blessing.'

'Thank you, dearest.' Rosalyn smiled and kissed his cheek. 'We shall be living abroad. You won't be forced to acknowledge us.'

'Ros…' Freddie protested, cheeks burning. 'I ain't such a damned snob. Wrexham might have…well, you know the story better than I, no doubt. But his family…at least, his *grandfather* was a decent sort. Earl Marlowe. Wrexham inherited the lot, you know: title, crumbling mansion somewhere near Hastings, I believe—and a load of debts. If you should need money…'

'I'm sure we shan't,' Rosalyn said. 'I have my own trust and I dare say Damian has what he needs. Money has never meant that much to me. I can be happy anywhere with the right person.'

'Yes, I know.' He smiled at her with affection. 'I haven't been much of a brother to you, Ros—but I do care about you. I would stand by you…if things didn't work out. You could always come home. Bea loves you—and that aunt of hers can…well, you know!'

The look of disgust on his face made her laugh. 'Freddie, dearest!' she admonished. She had been angry with him but was no longer. He had been afraid of losing Beatrice, and she could understand that. 'Please, there is no need to worry about me. I know exactly what I want and I am not frightened of the consequences.'

'No. You never were,' Freddie said, offering her his arm as they returned to the ballroom together. 'You should have been a man, Ros. You were always braver than me.'

Mrs Jenkins had recovered from her sickness by the next morning, but said it had been caused by too much racketing about town and declared her intention of returning to the country at once. At first she was determined to spend a few days at her home in Huntingdon before bringing Beatrice back to Cambridgeshire for the pre-wedding dance.

She was persuaded to relent after some tears from Beatrice, and a promise from Freddie that she could invite her brother to stay with them.

'Bernard wrote to me,' she told him in confidence when they were alone. 'He has some small difficulty with his financial affairs. I must discuss the problem with him in private.'

'I understood Mr Harrington was in town?' Freddie was surprised. 'Would it not be easier to ask him to call here, ma'am?'

'No, it would not. He can come down to the country if he wishes for my help!' she snapped, causing Freddie to bite his tongue and count to twenty lest he reply in like manner.

What Mrs Jenkins did not reveal was that her brother was a committed gamester, incapable of staying away from the tables for long. In the past, he had often won huge fortunes, but somehow they had slipped through his fingers. Of late, his talents, or luck, had seemed to desert him—perhaps because he had taken to drinking too much. She suspected that he frequented the kind of places she would think disgraceful, and was determined to drag him away from town if she could.

'Your brother is welcome to stay with us, ma'am. Pray write to him immediately.'

Freddie gave his promise easily, entirely unaware that his beloved Beatrice detested her aunt's brother—or that he was stirring up a hornets' nest.

'Ah, there you are,' Maria said, coming to kiss Rosalyn as she entered the house. 'Goodness! How bright you look, dearest. Have you had your hair trimmed at the front? It suits you very well.'

'No, I haven't had it cut,' Rosalyn replied, feeling amused by her cousin's expression. She knew that she was looking very much more the thing now that she had bought herself some fashionable clothes. 'It's just the way the wind has blown it. We had the carriage window down for miles. Mrs Jenkins was feeling unwell.'

'What a shame,' Maria said. 'Is that why she went straight to her room? Never mind, we can have a comfortable coze together. Just like old times.' She tucked her arm through Rosalyn's as they went into the parlour. 'It is so nice to have you home again.'

'You seem very cheerful,' Rosalyn said. She had taken off her pelisse and bonnet in the hall and, as Maria released her arm, glanced into an ornate wall mirror to tidy her hair. 'How is Sarah Jane? Where is she, by the way?'

'Oh, out with that dog, I expect.' Maria seemed uninterested. 'She has taken quite a liking to the wretched thing. She says it needs lots of exercise—and I must admit she is a different girl these days. Always helpful and polite. Her grandmother will hardly know her when she arrives next week.'

'Is Aunt Susan coming to fetch her?'

'Her letter said she would be staying for the dance but not the wedding. Unless Celia and her husband decide to come—in which case they will all be here for two weeks.'

'Goodness me,' Rosalyn said. 'I am not sure how we shall squeeze everyone in. Mrs Jenkins has invited her brother too.'

'I can always stay with a friend,' Maria offered and blushed. She hesitated a moment before making her confession, 'You will be amazed, Rosalyn. I was myself—but dear Mr Waller has…' Her colour deepened even further. 'He has asked me to be his wife and I have said I will…providing it does not upset you too much.'

'Upset me? Maria, you goose! I am delighted. I had thought you might quite like him. It is the very thing for you, and I do wish you happy, my very dear cousin.'

'Well, I think I shall be,' Maria said looking extremely pleased with things. 'But there is not the least hurry. I shall not leave you in the lurch. When you are settled I shall think of myself, but not before.'

'You need not worry about me.' Rosalyn laughed. 'No, I may not tell you just yet, but my own plans are almost set.'

They were prevented from talking further as first Beatrice and then Sarah Jane arrived. Gifts were exchanged, tea poured and everyone settled down to enjoy themselves.

'Where is Sheba?' asked Rosalyn when she had a moment to talk alone with Sarah Jane. 'Maria tells me you have been looking after her for me. That was very kind of you.'

'Oh…it was just taking her for walks and things,' Sarah replied, avoiding her eyes. 'Thank you for the riding habit. I've been out on one of the horses several times this past week, but now I shall be able to dress properly.'

'Your grandmother will be surprised when she comes to visit next week.'

'Yes, I expect so,' Sarah said. 'We can stay for the wedding, can't we? Beatrice has brought me such a lovely dress. She says I can be one of her bridesmaids if I like.'

'In that case you will have to stay,' Rosalyn said. 'I had better write and urge your whole family to come, though they had thought they would not wish to travel so far.'

She was thoughtful as she went away to write her letters. Everything was working out quite well. Maria was to be married, and Sarah Jane's family would take her home after the wedding.

And then, at last, Rosalyn would be free. She smiled as she remembered her last meeting with Damian, the way he had kissed her and told her he loved her.

Where was he now? Had he completed his business at last? How soon would he be returning to the country—and would she find a way of seeing him when he did?

Chapter Seven

Damian entered the gaming hall, glancing about him with distaste. It was the kind of place that attracted the worst types: hardened gamesters, ruthless sharps out to fleece any young idiot willing to be parted from his fortune—and worse. There *was* a sprinkling of respectable men, men with old titles whose dull, comfortable lives had driven them to find new experiences to enliven their routines. These were the men that might also be found at the Hellfire Club, another place of dubious reputation and frequented by the wilder elements of Society, but here there were also other men—men with desperation in their hearts who were close to destruction.

Had Bernard Harrington sunk to their level? Hugh Renshaw had spoken of debts and wild drinking bouts that had led to Harrington being excluded from the more select clubs where he had once been a member.

'He's had a run of terrible luck,' Hugh had confided when they spoke of Damian's quest to find the man. 'I've heard it said he's close to ruin. Davenport holds several of his notes, I believe. Not many will accept them now, so he has been forced to play elsewhere. His estate is mortgaged to the hilt—there can't be much left.'

The notes Davenport held were now with a firm of lawyers. Damian had purchased them for the sum of ten thousand pounds.

'Why do you want them?' Davenport had asked with careless interest, when requested to sell the notes at a private interview. 'I doubt Harrington can cover a half of that sum.'

'It is a personal matter,' Damian replied. 'One that should have been settled long ago.'

'Killed the wrong man, did you?' Charles Davenport arched his brows. 'I ain't a slowtop, Wrexham. You kept your mouth shut and that was damned decent of you, especially when you consider the way your father behaved towards you—but anyone with a grain of sense understood why you called Roderick Harrington out. We all knew you were like a brother to Renshaw—and, though they hushed it up, his sister's death was obviously a suicide. Add two and two and the reason for that duel becomes obvious.'

'Roderick and his brother were both involved, as it happens, but at the time…she named only one.' Damian frowned. 'I trust you will not speak of this to anyone? Ever?'

'You need not ask. I ain't one to gossip where a lady is concerned, but I have always felt you did the rest of us a service by ridding the world of that filth.'

Charles Davenport smiled. 'Yes, I will sell you the notes. My fervent wish is that Harrington will oblige us all by doing the decent thing and blowing his brains out—but I must tell you I doubt it.'

'Then perhaps I shall do it for him.'

'Planning on spending the rest of your life in India? He's hardly worth the sacrifice.' Davenport toyed with the intricate gold watch fob attached to his waistcoat. 'If you ever decide to assume your title and place in Society, I believe you would find yourself more welcome than you might think.'

Their conversation had taken place earlier that day; now it was evening. The gaming tables were full of hard-eyed, ruthless men, the air thick with the stench of sweat, stale smoke and spilt wine.

What an awful place! Damian was about to turn away when he heard the rumpus begin at the far end of the room. It was apparent almost immediately what had happened. Someone had been accused of cheating! The cardinal sin, even amongst these men. There was a lot of shouting and one of the tables was overturned.

'Damn you!' A man was on his feet. From his manner it was clear he had drunk too much wine. 'Call me a cheat, would you? You're the cheat, sir! No one has such luck as to win every hand.'

'By God! I'll have your apology for that or you will meet me for it. Name your seconds, Harrington.'

Damian's eyes narrowed as he studied the man swaying unsteadily on his feet. Was that Bernard Harrington? He could scarcely believe what he was seeing. No more than ten years Damian's senior, the man looked old, fat, his face puffy from too much drinking, late nights—and perhaps worse.

The room had gone silent, tense, as everyone waited to see what Harrington would do. He seemed to hesitate, blinked and shook his head as if suddenly realising what was going on, then he turned and stumbled away, knocking into tables and a waiter. The waiter's tray was sent flying, spilling its load of glasses on to the floor with an almighty crash.

'Damned fool,' muttered the man who had challenged Harrington. 'Won't come up to scratch. He's a coward and always has been.'

'I agree with you there,' Damian said. He had approached as the overset table was being righted. 'May I have a word with you, sir?'

The man stared at him for several seconds, then nodded. 'You're Marlowe's heir, ain't you? Someone pointed you out at Renshaw's affair the other evening. Sit down, sir.'

'Thank you. I don't believe I've the pleasure of having met you before?'

'No, we ain't met.' He offered his hand. 'Tamworth's the name. So, what can I do for you, sir?'

'I believe you may have something I want,' Damian said. 'Would you perhaps have taken Harrington's notes in lieu of coin?'

'Too damned many of them,' Tamworth said, a note of indignation in his voice. 'Tried to fob me off with another this evening. I already hold five thousand pounds—more than his entire estate is worth, I dare say.'

'And I now hold another ten thousand,' Damian said with a smile. 'Far more than Bernard Harrington could ever hope to pay. What do you imagine the outcome would be if I were to buy your notes and present the entire holding to a magistrate?'

'He would be arrested and taken to the debtors' prison until he could pay—which he couldn't, as far as I can tell.'

'Exactly.' Damian smiled wolfishly. 'What is the precise sum you are owed, sir? I shall engage to cover it and relieve you of the burden.'

'What has Harrington done to you?' Tamworth shook his head as Damian's mouth hardened to an uncompromising line. 'No, no need to tell me. I dare say he deserves it. Five thousand I'm owed.' He took some scraps of paper from his coat pocket and laid them on the table. 'Not worth a penny to me—but perhaps to you?'

'If you will furnish me with your address, sir, I shall send you a draft on my bank in the morning.' Damian pocketed the notes, shook hands once more, then hesitated. 'In the unlikely event that Harrington does name his seconds, my advice is to hold your fire until he discharges his own pistol, especially if you mean to fire into the air. Turn your back while he has a loaded pistol and...well, I leave the rest to your own good sense.'

He nodded and walked away, leaving Tamworth to stare after him.

'Well, what do you make of that?' he asked as an interested observer sat down on the chair Damian had vacated.

'Don't you know the story?'

Tamworth shook his head.

'Wrexham killed Harrington's younger brother in a duel years ago. He waited until Roderick had fired, then turned his back. Must have decided he didn't want to go through with it, I suppose. Roderick had another pistol inside his coat...tiny thing but powerful enough to nick Wrexham's arm as he walked away. Wrexham turned and shot him, put a ball dead between his eyes from thirty paces. It was pretty to see, so they said, took his time as he was entitled to do...and then fired.'

'Good grief!' Tamworth ejaculated. 'And now he's after the other one. What do you suppose they did to him?'

'It was all hushed up, but there was talk of a woman being abducted and raped. The thing was, Wrexham went after the wrong brother. Everyone knew Roderick might have had a hand in it—he was completely under Bernard's domination, always did as he told him—but he wouldn't have raped the girl. Not his style; tastes in a different category altogether, if you see what I mean.'

'So it was Bernard who raped the girl…and now Wrexham knows about it?' Tamworth nodded. 'Sounds as if debtors' row is too good for Harrington.'

'That's if he ever gets there. He has a sister. She was left a considerable fortune by her husband. Harrington will wheedle the money from her if he can.'

'He might be better off going to prison,' Tamworth remarked as he recalled the look on Damian's face. 'Unless he fancies a ball between the eyes.'

'Oh, Rosalyn,' Beatrice cried as she entered the parlour, 'he is *here*. I cannot imagine why Freddie told her to invite him. It will spoil everything.'

'Why, what can you mean?'

Rosalyn looked at her in surprise. Beatrice was obviously agitated. She paced about the room in distress for some seconds, before turning to face Rosalyn.

'Bernard Harrington is here! Aunt Patricia invited him without telling me. It seems he is in some financial difficulty. Oh, I do wish he had not come!'

'You cannot believe he would dare to embarrass you in *that* way?' Rosalyn said. 'Not now that you are to marry?' She saw the fear and revulsion in the girl's face and moved towards her instinctively. 'If he dared to lay a finger on you, Freddie would take a horse whip to him. You have only to tell him what you fear and—'

'It would cause a terrible scene,' Beatrice said, biting her bottom lip to stop it trembling. 'I really cannot tell Freddie—but you must promise never to leave me alone with Bernard. Please, Rosalyn. I should die if he tried to kiss me again. He makes me go cold all over. He is the most detestable man I have ever met. Truly he is.'

'Do you not think you might be overreacting?' Rosalyn asked, looking at her flushed cheeks. 'Could it not be that you have allowed a small incident to play too much on your mind?'

'No!' Beatrice shuddered. 'It is the way he looks at me as if… Oh, I cannot tell you. You must believe me! You must.'

Rosalyn could see she was nearly hysterical. She took her hands, holding them, calming her.

'I do believe you, dearest,' she said, 'and I shall do everything in my power to protect you.'

Rosalyn still felt it would be best if Beatrice were to confide her fears in Freddie, but she realised that would be too painful and embarrassing for the girl. Perhaps it would be better if nothing were said just yet, but if she considered Beatrice to be in danger, she would tell Freddie herself.

* * *

Rosalyn had thought Beatrice might be overreacting until she herself met the man later that morning. He was without doubt a repulsive creature, his face a pasty white and bloated, with dead, reptilian eyes that seemed to strip a woman naked.

No wonder Beatrice was frightened of him! Rosalyn was conscious of some apprehension herself, despite his many efforts to ingratiate himself with her.

'I have heard so much about you,' he said, bowing over her hand as they were introduced. 'You are far more lovely than the rumours…which I assure you are rife in town. They say Davenport and Forster were at each other's throats over you at Renshaw's ball.'

Rosalyn removed her hand from his moist grasp, barely repressing a shudder as she surreptitiously wiped it on her gown a moment or so later. It took all her resolution not to betray her extreme dislike of him, but for the time being she had no alternative other than to show him the politeness she owed to her brother's guests.

'You flatter me, sir. I am sure it was nothing but a friendly rivalry—a jest for the evening, no more.'

'I do assure you it is true, Miss Eastleigh. Do not tell me that neither of them came up to scratch? Can they be such fools?'

His attempts to flirt with her made Rosalyn's skin crawl. She saw Mrs Jenkins watching with a complacent smile. Good gracious! Could she be condoning his pursuit of a woman she had almost accused of having fallen from grace—of having consorted in the garden with a lover? Surely not! She would not consider Rosalyn a fitting wife for her brother, would she?

And yet there had been a subtle change in Mrs Jenkins's manner towards her. She was not exactly friendly...more watchful, wary. What could she be thinking?

Rosalyn's fortune was not exceptionable. Her trust provided her with a comfortable independence, but she imagined her capital could not be more than five or six thousand pounds. She had never bothered to go into details, but supposed it would be released if she married.

Surely the brother and sister could not be considering the idea? No, no, it was quite ridiculous! Rosalyn dismissed the thought...and yet an uncomfortable suspicion lingered as the days passed and he continued to pay her fulsome compliments.

Rosalyn did her best to ward off his unwanted attentions without being rude. She was better able to cope with his advances than poor Beatrice, who stayed as close as possible to Freddie and barely opened her mouth when Bernard Harrington was in the room.

Even Maria confided she could not like him, and Sarah Jane could not be brought to stay in the room if he was there.

'He is so ugly,' she told Rosalyn with a shudder. 'And those eyes—ugh! *You* have to be polite to him,

I suppose, but I don't. I am only a child. I'm not expected to understand Society manners.'

The look on her face was pure wickedness. Sarah Jane was not above claiming to be grown up when it suited her. However, she was seldom in the house these days. If she wasn't taking Sheba for a walk, she was out riding with one of the grooms. Her new regime of exercise suited her, bringing a fresh bloom to her cheeks.

Freddie's manner towards Harrington was at best brusque.

'I wish he would take himself off,' he confided to Rosalyn in a private moment. 'But I cannot ask him to leave.'

Only Harrington's sister seemed pleased to have him staying, so it surprised Rosalyn to hear them having harsh words when she came in from the garden the day before Beatrice's dance.

She paused outside the door of her parlour, not liking to enter when they were so obviously having an argument.

'I've told you before, Bernard,' Mrs Jenkins was saying. 'I am willing to pay any reasonable debts from tradesmen—but not your losses at the card tables. You must find some way of paying them yourself.'

'I would if I could,' he replied. 'Damn it, Patricia! I would not have come to you if there was any other way. I've mortgaged my land to the hilt. Even if I sold everything, I could not pay a third of what I owe. Now this damned lawyer is pressing me to settle my notes.'

'I thought you said they were owed to gentlemen who would give you time to sort out your affairs?'

'I thought they would, but apparently the notes have been sold on and the new creditor is determined to be paid. It is a damned nuisance, but perfectly legal. I am obliged to pay—or face the consequences.'

'Could you not see this person, ask him to be reasonable? Even if I were to pay a part of what you owe, I could not release the money for some weeks.'

'The lawyer has given me two weeks. After that, they will apply to the courts…and I'll be finished. I've given notes on property that no longer belongs to me, Patricia; land I have already mortgaged to the bank. That's fraud; I shall go to prison for it.'

'Then you must do something about it,' his sister said sharply. 'Marry Miss Eastleigh. Her capital is nearly fifteen thousand, though I doubt she knows it. I saw the papers in Sir Frederick's desk when we were in London. She can dispose of the money as she pleases once she is married.'

'She wouldn't have me. I dare say she could take a pick of half-a-dozen fellows if she cared to—but they say she does not wish to marry.'

'Then think of some way to persuade her…'

Rosalyn turned away in disgust, having heard more than enough. Mrs Jenkins should be ashamed of herself for trying to foist her brother on an unsuspecting victim—except that Rosalyn was neither unsuspecting or a victim. She would not in any case have married Bernard Harrington, and now she would take good care never to be alone with him.

Rosalyn was in her bedroom changing for dinner that evening when Sarah Jane burst in. Her hair was hanging loose about her shoulders, her gown had been torn and there was a scratch on her cheek.

'What has happened to you?' Rosalyn cried, terrible thoughts chasing through her mind. Had the girl fallen from her horse, or was there something more sinister behind her dishevelled appearance? 'Are you hurt, dearest? Did someone try to harm you?'

Sarah Jane was fighting for breath. 'No, I'm not hurt,' she managed to gasp out. 'It isn't me, it's Jared—they are trying to kidnap him. Two men…enemies of his father…'

'What?' Rosalyn laid down her hairbrush with a clatter. 'Tell me more details, Sarah. Two men, you say—where are they?'

'In the field behind the orchard,' Sarah said, recovering her breath. 'Sheba is with him, fighting them, but Rajib is hurt and I think they may kill Jared. He told me to run away, but I came to fetch you. We must help them. We must!'

'We shall certainly try,' Rosalyn said. 'And we must hurry.'

Her long hair was hanging loose about her face and

she was still wearing her blue silk wrapping-gown over her chemise. She did not stop to bother with her clothes. Instead, she went over to her dressing chest and took out one of a pair of pistols that had belonged to her father, which she had kept by her after his death. She had recently cleaned and loaded it, in case someone tried to pay an unexpected and unwelcome visit to her room. Picking it up, she looked at Sarah Jane.

'Find Freddie, if you can—but stay here in the house. Do not follow me. It may be dangerous.'

'What are you going to do?'

'Whatever is necessary,' Rosalyn said. 'Tell no one else but Freddie—and stay here.' She did not wait to hear the girl's answer.

It took only a few seconds to run down the stairs. Maria called to her, but Rosalyn did not look back as she left the house and ran across the lawns towards the orchard. Later, she would ask Sarah how she had happened to be with Jared when he was attacked, but for now all she could think of was that she might be too late. Damian had told her the youth's life had been in danger in India, but she had not dreamed there were would be another attempt on him here—and in broad daylight!

She ran faster, lifting the skirt of her dressing gown so that it did not impede her, heart pounding, lips moving in fervent prayer: let her be in time. These men must not be allowed to snatch Jared, for it would mean almost certain death for him. Please, God! Let her be in time!

Had it not been for Sheba, Rosalyn might very well have arrived too late. The terrifying scene that met her eyes as she left the orchard and began to run up the pasture land beyond was something she would always remember in her nightmares. Sheba was defending her friend with all her strength, growling and snapping ferociously.

Rosalyn saw the bitch jump at one of the men, biting his leg and shaking her head as if he were a rabbit. She heard the man's scream of pain. A second man carried a long, curving sword which he was using to try and fight off the brave animal. Before Rosalyn could reach them, she saw the blade flash out and suddenly Sheba lay still, her coat stained with the blood that was draining out of the deep wound in her neck.

Rosalyn saw one of the men try to grab Jared, who seemed stunned and could only stare at the lifeless body of the animal he had loved. Lying face down on the ground a few yards away was another man—a man Rosalyn imagined must be Jared's servant Rajib.

She did the only thing she could think of and fired in the direction of the second assassin, who was holding his leg and leaving the capture of Jared to his companion. Her ball went wide, as indeed it must, for she was not near enough, nor sufficiently skilled to hit him. However, her shot had a powerful effect on both the men. They stared at her as she took aim more carefully this time, then the injured one started screaming something in his native tongue; he began to hobble away as fast as he could, and was followed a few seconds later by his companion.

Rosalyn reached the top of the rise, steadying her right hand with her left as she aimed the pistol and fired once more. Her shot was close enough to cause a scream of fear as the ball whistled past the nearest man; it terrified him and both men fled as if the devil were after them. Her momentary feeling of elation faded as she turned to see Jared cradling Sheba in his arms. He looked up at her, tears streaming down his cheeks.

'She saved me,' he said in a choking voice. 'They would have killed me—but Sheba saved me and now she is dead.'

Rosalyn's eyes filled with tears as she saw it was true. Sadness swept over her. She had loved the noisy, tiresome creature—but not as Jared had, not with a love that hurt as his so plainly did. He stared up at her pitifully, his dark eyes reflecting the depth of his pain and anger.

'Sheba loved you,' she said, laying her hand on his bowed head. Her heart went out to him in his grief and loneliness: the bitch had been all he had to love. 'She was a brave dog and died as she would have wanted, saving her beloved master.'

'She was your dog, *mem-sahib*.'

'No, she was yours,' Rosalyn replied. 'She chose you—and I was happy with that choice.'

Hearing a moan behind her, Rosalyn turned and then went over to where Rajib lay on the ground. His clothes were heavily stained with blood. He had been stabbed several times in the chest and arm, having fought valiantly to prevent the kidnappers taking his master's son. She knelt beside him as he opened his eyes.

'It is all right,' she said. 'Jared is safe. But you are badly hurt. We must get you home.'

'My master's son…' Rajib looked beyond her, then sighed with relief as he saw Jared still kneeling by the dog; he closed his eyes again. 'I heard the shots. You came in time, *mem-sahib*. I owe you a debt of honour. If you had not come, if they had taken him, I should have died of shame.'

As Rosalyn had always suspected, he spoke perfect English, but until now he had not chosen to speak to her. She understood now his presence in her garden the night Sheba had attacked him, and his resentment at her interference: he had been merely doing his duty, trying to protect a wilful, unhappy boy.

'It was fortunate that Sarah found me so quickly,' Rosalyn said as she realised he was trying to rise. 'Can you walk if we help you? Or shall I send for someone to carry you on a gate?'

'I think I can walk…'

He groaned as he flopped over to one side and

managed to kneel, then, clearly in great pain, forced himself to stand upright. Rosalyn took his uninjured arm, helping to support him, and he muttered his thanks.

'Come, Jared,' Rosalyn said. 'We shall send someone to fetch Sheba later. She will be buried in the gardens of my home—but you can visit her grave whenever you wish. You must help me with Rajib. He needs urgent attention or he may bleed to death.'

'Yes.' Jared stood up. His manner was quiet and dignified as he came to stand with her as she helped Rajib to remain on his feet. He looked apologetically at his servant. 'You almost gave your life for me, too,' he said. 'Damian was right. I should not have disobeyed you. I should have stayed close to the house as you bade me. Will you forgive me, Rajib?'

'It was my duty to protect you,' Rajib said. 'I knew it made you angry—but my master bade me watch over you.'

'Thank you. Please lean on me, Rajib. Miss Eastleigh will help you if you put your arm over her shoulder.'

'It is not fitting, *mem-sahib*.' Rajib hesitated. 'You will get blood on your clothes.'

'Then I shall buy a new dressing gown,' Rosalyn replied. 'Please do not waste your breath in arguing, Rajib. We must get you home before you bleed to death—and before those assassins can return.'

'They will not come back,' Rajib said. 'To run from a woman will shame them. They will not return—but others will come in their place. Jared is not safe here. He will not be safe until his father takes a new heir.'

'Damian will take me away,' Jared replied. 'As soon as he knows what has happened…he will take me somewhere they cannot find me.'

It was a long, difficult process getting Rajib back to Orford Hall, but somehow they managed it between them. Rosalyn was less worried by the weight of his body, which almost caused her to stumble once or twice, than by her very real fear that he was losing too much blood and might die. However, when they were nearly at the house, a man came striding out to meet them, and she breathed a sigh of relief as Damian took the burden of the injured man from her.

'Rosalyn! My God! Let me help you,' he commanded. 'Rajib, lean on me.' He shouted and servants came running from the house to help. 'This man is badly injured. Take him inside and summon Nessa to tend him. I shall come in a moment.'

'I have failed you, *sahib*,' Rajib gasped weakly. 'I should have protected Jared. You should dismiss me—send me away.'

'You did all you could and almost lost your life in the process,' Damian said grimly. 'Do not talk now. Go with the others, Rajib. Your wounds must be dressed before you bleed to death. We shall speak later and decide what must be done to protect Jared.'

Rajib was silent, his head bowed in shame. In his own estimation he had betrayed the trust placed in him, and owed his life to the prompt action of an Englishwoman. Something that would not sit easily with his pride, but he held his tongue and allowed himself to be led away by the servants.

'Thank goodness you are back!' Rosalyn said when Rajib had been borne into the house by willing hands. 'I shall feel safer knowing you are here to watch over Jared.'

'What has happened?' He looked at her anxiously. 'Are you hurt also? And Jared? What has been going on?'

'After Rajib was wounded, Sheba tried to protect me—but they killed her and it was Miss Eastleigh who saved us,' Jared told him. 'It was my fault, Damian. I have disobeyed you by leaving the grounds every day. They knew where to find me. I made it easy for them.'

'That does not make it your fault,' Damian said grimly. 'It was my duty to protect you. I should not have stayed away so long.' He looked at Rosalyn's pale face. 'Will you come up to the house and let me give you something for the shock?'

Rosalyn hesitated, glancing down at herself. 'I ought to go back,' she said, realising all at once how she was dressed. 'I must see to poor Sheba—and explain to my family. They will be wondering what has happened.'

'I shall come with you—you cannot walk home alone.'

'You are needed here. The men who attacked Jared have fled. I shall be safe enough.' She lifted her hand, showing him her pistol. 'I believe I can protect myself if need be.'

'It seems you have already proved it.' His smile was so tender it almost overset her. 'Go then, if you wish. I shall come to the orchard tonight,' Damian promised. 'If you can slip away, meet me there. We must talk.'

'At half past eleven,' she replied, giving him a fleeting smile. 'Take care of them, Damian. Jared needs you now. Stay with him.' Then she turned and began to run back the way she had come, before she weakened and gave into the prompting of her heart.

Rosalyn did not want Damian to realise she was on the verge of an attack of nerves. Her thoughts on hearing of the danger threatening Jared had been solely for him, and afterwards she had known she must help the injured Rajib. Only now did she begin to think of her own situation. She was wandering the countryside improperly dressed. If any of her neighbours chanced to see her, they would think she had gone mad!

More worrying was what Mrs Jenkins would make of it! Rosalyn could only hope that no one would see her return. What must she look like? Her wrapping-gown was stained with blood, her hair blown into a tangle by the wind—and she was still clutching her father's heavy pistol!

The picture that presented itself to Rosalyn's mind was so funny that she laughed, and then the tears came. For a moment she was shaken by a storm of grief and delayed shock. Poor Sheba was dead. Rajib might yet die of his wounds—and she was beginning to feel decidedly odd. Oh, how very foolish of her! This really would not do: she must stop immediately.

She found a kerchief and wiped her face, smearing it where some of Rajib's blood had mingled with her tears, then she took a deep breath and lifted her head. There was nothing to cry about: it was all over! What a very silly woman she was to be sure, and how fortunate that Damian was not there to see her give way to weakness.

She blew her nose, feeling much restored, then slowed her pace to a walk as her home came in sight. There, she was almost home and could now put the whole incident from her mind.

It was not to be expected that she could reach her own room unobserved. Freddie was in the hall surrounded by servants, who were all making a lot of noise but doing nothing.

Maria was with them. She gave a shrill scream as Rosalyn entered.

'You have been hurt!' she cried as she saw the dried blood and thought the worst. 'Oh, I knew it—and it is all that foolish child's fault. If she had gone to Freddie as she ought…'

'Stop talking nonsense!' Rosalyn commanded. 'What is going on here? Freddie—Sheba is dead. Send someone to fetch her from the pasture, please. I shall have her buried in Mama's rose garden. I must go and change. I dare say dinner is already ruined.'

'Sheba has been found and I've had her brought back to the stables,' Freddie said, sounding relieved to have his sister returned apparently none the worse for her adventure. 'What happened, Ros? We thought you must have been kidnapped.'

'Thanks to Father's pistol I wasn't, nor was Jared,' she replied. 'The Indian servant—Rajib—was injured. Jared and I took him home. He could barely walk so it was a long and awkward journey. I am sorry if you were worried—but did you have to tell everyone, Freddie? I meant you to keep it to yourself.'

'Freddie was worried when he found the body of that poor dear dog,' Maria said, completely forgetting all the times she had called Sheba a wretched animal. 'We were wondering how best to search for you.'

Rosalyn nodded. She glanced beyond her cousin to where Mrs Jenkins and her brother were standing, watching the commotion in silence. Rosalyn saw disapproval in the other woman's face, and a look in Bernard Harrington's eyes that sent a cold shiver down her spine.

'I must apologise for my appearance,' she said, addressing the older woman. 'I was dressing when Sarah

Jane came to me—and there was no time to finish. I had to act immediately. Had I wasted even another second, I believe I must have been too late. I fired at the assassins just after they killed Sheba—I dare not think what might have happened had I delayed.'

'You should of course have informed Sir Frederick,' Mrs Jenkins said, her mouth screwed up into a sour look. 'However, if what you say is true, it would seem you have acted bravely and with no thought for yourself. We can only hope that no harm to your reputation is sustained from roaming about the countryside in…what is hardly suitable attire.'

'You are too harsh, Patricia,' objected her brother, a gleam in his eyes. 'For myself, I admire Miss Eastleigh. I take it you scared the ruffians off, ma'am?'

'Had I been closer I should not have hesitated to shoot them,' Rosalyn assured him. 'My father taught me to protect myself. He gave me a small pistol to take with me when I ride out alone—but I thought this would be more useful today.' She showed them the gun, which was an odd-looking thing with multiple chambers. 'You see, it fires more than once.'

'I have one of Mr Wheeler's contraptions myself,' said Bernard Harrington. 'An ingenious tool, but seldom reliable. You were brave to use such a weapon, Miss Eastleigh. It could have exploded in your face.'

'As you see, it did not.' Rosalyn was made uncomfortable by the look in his eyes, and very aware that every line of her body must be visible to his gaze through the soft silk of her wrapping-gown. 'Maria—please inquire if some kind of a dinner can be rescued. I must change, but I shall be down in fifteen minutes.'

She hurried away. If she could have followed her own inclination, she would have liked to lie down for an hour, but there had already been too much disturbance. The sooner everything was back to normal the better because, once they had all retired for the night, she would be able to slip away to meet Damian.

Chapter Eight

'Will this cause more trouble for you, my love?' They were in the orchard, alone in the moonlight. Damian stood with his arms about her, gazing down into her eyes. 'I ought not to have asked you to meet me, but it was such a shock when I saw you come back with Rajib: realising what a risk you had taken—what might have happened to you. You could have been killed, my darling.'

He looked so concerned that Rosalyn reached up to kiss him. His arms tightened about her, the kiss deepening to one of such intense passion that it shook them both.

'I love you too much to lose you now,' Damian murmured. 'I want you so badly—need you in my life. Come with me now, my darling. This very night. Soon, I am going to take Jared somewhere safe. Somewhere his enemies will not find him. You could come with us, then we need never be apart again.'

'I wish I could come with you tonight,' Rosalyn

said, her voice soft and full of longing. 'If it were not for Freddie and Beatrice, I would—but I have given my promise. Mrs Jenkins is capable of cancelling the wedding even now. At the moment she is being polite to me, perhaps because she hopes I will marry her brother. Of course I shan't, but…'

'My God!' Damian exclaimed, startled. His eyes narrowed, becoming angry. 'Is that man here? You do not mean to tell me that Bernard Harrington is actually staying at your house?'

'Yes. Yes, he is—why?' She saw the expression of anger and disgust on his face and her skin prickled with goose bumps. 'What is it, Damian? Please tell me.'

'He is evil,' Damian said in a voice thick with emotion. 'You must be very careful, Rosalyn. Take care never to be alone with him. Promise me, you will be very careful.'

Rosalyn's gaze became thoughtful. 'Beatrice told me he has made her afraid of him. I dislike him very much—but what has he done that you should call him evil?'

Damian hesitated, then inclined his head. He had kept the secret for so many years, but now he must speak out—for her sake.

'He raped a young woman. She was not much more than a child, only seventeen. A shy, delicate, pretty girl—very much like Miss Holland.'

'I thought it was his brother who did that? I have heard the old rumours, Damian—was that not the reason why you fought a duel with Roderick Harrington, over a woman?'

'It seems I have kept silence to no avail. You are not the only one to have guessed what I have tried so hard to keep secret. Yes, my darling, the duel was over a young woman. Helen was like a sister to me,' Damian said, his expression showing both remembered grief and outrage. 'We lived within a few miles of one another and I visited my friends often. One day, I found Helen weeping bitterly in the garden of her home. At first she shied away from me, would not tell me what was distressing her so much—then, because she had always trusted me, at the last she told me what had happened. Roderick forced her into his carriage when she was walking back from the village to her home. She fought him but he was too strong for her and she was so frightened that she fainted. Something unspeakable happened to her later that day; she would not tell me all the details, but I believed I knew.'

'That was wickedness indeed,' Rosalyn said, feeling sickened by the tale, 'but what has it to do with Bernard Harrington?'

'Nothing, or so I thought then. I comforted Helen, promised to avenge her and left her sitting there in the sunlight…by that evening she was dead. She had taken something poisonous…some plant or berry she had found growing in the garden.'

'Oh, that is terrible!' Rosalyn cried. She had not

realised the extent of the tragedy until this moment. 'The poor, poor girl…to take her own life! How unhappy she must have been.'

'She was ashamed,' Damian said grimly. 'I think she regretted telling even me. It was more than she could bear and so she took her own life. When I heard how she had died, I went after Roderick and forced a duel on him. I was young then and hot-tempered. I wanted to make him pay for what he had done. He tried to tell me he had not himself abused her, but I would not listen. It was only later that I learned the truth.'

'It was Bernard?' Rosalyn's face went white with shock. 'That is what you are saying, isn't it?'

'Apparently, he boasted of it to one of his cronies, and my father heard the story. He told me I had killed an innocent man, accused me of murder, then banished me. He did not tell me he knew Bernard was guilty. I learned that only a few weeks ago, from papers my father left when he died. All these years I have been tortured, not knowing for sure…wondering if I had mistaken Helen's meaning.'

'That was not kind of him.' Rosalyn sensed Damian's pain—and the guilt he must have felt when he discovered that he had forced a duel on the wrong man. Roderick was not innocent, but there was another more to blame. 'You must have been out of your mind with grief and guilt.'

Damian's expression did not change. 'Father never

cared for me, and he had lost a great deal of money to Bernard Harrington at the card tables. He blamed me for his losses.'

'How could it be your fault?'

'He said he could not refuse Harrington's challenge, because of what I had done, and that he had been cheated. He was angry, blaming me for having become embroiled in a matter that did not concern me.'

'Your father said he was cheated—did you believe him?'

'I was never sure, but now I think it may well have been the truth.'

Rosalyn asked what he meant, and he explained about the incident he had recently witnessed at the gaming hell.

'What are you going to do?' she asked, gazing up at him fearfully. 'Will you take revenge for what he did to Helen—and for your father's sake?'

Damian saw the anxiety in her eyes. He touched her cheek, marvelling at the softness of her skin, at the sweet perfume that seemed always to cling about her. There had been other women in his life over the years, but none had ever aroused such feelings in him before.

'Do not distress yourself,' he said, smiling at her. 'Mr Harrington will be brought to book for crimes other than rape—or cheating at the tables. I have purchased notes far above the worth of his estates. He will in time be arrested for debt and probably spend some time in prison. I believe he deserves at least that—and it will close the door on the past for me. I do not require revenge for myself, only that he should receive some punishment for his crimes.'

'I am glad you do not mean to fight a duel,' she said softly. 'I could not bear it if you were killed.'

'If we had not met, I might have thought it worth the risk,' Damian said in a voice caught with emotion. 'But now…' He drew her to him, kissing her tenderly once more. 'When I asked you to come away with me just now it was in a moment of madness, because I want you so much, but it was wrong of me. If you will have me, my darling, I should like to marry you.'

Rosalyn's face lit up with joy. 'Oh, Damian! You know I will. I would have lived with you as your mistress, but to be your wife is all the happiness I could ask of life.'

'We may have to go away for a time—to live abroad. I am thinking of adopting Jared as my own, of giving him my name. You would not object to that—to what others might think or say?'

'Of course not.' She touched her fingers to his lips, smiling at him with love in her eyes. 'I am already very fond of him. I am sure I shall come to love him as if he were my own. Besides, he needs to be loved—and I know you care for him.'

'I imagined you might say that.' Damian trailed a

finger down her throat, letting it rest for a moment on the tiny pulse spot at the base. 'You are so generous. Because of what happened today, I may have to take him away before the wedding—but, once he is safe, I shall return to claim you.'

'Must you go at once?'

'We cannot leave for a few days. Rajib is too weak to move just yet—but as soon as he is well enough, I shall leave. Perhaps without telling you. Do not fear that I have deserted you. I would never leave you—unless you told me to go.'

Rosalyn felt her love swell and grow within her. She could not imagine ever wanting him to leave her side.

'Shall we meet again before you leave?'

'It is Miss Holland's dance tomorrow evening, is it not? You will be too tired to meet me afterwards—but perhaps the following day? In the afternoon. I do not like the idea of your wandering about alone at night. Particularly as Harrington is a guest in your home.' He drew her close, kissing her again. 'Promise me you will be careful. If he harmed you—I *would* kill him!'

'Do not say such things.' Rosalyn laughed up at him. 'You are worrying for nothing. He saw Papa's pistol earlier this morning. He knows I am capable of firing it. You must not be concerned for me, Damian. Mr Harrington will not dare to harm me.' She leaned towards him, pressing herself against his body, offering her mouth for his kiss. 'How I long to be with you, my dear one, to know the sweetness of your love. Kiss me one last time, then I must leave you.'

Her honesty, her sensuality, was almost too much for him. He held her close to him; his need to have her, to know the intimate secrets of her lovely body, was overwhelming. Only his sense of honour, the caution that told him it was she who might suffer if he lost control, held him back. He wanted her so desperately, burned for her, but knew their plans might falter, be delayed. No matter how much he needed her, her safety came first. He must be strong now, because her love was so natural, so trusting, that she would willingly give whatever he asked of her.

'You must go back,' he murmured against her throat. 'I shall come with you, to make certain you are safe.'

'It is best if no one sees you. Come only as far as the shrubbery, Damian. You can watch over me from there.'

'Sheba was a better guardian than I thought,' he said, frowning. 'I wish you had her still.'

'Poor Sheba,' Rosalyn replied sadly. 'She was often a trouble to me, but she died bravely. Had it not been for her, I should surely have been too late. You must buy Jared another dog when we are settled, Damian. He needs something of his own to tend and love.'

'I have thought the same,' he said. They were walking with their arms about one another. 'It is a nuisance that I must take him away from here, but I have no choice. It is both my duty and my earnest wish to protect him from his enemies.'

'We shall be together soon,' she said and turned to him, reaching up to kiss him on the lips. 'Come no further, my love. Mrs Jenkins is an uneasy sleeper. She saw us in the gardens once before, and though I am decently dressed this time, I would prefer her not to see us together again—at least for the moment.'

'I shall watch until you are safely in the house,' Damian said, releasing her reluctantly. He did not want to let her go, was frightened that something would happen to part them—that he would lose this woman he loved with a passion that was so intense it shocked even him. 'Until the day after tomorrow—at three?'

'Wait for me in the orchard. I shall come to you as soon as I can.'

With that, they parted. Rosalyn ran across the lawn towards the house, but though she paused to glance back before entering through the French windows, she resisted the temptation to wave.

Damian was watching her. He would make certain she was safe inside the house. What neither of them could know was that someone else had seen her run across the lawns.

Bernard Harrington hid behind the curtains as Rosalyn locked the French windows after her. He could not be certain, but he believed he had caught a glimpse of a man standing in the shadows out there.

Why had Miss Eastleigh been walking alone at night? Had she been meeting a lover? His curiosity was aroused. Patricia's suggestion that he should marry her had perhaps held more merit than he'd imagined. Her fortune was not large, but it would stave off his ruin for a while—and his luck at the tables must surely change! Until the last year or so he had won almost as often as he lost, without resorting to cheating too often, though there had been times when he had considered it worth the risk.

With Miss Eastleigh as his wife, he could regain the respectability he had lost. He would be welcomed in the best houses again—and might soon recoup at least a part of his fortune. He had thought his cause impossible. The haughty Miss Eastleigh would dismiss an offer of marriage from him with the contempt it deserved—but if she had a lover there was hope.

She would have married the man if it were possible. He must be married—one of her neighbours, almost certainly. How long had it been going on? Harrington's thin lips parted in an unpleasant smile. It would cause a fine scandal if it all came out. She would do almost anything to prevent that—Miss Eastleigh and that pompous brother of hers. Harrington had seen the way they looked at him, known he was on sufferance only because he was Patricia's brother.

It would humble their damned pride if he threatened to expose Miss Eastleigh's little affair. From now on he would keep his eyes open—and if she slipped off on her own again, he would follow her.

Unaware of the plot being hatched against her, Rosalyn went swiftly up to her own room. She locked her door—something she had never thought necessary before—and began to undress. Her head was full of dreams as she sat brushing her hair before the dressing mirror. She had never felt so alive, so full of anticipation in her whole life.

In little more than a week, the wedding would be over. Once all the guests had gone, her life would be her own again, to order as she wished. She might have to wait for a little while for Damian to fetch her—but then she would go with him.

She had been willing to follow her heart, to live with Damian as his mistress, but now he had asked her to marry him. Her body felt as light as thistledown as she went to bed, leaning across to blow out the candle beside her bed.

She was smiling as she fell asleep.

'Are you enjoying yourself, Beatrice?' Rosalyn asked as the young woman came up to her. Her face was flushed from dancing a rather energetic polka with one of their neighbours. He was a hearty country squire, red-faced, good-natured but not an accomplished dancer. 'You look warm. Why don't you ask Freddie to take you outside for a few minutes?'

'Yes, perhaps I shall.' Beatrice looked nervously across the room. 'Mr Harrington asked me to dance with him next—but I really do not want to. His touch is unpleasant to me, Rosalyn, but I did not know how to refuse him.'

'Tell Freddie you are feeling over-warm,' advised Rosalyn, 'and tell him you do not want to dance with your aunt's brother. He will protect you. He will know how to handle it. You must let him do that for you, Beatrice—now and in the future. It will make things much easier for you.'

'*He* is coming this way,' Beatrice whispered. 'Oh, there's Freddie looking for me. I shall go to him.'

Rosalyn frowned as she hurried away. What had Bernard Harrington done to make her so nervous of him? It had surely been more than an attempt at a kiss?

Was it time she had a private word with her brother? After Damian's revelations, it was clear that Mr Harrington was more of a danger than she had supposed. It might be wise to put Freddie on his guard. Indeed, it was her duty to do so.

'I was about to claim Beatrice for this dance,' Harrington said as he came up to Rosalyn. 'Why did she run off like that?'

'She felt too warm,' Rosalyn replied, avoiding his eyes. 'I believe Freddie is taking her out for some air.'

'She was always a nervous girl, excitable and prone to fancies,' he said, a scowl of displeasure on his face. 'I dare say all this excitement and fuss has been too much for her.'

'Perhaps—though I would not have called her exactly nervous. No more than other young ladies of her age.'

'You, of course, are more worldly,' Harrington said, a sudden gleam in his eyes. 'I admire that in a woman, Miss Eastleigh.'

'I am older,' replied Rosalyn, wishing he would go away and leave her in peace. His next words told her that her hopes were doomed to disappointment.

'May I hope that you will do me the honour of standing up with me, Miss Eastleigh?'

Rosalyn would have liked to refuse, but she had no prior engagement for the dance now starting, and felt it would seem rude to refuse. He was a guest in her home, and she must try to be polite to him, little though she relished it. And, since it was a lively country dance, she would not be condemned to his company the whole time.

'Thank you, sir,' she said, allowing him to take her hand.

His grasp was moist, unpleasant to the touch, but Rosalyn was able to bear it for the duration of the set pieces she was obliged to perform with him. Afterwards, he thanked her and wandered off in the direction of the library, where card tables had been set up for some of the older guests who did not care to dance.

Rosalyn breathed a sigh of relief. Now that there was no further need to see or speak to Mr Harrington, she could give herself up to the pleasures of the evening.

'Rosalyn, my dear.' She turned as Mrs Buckley came up to her. 'You look very handsome this evening—that dress becomes you. Indeed, I have scarcely seen you look so well. I declare there is quite a new sparkle about you, my love.'

'That is because I am happy, Aunt.'

'You are in love!' Her aunt quizzed her with her lorgnette. 'At last! You cannot imagine how often I have longed for this. Tell me, who is the lucky man?' She laughed and tapped Rosalyn on the arm with her long-handled spectacles. 'No need, my dear. Unless I much mistake things, it is Mr Wrexham—or the Earl Marlowe, as he ought properly to be called. Where is he? Point him out to me. I am anxious to meet him.'

'Damian isn't here, Aunt.'

'Not here? Am I wrong?' Rosalyn shook her head. 'Why has he not come this evening?'

'Mrs Jenkins objects to his being in the house while she is staying. It was her younger brother—the duel all those years ago. One cannot blame her, it is a most unfortunate circumstance—and very awkward for us. You recall telling me something about the old rumours?'

'Yes, most certainly I do. I have discovered the

truth of it, Rosalyn—and I must tell you that I consider Mr Wrexham—as he then was—to have been unjustly treated by his whole family. They cast him out, when they ought to have honoured him for ridding society of a disgraceful rogue.'

'It was actually worse than you might imagine,' Rosalyn said. A shiver went down her spine as she recalled the dance she had been forced to share with Mr Harrington. 'I dare say you do not know the whole story. Indeed, I did not learn it myself until yesterday—and now is not the time to speak of such things.'

'No. You are very right to remind me.' Mrs Buckley frowned. 'Here comes Freddie, and Beatrice. She is a delightful girl—though I do not care for her relations. That woman is beyond bearing, so odiously top-lofty. Who does she imagine she is? I dislike the way she speaks to both Freddie and Beatrice.'

'She has been in the habit of having her own way,' Rosalyn said. 'Her husband left her very comfortably off, I believe, and Beatrice's mother left her to Mrs Jenkins's care when she died—so I suppose she thinks she has a perfect right to dictate to her.'

'If one has enormous wealth, one does not need to puff one's consequence in that way. She is very rude, Rosalyn. If she does not mend her manners, I may be forced to give her a set down.'

Knowing her aunt was capable of doing so, Rosalyn laughed. 'I am so glad you have come, Aunt

Susan,' she said. 'At least I have an ally in the house, and that makes me feel much better.'

'Have they been upsetting you, my dear?' Mrs Buckley studied her. In her opinion, Freddie had not always behaved as he ought towards his sister. 'You should not have let them, even for Freddie's sake. He has always done as he pleased. He should consider you more.'

'I am quite happy as things are, Aunt,' Rosalyn said and smiled at her. 'When we are alone, I may have some news for you.'

'Indeed?' Mrs Buckley arched her brows. 'If it is what I hope for, it will be good news.'

She turned her attention to Beatrice as she and Freddie came up to them, taking her hand and talking to her kindly.

'Will you dance with me, Ros?' Freddie asked. He frowned as she gave him her hand. 'You were dancing with that fellow Harrington earlier. I should not do that too often if I were you. I do not like him—nor the way he looks at Bea.'

'Neither Beatrice nor I wish for his presence here,' Rosalyn replied. 'I think she is afraid of him, Freddie. I am not exactly sure why—though I can guess. He does have a rather unpleasant way of looking at females. Especially young ones. Even Sarah Jane has complained of it.'

'Damn his impudence!' Freddie said, a glint in his eyes. 'If I thought for one moment—'

'I am sure nothing has happened which ought to disturb your peace of mind,' Rosalyn assured him hastily. Her brother could fly off the handle without warning sometimes. 'Nothing serious—but I believe he is capable of vile behaviour. The very worst. And you should make sure he never has a chance to be alone with Beatrice.'

'What?' Freddie glowered down at her. 'What do you know of Harrington? Why have you not told me this before?'

'Keep your voice down,' she cautioned. 'Now is not the time to discuss this, Freddie. Stop glaring at me. I have said nothing because I did not want to cause more trouble for you. Mrs Jenkins is fond of her brother. Had I not wanted to avoid another quarrel, I should have refused to dance with him this evening. You know how unpleasant Mrs Jenkins can be, dearest.'

'You do not imagine I would let that deter me?' Freddie saw the look in her eyes and flushed. 'No, no, you wrong me, Ros. This is a very different case. Had I been aware…I shall request Harrington to leave tomorrow.'

'And cause a breach with Mrs Jenkins? She may very well decide to leave—and take Beatrice with her.'

'Mrs Jenkins has given written consent. It would cause a scandal if she withdrew now, and I should make sure everyone understood why. I doubt she would risk it. She may disown Beatrice if she chooses—neither of us cares for that.'

'Do not quarrel with her without speaking to Beatrice, Freddie—and do nothing this evening, please. You do not want to spoil the dance for Beatrice?'

'No…' He was still frowning, though the first flush of anger was abated. 'No, of course not. I wish you had spoken to me sooner about this, Ros. It was very wrong of you not to confide in me—but I dare say no harm has been done. I'll think things through and speak to Bea tomorrow.'

Rosalyn said no more. It was not quite fair of him to blame her. Until Damian revealed the truth to her, she had not known anything of substance. Beatrice ought properly to have confided her fears to her fiancé, but Freddie would not think of it in that way. *She* could do no wrong in his eyes, and he found it easier to blame his sister.

Rosalyn was a little saddened by his thoughtless attitude, but it was not the first time it had happened. Besides, what could it matter? She had only to be patient for another week or so—and then she would be with someone who did care for her feelings.

For once in her life, Rosalyn decided to spoil herself and have breakfast in bed the next day, so it was well past noon when she finally emerged from her own bedchamber.

The house seemed very quiet, as if it were recovering from the rush and tear of the previous day. When Rosalyn went downstairs, she found Maria removing dead flowers from a vase in the parlour.

'Working again?' Rosalyn chided her with a smile. 'You should have slept in as I did, Maria. I am sure you must be tired. You did so much to make the dance a success last night. I am sure both Freddie and Beatrice are grateful for all your efforts.'

'Yes, it did go well, did it not?' Maria smiled in a contented way. 'Mr Waller—that is to say, Edward and I have decided we shall be married the week after your brother. It will be a very quiet affair, of course, but I should like you to be there if you will.'

'If I can,' Rosalyn promised. 'I am going to tell you something, Maria, but you must not tell anyone—no one at all. Please give me your word?' Her cousin nodded, eyes wide with curiosity. 'I am going away with Mr Wrexham. We shall be married, but not before we leave England, and not until after my brother's wedding. Damian is anxious to settle Jared in a place of safety first, and then he will return to fetch me.'

She had expected Maria to look shocked, but her cousin surprised her by coming to kiss her cheek.

'I have thought there was something, dearest. You seemed so much happier than you had for a very long time. I am exceedingly glad for you—and I wish you happiness. I hope you will keep in touch—write to me now and then?'

'Yes, of course I shall,' Rosalyn said. 'You have been a good friend to me, Maria. Indeed, I do not know what I should have done without you.' She kissed her cousin again. 'Have you seen Freddie this morning, by any chance?'

'He went out half an hour ago,' Maria said, giving her an odd look. 'He was most unlike himself, Rosalyn. Seemed to be in a bad humour. I asked him what was wrong and he told me it was not my concern—quite sharply. I was a little upset, though I am sure he did not mean to be harsh.'

'Oh, dear.' Rosalyn was disturbed by the news of her brother's ill temper. 'I know he has things on his mind just now, but he should not have been rude to you.'

'Oh, he was not exactly rude,' Maria said. 'At least, I do not mind that; it was just a careless moment, and Sir Frederick does sometimes…well, you know, my love. I was merely concerned that he seemed upset over something. I do hope he has not quarrelled with Beatrice.'

'He was not really annoyed with you,' Rosalyn said, excusing her brother. 'I expect it is all this fuss over the wedding. Men do not enjoy it in their hearts.'

'Yes, perhaps that is so…' Maria glanced up as the housekeeper entered the room. 'Did you want me, Mrs Simmons?'

'It is Mrs Jenkins,' the housekeeper replied, her mouth twisting wryly. 'It seems she has been ill in the night—in pain and vomiting. She says she does not want a doctor—but she looks proper poorly to me, Miss Eastleigh. I wondered if you would take a look at her?'

'Very well, I shall come and see her now,' Rosalyn said. 'It might be wise to send for the doctor—but I shall hear what she has to say.'

She ran hurriedly up the stairs. This was the second time Mrs Jenkins had suffered such an attack—or had it happened more often?

Rosalyn was shocked by Mrs Jenkins's appearance. She had dark violet patches under her eyes and they had an unnatural staring look. It was clear that she was quite ill. Very sick, much more so than she had been in London.

'I am sorry to be so tiresome,' she apologised in such a fading voice that Rosalyn was alarmed. 'I am prone to these attacks. I have my powders, but of late they seem not to help—indeed, I have wondered if they make me worse.'

'You must rest,' Rosalyn insisted. She sat on the edge of the bed and reached for Mrs Jenkins's hand, patting it soothingly: it felt moist and over-warm. 'You are no trouble to us. I am only sorry you feel so unwell at this time.'

'You are…generous.' Her eyes dropped before Rosalyn's clear gaze. 'I am sorry…' She turned away to press a handkerchief to her mouth. 'Forgive me. I feel sick again.'

Rosalyn reached for a small china bowl and held it for her; she waited patiently as she vomited several times, then handed her a damp cloth to wipe her mouth.

'I shall leave you to rest, ma'am,' she said after emptying the bowl into the waste bucket in the pot cupboard and fetching a glass of water. 'A sip or two of this may help. But I think we should have the doctor. He may be able to give you some different powders, which will ease the nausea.'

Mrs Jenkins was too demoralised to protest. The woman she had treated as an enemy, had insulted and threatened, had just shown her more compassion than she could have expected. She felt embarrassed and slightly ashamed, turning her head away as the tears filled her eyes.

In all her life, Patricia Jenkins had only ever loved one person: her brother Roderick. She had done her best to love Bernard. God knew, she had paid enough of his debts—but she could not love him as she had her beloved Roderick. *His* death at such a young age had almost killed her, turning her into the sour woman she now was.

Rosalyn could, of course, know nothing of the older woman's thoughts. Her sympathy had been aroused when she'd seen how unwell Mrs Jenkins was, and she had acted instinctively. She did not consider herself to have been particularly kind. Indeed, she had given no thought to anything other than her guest's comfort.

The stable lad was sent to fetch a doctor. Mrs Simmons was instructed to give every attention to the invalid, and Beatrice was told not to worry.

'It is probably best that you do not go up to Mrs Jenkins for the moment,' Rosalyn advised. 'I do not believe your aunt's illness is infectious, but we must be careful. You would not want to take an infection so close to your wedding.'

'No, of course not.' Beatrice looked anxious. Her face was pale and Rosalyn suspected she might have shed a few tears. 'Have you seen Freddie? He—he was so cross with me earlier. I have been looking for him, but I cannot find him. He is not in the house, or the gardens. Where can he have gone?'

'Maria said he went off earlier. He may have taken one of the horses out.' Rosalyn saw the girl was in a state of acute distress and frowned. What could have happened to make her so upset? 'She said he was in a temper—surely he did not quarrel with you?'

'He...asked me about Bernard,' Beatrice said in a faltering voice. She bit her lip and tears started to her eyes. 'He does not like the way Bernard looks at me...so I told him.' She drew a shaky breath. 'I told him everything, Rosalyn. It was terrible! I was so embarrassed and Freddie was furious. He shouted at me. He has never done that before. He said I ought to have told him all this at once—and that he would not have such a vile creature in his house.'

'I am afraid it is my fault,' Rosalyn said regretfully.

'He said something particular to me last night, and I felt obliged to tell him you were nervous of Mr Harrington, but not why. Indeed, I do not know, for you have never said exactly what he did to upset you.'

Beatrice told her in a shame-faced whisper. The words came out haltingly and obviously caused her pain in the telling.

When she had heard the girl's story to its end, Rosalyn was not surprised her brother had flown into a temper: it was far worse than she could ever have imagined. How could Mr Harrington have behaved so badly towards a girl who was a guest in his own sister's home? Yet had he not done something far worse to another young girl? Perhaps Beatrice had been lucky to escape with a fright.

'He actually came into your bedroom and tried to get into bed with you? He put his hands on you? Oh, Beatrice, my dear! That must have been a terrible shock. What did you do?'

'I called for my maid. I had asked her to sleep in my dressing room because I was afraid he might…' Beatrice blushed for shame. 'Alice rushed in and hit him on the shoulder with a hairbrush. He ran off then, but the next day he threatened to tell Aunt Patricia that I had enticed him. He said she would believe him instead of me and I think…I think perhaps she would have.'

'Oh, my dearest girl,' Rosalyn said. 'Surely she could not be so prejudiced—or so stupid? It was a terrible experience for you. And you had no one you could tell, no one to comfort you. No wonder you cannot bear to be near him.'

'I was too ashamed to speak of it,' Beatrice said, smothering a sob. 'I felt that I must have done something wrong, though I could not think what. I never once gave him cause to think me willing, I swear it. It has hung over me like a black cloud—and now Freddie is angry with me.'

'Leave him to mull things over,' Rosalyn advised. 'You have done nothing of which to be ashamed, Beatrice. Freddie is angry because he unwittingly allowed you to be exposed to danger and he feels guilty. He does not blame you, I am sure of it.'

'I really did not give Bernard encouragement to think I might welcome his advances,' the girl said, her lip trembling. 'Not ever. You must believe me. You *must*!'

'I do,' Rosalyn replied and smiled at her encouragingly. 'I have no idea where Freddie has gone, but when he returns I shall tell him something he ought to know.'

'Good God! I can scarcely believe it.' There was revulsion in Freddie's eyes as he looked at Damian across the drum table in the library of Orford Hall. Beatrice's story had shocked and angered him. Furious, and afraid of doing something he might regret, he had rushed out of the house and ridden hell for leather to the Orfords' house, knowing that one person could tell him for certain what he needed to know. 'Do you mean to tell me that I have been harbouring a rapist in my house? And no one told me!' He banged the table with his fist. 'This is monstrous. I had a right to know! Rosalyn should not have kept this from me.'

'You have no reason to blame your sister,' Damian said, frowning. 'Rosalyn did not know herself until the night before your dance. She was shocked and distressed herself. I imagine she wanted to tell you—but was not sure of your reaction.'

'What do you mean? Not sure of my reaction…' Freddie glared at him, expressions of anger and shame warring for supremacy in his face. 'You are thinking that I would have ignored this for the sake of peace? Damn it, Wrexham! I am not such a fool. This cannot be brushed under the carpet. It is too serious, too dangerous. Besides, no matter what her aunt does, Beatrice will marry me. Even if we have to elope. She has assured me of it several times.'

'I am very glad to hear it.' Damian allowed himself a smile. 'You would soon have found Mrs Jenkins had too much influence in your matrimonial affairs had you let her continually have her way.'

'I was concerned for Beatrice's inheritance,' Freddie admitted, looking ashamed. 'But she does not care a fig for it and nor do I. All I want is to be left in peace with her. I'm damned if I'll have that fellow in my home another night. To think that

Beatrice has been forced to be polite to him! I can tell you, it turns my stomach, Wrexham. The man ain't fit to live. If I had my way I would take a horse whip to him.'

'He will be punished, you may rest easy on that—but perhaps not in quite the way you suggest.'

'I don't care what happens to him once he's out of my house!'

'I confess I shall feel easier in my mind if he has gone,' Damian said. 'It is my intention to meet Rosalyn in…' he glanced at the gold pocket watch which hung from a chain attached to his waistcoat '…just about an hour's time. After that I shall not be able to see her for some days. The attack on Jared makes it important that I move him to another location—but when I return I shall claim your sister. We shall be married, but not until we have reached our destination. You have my word that my intentions are honourable, and that I shall do my best to make her life as comfortable and happy as possible.'

'And where will you live?' Freddie looked sceptical. 'Some outlandish place abroad, I suppose? Why can you not wait and marry her here? A proper wedding with all her friends about her. Do the decent thing, Wrexham. You cannot expect her to give up everything she knows and loves for your sake?'

Damian hesitated before he answered. 'I believe Rosalyn is well able to make her own decision, Eastleigh. I have a duty to Jared and it may be some years before I could return to this country to live. I do not imagine it would suit her to be kept waiting that long. Indeed, she has told me that she has often longed to travel.'

'I suppose if it is what she wants…' Freddie reluctantly offered his hand '…then of course you have my blessing. But I do not like it. I tell you frankly, sir, it ain't what I want for my sister. She belongs here amongst her friends and family.'

Damian inclined his head, accepting his hand. Sir Frederick was right, of course; what he had to offer was not good enough for a woman like Rosalyn, but he believed he could make her happy. She would have his name, his fortune and his love. It was all he could give her.

Would it be enough? Only time would tell.

Chapter Nine

Rosalyn was detained by her aunt just as she was about to slip away from the house to meet Damian. Mrs Buckley was in high spirits and kept her talking for several minutes, so it was almost a quarter past the hour when she reached the orchard. She had hurried, fearing that Damian might be gone, and was breathless. When she saw him leaning against an apple tree, waiting for her, her heart took a flying leap. How handsome he was—and how very much she had come to love him!

'I am late,' she said as he reached for her hands, holding them and gazing into her face, before bending his head to kiss her lips. Her pulses raced with excitement as he caught her to him. She smiled, looking up at him. 'Forgive me? My aunt had so much to say that I thought I should never manage to get away.'

'Did you not know I would wait?' His eyes teased and challenged her. 'Did you think I should fly into a temper because you were a few minutes late and leave without seeing you?'

'I was not sure. No, of course I did not think that, but you might have been in a hurry to start on your journey.' Rosalyn recovered her breath and laughed at herself. 'I should have known—but I was eager to see you. No, do not laugh at me! You must know I have been longing to see you—that my haste was because I was eager to be with you.'

'No more eager than I to see you,' Damian said, looking deep into her eyes as if he sought her very soul. His wicked smile had gone and now he was serious. 'It will be the last time for a few days. I wish I did not have to leave you, my love—but I fear I must. Jared grows impatient at being almost a prisoner in the house, and who can blame him?'

'No one. Of course you must think of his safety first. It must be almost unbearable for him to stay closed in—especially when the weather is so fine,' she said. 'Where will you take him?'

'To France for the time being—and perhaps we shall all travel on to Spain in a few weeks. Jared will be happiest in a warmer climate. I too have grown accustomed to the heat from my years in India…'

'And I have always loved the sunshine,' Rosalyn said, answering the question in his eyes. 'How exciting it will be, Damian. To see places I have only read of in books, to experience new cultures and meet new people. I have often thought I should enjoy travelling.'

'I believe it will suit you,' he replied with a strange

little twist of his lips. 'You are no pale English rose to wilt in the heat of summer, but a more exotic bloom—one best suited to growing wild.'

'How well you know me! Perhaps too well. I shall never be able to have secrets from you.'

Rosalyn's laughter rang out. She went into his arms willingly, lifting her face for his kiss. It felt so right, being held close to him. She had never known such sweetness, such content. Her body swayed into his, melding with his in the heat of their desire.

'I want you so much, my darling,' he whispered huskily into the softness of her fragrant hair. 'I shall always love you. Always want and need you.'

'And I long to be yours.'

Rosalyn felt as if her heart was being drawn from her body as they kissed. She was no longer a separate being, but a part of Damian: without him, she would wither and die like a vine in arid soil.

'You will come back soon?'

'The journey there and back should take me no more than a week,' Damian promised, his thumb smoothing the lips he had just kissed so thoroughly. 'Look for me in the gardens on the eve of your brother's wedding. If I do not come then, I shall the following night or without fail the next.'

'It does not matter. I shall be ready when you come,' she promised. 'Once Freddie is married, there will be nothing to hold me here. We can leave the moment you are ready.'

'It cannot be soon enough for me,' Damian said, drawing her into his arms once more. 'Take care of yourself, my dearest. And remember, I love you. No matter what anyone says to you—I love you and I believe we shall be happy together.'

What did he mean—no matter what anyone said to her? Rosalyn would have asked, but he was kissing her again, kissing her with such tender passion that she let it go. Damian must know that no one could say anything which would make her change her mind about him.

'And now you must go,' he said as he released her. 'You will be missed—and I have work to do if we are to leave this evening.'

'This evening? You mean to travel by night?'

'Jared and I leave on horseback after sunset,' he replied. 'Rajib and Nessa will follow by coach in the morning—that way I hope to avoid being seen and followed by anyone who might try to harm Jared.'

'Do you think the men who attacked him are still around, waiting for another chance?'

'No, I think they have been frightened off—but it is best to be careful. There may be others willing to take their place.' He smiled as he saw her anxious look. 'Do not worry, my love. Nothing will happen to us, I promise you. Jared was attacked because I was not there to protect him. In India I was known for the accuracy of my shooting—a skill much appreciated by villagers being attacked by renegade tigers, I assure you. You need have no fear for my safety.'

'No, of course not.' She smiled at the picture his words conjured up, realising there was so much she did not know of him or the life he had led in India. She reached up to brush her lips over his in a farewell kiss. 'I must go now, but I shall be thinking of you until we meet again.'

From somewhere high above in the branches of an apple tree, a blackbird trilled its song. Rosalyn stood back, gazing at him for a moment longer, then turned resolutely.

She began to walk away, looking round to wave once more before leaving the orchard. Damian was still standing there, feet apart, eyes intent, watching her—as if he were reluctant to leave even though they had said their farewells.

Rosalyn knew an urgent longing to run back to him, to tell him she did not care about her brother's wedding and would go with him that very moment. She fought the urge down, telling herself that she was being very foolish. In a week, Damian would return to her. She could not break her promise to Freddie, nor must she do anything that might spoil Beatrice's wedding day. That would be extremely selfish of her, and might lay heavy on her conscience. No, no, she must be patient a little longer.

Lost in her own thoughts, Rosalyn walked slowly through the shrubbery that led towards the back lawn which in turn led up to her parlour. If she could gain the house without being seen, she might be able to snatch a little time for herself…time to dream, to think of Damian and remember what it felt like to be in his arms, what it would be like when they were married.

Because she was wrapped up in her plans for the future, she was completely unaware of Bernard Harrington until he suddenly stepped out in front of her, blocking her path.

'Oh!' She was startled to see him. 'Mr Harrington. Where did you come from?'

There was such an odd expression in his eyes! It made her uncomfortable. Why did he look so very pleased with himself?

'I have been watching you,' he said, a sneer of mockery on his lips. 'I saw you meeting your lover in the orchard…'

'You have been spying on me!' Rosalyn was shocked, a feeling of unease going through her as she looked into those cold, merciless eyes. He was so evil! 'That was impertinent of you, sir. What gives you the right to follow me?'

'I saw you alone in the gardens the other night,' he said. 'I guessed then that you had a lover—and so I followed you this afternoon when I saw you slip away. I saw you meet him. Who is he…the husband of one of your neighbours? What a deceitful little slut you are to be sure, the haughty Miss Eastleigh throwing herself into the arms of a man like any common bitch on heat.'

'How dare you!' Rosalyn's hand shot out, striking him across the face. 'How dare you insult me, sir?'

'Whore!' he snarled, catching her wrist. 'I'll teach you to respect your betters! You looked down your nose at me. I saw the disgust in your eyes, as if I were beneath you, some kind of filth from the gutters—and all the time you were sneaking out to meet a lover.'

'You had no right to follow me,' Rosalyn cried, twisting and turning furiously as she tried to break free of his grasp. 'Take your hand off me, sir. What I do is not your affair.'

'I have made it so,' he said, his grip tightening on her wrist, bruising and hurting her as he swung Rosalyn round so that her back was to him. She cried out as he twisted her arm, pressing it hard up against her shoulder blade. He put his other arm about Rosalyn's waist, so that she could not move as he pressed his face close to her ear, spewing out his spiteful threats. 'I have decided you will make me a fine wife. I like women with spirit—and I need your inheritance, my dear. Marry me, and you need never reveal your shame—refuse me and I'll ruin you.'

'I would as soon wed a snake,' Rosalyn spat at him. She kicked out hard at his shins, making him curse and let her go. She retreated but, instead of running, from a safe distance she turned to face him, her eyes bright with anger. 'Do your worst, sir. I care nothing for your blackmail or your threats. I shall be married as soon as Freddie's wedding is over. Damian is coming for me and—'

'Damian…' His eyes narrowed to dangerous slits. 'You mean Wrexham—that murderer? Patricia told me she had seen him here in this house…that you had invited him.'

'Damian is not the murderer,' Rosalyn cried shrilly. 'You were your brother's murderer, sir. It was you who raped that girl—you who drove her to take her own life because she was so ashamed… ashamed of what you had done to her. Your brother kidnapped the girl, but you were the instigator of that foul deed. Damian killed your brother fairly in a duel—but it should have been you, not Roderick, who died that day. You let him die in your stead rather than confess your guilt. You killed your brother, sir—his blood is on your own hands.'

'What do you know of this?' Harrington's voice was a dry rasp. 'What lies have you been spreading, bitch?'

'I have spread no lies,' Rosalyn said, lifting her head proudly. 'You will be brought to book for your crimes, sir. If not for rape, for—' She broke off as he snarled and lunged at her, retreating before the fury in his face. 'When I tell my brother of your attack on me, he will request you to leave our house at once. You are no longer welcome here, sir. Besides, Freddie knows that you tried to abuse Beatrice—that you went to her room and attempted to get into her bed.

Her maid drove you off, but you threatened to tell your sister that Beatrice had encouraged you, thereby ensuring she would not dare to speak out and accuse you. You are everything despicable, sir. Everything any decent woman would revile and refute.'

Bernard hesitated, staring at her in frustration. How dare she defy him? He would have liked to take the bitch by the throat and break her neck, but her screams would rouse the household. Besides, he had other more important business for the moment. He had known when the lawyers began to press for payment that he must have an enemy, but had not suspected the man's identity until this moment. He needed to confirm who held the notes that would send him to the debtors' prison, and to teach that person to keep his nose out of his affairs—time enough to take care of this woman when he had dealt with the instigator of his troubles.

'There is no need for your brother to ask me to leave,' he said with a curl of scorn about his mouth. 'I cannot wait to shake the dust of this accursed place from my boots. Be damned to you and your brother, Miss High-and-Mighty Eastleigh! I came here only because Patricia commanded it, but for all the help she's given me I might as well have stayed in London. She clings so tightly to that damned money of hers, I doubt I'll see a penny of it until she's dead. And the sooner that happens, the better as far as I'm concerned.'

He walked off, fuming. Be damned to the bitch and to his own sister! Patricia could have given him the money and not missed it, but she was too tight-fisted. He needed to cool his temper before returning to the house or God only knew what he might do!

Rosalyn stood where she was for several seconds after he had walked away from her. She discovered she was trembling; the encounter had upset her more than she cared to admit. When he'd held her imprisoned in his grasp, she had feared what he might do. His strength was such that he could have killed her if he had chosen to do it, and she could feel the imprint of his steely fingers on her flesh. She would no doubt have bruises to show for his rough handling of her.

Taking a deep breath to steady herself, Rosalyn lifted her head and looked up at the windows of the house. In that moment, she saw something move. Someone had been watching and—since the window had been opened slightly at the top to let in air—they could also have heard every word she had exchanged with Mr Harrington.

It was the window on the landing at the top of the stairs, not one of the bedchambers—so it could have been anyone: a servant, Maria, Freddie…any one of them. Rosalyn went quickly into the house. She must hurry. Her most urgent thought was that she must stop whoever it was from speaking of this if she could…but when she reached the top of the stairs whoever had been standing there had gone.

She was too late. She had hoped to prevent any gossip reaching Mrs Jenkins's ears, but there was nothing she could do about it now. Any mention of that unpleasant scene in the garden to other members of the household would only bring about that which she hoped to avoid.

Who could it have been? Rosalyn looked about her. It had taken her a few seconds to come in from the garden, plenty of time for the person who had been observing her quarrel with Mr Harrington to have gone downstairs or into one of the bedrooms.

What a nuisance! She frowned in annoyance. If only she had been in time. She must simply pray that whoever it was, would have the sense to keep what they had seen and heard to themselves.

Rosalyn sighed. The damage had been done. She dare not think what Mrs Jenkins would make of it if she learned of the unpleasant incident. She was bound to blame her—or Damian, of course. Beatrice had spoken of her aunt's fondness for her brother, so it was unlikely Mrs Jenkins would believe a word of what Rosalyn had said, even after his harsh words concerning his sister—but it could still cause trouble. She would be very angry that the accusation had been made, and might even call off the wedding as she had threatened once before.

Thinking of Mrs Jenkins made Rosalyn remember how sick the poor woman had been. The doctor had visited earlier, but perhaps she would just look in and see how she was now. She glanced at herself in a wall mirror, smoothing her gown and a few stray wisps of hair, then she went down the hall and knocked at Mrs Jenkins's door.

Several seconds passed and she was about to turn away when she heard something and then the door was opened. Mrs Jenkins was dressed and, although her skin still looked slightly yellow, seemed better, more like her usual self.

'I am sorry to disturb you,' Rosalyn said, startled by the look of anger in the other woman's eyes. She was clearly very disturbed about something. 'I just wondered how you were feeling—if you needed anything?'

Mrs Jenkins gave her a cold, proud stare. 'Thank you, no,' she said. 'I am much recovered, Miss Eastleigh. I believe I shall come downstairs in a little while.'

'I am very pleased to hear that,' Rosalyn said and hesitated. 'Without wishing to intrude, may I ask what the doctor said was the cause of these unfortunate attacks?'

'He said the powders I have been using for my indigestion had a peculiar smell to them and might have gone bad,' she replied, a very odd expression in her eyes. 'He took them away with him and gave me something different to use.'

'Then I hope you will find an improvement in your health,' Rosalyn said. 'It would be a shame if you were ill and we had to postpone the wedding. Beatrice would be so upset.'

'You need not fear that,' Mrs Jenkins said, surprising her. 'I am determined that nothing shall stand in the way of Beatrice's happiness.' She saw Rosalyn's expression and smiled strangely. 'I dare say you may find that difficult to believe, Miss Eastleigh—but I happen to be very fond of my niece, regardless of what either she or anyone else may think.'

'I am sure…' Rosalyn found it almost impossible to answer. 'I am sure she knows it, ma'am.'

'No, do not lie to me,' Mrs Jenkins said. 'I have come to appreciate your honesty, Miss Eastleigh. I know I am a difficult woman, but I do care for Beatrice and I shall do nothing that might harm her. She will be happy and safe with your brother, and that is all that I desire for her.'

Rosalyn smiled, making no comment; it was best to leave the conversation there for the moment. She merely repeated her hope that Mrs Jenkins would soon be fully recovered and said that she was about to take tea in her parlour.

'We shall all be very happy if you were to join us, ma'am.'

'Thank you. Perhaps a little later…I have something I need to do for the moment.'

Rosalyn went away. She was thoughtful as she walked down to the parlour. What had changed Mrs Jenkins? She had seemed very angry when she first opened her door, but her manner had softened as they talked—and she had so far unbent towards Rosalyn as to become almost friendly. Her promise that she would do nothing to spoil the wedding was reassuring.

At least one thing seemed clear: she could not possibly have been at the window to witness the quarrel between Rosalyn and Mr Harrington. No, that must have been someone else. Who? Rosalyn wrinkled her brow. One of the servants—or Maria? Perhaps it did not matter. Providing no one said anything to annoy Mrs Jenkins, the wedding would go ahead without any further upsets.

Rosalyn sighed as she recalled her brief meeting with Damian that afternoon. How she wished she had been able to go away with him at once. She felt a coldness pass over her skin, a premonition of something frightening making her shiver.

Now she was being silly. Nothing was going to happen. Damian would only be away for a few days, and then they would be together for the rest of their lives.

Very early the next morning, Rosalyn woke suddenly. She had been dreaming, a dream so clear and vivid she could recall it as if it had been real. She had been lost in a mist, running, trying to find…Damian.

Her cheeks were wet with tears. In her dream, she

had seen him but she had not been able to reach him. He had been somewhere in the mist, so near that she knew if she just reached out she could touch him, but something was stopping her, holding her back. Invisible chains…the chains of duty.

Rosalyn got out of bed and went to the window, looking out at the garden, which was shrouded in a fine morning mist. A shiver went through her. She longed for Damian, wished that she had gone with him when he asked.

'Damian, come back to me, my darling,' she whispered. 'I love you so—and I am so afraid…so afraid of losing you.'

What a very foolish woman she was, to be sure! Rosalyn laughed at her own fears as the sun began to break through the mist. It was just a dream… nothing terrible was going to happen, nothing that could prevent her leaving with Damian when he came for her.

It seemed that Mr Harrington had departed without a word to anyone, except perhaps his sister. He did not come in for dinner that evening and Rosalyn took it for granted that he had left as he intended. As no one asked her, she did not speak of the incident in the garden, preferring to put it out of her mind as though it had never happened. Beatrice and Sarah confided privately that they were glad he had gone, and Freddie seemed distant from everyone except his fiancée.

Mrs Jenkins made no mention of his departure to anyone, so if he *had* taken leave of his sister, whatever had passed between them could not have included a revelation of the quarrel between him and Rosalyn. Indeed, Mrs Jenkins seemed to have made a remarkable recovery—of her health and her manners. She went out of her way to be pleasant to Rosalyn and her aunt, revealing a side of her that no one had previously guessed was there.

'You might almost think her a different woman,' Mrs Buckley remarked in private. 'Now, what do you suppose could have brought about such a change?'

Rosalyn laughed. 'I have no idea. I am just glad of it for Beatrice's sake, and Freddie's, of course.'

The next few days passed so pleasantly that Rosalyn was able to forget her fears of exposure and enjoy all the celebrations leading up to the wedding itself. The only altercation was when one of Mrs Simmons' staff upset Monsieur Maurice and caused the great artist to throw a tantrum in the kitchen, as well as several heavy copper-bottomed pans, which were aimed at the unfortunate maid who had aroused his wrath, but happily they missed and caused nothing more than a few tears.

His threats to resign immediately threw Freddie into a panic, for how could the wedding reception go ahead without him? Rosalyn was called, and, after several minutes spent soothing feathers and tending injured pride, was able to restore a smile to the chef's face.

'You understand me,' he said, placing a hand on his heart. 'You understand what a great chef must suffer in the cause of his art—and if that stupid woman does not understand when I say the onion must be chopped just so, she has no soul.'

'She is young and silly,' Rosalyn said to placate him. 'You who are so much wiser must find it in your heart to forgive her.'

'So beautiful and so wise.' He bowed over her hand, kissing it and sighing. 'If only you did not live in the country, Mademoiselle Eastleigh—what a joy it would be to serve you.'

'Sir Frederick would be devastated if he lost you,' Rosalyn said, smiling inwardly as she imagined his reaction if the chef transferred his loyalties to her. 'You must not think of deserting him. Besides, you will have far more opportunity to practise your art in his service than you could in mine. No, no, you would be wasted here.'

As Monsieur Maurice nodded over the wisdom of this, Rosalyn made her escape. No matter how wonderful his food was, she thought she could not have put up with his tantrums for very long. She apologised privately to the kitchen maid, and told her she could have the afternoon off to recover from her fright.

'You should be the mistress of your own home,' her aunt told her when they laughed together over the incident in the privacy of her parlour later that day. 'I wonder how Beatrice will cope with the *artiste*'s tantrums when she is mistress of Freddie's household.'

'I dare say she will manage better than you may imagine,' Rosalyn replied. 'I think there is more to her than any of us yet guesses. Poor Freddie may well be in for a surprise.'

'Yes, perhaps…' Her aunt smiled and nodded. 'Well, tomorrow is the big day. It will soon be all over.'

Rosalyn smiled happily. Every day that passed brought her closer to the moment Damian would return to claim her.

'Yes, tomorrow is Bea's wedding day. I was sorry Celia did not feel up to coming—but I am glad you and Sarah stayed on, Aunt Susan.'

'I wanted a little time with you,' her aunt replied. 'I know we do not often visit one another, but I shall miss you. It would have been much nicer if you had married Mr Wrexham here amongst your friends and family, my love—but I do understand how you feel. I hope you do not mean to desert us altogether? You will visit from time to time?'

'I shall write, of course,' Rosalyn said and touched her hand affectionately. 'But I am not sure whether we shall visit England again. I dare say it may not be for some years.'

Rosalyn hugged her thoughts to herself. Damian had told her to meet him in the garden that night. He would come if he could, and if not he would be there the following night or the next. There was not long to wait now. Soon she would be with him, and then they would never part again.

'Freddie has some visitors,' Sarah Jane announced as she came into the parlour just before tea, and flopped down on the sofa. 'They looked very odd when they arrived, very serious and grim, as though something unpleasant had happened.'

'Oh, dear,' Rosalyn said. 'I do hope it isn't bad news.'

'No, I'm sure it isn't,' her aunt reassured her. 'What could possibly go wrong? Unless they have come to arrest Monsieur Maurice for attacking the kitchen maid?'

'Oh, Aunt,' reproached Rosalyn with a smile. 'How can you make a jest of…?' Her words died on her lips as the door opened and her brother walked in. One look at his face told her that something was very wrong. She rose to her feet, her heart beating very fast. 'What is it, Freddie? What has happened?'

'Sarah Jane,' he said, his expression that of a man struggling against his emotions. 'Would you be kind enough to go and find Beatrice for me, please? I believe you will discover her in the garden picking roses.'

'Must I?' Sarah Jane hesitated. It was obvious to her that she was being sent away because Freddie had some important news to impart—news he did not want her to hear. However, the unusually stern look on his face made her obey without further protest. 'Oh, all right, if you like…I'll go, I am going now.'

Rosalyn waited until the door had closed behind the girl. 'Tell us,' she said, sitting down next to her aunt on the large sofa because her legs had begun to shake. 'Something awful has happened, hasn't it? It is bad news, isn't it, Freddie?'

'I have just received a visit from an officer of the law, Rosalyn,' he said and she saw his hands clench at his sides. 'It appears that…there has been a murder.'

'A murder!' Mrs Buckley cried, her face draining of colour. 'Who has been killed? For goodness' sake, Freddie. Explain yourself. Who has been murdered and why did those men come here? What can this possibly have to do with us?'

'The body was found yesterday by a man walking his dog along a seldom-used country lane between the village and the boundary of our estate,' Freddie said, a flicker of something that might have been disgust…or fear…in his eyes. No, surely not fear, thought his sister, dismissing such a ridiculous idea immediately. 'It was the body of a man who had been shot at close range…at least two or three times. There was no doubt it was murder; it could not have been anything else.' Freddie seemed to look at Rosalyn in a very strange way as he paused.

'Who was it?' she asked, but the coldness seeping through her was already warning her that she would not like the answer. 'Please tell us, Freddie. Who has been murdered?'

'Bernard Harrington,' Freddie replied hoarsely. 'It

appears he has been dead for several days…perhaps since the day he left here. They cannot be sure, naturally, but he has been dead for some time.'

'How do you know?'

'Apparently…' Freddie looked sick and avoided looking at her or their aunt. 'This *is* the countryside, Ros. We *have* foxes. I shall not go into details. Sufficient to say that it was not a pretty sight for those who had to deal with it. Identification was only possible from certain personal items—which I was able to say quite positively belonged to Mr Harrington.'

'So he was shot after he left here…' Rosalyn stared at her brother, her face white. 'And they think it could have been that very day…'

'But who would want to do such a thing?' Mrs Buckley asked, looking puzzled. 'I know he was not a very likeable man, but murder…that is horrid! I can hardly believe it.'

'Do they have any idea of who might have done it?' Rosalyn said. Freddie looked down, refusing to meet her questing gaze. 'Were there any clues—any witnesses?'

'None as far as I could tell,' replied her brother. He was clearly disturbed and did not know how to answer her. 'Robbery would be the usual motive for such a crime—but he still had his purse and his watch. Which makes it difficult to know why he should have been attacked—and so close to our estate.'

'What are you thinking?' Rosalyn's hand crept to her throat as she realised why he was looking at her so strangely. He could not think…but she could see by his face that he did! 'No, Freddie, you are wrong. Damian left for France that same night. He would not have had time to do it. Besides, he would never had killed Mr Harrington in such an underhand way. If he had wanted him dead, he would have challenged him to a duel.'

Rosalyn remembered her nightmare, and she felt cold all over. She had sensed that something terrible might happen. No, no, she must not let herself be frightened. Damian was not a murderer. Nothing could part them.

Freddie could not look her in the eyes. 'I did not say it was him… Indeed, I told the officers that I had no idea who might want to kill Harrington—that it must have been a stranger. A gypsy or some other itinerant passing through the county.'

'But you thought it! I can see it in your face,' Rosalyn cried, jumping to her feet as the anger rose in her. 'How can you, Freddie? How can you! There was no reason…' her voice died away as she recalled the scene in the gardens, the moment when Bernard Harrington had attacked her. If Damian had seen that, there was no telling how he might have acted! 'No, no, he wouldn't…I was not harmed. I know Damian would not, could not have done this terrible thing.'

'What did Harrington do to you?' Freddie's eyes

narrowed as he saw her expression. 'Did he attack you—or Beatrice?'

'He tried to blackmail me into marrying him,' Rosalyn said slowly, her throat tight with emotion. 'He had seen me with Damian, and he called me a…whore. I slapped him and he twisted my arm behind my back. For a moment I thought he might attempt to…but I managed to break away from him, and I accused him of his crimes. I told him you would not tolerate his presence in this house another night, and he said he did not wish to stay—that he had come only to ask his sister for money and, since she would not give it, was leaving of his own accord. Now I think of it, he did not go towards the house, but past me towards the orchard—and could have found his way to the lane from there.'

'Did you speak to him again after that?'

'No, Freddie, I did not. I assumed he had left…why?'

'His things are still in his room,' her brother replied. 'Mrs Simmons told Maria apparently, but she assumed he would be returning for the wedding so said nothing of it to anyone. As far as I can ascertain, he told no one but you of his intention to leave.'

'You think he was killed soon after the attack on me?' Rosalyn felt cold all over. Her skin prickled with goose bumps as she saw the expression in her brother's eyes. 'You *do* believe Damian killed him, don't you?'

'What I believe does not matter,' Freddie said,

refusing to meet her eyes. 'The man was undoubtedly a menace. Had I known what he had done, I should never have invited him here. I cannot pretend to be sorry he is dead—my only fear is that it will bring scandal on the family. For heaven's sake! I am supposed to be getting married tomorrow. This could ruin everything…if it gets out. If it is known that my own sister is meeting the man who killed Harrington's brother, that she intends to go away with him—what do you imagine people will say? They will think it odd Harrington was murdered here—and assume Wrexham left the country because he was guilty. Our name will be dragged through the mire with his. Especially if you—'

'You need not fear that,' Rosalyn replied, her face revealing more of her feelings than she realised, making Freddie flinch at his sister's scorn. 'Damian will be coming for me very soon, and I shall go with him. You can always disown me.'

'You will still go with him—knowing that he may be a murderer?' He stared at her in disgust. 'Surely this changes things? You must see you cannot marry him now?'

Rosalyn felt the sting of tears. How could Freddie say such things to her? She lifted her head, looking into her brother's eyes.

'No, I do not see it,' she said. 'I would go to him even if I believed him capable of murder—but I do not. I know Damian would never kill a man in the way you describe, Freddie.' She stood up, her expression stiff with pride. 'I am going to my room. Please excuse me.'

'Ros…' The cry was wrung from her brother as she left the room. 'I'm sorry…but it all points to him, you must see that?'

She stood in the doorway and looked back at him, her scorn making him turn pale. 'Does it, Freddie? I think there are others who might feel anger against him…others not far from where I stand. Where did you go that day, tell me that if you can?'

She knew the accusation was unfair even as she made it, but could not help herself. How could Freddie point the finger at Damian, knowing as he must that she was in love with him? Any consideration for her must have forced him to keep silent, even if he suspected Damian of wrongdoing.

Freddie was stunned to silence. He stood staring after her as she closed the door. Was she saying that he…? Be damned to that! He would not stand for her insults in his own house! But his aunt was speaking to him, claiming his attention.

'You had no right to make such accusations, Freddie. You owe Rosalyn a great deal, and you have not always treated her as you ought. This house was her home and you have forced her from it without a thought for her feelings. I think you should go after her, apologise. Ask her to forgive you. If you do not, I fear it will create a breach between you—one that may never be healed.'

Freddie turned to stare at his aunt, the fury beginning to mount inside him. 'Apologise after what she just said to me?' he cried, his face white with temper. 'I think you much mistake the matter, Aunt. I shall leave her to think better of things and then she may apologise to me if she wishes.'

With that he turned and left the room, slamming the door behind him.

Mrs Buckley frowned. She would have done better to keep her silence, but she had been provoked into making what she felt was a well-justified comment. Freddie had jumped to conclusions—conclusions that besides being very unlikely had been hurtful to his sister.

Did he not understand that Rosalyn had fallen in love for the first time in her life? And so deeply that she was not likely to recover from it if forced to give up the man she loved. He could not expect her to do so simply for the sake of what people might say? Freddie should have thought things through more carefully before making such a statement…unless Rosalyn had hit upon the truth and he was hiding his own guilt.

Was Freddie capable of such wickedness? For that was what it was if he had blamed Mr Wrexham for his own deed.

Rosalyn had told her in confidence of the reason why Beatrice stood in fear of the objectionable Mr Harrington. It was just possible that, knowing the man had once attacked his fiancée, Freddie had come back from his ride that afternoon and seen the quarrel between Harrington and his sister…and his fury had been such that he had followed the man and, possibly, in a rage, killed him.

Upstairs in her bedchamber, Rosalyn paced the floor in a turmoil.

'Damian…oh, my love,' she whispered, her face pale and distressed. 'I know you are innocent of this crime…I know it.'

But someone had killed Harrington. Someone had seen the quarrel between her and Bernard Harrington that afternoon. Someone had heard every word that was spoken—and that person had killed Harrington because of something that had been said or done.

Could it have been Damian? Had he decided to follow her through the orchard…he had seemed to linger as if unwilling to leave her, had still been standing there when she looked back. He had once said he would kill Harrington if he harmed Rosalyn…but she had not been harmed, apart from a few minor bruises.

For a moment Rosalyn was racked with agony. Was the man she loved so much capable of murder?

No, she would not believe it. Damian would have called the man out, as he had Roderick all those years ago—so someone else had followed Bernard as he left the estate that afternoon. Someone else had taken a gun and killed him, leaving his body lying on the ground to be discovered by anyone who chanced to find it.

Who would do that? The lane was seldom used because it led only to the estate and the body had lain undiscovered for some days, covered in part perhaps by the hedges that grew thickly there.

Why had no attempt been made to hide the body? Had a grave been dug it might never have been found.

Rosalyn tussled with the problem, then dismissed it—it was not important. She felt sickened that her brother had not hesitated to blame Damian. How could he say such things to her? How could he expect her to give up her only chance of happiness?

Unless he had done so in order to cover his own guilt? She had seen something in his face which had made her wonder if he was frightened. No, surely she was mistaken? Freddie would not… She shook her head, feeling sickened by the thought. Even if he had been driven into an act of violence, he would not seek to cover it by blaming someone else—or would he?

Rosalyn paced the floor of her bedchamber. She was distressed by the idea, but could not quite rid herself of it. Freddie had always been selfish and inclined to think first of his own comfort, but surely he would not do anything so wicked?

It was as difficult for her to believe ill of her brother as it was of Damian. She could not think that either of them would murder in cold blood. Her brother might have carried out his threat to take a horsewhip to Harrington, and Damian might in anger have challenged him to a duel…but murder? No, she did not, would not believe it of either of them.

Oh, Damian, she thought, I wish you were here. Here to defend yourself—and to hold me. I need you so much!

All at once Rosalyn stopped her pacing. What was she thinking of? This was so selfish of her. Her own distress at what had happened could be nothing compared to what Mrs Jenkins must be feeling. Had anyone thought to tell her? Freddie was hardly likely to do it, might even wish to conceal the facts in case she demanded the postponement of the wedding, as was her right—but it could not be kept from her. She must be told immediately, and in the kindest way possible.

Rosalyn splashed her face with cold water and dried it on a towel. She tidied her hair, squaring her shoulders as she prepared to go down the landing and speak to Mrs Jenkins, but even as she turned to leave, there was a knock at her door.

'Come in,' she said, expecting Freddie and preparing to meet her brother's recriminations. He had no doubt come to argue with her again. She was surprised as the door opened and Mrs Jenkins entered. 'Oh…I was just about to come to see you, ma'am.'

'Forgive me for disturbing you,' the older woman

said. 'Mrs Buckley gave me the news of…' Her voice almost failed her, but she lifted her head, meeting Rosalyn's sympathetic gaze with determination. 'I have been told of my brother's unfortunate accident.'

'Accident…' Rosalyn was surprised by her calm manner. She had expected something very different. Anger, indignation, distress—but not this iron control. 'Oh, I am so sorry. I meant to speak to you myself. My aunt has told you how he died?'

'He was shot by a poacher or some such person, I dare say,' Mrs Jenkins said, a tiny nerve flicking in her throat. 'Or perhaps one of his many enemies followed him from town. My brother did have enemies, Miss Eastleigh. I believe several threats have been made against his life at various times. I regret to say it, but he had recently begun to mix with very low company. Although it may have been a poacher. Bernard would have remonstrated with anyone he saw shooting your brother's game; he was very strict with poachers on his own land at one time…before he took to gambling so much.'

'I…' Rosalyn stared at her, uncertain of what to say. She had not thought of such a solution, but she saw at once how much better it would be for everyone if it were true. 'I—I believe you must be right, ma'am. It was most unfortunate. Especially at this time. I do understand that you are very upset—and if you intend to postpone the wedding I shall support you.'

'No, no, not at all,' Mrs Jenkins said. 'I do not wish to cause distress for Beatrice or your brother. It is not yet generally known that Bernard has...met with an accident. Therefore, I believe the wedding should go ahead as though nothing has happened. Later, I shall insert a brief notice of my brother's death in *The Times*. I think that should suffice.'

'That is generous of you—and very brave.'

'I have caused enough grief in this house, and so had Bernard,' Mrs Jenkins replied in a dignified tone. 'The least I can do is allow the wedding to go ahead.' She hesitated, then said, 'If my brother importuned you with his attentions, I must apologise. I suggested that he might solve his financial problems with your fortune—that was wrong of me. Please forgive me. I was not thinking properly at the time.'

'It...does not matter.' Rosalyn frowned. There was something very odd here. Why had Mrs Jenkins changed so much of late? 'I am glad you have come to me, ma'am—and I am sorry that such a terrible thing should have happened to your brother.'

'Please do not...' Mrs Jenkins held up her hand. 'I have been aware for some time that Bernard...' She paused, took out her kerchief and blew her nose. 'I loved my brother Roderick very much. When he died, I was devastated. It made me bitter. I have tried to love Bernard, but could not—not as I had loved Roderick. I am sorry it has come to this, of course, but you must not imagine I am suffering too much grief, Miss Eastleigh. Let me assure you I am not.'

'I see...' Rosalyn felt chilled for some reason she could not decipher. 'Then we shall say no more of this, ma'am. Have you told my brother the wedding is to go ahead?'

'I thought perhaps you would do that for me,' Mrs Jenkins said. 'If you will excuse me, I shall stay in my room this evening—though I shall of course attend the ceremony tomorrow.'

'Are you unwell? Has the sickness returned?' Rosalyn asked, a little puzzled by her manner.

'No, no, I am quite well. I believe it was as your doctor thought, Miss Eastleigh. My powders had gone stale...that is why they made me sick. Now that I have replaced them I think I shall be quite well again. Yes, I am perfectly certain the nausea will not return...now.'

Rosalyn sat down for a few minutes after Mrs Jenkins had left. Such a terrible thought had come to her that it made her feel unwell...but she was letting her imagination run wild. It was not possible. No, no, she was entirely wrong. Mrs Jenkins was right...the shooting had probably been an accident and not murder at all.

She stood up, lifting her head. She must speak to Freddie. He would be worrying about the wedding, and she did not want him to disturb Mrs Jenkins. No, that would never do...not until she had had time to rest and recover her composure.

Chapter Ten

It seemed ages until that evening. Rosalyn could not wait for Damian's return. She was on tenterhooks and longed for the chance to talk to him, to tell him what had happened.

'Damian, I need you so…' The words were only in her mind. 'I need you so…'

Perhaps he would meet her in the garden that evening? Her desire to be with him made her restless and impatient, very unlike her usual self. Even her quarrel with her brother paled into insignificance beside her need to see Damian, to be held in his arms. She did love him so very much!

Rosalyn saw Beatrice looking at her oddly throughout dinner that evening. She too was on edge and clearly suspected something was being kept from her. At Freddie's insistence, she had not been told about the death of her aunt's brother—nor the quarrel between her fiancé and his sister.

The interview in the library between brother and

sister had been very formal. Freddie had thanked her for the news that the wedding was to go ahead, but he had not apologised for his behaviour and Rosalyn had made no move to heal the breach between them. Indeed, she was very angry with him. Had it not been for her very real affection for Beatrice, she would have left the house immediately afterwards, but, meeting the girl in the hall as she came from the unpleasant interview, had been forced to smile in answer to her greeting.

Fortunately for Rosalyn's peace of mind, Freddie took himself off after dinner. Although not intending to indulge in a pre-wedding fling, he was staying overnight with a friend so as not to see his bride before they met at the church the next morning. Because he was not there, Rosalyn was able to sit with her aunt, Beatrice and Maria in the parlour and make comfortable conversation, though Mrs Jenkins had remained in her room, refusing even the light repast Mrs Simmons had carried up to her.

They were all ready for an early night after the hectic celebrations of the previous few weeks, and of course Beatrice wanted to be fresh for the wedding itself. She embraced Rosalyn before they parted, thanking her for everything she had done to make things easier for her.

'I hope you know how fond I have become of you, dearest Rosalyn?' she said. 'I am so glad we are to be sisters—and I hope we shall often meet.'

Clearly, Freddie had made no mention of Rosalyn's plans to marry. Perhaps he hoped his sister would change her mind?

Rosalyn merely smiled and kissed her. Let Freddie tell her the truth after they were married, if he chose.

Alone in her own room, Rosalyn took the pins from her hair and brushed it, letting it hang loose on her shoulders. She packed a few possessions while she waited for time to pass; some of her clothes could perhaps be sent on later. Many of them would not be suitable for her new life. She had decided she would take only a few of her newest garments, and her personal treasures, things given her by her parents:

her mother's jewellery and items she had kept for various reasons.

She went to the drawer where she had kept her father's pistols. One of them was missing. She stared at the empty aperture in the box—surely she had replaced the weapon after using it to drive off the men who had attacked Jared? Yes, she was sure it was missing—and the box containing the balls used as ammunition was almost empty. When she last used it, it had been half-full.

A cold chill ran down Rosalyn's spine. Where had the pistol gone? Someone had taken it—could it have been Freddie? Or someone else? Had the pistol been used to kill Bernard Harrington?

That thought made her feel slightly sick, and she

could not wait to unburden her thoughts to the only person she could tell of her suspicions.

It must be time, surely? If Damian was coming, he would be here by now. Rosalyn picked up a branch of candles and looked out of her door to make sure she was unobserved. There was no reason why she should not meet Damian, yet even now she would do nothing to disoblige her brother if she could help it.

She went down to her parlour, unlocked the French windows and slipped out. The moon was bright, its silver light giving the garden an air of romance and mystery. Was Damian here? Was he back yet? Her heart beat faster in the hope of seeing him, but though she called softly and waited for nearly an hour, there was no sign of him.

'Oh, Damian, where are you? I need you. I need to talk to you, to hold you. I need you so very much…'

Rosalyn sighed her disappointment and went back inside. Perhaps he would come tomorrow.

The morning of the wedding was fine and warm. Beatrice looked as beautiful as everyone expected, her face alight with happiness as she walked down the aisle to stand beside Freddie and take her vows.

Rosalyn watched her. She surreptitiously wiped away a tear, smiling as she saw her aunt doing the same thing.

'I do hope she will be happy,' Aunt Susan whispered. 'Do you not think Sarah Jane looks very grown up, my dear?'

Rosalyn nodded. She suddenly found she could not speak, because as she turned to watch the newlywed couple leaving the church, she saw that a man was standing at the very back. He had taken his place behind a pillar so as not to be seen too clearly, but Rosalyn knew him at once and her heart began to race wildly.

Damian was back! He was back. It took all her resolution not to go to him at once. As she followed her aunt and the other guests out into the sunshine and the peal of joyful bells, Rosalyn saw that Damian had moved away to a far corner of the churchyard and was watching her. She smiled and moved as if to go to him, but he shook his head and mouthed the word 'later' to her. She nodded, her spirits soaring. Damian was right. She had waited this long, she could wait a little longer.

Yet it was so difficult to keep a smile on her face, to listen to all the chatter and laughing jests made by the guests at her brother's expense, when she wanted to put all this behind her and go to her lover.

At last they were back at the house, and the reception was under way. The table in the dining room had been set out with all manner of delicious trifles. Monsieur Maurice had surpassed himself, Rosalyn thought as she moved amongst the guests, making polite conversation.

'And when shall we have the pleasure of your company in town again, Miss Eastleigh?'

'I do not know, Mr Carlton,' she replied. 'I have no plans to return for the moment.'

'That is a pity. I had hoped to see you there this season.'

Rosalyn smiled and shook her head, moving on to various guests. She was sure Damian would be waiting for her in the garden. Dare she slip away to meet him for a few minutes? Why not? She had done her duty. No one would miss her. There were plenty of others to entertain Freddie's guests.

She made her way unhurriedly through the crowded rooms, leaving by the French windows of her parlour. There was no sign of Damian. He would not risk being seen, of course, but as she hurried across the lawn to the shrubbery, he came out and caught her in his arms. Her heart leaped as he held her close, gazing down at her hungrily.

'You came,' he said, bending his head to kiss her on the mouth. 'I was not sure you would manage it until this evening—but I could not stay away. I have been longing for you, my darling.'

'And I for you,' she said, pressing herself against him, surrendering her mouth to his as the heady desire swept over her. 'I have everything ready. I can leave as soon as Freddie and Beatrice have gone—' She stopped as she saw the way his eyes were looking at something behind her. 'What…?'

Swinging round, she saw her brother striding towards them, his face tight with anger.

'I thought I should find you with him,' Freddie said coldly. 'Are you so mad for him that you care nothing for your reputation, Ros? If what people say of you matters not to you, then at least have a thought for my wife's good name.'

'Freddie!' Rosalyn felt as if he had slapped her. This was so unfair. She had done all she could to make things easier for him—and now he had so unjustly accused her of thinking only of herself. 'No one has seen us. Besides, we shall be leaving soon. You are married now—what can it matter if someone does see us?'

'It matters to me if my sister is seen embracing a murderer.'

'Freddie!' she cried, dismayed. 'How can you say such things?'

'What is this?' Damian's eyes narrowed. 'You are not speaking of the duel, Eastleigh? Damn it, you cannot believe I was responsible for Bernard Harrington's murder?'

'So you do not deny it was murder?' Freddie glared at him. 'I was prepared to accept the situation between you and my sister as things stood—a duel is not murder—but this changes everything.'

'I give you my word I had nothing to do with this,' Damian said, eyes cold, proud. He was very still, watchful. He glanced at Rosalyn. 'Do you believe me?'

'Yes, of course,' she said quickly. 'I know you did not do it, Damian.'

'You are being foolish,' Freddie said glaring at her. 'You have only his word that he did not shoot Harrington. How can you marry him, knowing he may be a murderer?'

'I would marry him whatever he had done,' Rosalyn said quietly. Her back was very straight, her manner calm and dignified. 'Damian loves me—that is something you have never done, Freddie. You are not my legal guardian. I can marry whom I choose.' She lifted her candid eyes to meet those of the man she loved. 'I am going to fetch my things now, Damian. Please wait for me. Everything I want is packed. It will take me only a few minutes to fetch them.'

'Are you sure?' he asked.

'Quite sure. Please be here when I return.'

'If you leave with him now, I've finished with you,' Freddie said, lips white with fury. 'You can never come back. I shall forbid Beatrice to speak to you ever again.'

Rosalyn lifted her head, her face pale. She was tense but determined. 'I shall not wish to return,' she said with painful dignity. 'This is no longer my home—and you are no longer my brother.'

She walked away, refusing to glance back even when her brother called to her. How dare he? How dare he say such things to her—to Damian? She would never, never forgive him.

As she disappeared into the house, Freddie turned on Damian in fury.

'Do you know what you've done?' he demanded. 'You've ruined her. You may think you can get away with murder, Wrexham—but people will talk, they will believe you killed Harrington. Some of them will think in private that you've done the world a service, but in public they will refuse to know you. You will be tainted—and so will Rosalyn. You have dragged her down to your level—I hope you are satisfied?'

Damian curled his fists at his sides, willing himself to control his temper. If he struck Rosalyn's brother in anger the breach would never be healed—and that would hurt her. She was angry with Freddie now, but perhaps in the future she would begin to miss him, to miss all her family. He must not do anything which might make it impossible for her to return to her home one day.

'If you were not her brother, I would call you out for that,' Damian said. 'If you ever do anything to hurt her in the future I shall take a horsewhip to you. Say what you like to me—but never hurt her like that again.'

'Damn you!' Freddie yelled. He lunged at Damian, throwing a wild punch and missing. As he came at him again, Damian's fist connected with his chin, sending him down. He sprang up again, angry and ashamed. 'You devil…I'll teach you.'

'You had best take yourself back to your bride before I make it impossible for you to play your part on your wedding night,' Damian said. 'Think yourself lucky I do not thrash you as you deserve. One day I have no doubt you will come to your senses, and you may wish to apologise to Rosalyn—'

'Never!' Freddie yelled, beside himself with anger. 'She has made her bed—and she can damned well lie on it.'

He turned and began to stride across the lawn, disappearing into the house without looking back.

Upstairs in her room, Rosalyn took a last glance around her, then picked up the two cloak bags she had packed herself. She had her father's pearls and a ring that had been her mother's, that was all she really wanted—and enough clothes to take her as far as France. She could buy anything she needed there; at least Freddie could not control her money, her father had seen to that.

She was about to leave when her aunt came in. Mrs Buckley saw her white face and the bags and took in the situation immediately.

'Freddie is in a terrible mood,' she said. 'Have you quarrelled with him again?'

'He forbade me to go with Damian—but I cannot obey him, Aunt. He says that he has finished with me, that he will forbid the family to acknowledge me—but I do not care. Nothing can stop me leaving. I must go with Damian. I love him.'

'Of course you do,' her aunt said. She moved to embrace Rosalyn. 'You have my blessing, my dear—and if you ever need a home I shall always be happy to receive you.'

'Thank you—' Rosalyn broke off as Maria came rushing into the room, her face white.

'You were not going without saying goodbye?'

'No, I was going to ask my aunt to tell you to meet me in the garden,' Rosalyn said and went to embrace her. Maria was crying. 'Forgive me. I cannot stay for your wedding, my dearest cousin—but I shall write to you as soon as we are settled.'

'You will visit sometimes?'

'Yes—if we can,' Rosalyn promised. She looked from Maria to her aunt. 'I am sorry, I must go. Damian is waiting.'

'Yes, of course,' Mrs Buckley said. 'Would you let me come with you, Rosalyn? I should like to meet him—to tell him that he has my blessing.'

'And mine,' Maria said. 'I do not care what Freddie thinks. He has behaved very badly towards you, and I shall tell him so.'

'Yes, come with me,' Rosalyn said. 'I should like Damian to know that not all my family are against him.'

She went ahead of her friends, her emotions in turmoil. Would Damian be waiting? Surely he would not leave without her? Please God, let him not have taken Freddie's rudeness too much to heart!

She saw him standing where she had left him. Sarah Jane was with him, laughing at something he had said to her. The girl turned as they approached.

'I have been giving Mr Wrexham a message for Jared,' she said. 'I shall go in now, Rosalyn. Beatrice will be wondering where I am.' She came to kiss her on the cheek. 'I shall never forget how kind you have been to me—and I hope we shall meet again one day.'

'I am sure we shall,' Rosalyn said. She turned to Damian as the girl ran off. 'My aunt—Mrs Susan Buckley—wanted to meet you. And Maria would like to say goodbye.'

'I could not let you go without wishing you both good luck,' Maria said, a faint blush in her cheeks as Damian took her hand to kiss it. 'Please take good care of Rosalyn for us. We are very fond of her—but of course I know you will.'

'You will be welcome to visit us when we are settled,' Damian assured her. 'And perhaps one day we shall visit you.'

Their farewells over, Damian took Rosalyn's cloak-bags from her and slung them over his shoulder, a questioning look in his eyes.

'Ready?'

'Yes. Quite ready.'

'We must walk as far as the Hall. I was not expecting to leave quite this soon.'

'Nor I,' she admitted, giving him a smile that was

perhaps a little too bright. 'Do not be concerned for me, Damian. My brother has behaved badly, but we shall not allow him to upset us.'

Was she simply putting on a brave face for his sake? Damian was not sure. They had known each other such a short time, and this was a huge step for Rosalyn to take. What had happened had perhaps been inevitable from the start. Love had flared between them almost instantly, creating a need that could not be denied—but would love be enough to compensate for all she had given up?

He offered her his hand. 'Come,' he said, his strong fingers curling about hers. There could be no place for doubt or regret in their lives. 'We should go, my love. We have a long journey before us.'

It was dark long before they reached Dover. Rosalyn had slept for a part of the journey, her head against Damian's shoulder.

At first they had talked of the future, and the new life they had entered together. Damian told her about the house he had taken on the outskirts of Paris.

'It is just for a week or two,' he said. 'I think you will like it—it is away from the bustle and noise of the city, but near enough to enjoy all the benefits. We shall go shopping together, my darling. I want to buy you lots of beautiful things.'

'Why? I have the money from my trust. I can arrange for that to be paid into any account I choose.

Freddie has no control over my income. You do not need to buy me things, Damian.'

'Will you deny me that pleasure?' His brows arched. 'For years I have done nothing but accumulate wealth. Now that I have someone on whom to spend the money, may I not do so?'

'Are you very rich?' Rosalyn was surprised. She had not considered it before, taking him to be a man of modest means.

'I fear so,' he replied, a naughty glint in his eye. 'My years in India were put to good use. Do you mind?'

She shook her head, the hint of a smile on her lips. 'It is not important either way. But if you wish to lavish your money on me, I must tell you I am extremely fond of good horses. It is a passion I have often wished to indulge—and I should warn you that you may find me extravagant where they are concerned.'

'Horses?' Damian laughed. 'Then we have more in common than I knew. You shall have the very best, Rosalyn—both for your carriage and for riding.'

She smiled but said nothing more on the subject. 'How long shall we be in Paris?'

'Long enough to be married,' he said, taking her hand in his. 'Jared has gone down to a secret location in the country and we shall join him there in a week or so—but I thought we could be married in Paris? We could of course marry before we leave England, but it would be a rushed, makeshift affair. In Paris I have friends. We could have a small reception—and you would have the chance to buy a pretty gown for the occasion.'

'Then we shall wait until you can arrange it all,' she said, looking at him curiously. 'I did not know you had friends in Paris, Damian.'

'It is only in England that I have been cast out by society,' he replied, a flicker of amusement in his eyes. 'Edward and Charlotte Forrester were with the British Company in India for seven years. We became close friends—and they have often asked me to visit them at their home in Paris.'

'Then I shall look forward to meeting them.'

'And I know they will be delighted to meet you. Charlotte has been nagging me to marry for years, but until now I had no wish to oblige her.'

Rosalyn laughed at the wicked look he gave her. The slight constraint, which had arisen over the suggestion that he wished to lavish her with gifts, vanished as though it had never been. She was not quite sure why she had objected; it was natural for a husband to spend money on his wife—but she did not wish to be bought. Her love had been given freely and she required only love in return.

It was her wretched independence again! Rosalyn scolded herself mentally. She would soon be married, and must get used to the idea of being a wife.

She had slept after a while, lulled by the comfort

of the well-sprung carriage and her sense of being safe and cared for; she was vaguely aware that Damian's arm was about her, supporting her. When she woke it was dark and the carriage was pulling into the yard of a busy inn. She could hear the sounds of ostlers shouting to one another, the clatter of wheels on cobblestones, and the hissing of flaring lanterns in their scones on the walls; then their groom opened the door and the steps were let down.

'I had booked two rooms here for tomorrow evening,' Damian said as he gave her his hand to help her from the carriage. 'We must hope the host has accommodation for tonight. There are other inns, of course, but this is the best.'

'We shall find something.'

Rosalyn smiled as she took his arm. She was determined not to make a fuss whatever the case. Besides, this was the beginning of a great adventure. No matter what happened now, she was with the man she loved. There was no going back, no return to her old life, nor did she want there to be. Despite some natural apprehension, she felt alive in a way she never had until now.

It was clear that the inn was extremely busy. The yard was littered with bags and trunks, several carriages having arrived almost simultaneously. Inside, in the welcoming parlour with its oak panelled walls and comfortable settles, Damian was forced to wait his turn for attention, and was eventually told that there was only one room available that night.

He frowned as he turned to Rosalyn, who had found a place to sit and was idly contemplating a magnificent painting of a stag. 'I am sorry, there is only one room. It seems we must try elsewhere.'

'Why? I believe one room will be sufficient for our needs.'

As he saw the glow in her eyes, his own lit with fire. 'You are sure?'

'Quite sure.'

Damian nodded, making no further objection. He booked the room, which the landlord assured him was one of their best, then led her into the crowded dining parlour, where they were fortunate to find a table by the window.

Rosalyn had eaten very little at her brother's wedding reception, and she enjoyed the poached salmon and asparagus spears in a light, creamy sauce that were served her. She drank two glasses of the delicious white wine Damian ordered; it went to her head a little, combining with excitement to bring a brilliant sparkle to her eyes.

She noticed that Damian ate sparingly, merely sipping his wine. He seemed a little reserved, a rather odd expression in his dark eyes. What could be troubling him? Rosalyn experienced a moment of unease. She did not really know this man to whom she had entrusted her life. The future would no doubt be a journey of discovery.

'Would you like to go up now?'

Rosalyn felt a tingling sensation at the nape of her neck. She looked across the table, seeing the question in his eyes. Her cheeks took fire and she was aware of butterflies fluttering inside her. Now that the moment had come, she could not help being a little nervous—as all brides must be on their wedding night, surely? For though she was not yet wearing Damian's ring, this was the first night of their marriage—the night when they would truly become one.

Rosalyn smiled and stood up. 'Yes, I am ready,' she said, and gave her hand into his keeping.

Alone in their room, which was clean and perfectly comfortable, Rosalyn untied the strings of her bonnet and laid it with her velvet pelisse on a small sofa by the window. She stood for a moment looking down at the inn yard, which was almost silent now, then reached up to draw the heavy curtains, shutting out the night. When she turned, she saw Damian watching her; again his expression was so strange that her heart caught with fright.

What could have brought that haunting sadness to his eyes?

'Is something wrong?'

'No…nothing is wrong.' He moved towards her, reaching out to touch her cheek with his fingertips. 'I was just thinking how lovely you are—and wondering what I had done to you.'

'What do you mean?' Rosalyn gazed up at him, her eyes dark with anxiety. 'Damian? Don't look at me so…it frightens me.'

'Forgive me, I meant not to make you anxious. Are you certain this is what you want? It is not too late to change your mind.'

'Do you wish to change yours?'

'No, of course not.'

'Then why should I? Do you doubt my love?' She frowned. 'Is this because of something my brother said?' She read her answer in his face and was angry. 'Freddie had no right to interfere—no right to say the things he did to you.'

'He accused me of murder…'

She pressed her fingers to his mouth. 'Hush, my love. I know you did not kill Bernard Harrington. No matter what Freddie or anyone else may say—I know you are innocent.'

'Have you so much faith in me?'

'I have no choice,' she replied. 'I love you—would love you, whatever you had done. Nothing else matters. Surely you must see that?'

'Then nothing can harm us,' he said and reached out to draw her into his arms. 'My lovely woman… my life.'

Rosalyn felt the heady desire move in her as he kissed her lips, her white throat and the sweetly shadowed hollow where her gown dipped to reveal a glimpse of her breasts. She turned, lifting her hair so that he could release the fastening of her gown, letting it slip down over her hips to the ground where it lay unheeded. Her chemise followed so that in a moment she stood before him in all her womanly beauty, the soft contours of her body arousing such a fierce need in him that he groaned and swept her up, carrying her to their bed.

Then he too was naked, his clothes cast away, his manly arousal so evident and needy that she gasped in wonder at the power of him. She yielded to him as he began his tender assault on her willing flesh, lavishing her with his tongue and lips to bring her swiftly to a quivering acceptance of his loving. So urgent was their mutual desire that Rosalyn knew only pleasure; the piercing of her maidenhead was a fleeting pain scarcely felt as she clung to him, her body arching, opening to accommodate him, to welcome him, deep inside her. Love consumed her in a golden flame, carrying her to a far distant place where she had never been.

When it was over, she nestled into him, her face buried against his chest. She loved the scent and taste of him, the tickle of masculine hair and the smooth hard contours of his shoulders as her hands roamed and explored him. To be held like this in the warm intimacy of love was beyond her expectations, opening up new possibilities, new realms of emotions and experiences. She had never been this close to anyone, never understood what love could mean—the pleasures it could bring.

Damian touched her cheeks and found them wet. He leaned over her, looking into her face, seeking the reason for her tears.

'Crying?'

'Tears of happiness.' she assured him. 'I did not know it could be this way—that I could feel such pleasure, such content.'

'You are a very special woman,' Damian said and kissed her lingeringly on the mouth. 'I was lucky no one else had snapped you up long ago.'

Rosalyn smiled but made no answer. What need for words when such glorious sensations were flooding through her whole body? She moaned with pleasure, giving herself up to his loving once more as his hands moved down to cup her buttocks, squeezing them gently, lifting her to ease himself inside her, gently, slowly, beginning to tease her until she whimpered and quivered with pure delight.

They had the rest of their lives to talk, time to tell him that she had never wanted any other man, that she had always believed her soulmate was waiting somewhere—that one day they would be drawn together by fate. She had refused to settle for less, to take a husband she did not love for the sake of comfort and her own home as so many women did—and now she understood why.

Chapter Eleven

'At last! You cannot imagine how often I have hoped for this day.' Charlotte Forrester enveloped Rosalyn in her warm, perfumed embrace. 'My dear girl! You are beautiful. I can see why you achieved what none of the young ladies I thrust endlessly under Damian's nose even came close to—though I must admit that some of them were exceedingly pretty.'

'I am not pretty,' Rosalyn protested with a laugh. She looked at herself in the large oval wall mirror, admiring the exquisite fit of her new evening gown. The colour was a wonderful sea-green, the material a fine silk that moulded itself to her figure in flattering swathes. 'But Madame Yvonne has done her best to make me stylish—and I believe she has succeeded.'

'She is an artiste,' agreed Charlotte, 'but she told me she has seldom had a better figure to dress. I only wish mine were half as good!' She pulled a face at herself in the mirror.

Fair-haired and possessing a perfect English-rose

complexion, Charlotte was what her husband termed 'a luscious armful' in their private moments. Reaching only as far as his shoulder, she was a little too plump—at least in her own estimation. However, she had such an infectious smile and her manner was so engaging, that she was generally admired and spoken of as a beauty.

'You *are* pretty,' Rosalyn said warmly. 'And so kind to me. I was afraid you might think me shameless, for you must know Damian and I are lovers…' She faltered and blushed.

'That is not so very terrible. Especially after the way your brother behaved towards you, forcing you to leave your home so suddenly…' Charlotte pulled a face. 'Besides, you are to be married next week. As long as you are happy, my dear. Why should we quarrel over trifles?'

Although they had known each other only a few hours, Rosalyn realised it was typical of Charlotte to dismiss their unusual living arrangements as a trifle. It would, as she knew only too well, have shocked most women of her class, but once Rosalyn and Damian had made love at the inn, it would have been ridiculous to have insisted on separate rooms in their own house. Besides, she did not wish to sleep alone—why should she when she could be in his arms?

She had known more happiness in Damian's arms than she could ever have expected, and if, sometimes, she still sensed that inner sadness in him, she accepted it as a part of the man she loved. She did not pry, for if Damian had a secret he would tell her when the time was right. It was enough that she loved and was loved in return.

'Well, my love—shall we go?' Charlotte asked, taking her hand to lead her from the bedchamber. 'I am sure the gentlemen are becoming impatient. I must tell you that the play we are to see is a little naughty, but you will not mind that? Everyone says it is wickedly funny.'

'Oh, I have read Mr Sheridan's plays,' Rosalyn said. 'I like them.'

'But you have not seen them performed in quite this way,' Charlotte said with an enchanting lift of her fine brows. 'The French manage to make everything that much more risqué.'

Rosalyn laughed but said no more on the subject. Since their arrival in the city some days earlier, Damian had already taken her to several of the Cafés Concerts, where the atmosphere was slightly decadent and the dancing girls so daring that she had felt her cheeks grow warm watching them. Yet she loved those nights, as she loved the days spent exploring the wonderful city of Paris on Damian's arm, strolling in the warm sunshine amongst the busy streets with their flower sellers, artists and the constant flow of life. It was all so colourful, part of the new experiences she was soaking up, and she found everything so exciting, so different from the quietness of her family home.

Life was so much fuller for her now. She had not had time to look back, or to regret—for what was there to regret? Perhaps the quarrel with her brother, but that was his fault, and she would not let it spoil her happiness.

They were driven to the theatre in the Forresters' carriage. Damian had not yet set up his own equipage. He was looking for the right horses, which were to be his special wedding gift to Rosalyn—though he had already given her so many gifts. Almost too many for her comfort.

Inside the foyer of the large and impressive theatre was a lush décor of crimson and gold with a grand, carpeted stairway leading to the private boxes. Ladies and gentlemen in evening dress were moving to and fro, meeting acquaintances or taking a glass of chilled champagne in the refreshment area. In the background, Rosalyn could hear the music of an orchestra.

'This is wonderful,' she whispered to Damian as she clung to his arm. 'I am so glad you chose this gown! I should have felt positively dowdy in my old one.'

'You could never look anything but lovely,' Damian replied. 'I think we should be finding our box. The play will be starting at any moment.'

'We must not miss the opening,' Rosalyn said. 'Charlotte told me it is very naughty.' Their friends were ahead of them, almost halfway up the stairs. 'I am looking forward to the performance.'

Damian smiled. She sensed that he was about to say something concerning the play, but instead he became very still, a little nerve twitching at the corner of his mouth. She followed the direction of his gaze, feeling a coldness seep through her as she saw Freddie and Beatrice moving their way.

It was quite obvious that Freddie had seen them. He was glaring furiously, as though outraged that they should have the audacity to come to the theatre at all. Rosalyn hesitated. How unfortunate that this should happen. If she had ever known, she had forgotten that her brother intended to bring his wife to Paris on their honeymoon.

What ought they to do? She glanced at Damian uncertainly. He looked angry, but seemed to be hesitating. Then Beatrice noticed them. She touched Freddie's arm, her manner indicating that she was urging him to go up to his sister. As Rosalyn watched, she saw Freddie say something sharp to his wife, then he took a firm grip on her arm and steered her away. Beatrice looked back, her expression one of both apology and acute distress as she was forced in the opposite direction.

Freddie had deliberately cut her! The hot colour washed into Rosalyn's cheeks and then faded, leaving her pale and sick to her stomach. How could her own brother behave so badly?

'I am sorry,' Damian said to her. He held her arm protectively, his eyes glittering with anger. 'That was a disgusting thing for him to do.'

'It doesn't matter,' Rosalyn replied, lifting her head proudly. 'I had thought Freddie might have got over his temper and regretted his hasty words—but it seems he has not.'

'He could at least have acknowledged you.' Damian was furious. He was tempted to go after Freddie and demand that he acknowledge his sister. 'He was abominably rude to you.'

'Let us forget him,' Rosalyn said, her hand tightening on his arm. The incident had shocked and distressed her, but she did not wish to make a fuss about it. 'Charlotte will be wondering where we are. It is not important, Damian. If my brother chooses not to know me, that is his affair.'

Damian said no more as they continued on up the stairs. Rosalyn was pretending not to mind, but he knew the incident had hurt her. He was so angry for her that it almost choked him. He would have liked to pursue Freddie, to force him to apologise, even if he had to thrash him—but that would have ended in a terrible scene and made things worse than they were already.

Damian hardly heard a word of the play. He sat watching Rosalyn as she went through the motions of enjoying herself, knowing that the evening had been spoiled for her, and his inner turmoil mounted.

What had he done to the woman he loved? She had given up so much for him, and he had so little to give her in return.

During their first few hectic days in Paris, he had bought her more clothes than she could possibly wear. She had a magnificent diamond and emerald ring, which matched the necklace and earrings she was wearing that evening—other costly jewels lay in their boxes, as yet unseen by her eyes, waiting for the right moment to be presented. She always smiled and thanked him warmly for his gifts, yet he knew she did not need them: no jewels could match the beauty and grace of this special woman. It was he who needed to give, to make up for all she had lost by coming away with him—but what could make up for the hurt she had suffered that evening?

Rosalyn too was thinking deeply. She knew that Damian was angry. She was aware of him watching her as she struggled to control her seething emotions. Damn Freddie for spoiling things! It was so like him to go his own way with no thought for her. She had been hurt many times in the past by her brother's careless attitude, but never again. This was the very last time she would allow herself to care what Freddie said or did to her.

Rosalyn sat in her fine silk nightgown, brushing her hair. It fell like a shining curtain about her face, tumbling on to her shoulders and reaching almost to the small of her back. Hearing the door open, she turned to look as Damian came in. He had remained downstairs after their return from the theatre, and, as he came to her, she could smell the brandy on his breath. He did not often indulge in strong drink, and she knew she had her brother to thank for this: Damian's pride had naturally been hurt, and he was upset for her sake. Somehow she must make him forget the unpleasant incident.

She stood up and moved to meet Damian, holding out her arms; the scent of her perfume enveloped him, filling his senses and driving the anger to a corner of his mind.

'I was wondering where you were,' she said as he drew her close, his lips moving against her neck. 'Hold me, my darling. Love me. I want you, need you so very much.'

'Rosalyn…' He made a moaning sound in his throat, catching her to him in a desperate embrace. 'My lovely woman.'

'Make love to me,' she murmured huskily. 'Love me, Damian. Love me always. Never leave me.'

His answer was to carry her to the bed. Laying her down on cool, sweetly scented linen sheets, he lavished kisses on every tender, intimate place of her quivering body. His tongue teased and flicked at the deep rose of her gently swollen nipples, while his hand moved between her soft thighs, stroking and invading the centre of her femininity. The warm moistness of her invited his entry and, driven by his urgent need, he thrust himself inside her, deeper and deeper until she moved with him, gasping out her frantic pleasure as their passion intensified.

'Damian…ahhh! Damian…my love.'

She screamed his name, arching her back to meet him, her nails scoring his shoulder as she felt herself falling into space: falling…falling into a state of being where she knew nothing except the endless, aching pleasures of love, which seemed to go on and on until she lost all sense of time and place.

'You little witch,' Damian murmured huskily against her throat when they lay finally entwined, exhausted and at peace. 'My back feels as if I have lain with a tigress.'

'Have I hurt you?'

She attempted to rise and look at his shoulder, but he laughed and rolled her back into the pillows, holding her there as she half-heartedly struggled to free herself.

'Be still, witch,' he said. 'I was teasing you. I love it when you scratch me. I love it that you never hold back when we are together like this—you are a very giving, passionate woman.'

She gazed into his face, suddenly almost shy. 'Are you saying I'm wanton? Is that a good thing in a wife, Damian?'

'Very good.' He grinned at her wickedly. 'With you in my bed, I'm not like to look for a mistress. I wouldn't have the energy.'

'I am your mistress.'

The smile left his face as though it were a slate wiped clean. She saw anger spark in his eyes before he rolled away from her.

'Only because I could not arrange the ceremony sooner,' he said. 'It was your choice, Rosalyn. I would have waited.'

She knew that she had unwittingly touched a raw nerve. She lifted herself on one elbow, her hair hanging forward so that it brushed his face and chest as she looked down at him. What lay beyond that closed expression? Why torture himself so?

'I did not wish to wait,' she said softly. 'Do not be angry, my love. Wife or mistress, I love you—and I know you love me. Believe me, I do not feel used, nor have you taken advantage of my innocence. I came to you willingly, because I love you. All I want is to be yours, totally and forever.'

For a moment he stared at her, his expression hard, unchanged, then he reached up, tangling his fingers in her hair as he drew her face down to his and kissed her with a fierce hunger.

'I shall always love you,' he said as she slid down beside him, burying herself in the curve of his shoulder, melding her willing flesh with his. 'You may come to wish one day that you had thought twice about leaving your family but—'

'Never!' Rosalyn said, nipping at him with her sharp teeth. 'Do not be foolish, Damian. I love you…you are all I need, all I shall ever need. I want only you. You are my life.'

'I know. Forgive me.' He kissed her forehead, stroking her hair, letting it slip through his fingers as she pressed herself closer to his side. 'I was angry earlier, but not with you. Go to sleep, my darling. I am a strange, foolish creature, but I love you.'

Rosalyn muttered something against his shoulder. He smiled as he realised she was almost asleep: she possessed that enviable gift of being able to curl up like a kitten and sleep when she was comfortable. The fresh, clean scent of her hair filled his nostrils as she filled his senses. He could feel desire stirring deep within him again, but he quelled it with an iron control. She was always responsive to his needs, but he would not wake her. Let her sleep. He was too angry to let sleep claim his mind—angry with the man who had hurt her, and himself for being unable to prevent it.

When Rosalyn whimpered in her sleep, his anger deepened. She would never give him reason to think her unhappy, but he could not rid himself of his guilt. He had taken her from her home and family. She was content enough for the moment, but what of the future? Would she come to regret all she had lost? Would she begin to wish that she had never met him, never thrown her hat over the windmill for the sake of love?

Damian had known the pain of exile. Although he

had finally won fortune and friends in India, he had never quite forgotten the hurt of being cast out by his family. Now, because of him, Rosalyn too was an outcast—at least as far as her brother was concerned.

What made Damian feel so frustrated was the charge of murder. This was the second time such a charge had been levelled at him, and it rankled deep in his soul. The first time he had believed in his heart that he was indeed guilty—guilty of killing the wrong man, and that had lain heavily on his conscience for many years. But this time he was innocent. Yet there was nothing he could do to refute the charge, no way he could clear his name—the name he was about to give to Rosalyn.

He had taken her from home and family, and all he could give her was a tainted name.

'Will you be all right by yourself?' Damian asked for perhaps the tenth time that morning. 'I hate to leave you, my dearest, but it is business. I have several calls to make, and you would be kept waiting for ages.'

'Of course I do not mind,' Rosalyn said. 'You do not need to be with me all the time. I am quite capable of amusing myself for a few hours. I shall write to Maria and Aunt Susan. I ought to have done so sooner, but we have hardly been in the house.'

'Give *poor* Maria my love,' he said with a twitch of his lips. 'Tell her we shall be leaving Paris after our wedding. We must go to Jared soon or he will think himself deserted.'

'I have enjoyed our stay here very much,' Rosalyn told him. 'But I shall not be sorry to be in the country again.'

Damian nodded and kissed her. After he had gone, Rosalyn sat down at the pretty little inlaid writing desk in the back parlour; it was set in the window embrasure and looked out at a garden with rose-beds and secret arbours. The top of the desk was littered with expensive trifles Damian and she had bought during their stay in Paris. She had just picked up a rather attractive gold and enamel pen to begin the first of her letters when she heard the front door-knocker.

Now who could that be? They had made several new acquaintances in Paris, but she did not expect any of them to call that morning, especially as she knew for certain that Charlotte had a previous engagement.

Hearing voices in the hall, Rosalyn got to her feet, her heart beginning to beat uncomfortably fast. Surely that was Freddie! Why had he come here? The maid entered to announce him. Rosalyn stood stiff and straight, the colour draining from her face as she saw the look on his. He was in one of his black moods, and clearly still angry with her.

'This is not a social call,' he said as the maid withdrew. 'There is a small business matter which needs attention. Father's will provided for the release of your capital on your marriage…' His eyes went to her left hand and his lip curled scornfully. 'I see that has not yet taken place…'

'It is arranged for next week,' Rosalyn said, her chin lifting with pride. 'Will you sit down, Freddie? Beatrice is not with you?'

He remained standing, his manner indicating that he was here only because it was necessary.

'You think I would bring my wife here—to this house?'

The note of contempt in his voice made Rosalyn flinch.

'That is enough!' she cried, a flash of anger in her eyes. She would not stand for this in her own home. 'I do not intend to let you insult either me or Damian again. Say what you have to say and leave.'

'Very well. I had hoped you might have come to your senses—but I see you have not. You were always headstrong and stubborn. I am sorry for it and hope you will not regret your choice.'

'You have no need to fear for my future, sir. I am happier than I could ever have hoped.'

He inclined his head. 'I shall leave you these papers, which are in accordance with Father's will. You may look through them and return them to my lawyers when you have signed them. This will mean there is no need for further communication between us.'

'As you wish.'

Rosalyn felt cold with anger. How selfish he was! How uncaring!

'I have forbidden Beatrice to write to you. I do not wish my wife to associate with the wife of a murderer.'

Oh, how could he? Rosalyn itched to slap him, but maintained her dignity. 'I am ashamed of you, Freddie,' she said, giving him a look filled with contempt. 'I would never have believed you could be so cruel—so unfeeling. You were always selfish, but I thought you loved me as a brother should. I see now it was not so.'

'You chose to cut yourself off from your family. You are the arbiter of your own fate.'

'Am I, Freddie?' Her candid gaze caused him to look away. 'You accused Damian of murder—but I think it was in your own heart at one time. Look into your heart, brother, and see if you can find a part of what was once there, for if you do not, I believe you will suffer for it.'

Freddie refused to look at her. 'I have said what I came to say. Mrs Forrester told me where you were living. I know her husband slightly. We both belong to White's Club. Should you need to contact me in the future, you may do so through my lawyer.' He gave her a brief nod, turned and walked from the room without another word.

Rosalyn remained standing as the door closed behind him. Then she gathered up the papers he had left and thrust them into her writing box. She could not face them now, or the letters to her family.

She would go out into the garden and walk in the sunshine.

'Oh, Damian, they are beautiful! Thank you so much. I could never have wished for anything better.'

Rosalyn stood at the head of the pair of magnificent carriage horses Damian had purchased for her. They were both black with a flash of white on their noses, as close to a perfect match as it was possible to find and both spirited, handsome creatures. She knew at once that he must have gone to a great deal of expense and trouble to find them for her.

'I am glad they please you,' he said, smiling at her evident pleasure. None of his other gifts had brought such a sparkle to her eyes. 'When we are settled, I shall buy more horses for you…' His brows arched in inquiry. 'I thought perhaps you might like to set up your own breeding stables… thoroughbreds you could ride yourself or race if you chose?'

'Could I really do that?' She looked at him in wonder, her face alight with excitement, eyes glowing. 'How did you know it was what I have always wanted?'

'I did not know,' he said, bending his head to brush his lips lightly over hers. 'I merely hoped the idea might appeal to you—give you something to fill your days, to amuse you.'

To make up for the loss of family and friends.

'It is what I should like of all things,' she assured him, laying her face against that of the horse she was fondling. 'Oh, you beauty!'

'They are called Blackberry and Midnight,' Damian said. 'But you may choose new names for them if you wish.'

'It would merely confuse them,' Rosalyn replied. 'If we are to breed horses, I shall have the naming of many horses in time.' She stood back as their new coachman led the horses away, slipping her arm through Damian's. 'Where on earth did you find them?'

As they went into the house, Damian spoke of the contacts he had made, confessing that he had seen more than a dozen matched pairs before making his final choice.

'I wanted them to be perfect,' he said, glancing at her face which still carried the glow of surprise and delight. 'So—what have you been doing, my love?'

'Sitting in the garden for most of the time,' she answered, avoiding his penetrating gaze. She did not wish to spoil his surprise by speaking of the visit from Freddie. 'I did write my letters eventually.'

Damian sensed she was not being quite open with him, yet he could not think what she could be keeping from him. Perhaps it was merely that the act of writing letters to her family had made her realise exactly what she had done—what she had lost?

'Did you finish all your business?' she asked as he was silent.

'Yes—everything.' Damian frowned. 'There were letters waiting for me at the Embassy—the news is not good as far as Jared is concerned, I am afraid.'

'Letters—from his father?'

Damian nodded, his mouth thinning. 'It seems he has decided to bow to the wishes of others. He has officially cast off Jared and made his second son his heir.'

'Oh, how unkind of him!' Rosalyn's concern was all for the youth who had been forced into permanent exile by this act. 'How could a father do that to his son?'

'I do not believe Ahmed had much choice at the end,' Damian said. 'He has acted properly as far as Jared's inheritance is concerned. Besides the jewels we brought with us, he has lodged a large sum of money with a bank in Paris for Jared—enough to make him a wealthy young man one day.'

'Can money ever replace a father's affections?'

'No, of course not—but I hope to do that in some small measure. I wrote to Ahmed some weeks ago and asked for his permission to stand as a father to his son—and he has granted me the right to give Jared my own name. This means that Jared will now be safe from further attack—and that was perhaps the main reason for Ahmed's decision.'

Rosalyn reached up to kiss his cheek, her eyes soft with love. 'I am glad Jared has you,' she said. 'I just hope that he will not be too hurt by what his father has done.'

'I shall tell him myself,' Damian said, 'which means that it will be best if we leave for the country immediately after our wedding.'

'Yes, of course,' Rosalyn agreed. 'I am ready to leave when you are.'

She recalled the papers Freddie had tossed down, which were still tucked into her writing case, unread. Her brother had expected her to return them to his lawyers within a few days, but it could make no difference either way. She did not need more than her allowance; the papers could wait until she was ready to look through them.

'You look lovely,' Charlotte said and kissed Rosalyn on the cheek. 'I am so happy Damian has found you, my dear. There was a time when I believed he would be haunted by his memories… that he would never forget her…' She pulled a wry face as she realised what she had said. 'What am I saying? And on your wedding day! My foolish tongue!'

'Who was it you thought he would never forget?' Rosalyn frowned. Was this what lay in Damian's past? Was it his memories of a woman he had loved and lost that brought such a bleak look to his eyes sometimes?

'Helen…surely he has told you? You must know why he fought that duel?' Charlotte looked puzzled, contrite. 'Forgive me, I believed you knew his story.'

'I knew about the duel…' Rosalyn turned away to pick up her white gloves. 'I thought Helen was his friend's sister.'

'Yes, she was…' Charlotte was instantly remorseful. 'I should not have mentioned her. Especially today—but I meant only to say how pleased I am that Damian has finally put the past behind him and found happiness.'

Rosalyn smiled, her head slightly raised, hiding her confused emotions. Charlotte had not meant to hurt her, nor to raise doubts in her mind. She would not allow the knowledge of Damian's love for the girl who had taken her own life out of shame to spoil her special day. She ought to have realised sooner that he would not have fought a duel unless the girl meant a great deal to him—but she had never suspected that he had carried the memory of his lost love in his heart all these years.

Did it matter? Rosalyn told herself it did not; she had proof enough of Damian's love for her. It would be foolish to let herself be haunted by jealousy of a long-dead girl. No, no, she was far too sensible to let such a trifle distress her.

'Have I upset you with my foolish chatter?' Charlotte asked anxiously.

'No, of course not,' Rosalyn said, giving her a bright smile. 'I have known about Helen for a long time.' She pulled on her gloves. 'I think we should go now, Charlotte—or Damian will believe that I have changed my mind.'

The ceremony was quite brief, witnessed only by a handful of friends, the chief of whom were the Forresters. A brilliant sun hung in the sky as Rosalyn left the small church on Damian's arm to the sound of bells pealing and a shower of rose petals, which floated on the breeze.

The reception was held at a hotel, just a simple meal shared with friends who toasted them in the finest champagne and then waved them off in the splendid new carriage Damian had purchased for his bride.

Once their journey was under way, Damian leaned across to kiss his wife on the lips.

'Happy, my lady?'

'Yes. Very.'

Rosalyn laughed. Damian had used his title for the wedding ceremony, and she was now the Countess Marlowe, something that she found amusing in the circumstances.

It occurred to her that if she were ever at a dinner party where her brother was being entertained, she and Damian would take precedence. Had she been of a spiteful nature she might have gained satisfaction from the thought but, possessing a certain kind of humour which saw the ridiculousness of such conventions, she merely smiled to herself.

'Why are you smiling like that?'

'No particular reason,' Rosalyn replied. 'Except that it seemed so odd to hear myself addressed as Lady Marlowe.'

'I wanted there to be no doubt about the legality of our marriage,' he said, a wry expression in his eyes. 'The title means nothing to me—but you are at liberty to use it if you wish.'

Rosalyn shook her head. 'I am content to be your wife—by what name I am known, I care not.'

The subject was dropped, and they turned to idle chatter and to staring out of the window at the changing scenery: fields, sloping hillsides covered with vines from which the rich wines of France were created, sleepy little villages drowsing in the evening sun—and then the cobbled yard of the inn where they were to stay for the night.

That night Damian's love-making reached new heights, as if by making her his wife he had reached firmer ground and found peace of mind. Rosalyn slept in his arms, content and happy. By the following evening, they would arrive at the house which was to be their home for the next few weeks, though eventually they would travel on to Andalucia and their future.

Chapter Twelve

'Here we are, my love,' Damian said as the carriage turned into a long drive. 'I hope you will like the house I have chosen. It is quite old, but adequate for our needs for the time being. We shall not stay here too long.'

Rosalyn looked out of the window as the house came in sight.

'It is lovely,' she said. 'A charming house.'

A groom opened the door of their carriage, and Damian got out first, turning to help his wife down.

'Ah, I see our arrival has been anticipated.'

Rosalyn looked and saw Jared walking towards them.

'I have been waiting for you,' he said, coming out to meet them. The evening shadows were just beginning to fall across the old courtyard, and the rays of a dying sun had turned the stone walls to rose. 'It is beautiful here, is it not? Can you smell the fragrance of the flowers? That's the jasmine, it always smells beautiful at night.' He stopped and looked at Rosalyn a little shyly. 'I do not know what to call you—should it be Lady Marlowe?'

'No, indeed it should not,' she said and leaned towards him, kissing his cheek. 'We are to be a family, Jared—and my family call me Rosalyn. I should be happy if you were to use my name.'

She saw her suggestion had found favour. He bowed to her, offering his arm, every inch the fashionable young gentleman he was fast becoming. She had noticed a distinct change in him, but perhaps it was just that he was growing up. He seemed to have shot up at least two inches in a few weeks, and she told him so. They went into the house together, laughing and talking as Rosalyn described Paris in lively detail, telling him of the places they had visited and the sights they had seen.

'I have bought several small tokens for you,' she told the youth. 'Just trifles I thought would amuse you. If we return to Paris before we leave France, you must come with us, Jared. I am sure you would enjoy the experience—though I know you love the freedom of the countryside…'

Rosalyn glanced about her, taking stock of her surroundings.

It was a large, old house which had obviously been important in its day, but was now fading into genteel decay. She supposed Damian had chosen it for its beautiful grounds, which he had told her led down to a private beach. There was plenty of room here for

Jared to roam at will in safety…though there would be less need for security in the future. It was most unlikely that further attempts would be made on his life now that he was no longer his father's heir.

Rosalyn wondered how Jared would react to the news that his father had cast him off, and her concern made her redouble her efforts to amuse and please him.

She began to tell Jared about her plans to breed horses in Andalucia, and his enthusiasm for the project was such that they were on excellent terms as they went into one of the shabby but comfortable salons, where refreshments had been prepared for their coming.

Their lovemaking that night was perhaps more special, more passionate and deeply felt than it had ever been. Afterwards, Rosalyn lay entwined in her husband's arms, her face pressed against the moist warmth of his shoulder. He had been all hers while they were making love, but now she sensed a withdrawal in him.

'What is wrong, Damian?' she whispered. 'Is something the matter?'

'Nothing, my dearest,' he murmured and kissed her. 'Everything is perfect. Go to sleep now.'

Rosalyn said no more. She slept in his arms for a while, but woke when he left the bed. For a moment she lay with her eyes closed, then when she heard the door close softly behind Damian, she'd sat up, waiting for him to return. Something was bothering him, and she needed to know what.

Could it be that despite his feelings for her, he could not forget Helen? Did the terrible fate of his lost love still haunt him?

Rosalyn felt the pain twist inside her. Would Helen's ghost always be between them?

She waited for Damian to return for a long time, but he did not come and at last she slept. When she woke the next morning it was a new day, and she made up her mind to put the past behind her.

If Damian had his ghosts, he must be the one to speak of them. All she could do was to show him how much she loved him.

'Oh, you are too good for me!' Rosalyn laughed as Damian's ball knocked hers aside. They had been playing croquet on the lawn at the back of the house. Now she threw down her mallet and went to sit in one of the basket chairs overlooking the sea. 'It is too warm to play any more,' she said as he came to look at her inquiringly. 'Is that Jared down there on the shore?'

Damian looked down at the beach and frowned. 'Yes, I think so. He went off in a mood after I told him about his father's decision. As I feared, it upset him a great deal.'

'He isn't wearing a turban.' Rosalyn shaded her

eyes as she looked up at Damian. 'Why has he taken it off? I thought it was a part of his religion?'

'Perhaps he has decided to cast off his past life entirely,' Damian suggested. 'We must leave him to find his own way, Rosalyn. He is torn between two worlds—and perhaps it will be easier for him if he makes a new world for himself. Indeed, he must, for he can never return to the old one. He would not be welcomed and his life might be in danger from those who feared his influence.'

'I think I shall go down to him,' Rosalyn said. 'This has been very hard for him, Damian. He needs to know that we care if he is to make this transition. Do not be concerned, I shall not try to persuade him either way, now or in the future.'

'I believe he has begun to see you as a stand-in for Anna,' Damian replied. 'He is beginning to love you, Rosalyn.'

'I want only that he should be happy,' she said, and reached up to kiss Damian's cheek. 'As happy as we are.'

'You are happy?'

'Of course. Why should I not be?'

'No reason.' He smiled wryly. 'Do you want to go to this party tonight? These people are friends of Charlotte's. We met Devere's younger brother and his wife in Paris, if you recall?'

'Yes, of course. I liked them,' Rosalyn replied. 'I remember Monsieur Devere speaking of the *comte* once or twice. It was courteous of him to invite us to his house when he discovered we were living near by. I think we should go, Damian—unless you do not wish to?'

'It does not matter to me one way or the other,' he said, reaching out to tuck a wisp of wayward hair behind her ear. 'I care only for your happiness. Go down to Jared, my love. I have some letters of business to write.'

She smiled and nodded. As he went into the house, she began to make her way leisurely down the gentle wooded slope to the beach below. Jared had been throwing sticks into the sea, but, hearing her voice calling to him, turned to greet her. She saw that his hair had been cut quite short, changing the appearance of his features so that he looked even more European than before.

'I have cut my hair,' he said, a defensive look in his eyes as she came up to him. 'Nessa was angry with me—and Rajib said nothing. He is angry, because he thinks I have betrayed him and all that he believes in, but I do not care. I have told them that they should return to India. I am no longer a child. I do not need a nurse.'

'Your hair suits you like that,' Rosalyn said truthfully. 'But you must not turn against those who love you, Jared. Especially your father. He did not want to disinherit you, he had no choice—what he did was for your own sake.'

'He put me aside to favour the son of his new wife,' Jared said bitterly. 'He has betrayed both me and the memory of my mother.'

'Yet you must try to forgive him if you can, dearest.' Rosalyn saw the tears glistening in his eyes. Despite his grown-up ways, he was still a child and he had been hurt. She understood how it felt to be cast off by the family one had loved and opened her arms to him invitingly. 'You are not alone—we love you. Damian and I think of you as our own,' she said. 'I know what has happened hurts but—'

She got no further. Jared rushed into her arms, sobbing out the grief he had held inside him for so long. Rosalyn's arms closed about him, holding him, rocking him as he sobbed. She kissed the top of his head, and stroked the rather roughly shorn hair, comforting him until he was still, his grief spent.

'It will get easier,' she promised him. 'In time you will come to understand that your father did what he thought was best for you. Try not to become bitter, my dear. Nothing will be gained by hating your father.'

Jared drew back from her as the storm of grief subsided. His head lifted and there was pride in his face. 'You are very wise,' he said. 'I shall try to do as you say—but it is very hard.'

'Let us go back and have our tea,' she said, giving him her hand as they began the climb up to the house. 'Damian and I have been invited to a grand party this evening by the Comte Christophe Devere—tell me, should I wear my green gown or the crimson?'

'You always look beautiful,' Jared told her as she put an affectionate arm about his waist. 'But I think the crimson gown is very elegant. If there are to be important guests, you should wear that—with the diamonds Damian gave you yesterday.'

'I shall look very grand, shan't I?' Rosalyn was laughing as she entered the house, her arm still loosely about him. 'Yes, I think you are right, Jared. I shall wear the crimson gown…'

Damian came into the bedroom as Rosalyn was changing for the evening. She smiled at him, turning her back so that he could fasten the hooks at the neck of her gown.

'Jared thought I should wear this tonight,' she said. 'Do you like it?'

'You are always lovely, whatever you wear. Surely you know that?'

There was an odd note in his voice which made her look at him more intently. She remembered the night he had left her bed and not returned.

'Is something wrong, Damian?'

'Why should anything be wrong?' He took the diamond necklace she was trying to fasten and slipped the catch into place, then kissed the top of her shoulder. 'Why do you ask?'

Rosalyn turned to face him. There *was* something wrong, but he obviously did not want to talk about it. Perhaps it would be better to leave well alone for the moment? If he was still in this same mood when they came home from the party, she would ask him again then. She felt that he was shutting her out and it hurt, but she was determined not to let him see it.

'No reason, it does not matter. Are you ready to leave?' she asked. Her manner, though she did not know it, was a little reserved. Damian noticed it at once, but made no comment. He nodded, holding her velvet wrap to place it around her shoulders. 'I wonder what the *comte* will be like. Have you ever met him, Damian?'

'No.' He frowned, thinking how magnificent she looked in the crimson gown. She had always been beautiful, but of late there had been a new glow about her. She would draw all eyes—just as she had at the ball in London, when he had felt so jealous. 'No, I have not met the Comte Devere, but I have heard of him.'

'Oh…?'

She moved towards him, her perfume so intoxicating that he felt an urgent need to make love to her. He wished they need not go to this dinner party, yet perversely was pleased that they had been invited for her sake. She had every right to shine in society, and he was proud of his wife.

'He is as yet unmarried,' Damian answered her question with a wry twist of his lips. 'Rich, handsome and charming, so they say—but determined to remain single despite the best efforts of a legion of young ladies.'

'Ah…' Rosalyn laughed. 'I see. It will be interesting to meet this paragon, do you not think so, my love?'

'We shall see…' Damian smiled. 'Your carriage awaits, my lady.'

Rosalyn was surprised by the richness of the *comte*'s château, which was filled with treasures of every kind. Paintings by the old masters adorned the walls, and the furniture was as fine as that she had seen at Versailles and the Louvre in Paris, both of which she had visited with Damian. The *comte* was obviously very wealthy, and a connoisseur of beautiful things.

Rosalyn and Damian walked up the grand staircase to be greeted by their host in an even larger and more lavishly decorated salon than the one downstairs. Her first sight of Christophe Devere told Rosalyn that Damian had not exaggerated when telling her the stories about this man. He had raven black hair and eyes so blue they rivalled the Mediterranean on a summer's day. He was dressed with exquisite care, his cravat falling in folds of the finest lace and pinned with a diamond so large that it dazzled the eyes when caught by the light of the crystal chandeliers. However, it was his only extravagance and the elegance of his attire came from its simplicity.

His manners were perfect. He bowed over Rosalyn's hand, kissing it briefly but holding it a fraction of a second longer than necessary. His look told her that both she and her gown, which was cut quite daringly low over her breasts, had found favour in his eyes.

'Enchanting, *madame*,' he murmured huskily. 'Seldom have I seen such perfection…such poise.' His eyes mocked her slightly. 'They told me you were English—but surely not?'

'I am indeed English,' Rosalyn replied, amused despite feeling wary of this charming predator. She had met his kind before, and was well aware of the danger they posed for women foolish enough to be taken in. 'But I believe I do not have the English rose style.'

'A far more exotic bloom,' the *comte* replied. 'My lord, you are to be congratulated in your choice of a wife. She is exquisite.'

'Yes, so I have always thought,' Damian replied drily. 'I count myself very fortunate that she chose to marry me instead of one of several devoted admirers.'

His tone made Rosalyn glance at him in surprise. He sounded as though he were warning the other man off. Surely he could not be jealous? He could not imagine that she would be in the least interested in any other man? He must know she loved him, and only him! Yet there was a dangerous glitter in Damian's eyes, which disturbed her. She gave him a little warning frown, but he had turned away.

The *comte* bowed but made no further comment. They passed on, mingling with the other guests milling around the huge reception chamber until dinner was announced. The long dining table was a work of art, set with fabulous silver-gilt epergnes and dishes, delicate glasses with fine air twist stems, and an array of flower displays which perfumed the air.

Rosalyn discovered that she had been placed at her host's right hand; Damian was much further down the table on the same side, which made it difficult to look at each other. She saw that there was an attractive lady on each side of him, and hoped that would be enough to make him content with the arrangement. She herself was very conscious of her attentive host, who made it the business of the evening to attend to her every need, pressing her to try each new delicacy offered.

'Tell me, Lady Marlowe,' the *comte* said, leaning close to whisper in her ear after they had been at table for some twenty or thirty minutes. 'Is your husband always so possessive of you? Not that one can blame him. Such a treasure must always be closely guarded.'

Rosalyn felt that he was mocking Damian and frowned reprovingly. 'My husband does not think of me in those terms,' she said. 'We are happily married, sir.'

'Then he is even more to be envied,' the *comte* replied, a hint of laughter in his mesmerising eyes. 'Wedded bliss is even rarer than the treasures I pay a fortune to acquire for my collection. May one inquire how long you have been married, *madame*?'

'A few weeks. '

'Ah…then the novelty has not yet worn off,' he murmured. 'It is a pity we should have met at this time. A beauty such as yours should not be wasted on one man…unless that man has the eye to appreciate it, which I take leave to doubt.'

The look in his eyes left her in no doubt of his meaning.

'No more of this, I beg you,' Rosalyn said, beginning to feel distinctly uncomfortable. She glanced at Damian, but he seemed engrossed in his conversation with the lady sitting beside him. 'I do not care for foolish compliments.'

'No? An unusual woman indeed.' A wolfish smile played over the *comte*'s mouth. He gave her a speculative look. 'What would appeal to you, *madame*? I wonder.'

Rosalyn shook her head but did not answer. It was clear the *comte* had decided to hunt her, probably because she had shown reluctance to be flattered. It was no doubt a game with him, a game he played to alleviate the tediousness of a life which contained no real purpose. Although he could be charming, she considered him a rather vain and foolish man, and wished he would not be so intense towards her.

Her wish was not to be granted. The *comte* continued to give her his undivided attention throughout the meal, as course after course of delicious food was brought to table.

At the end of the long meal, a huge sugar confection was carried in, accompanied by cries of delight and polite clapping. It depicted a scene from a Greek legend and included nymphs, satyrs and men fighting mythical beasts—a triumph of the chef's art that even Monsieur Maurice would have found difficult to surpass.

After this, the ladies were led to a separate salon by the *comte*'s sister, Madame Moreau, leaving the gentlemen to their brandy or port. Rosalyn found herself singled out for attention over the teacups by the *comte*'s sister, who seemed to imagine her a favourite of her brother.

'Christophe has never married,' she told Rosalyn. 'I fear he is spoiled, *madame*. He loves beautiful things but he has never found a woman to grace his home. I tell him he is too particular. It is time he married and provided an heir for the family.'

'Yes, of course. I suppose you must wish for your brother to be happily settled,' Rosalyn replied dutifully. She did not particularly care for the *comte* or his sister—neither of whom were as pleasant as their brother, whom she had met at Charlotte's house in Paris. She was beginning to find the evening tiring and wished the gentlemen would join them so that she could ask Damian to take her home. 'With such a treasure house as this, your brother must wish for an heir to follow him, I think. There are so many beautiful and rare things here, are there not?'

'What do you particularly admire, Lady Marlowe?'

'Oh, there is far too much to pick out any one thing,' Rosalyn replied. 'But I suppose the cabinet with the collection of gold and enamel curios is very interesting.'

'You have a good eye,' the older woman replied with a satisfied smile. 'My brother has collected pieces from Italy, Russia and the Orient. Yes, there are some very valuable things in that particular cabinet.'

Rosalyn smiled but made no further comment. She was uninterested in the value of the *comte*'s collection, and she had just seen Damian enter the drawing room. She sent him a look of appeal, which brought him immediately to her side.

'Can we go home?' she asked in a whisper. 'Are you ready?'

'They are about to set up the card tables,' he said. 'Do you wish to leave so early?'

She did wish it but could see he was not ready to leave. He was obviously in the mood to gamble, and as the card tables were being set up, she was herself obliged to join the *comte*'s sister in a four at whist.

Rosalyn played with mixed success, something that annoyed her partner, and for which she was quick to apologise.

'I fear I have never excelled at cards,' she explained. 'My father and I were more inclined to play at chess in the evenings.'

After some hands, her place was taken by another lady, and, seeing that Damian appeared to be enjoying himself, Rosalyn got up and wandered over to the window. She was staring out at the night, and a sky that was sprinkled with stars, when she became aware of someone standing close behind her. Turning her head to look, she saw it was the *comte*: the look in his eyes was speculative and sent a shiver down her spine.

'You do not care for cards, *madame*?'

'Not very much,' she admitted. 'I was taught chess by a master and much prefer the challenge of pitting one mind against another, instead of relying on the cards one is dealt.'

'Ah, I see…you like to take your destiny in your own hands.' He nodded, seeming pleased with the interpretation. 'Then perhaps you would care to see one of my special treasures? I have a rather splendid chess set in my own private parlour. If you wish, we could go there now.'

Rosalyn hesitated, not wanting to offend him, yet determined not to be lured into an obvious trap. She glanced towards Damian, who had just won the game he had been playing. He had turned in his chair to look at her, his expression unreadable.

'You must forgive me, sir,' Rosalyn said to the *comte*. 'I believe I shall ask my husband to take me home now. I have a slight headache.'

'I am sorry to hear that.' The *comte* arched his brows. 'Perhaps another day you will favour me with a game of chess? I have seldom found an opponent worthy of my time—but perhaps you…?' He left the question open, inviting her comment.

Rosalyn merely smiled. Damian was rising as she walked to join him.

'Do you want to go home?' he asked.

'Yes, please. If you are ready. I have a slight headache. I have explained to the *comte*.'

'You should have said something earlier.'

'I thought you wanted to play cards?'

'I felt obliged once asked,' he replied. 'But I do not care to continue. Gambling is something I can take or leave.'

Rosalyn said nothing. His father had been ruined at the tables. The fever might be in his blood for all she knew. That evening he had played for small stakes and risen a modest winner, but in other circumstances he might not have been so prudent. How could she know?

There was so much she did not know about him, and his recent moods had made her feel there was an invisible barrier between them.

Their carriage having been sent for, they took leave of their host and fellow guests. Damian helped her into the carriage and settled into the seat beside her, leaning his head back against the squabs and closing his eyes.

He did not speak once during their journey home. She sensed he was angry about something, but did not feel inclined to ask what was wrong. If he was jealous of the *comte* paying her attention, it was his own fault. She had done nothing to court that attention, but had been forced to respond politely to her host's civility. Besides, Damian had been in a mood even before they left the house.

He was perfectly civil as he wished her goodnight before she went up, but he did not kiss her and he made no attempt to follow Rosalyn to their bedroom. At the top of the stairs, she paused to look back and saw that he was staring after her, his face set in an expression that chilled her.

What on earth could be wrong with him? Damian had once said that she might regret marrying him—was he beginning to have regrets himself? Had he discovered he was still unable to forget Helen, despite his marriage? Was that the reason he left her bed while she slept, because he wished she was Helen?

It was a bitter thought and one that, despite all her efforts, refused to leave her.

Rosalyn slept alone that night. It was the first time since they had left her home in England that Damian had not come to her. In thinking about it, she realised with a shock that she had not seen her womanly flow since before that time.

Could she be carrying Damian's child? It was surely too soon? And yet she had always been so regular.

Rosalyn thought about the very real possibility. She was not sure whether she was pleased to have fallen so quickly or not. It might have been better if she and Damian had had more time alone, before all the complications that childbearing must bring.

Would Damian be pleased? She was uncertain, not of his love for her—but of his needs and hopes for the future. He did love her, she believed that, of course she did. She must believe it or she was lost! Damian cared for her, but something was playing on his mind, giving him no peace. Or perhaps it was just a part of his nature to be restless?

Rosalyn decided to keep her suspicions about the child to herself for the moment. She could not be sure that he would welcome her news, and she might be wrong. No, no, better to be certain before speaking of her hopes to Damian.

Why had he not come to her that night? Why had he seemed angry? His mood had started before they left for the *comte*'s dinner party—after they had parted, Damian to write some letters and she to meet Jared on the beach.

What had annoyed him? Rosalyn could find no reason for it. They had been happy enough earlier, playing at croquet. Why had that haunted look come back to his eyes?

What was it that worried him so? The thoughts went round and round in her mind, tormenting her.

Damian went for a long, hard ride before Rosalyn was awake the next morning. He had stayed up late, drinking alone in his study, cursing himself for his foolishness in allowing his jealousy to show. Rosalyn's headache was surely a sign of her displeasure? She had always valued her independence, she would not take kindly to having her freedom questioned.

He had behaved like a heavy-handed husband, when he ought to have been amused by Devere's attempts to seduce her—attempts which had been given the dismissive treatment they deserved. He was well aware that Rosalyn had given the man no encouragement; he had nothing to blame her for…nothing to cause the foul mood which had come over him when he'd noticed her standing near the window with Devere and seen the predatory look in the other man's eyes.

It was not unexpected from such a man. Devere wanted her the way he desired one of his rare *objets d'art*. He was attracted by her beauty—and because she was out of reach. The *comte* had become accustomed to taking his pick of pretty women; they fell over themselves to please him—the girls looking for marriage to a wealthy man and the bored wives who were flattered to be invited into his bed.

Rosalyn was different; there was something exciting about her, something that made men want her. She had aroused the *comte*'s hunting instincts. Damian had sensed danger from the beginning. One part of him had wanted to carry her off immediately, back to the safety of their home: the other, saner side knew that she was quite safe as long as she did not allow Devere to lure her into a compromising situation.

Damian laughed at himself. What a fool he was to worry! Rosalyn's quietness of late meant nothing. He was wrong to think she was brooding, regretting the impulse which had made her throw away all that she held precious for his sake.

Rosalyn was not Helen. She would not fall victim to abduction or seduction as that innocent child had all those years ago; she would not take her own life because she was unhappy. He had no need to fear it. Yet he could not quite rid himself of the idea that she might be in danger, that he might lose her.

'Damned fool!' Damian cried aloud. Would he never rid himself of the past? Of his feelings of guilt…the nagging fear that he did not deserve to find happiness, that any attempt to do so would be punished by the fates who ruled man's destiny.

It was not Damian's fault that Helen had taken her own life, but he had never been able to forgive himself for not preventing the tragedy. Although he had learned to live with his failure, it had remained at the back of his mind—and the business of Bernard Harrington's murder had made all the old sores fester once more.

He knew that he had been given something infinitely precious. Rosalyn was all that he had ever desired in a woman and more, but he was haunted by the fear that it would not last: that she would grow tired of living in exile and long to return to her old life, a life that was now denied to her. He was afraid that she might already have begun to regret her hasty action in leaving England with him.

Damian had the previous afternoon, when looking through his wife's writing box for a stick of sealing wax, accidentally discovered the papers relating to Rosalyn's capital, which was released on her marriage under the terms of her father's will. They had not been signed by her, but the date stamped in the official wax seal told him that she must have seen her brother in Paris. Why had she not mentioned it to him?

It seemed to Damian that she had deliberately kept the meeting with Freddie a secret. Why? Had her brother agreed to see her, providing she met him alone? The thought rankled, bringing a bitter taste to his mouth. Rosalyn had a perfect right to see her brother if she wished—but he would have preferred it if she had mentioned it.

Now he was being stupid! Damian was angry with himself for allowing such a small thing to matter. This business of the Comte Devere was far more important. He must warn Rosalyn to be vigilant…and yet she had shown herself well able to handle the *comte*. Perhaps it was better to say nothing. They would in any case be leaving France for Spain in a few weeks…and yet he carried a nagging fear that would not let him be.

Chapter Thirteen

Rosalyn discovered the prettily wrapped package on her dressing table. Another gift! Damian gave her presents all the time, but she was growing used to it and had discovered that she enjoyed being spoiled. After all, why should she mind that the husband who loved her liked to buy her things?

She picked up the box, turning it over in her hands, speculating on the contents. Could it be yet another piece of jewellery? It felt a little too heavy. She smiled as she untied the ribbon and took off the outer wrapping, looking for a card and failing to find one. That was unusual. Damian normally wrote funny, tender messages of love, slipping them inside the paper, but this time there was none.

She frowned as she took the lid off the box and saw what was lying inside. It was a delicate object made of gold and some kind of pink crystal, which she thought might be quartz. The stem was of twisted gold wire and bore a cluster of flowers made from the pink stone; the centres were studded with rubies and the leaves were probably jade, she thought. It was an exquisite thing, and quite different to anything Damian had given her previously. She set it down on the dressing table as the door opened and he came in.

'Damian,' she said, holding out her hand to him. 'Thank you for your gift, my darling. It is exquisite—'

'Gift?' Damian saw the pretty trifle amongst the discarded wrappings on her dressing table and frowned. 'Where did that come from?'

'Did you not leave it for me?' She looked at him in surprise. 'It was on my dressing table when I woke. I thought you must have left it there.'

'That did not come from me,' he said, a little nerve flicking at the corner of his mouth. 'You must realise who sent it, Rosalyn. Did you not see other similar pieces last night?'

'Comte Devere sent it?' She stared at him in dismay. 'One of the maids must have brought it up while I was sleeping. I cannot accept such a gift from the *comte*. It is far too valuable. I shall have it packed and returned immediately.'

'You would certainly be well advised to do so,' he said. 'Unless you wish to encourage his pretensions?'

'Damian!' Rosalyn had risen at his entrance. She took a step back, shocked that he could even suggest such a thing. 'You must know that I do not? I am your wife.'

'Which would make it all the easier for you to have an affair with the *comte* if you wished, would it not?'

It was accepted that married women sometimes had affairs, whereas the same behaviour in single ladies was frowned upon—but the idea that Damian should think she might be willing was so distressing to her that she could only look at him in horror. Surely he could not mean that? How could he insult her so?

The pain whipped through her. Why was Damian being so harsh towards her? He could not imagine she wanted the *comte*'s gift?

'That is a wicked thing to say,' she said, eyes mirroring her hurt. She raised her head, looking at him proudly. 'I cannot believe that you have said such a terrible thing to me.'

Nor could Damian. The words had come out of his jealous confusion. He knew them to be both cruel and unworthy and regretted them the instant they left his tongue.

'Forgive me,' he said, his manner stiff and reserved. He wanted to apologise abjectly, but pride—or jealousy—held him back. 'You are right to be angry, Rosalyn. It was wrong of me to say that. I know you would not consider…but you must realise that the *comte* intends to make you his mistress if he can?'

'That is nonsense,' she retorted, angry in her turn. Did Damian imagine that because she had gone to him before marriage, she had no morals—that she would contemplate being another man's mistress? How could he! 'The *comte* was merely being a polite host last evening—and this gift is the thoughtless impulse of a generous man.'

Even as she spoke, Rosalyn knew she was being untruthful. The gift was bait to lure her into a gilded trap. She had no intention of accepting it, none at all.

'Then keep it,' Damian said coldly. 'It seems to please you more than anything I have given you.'

He turned on his heel and left the room. Rosalyn stared after him, feeling stunned and disbelieving. What was wrong? Damian had never been like this with her. It was their first serious quarrel and it hurt her, it hurt her so much that she felt as if he had struck her.

What had she done that he should be so distrustful of her? Rosalyn blinked back her tears. It was not her fault that the *comte* had decided to pursue her; she had given him no encouragement: indeed, she had done her best to make him see that she was not interested in him.

Hot tears stung her eyes, but she held them back. She would not give way to her emotions.

Rosalyn rang the bell, summoning a maid. She gave instructions for the box to be wrapped and returned to the *comte*—and that any further gifts from him should be sent back immediately.

The maid dismissed, she began to brush her hair. She was about to ring for her personal maid to help her dress when the door opened again and Damian came in. He hesitated in the doorway, giving her a look full of contrition.

'I am sorry,' he said in a husky voice. 'I am a jealous fool. It made me angry to see the way Devere looked at you last night. When you were pleased with his gift, I lost my temper. I have behaved stupidly—will you forgive me?'

'Of course. I sent his gift back. You could not think I meant to keep it?' She rushed to his arms as he shook his head, a surge of relief rising in her. She was not sure she could have borne it if their quarrel had continued. 'I love you, Damian. No one else. You must know that?'

'Yes. I did not truly doubt you.' He touched her cheek, a rueful look in his eyes. 'Forgive me. I cannot help my jealousy, Rosalyn. It is a demon I must try to control in future—but you will take care? Devere is not to be trusted. If anything were to happen to you…I should not be able to answer for my actions.'

She gazed up into his face. His expression frightened her. He looked almost desperate. It made her wonder what he might be capable of if the *comte* attempted to seduce her…would he kill for her sake?

Had he already done so?

She had been so certain he could not have shot Bernard Harrington, but now she had begun to wonder…

Rosalyn kept her thoughts to herself. Over the next two days, Damian was very attentive and concerned for her. He put himself out to please her, taking both her and Jared to an English fair that had come to the district.

It was a warm, sunny day, without a cloud in the sky. They wandered around the stalls, Rosalyn delighting in the various trinkets and games that were on offer. She watched Damian bowling in vain for a pig, laughing as all his efforts failed to win the prize—but when it came to the shooting range, it was a different matter.

Each shot struck its target in the exact centre. Jared was excited and applauded enthusiastically.

'Damian was the best marksman at my father's palace,' he told her. 'Everyone knew that he would always win if there was a competition. And when a tiger attacked the villages, he was always the one who was called upon to kill it. He was fearless, and he saved my life when the assassins tried to kill me. There were three of them, and he shot them all…'

Jared's tale sent shivers down Rosalyn's spine. What did she really know of the man she loved?

Damian was obviously skilled with guns of all

kinds. Rosalyn smiled and accepted the china fairing he won for her, but she could not help wondering if he would kill a man as easily as he shot at a target.

He had killed Roderick Harrington because of what he had done to Helen, but it was truly Bernard who had shamed the innocent girl. Had Damian killed him because of that…had he taken his revenge coldly and without mercy?

Rosalyn had believed him innocent of the crime. She had been almost sure that she knew the identity of the real culprit, but now she was not sure. Damian's moods could come so suddenly, and while they lasted he was capable of anger.

If only she could understand what it was that haunted him. She longed to ask him, and yet she was afraid that she might not like the answer.

Their quarrel had been soon mended, but she sensed Damian's growing frustration and it made her afraid.

She woke one night from a dream…the dream she had had once before. She was running in a mist. Damian was there, just ahead of her, but she could not reach him. She cried his name aloud, but when she opened her eyes and turned, needing to touch him, to feel the reassurance of his arms about her, he was not there.

'Oh, Damian,' she whispered into the darkness. 'Do not leave me, my darling. Come back to me. I need you…I need you so much.'

She was afraid that they might drift apart, that she might lose him. And she could not bear it.

'Madame Moreau,' announced the parlour maid. 'And Comte Devere.'

Rosalyn glanced round as the new arrivals entered her sitting room where she was presiding over the teacups. Since the *comte*'s dinner party three days previously she had received a steady stream of callers, most of them ladies who were curious to discover more about the woman who had commanded so much attention from Comte Devere.

'*Madame—monsieur.*' Rosalyn rose to greet her guests. 'It is a pleasure to welcome you here.'

Madame Moreau was looking about her in a superior way, obviously thinking that the house did not compare to her brother's.

'Madame.' The *comte* bowed over Rosalyn's hand, a gleam of appreciation in his eyes. 'You grow more lovely each time we meet.'

Rosalyn had wondered if the prompt return of his gift might offend him, but judging from the way he was looking at her—like a hungry wolf stalking its prey—she sensed that it had merely intensified his interest in her. The *comte* clearly enjoyed the thrill of hunting his intended conquests.

She wished that Damian had been at home to support her that afternoon. However, he and Jared had gone to an isolated estate some distance away, to look at a stallion they had been told was particularly fine.

'If it is what we want I shall buy him,' Damian told her. 'We can take him with us when we leave for Spain.'

'When are we leaving?'

'Soon,' he promised. 'I am waiting for my lawyers in Paris to complete the papers necessary for Jared's adoption, then we shall go.' He had smiled and kissed her. 'I already have agents looking for the right place for us…somewhere with good grazing for the horses and plenty of water.'

Rosalyn had still said nothing to him of her suspicion that she might be with child; she was not yet certain, though her conviction grew with each passing day. She hoped they would be settled in their new home before her condition began to make things uncomfortable.

She had let Damian go with a smile and a kiss that morning, but now she felt suddenly alone and vulnerable. No, no, that was ridiculous! She had a house full of servants, and half a dozen guests to keep her company. There was not the slightest need to be uneasy.

Yet as her other guests began to say their farewells after the customary twenty minutes or so, her anxiety intensified. Why must the *comte* keep staring at her in that particular way? Why was she beginning to feel trapped?

Eventually only Madame Moreau and the *comte*

remained. When the sister stood up, telling her brother that he must not leave on her account, Rosalyn knew a moment of panic.

'No, no, Christophe,' Madame Moreau said to him. 'I know you wish to talk privately to the countess so I shall leave you together. I am perfectly well able to find my way home.'

She gave him such an arch look that Rosalyn was angry as the Frenchwoman swept from the room. It seemed clear to her that Madame Moreau was a party to her brother's plans for seduction. She suspected the pair had played this game before.

Well, it would not work this time! She was no innocent to be deceived by a philanderer.

As soon as the *comte*'s sister had gone, Rosalyn got up and went to ring the bell for the maids to clear the tea things. She turned to look at the *comte*.

'You will forgive me if I ask you to leave now, *monsieur*?' she said. 'I have a little headache and I wish to rest for a while.'

'Another headache?' The *comte* looked amused. He arched his brows. 'I am alarmed, *madame*. You are perhaps ill? Will you allow me the privilege of recommending my own physician?'

Rosalyn was prevented from answering by the arrival of the maids. As they began to clear the used tea things, she walked out to the open French windows and went out to the stone terraces. She walked down three steps to the lawns below. The *comte* followed her.

'Yes, you are very wise, *madame*. Fresh air will often cure a headache, I believe. Perhaps more so than lying down in an airless room. Unless of course one had company to ease the tedium…'

His meaning was so clear that she turned on him, eyes sparking with anger. 'Very well, sir, you force me to speak plainly. I do not wish to be alone with you. Your attentions are unwelcome to me.'

'You returned my gift,' he said, ignoring her outburst. 'Did it not please you? I was told you had a preference for such trinkets, but if you would prefer something else you have only to ask. Tell me, *madame*, what can I offer that would make you smile for me? Both my person and my fortune are yours to command.'

'Nothing. I want nothing you can give me.' Rosalyn glared at him. Was the man so thick skinned that he could not be told? 'Please leave now and do not bother me again.'

She walked away from him, across the lawn. The sun was hot and she had not lied when she'd said she had a headache. It was a dull, heavy feeling that had been pressing down on her for a while.

When she realised the *comte* was still following her, she swung round, temper flaring.

'Will nothing I say make you understand?'

He smiled his disbelief, so used to having his way that he could not believe her refusal to be final.

'You are magnificent when you are angry,' he said,

his voice husky with desire. 'Such a woman as you would be worthy of my home. If I have given you the impression that I want only a brief affair, I must beg you to forgive me. If you were free I would marry you—as my mistress you would have a king's ransom at your command.'

'I have no wish to marry you or to become your mistress. Nor am I interested in your wealth, *monsieur*.'

She was beginning to feel very uncomfortable. The pressure in her head was becoming hard to bear.

'But you will be mine,' the *comte* muttered, angered by her apparent indifference. An ugly lust twisted his features as he made a grab at her. 'I shall taste the honey you deny me…if only briefly…'

Rosalyn was so shocked that he should physically assault her in broad daylight and in the very gardens of her home that she did not react fast enough. His arms closed about her, pulling her, resisting, against him. She beat at him with her fists as he bent his head to take possession of her mouth in a hateful, greedy kiss that filled her with disgust. Such was her horror that she summoned all her strength, wrenching away from him and wiping the back of her hand across her mouth to take away the taste of him.

'How dare you? How dare you insult me so?'

'That was only the beginning.' His eyes narrowed. Unused to being thwarted and denied his pleasures, her resistance had brought out the worst in him. He had heard rumours about this woman that had made him think she might be available and his disappointment at being rejected was all the stronger. 'I always get what I want in the end, believe me. You were Marlowe's mistress before he married you—why not leave him and come to me? I can give you far more—'

'Never!' she cried. 'Please—leave me alone.'

'Why not make this pleasant for us both? I can be a bad enemy if I choose. I want you—and I intend to have you, if I have to abduct you and kill your husband.'

He could not mean it! Rosalyn was too shocked and confused to think clearly. 'No…' she whispered, as his face began to go fuzzy before her eyes. She was feeling most unwell. This could not be happening: it was like a nightmare playing out in slow motion. She pressed a hand to her forehead as the garden began to spin around her. 'No…you must not say such…' Through the mists, which were closing in on her, she was aware of danger and she cried out to Damian. 'Please help me…help me…'

Everything was going black. She was falling… falling into a bottomless void…

When Rosalyn came to her senses some time later, she was lying on a sofa in the parlour. Nessa was bending over her, bathing her head with a cloth wrung out in cool water, and a maid was hovering in the background: there was no sign of the *comte*.

'What happened?' she asked, a faint moan escaped her. 'How did I get here?'

'The *mem-sahib* fainted,' Nessa said. 'You were kissing that man—and then you fell to the ground. Rajib was in the garden; he saw what happened and went to your assistance. It was he who carried you here.'

'I must thank him…' Rosalyn put a hand to her head as she tried to sit up. 'The *comte*…' The room still seemed to be moving and she lay back, sighing and closing her eyes. 'He…forced himself on me. I did not kiss him. He threatened to…' She recalled Devere's threat to kill Damian and a thrill of fear went through her. 'My husband must know nothing of this. If he knew what the *comte* said to me, he would—'

'What would I do?'

Rosalyn's throat caught as she looked up and saw Damian coming towards her. His expression was so stern. When had he returned? What had he seen or heard that had made him look like that?

'Damian…' She faltered, feeling nervous. Was he angry with her again? 'I did not know you were home.'

'Did you not, my dear?' His tone was so cold, so angry. 'Perhaps it is fortunate that I did return a little sooner than planned. Otherwise I might not have discovered what has been going on.'

'Damian…' cried Rosalyn in distress. 'You cannot think…'

She pushed herself up against the pillows someone

had placed behind her. Why was he looking at her in that way? She stared at him, the coldness spreading through her as she sensed his fury. He had already sent the maid scurrying from the room; now he jerked his head at Nessa, dismissing her.

'I said leave!' Damian glared at the old woman. 'I want to be alone with my wife.'

'Damian—there is no need to shout at her,' Rosalyn protested. 'She was helping me, because I had fainted.'

'And why did you faint, my love?' Damian asked as Nessa went from the room. 'Was it at the prospect of becoming the *comte*'s mistress—or your disappointment that you had not waited and married him?'

There was such bitterness in his face!

'How can you?' Rosalyn stared at him, tears she refused to shed stinging her eyes. What had happened to him? He was like a stranger. A hard, cold man she had never before seen. 'Comte Devere called with his sister. I was obliged to entertain them.'

'I met Madame Moreau's carriage as she was returning to her home,' Damian said, a hard glitter in his eyes. 'When I reached the house, I was told the *comte* was with you—but before I could come in search of you, Rajib told me you had fainted. I came at once...in time to hear you beg Nessa to help you conceal your indiscretion.'

'No, that is not true. You do not understand,' she cried. 'This is unfair, Damian. You accuse me without having heard my story. It was not what you think. You must believe me!'

'Then tell me. I shall be interested to hear what Devere said to you.'

Rosalyn got to her feet. She was still feeling unwell, but she could not allow this misunderstanding to continue.

'Listen to me,' she begged. 'Please listen, Damian.' There was no chance of concealment now. She must tell him the whole story and hope he would not lose his temper again. 'I did not wish you to know, because I feared you might force a duel on him and I do not wish…'

'You feared for his life? You would do well to do so.'

'Do not be ridiculous!' Anger helped her stand straight despite the fuzzy feeling in her head. 'I cannot believe you think so ill of me, Damian. Have you lost your senses? The *comte* insulted me. He told me he knew I had been your mistress—and promised me a king's ransom if I left you for him. When I naturally refused, he became resentful and seized me. He kissed me but I fought him off. Then he became abusive…he said he would have me if it meant abducting me and killing you. I was feeling most unwell and called for you to help me—and then I fainted.'

Damian was staring at her oddly; the fierce anger

had died out of his face to be replaced by an expression of shame. He had been incensed when he heard her telling Nessa to keep the incident from him, but now he saw why she had done so: it was entirely for his sake, to protect him from the duel he was in honour bound to fight. He must certainly fight: he could not allow this insult to his wife to go unchallenged. Damian acknowledged the whole thing was his fault: by making her his mistress before they married, he had opened the way for an insult of this kind.

'Forgive me,' he said. 'I should not have said such terrible things to you. I most humbly beg your pardon, Rosalyn. This is all my doing. All my fault. None of it was of your making.'

'No, it was not, nor should you have accused me so unkindly,' Rosalyn said. Her head was going round and round so fast that she could scarcely see his face. She felt very ill and did not know what she said, 'If you are going to be so jealous…so angry…every time a man looks at me, I do not think I shall be able to bear it.'

'Rosalyn…' She sounded so odd, so detached—as if his behaviour had so disgusted her that she had begun to regret their marriage. 'Forgive me… please?'

Damian was about to explain his reasons for being so overwrought when she made a little sighing sound and fainted again. He moved swiftly to catch her in his arms, fear coursing through him. Everything else faded into insignificance as he realised she must be ill. If Devere's despicable behaviour had caused her to faint once that would not have been surprising, but this was different.

Carrying her in his arms, he went swiftly from the parlour and up the stairs. He called loudly for assistance, sending a footman scurrying to fetch a physician from the village, and two maids to prepare the bed. As he laid her gently down, she moaned and fluttered her eyelids. He stroked the damp hair back from her forehead, cursing himself for quarrelling with her when she was ill. What a thoughtless brute he was! And all because he was afraid of losing her.

'Rosalyn dearest,' he whispered as he sat beside her, bathing her head with cool water. 'I am a wretch to upset you so, my love. I am so sorry…so very sorry.'

Her eyes opened at that, and she caught his hand. 'You won't call him out, will you? Please, Damian! You must not fight him because of what happened this afternoon. I was not really harmed…and he has sworn to kill you. I could not bear it if…'

So he had not quite killed her love! Damian felt the relief sweep through him. He had allowed his fears to drive a wedge between them, but it was not too late. She still loved him.

'I shall not be killed,' he reassured her. 'Rest, my darling. Nothing will happen to me. All that matters is that you should be well again. I have sent for the doctor. He will soon be here.'

Her head was beginning to clear at last. She smiled at him, sensing his anxiety, his guilt for having been angry with her. Her fingers entwined with his lovingly.

'I believe I may know what is wrong with me,' she told him softly. 'I think…it may be that I am carrying our child, Damian.'

'Carrying our child?' Damian stared at her, first in disbelief and then in dawning wonder. If this was true, it was so much more than he had hoped for! 'Do you mean it, Rosalyn—you are carrying our child?'

'Yes…I think I must be,' she said, a strangled laugh escaping her as she saw his joy. And she had wondered if he would be pleased by the news! 'I cannot be certain until I have consulted a physician, of course, which is why I did not say anything before this—but I do believe it to be so.'

'No wonder you fainted,' Damian said, a rueful look in his eyes. 'And I was so unkind to you—can you forgive me?'

'Yes, I can forgive you,' she said, clinging to his hand, 'but I do not understand your anger, Damian. You cannot for one moment think that I encouraged the *comte*'s advances?'

'No…' A little nerve flicked in his throat. 'No, Rosalyn. Despite what I said to you downstairs, I did not truly think it. Not in my heart—only with my jealous mind.'

'But why?' she asked. 'Why should you be jealous? You must know why I came with you? You must know that I love you?'

'Yes…' He stood up and walked away to the window, looking out into the garden. How to tell her when he did not truly understand himself? 'It makes no sense…I do not know how to explain it to you.'

'Won't you try, Damian?'

'I suppose I feel that I do not deserve you,' he said, and turned to face her. She saw that the bleak look was back in his eyes. 'That…if I allow myself to be happy, it will all go away.'

'But why? Why should you not deserve to be happy? Please tell me, my love.'

Damian was silent. She sensed that he was struggling with himself, trying to find the words to tell her what was in his heart, but before he could do so, one of the maids came rushing in to tell them the doctor was on his way upstairs.

'Another time, my love,' Damian said and bent to kiss her forehead. 'I shall wait downstairs while the doctor examines you.'

Rosalyn nodded, sensing that the moment for explanations had passed. She wanted to beg him not to leave her, but could not. He pressed her hand, turning as the doctor came in.

He was a fussy little man in a black frock-coat and striped trousers.

'Well, well, what have we here, *madame*?' he said, giving her an indulgent look. 'They tell me you have been fainting. Have you been sitting too much in the sun?'

Damian smiled and left her alone with the physician.

Why had he found it so difficult to put his thoughts into words? She deserved an explanation for behaviour she must think unreasonable. How could he tell her that he was haunted by his fear…that because he had failed Helen, he would lose the woman he loved?

It was not a rational fear. He had tried to tell himself so many times that it was not his fault Helen had taken her own life, and yet the guilt remained even after all these years.

If he had not left Helen there, sitting alone on that bench in the garden of her home, she might still be alive. She had begged him to go, told him that she felt much better, that she needed a little time alone—but he should not have listened. He should have taken her to her family, made sure that she was being cared for.

His own anger and disgust at what had been done to her was such that he had not been able to think sensibly; he had shown his feelings too clearly, and as a consequence of his neglect a girl had died. He had killed a man because of that—but it had not brought her back, nor had it eased his own guilt. Indeed, when he had discovered the wrong man had paid a cruel penalty, it had made his burden harder to bear.

But that was so many years ago! It was foolish to

let the old memories haunt him still. No more! He would put them from his mind, crush the fears that lingered and take the happiness Rosalyn had brought him with both hands.

Damian waited alone in the parlour, to have a word with the physician when he came down after examining Rosalyn.

'Is she ill, sir?' he asked, torn with anxiety. 'Has she been doing too much?'

'Your wife seems to think she is with child,' the physician replied with a reassuring smile. 'Although too soon to be certain, I think she is possibly right in her diagnosis. It is not unusual for ladies to faint in this condition. However, you would do well to keep an eye on her—and she should rest for an hour or so in the afternoons.'

Damian thanked him, asked him to call again in a couple of days and then went back into the parlour. He sat down at the elegant rosewood desk he had bought for his wife in Paris. Rosalyn liked to sit at it when writing her letters, so that she could gaze out at the garden. What to do now? Rosalyn had begged him not to call the *comte* out, but Devere could not be allowed to insult her and get away with it.

Frowning, he looked down at the desk and saw there was a little pile of letters waiting for his wife. The franking showed that two of them had come from England, the third from Paris. He could smell

Charlotte's perfume on that one, but who were the others from? He looked at the writing. One of the hands seemed familiar—he thought it had probably come from Maria—the other was unknown to him.

He rang the bell, summoning a servant. Letters from home were always welcome to his wife. Rosalyn would enjoy reading these while she was resting.

A maid had come in answer to his summons. He gave her the letters for Rosalyn, requesting her to take them up to her mistress immediately.

'Please tell my wife that I have had to go out,' he said. 'I may not be back in time for dinner. Tell her that I think she should stay in bed and rest. I shall see her in the morning.'

'Yes, sir.'

Damian left the parlour after the girl had departed. There was something he needed to fetch first, and then he would pay Comte Devere a little visit.

He went into the room he used as a study, taking a polished mahogany box from his desk and opening it. Inside lay a pair of perfectly matched pistols. It would be Devere's right to provide the pistols, or indeed to use swords if he so wished—but Damian thought it best to be prepared. He doubted the *comte* had killed a man in his life—and certainly not a maddened tiger at close range. It took a certain kind of man to hold his nerve under those circumstances. If Damian were any judge, the *comte* was not the type to wait until his opponent had fired.

Devere might be able to hit a practice target, but not many had the courage to put a ball in a man's heart. A grim expression drew Damian's mouth into a hard line. If he chose, Devere could die this night. No matter what the cost, this business must be settled for once and all.

Chapter Fourteen

Rosalyn took the letters from her maid without enthusiasm, scarcely glancing at them before laying them on the chest beside her bed. She had recognised Maria's hand but did not feel in the mood for reading her cousin's letter. Her head had cleared a little. She realised she was at last beginning to feel better, and would have liked to talk to Damian.

It was time they talked. Something had been bothering him for a while now. He had confessed that he did not truly believe she had betrayed him, even in her thoughts—so what was it that lay behind the moods that had come on him since they left England?

Was it possible that he had killed Bernard Harrington? Had he done so to protect her—and was it the act of murder which lay heavy on his conscience?

Rosalyn shook her head. No, for a while she had wondered, but she was able to think more clearly now and she would not believe any such thing! She had dismissed the idea as impossible from the beginning, even thinking that Freddie might have been the culprit for a while, and then something very different had occurred to her. Her doubts had been roused by Damian's haunted expression, but she believed there was a different explanation for his moods. Damian was innocent of murder—but something was causing him to be uneasy.

Was it his memories of the woman he had loved and lost? Had he been unable to forget, despite his love for Rosalyn? She knew a moment of terrible jealousy but fought it. This was unworthy of her. She could not be jealous of a girl who had died of shame!

The maid had told Rosalyn that Damian would be out for the evening. He had requested that she should rest, have her supper sent up to her on a tray, but she did not feel like eating. Nor did she want to stay in bed now that the dizziness had passed.

Where had Damian gone? Had he decided to challenge the *comte* to a duel for insulting her? She was suddenly sure in her own mind that he had gone out for that very purpose.

Rosalyn felt cold all over. How foolish of him! Surely it was not necessary? She had been upset at the time, but no real harm had been done, and now she thought about it calmly, she did not believe the *comte* would have carried out his threats to abduct her and kill Damian. He had spoken in the heat of the moment and would surely reconsider his hasty words once he'd had time to reflect. He did not love her, he had merely wanted to add her to his collection—which was not worth the risk of fighting a duel.

Unable to rest, Rosalyn threw off the bedcovers and went over to her dressing table. She brushed her hair; the action was soothing, easing the headache that had plagued her since her fainting spell.

She felt restless. It was impossible to sit here in her room, not knowing where Damian was or what he was doing. She would go downstairs and wait for Damian. Surely he could not be gone all evening?

If her husband had gone to fight a duel, he might be killed.

The thought filled her with terror. She could not bear it if he died. Oh, why must men be so foolish? It was such nonsense, to fight a duel for so small a thing!

Alone in her parlour, Rosalyn ran her fingers over the ivory keys of a pretty little spinet. She sighed, wishing that Damian would come back and take her in his arms. She was missing him, the more so because they had come close to quarrelling again, and that distressed her. Why was Damian behaving so oddly of late? Was it only jealousy?

She turned as she heard a sound behind her. Rajib was standing in the doorway, staring at her strangely.

She felt a sudden coldness at the nape of her neck.

'Yes, Rajib—what is it?'

'I wanted to speak to you, *mem-sahib*.' His dark eyes were intense as he looked at her. 'May I speak openly?'

'Yes, of course.' She rose to her feet, waiting for him to begin.

'I have decided to return to India, and Nessa is to come with me.'

'Oh…' Rosalyn hesitated. 'I do not quite understand. You should properly say this to my husband—or to Jared.'

'Jared knows of my decision. He has grown away from us. We are no longer needed.'

Rosalyn heard the resentment in his voice. 'I am sorry that you should feel rejected,' she said. 'I know you love Jared—both of you.'

'He is my master's son.' Rajib said. 'I did what my master bid me. Now I must go home.'

'But you are angry?'

Rajib's eyes met hers, then he inclined his head once. 'You are not to blame. Nessa blames you for taking Jared's love, but I do not. I came to tell you this—and one other thing.'

'Thank you for your confidence,' Rosalyn said. 'What else did you wish to tell me, Rajib?'

'The *sahib* has gone to fight a duel with the man who came here today. I thought you should know.'

'A duel…' Rosalyn stared at him in dismay at having her fears confirmed. 'How do you know this?'

'He took his pistols with him. Besides, it is a matter of honour. The man who came here today attacked you. The *sahib* must kill him. It is his destiny.'

'No!' Rosalyn cried, her heart standing still with fright. 'Please, do not say so. He must not fight the *comte*. He could be killed.'

'The *sahib* will not die,' Rajib said and bowed his head to her. 'I shall not see you again, *mem-sahib*. In the morning Nessa and I will be gone.' He was about to turn away when Rosalyn stopped him.

'I should like to thank you,' she said. 'For what you did earlier today.'

'You saved my life,' he said. 'I have only given back what was owed.'

Rosalyn felt the barrier in place between them. It had always been there, though once for a few moments it had lifted—but they were from different worlds.

'Goodbye,' she said softly. 'I wish you and Nessa good fortune, Rajib.'

He bowed his head, his dark eyes giving nothing away. Then he turned and left her standing there alone.

Rosalyn felt suddenly light-headed. She was so tired! She sat down on the elegant daybed, gathering the cushions so that they made a pillow for her head.

She was concerned for Damian, but knew there was nothing she could do, except pray for his safety. She must think of her child and rest—but she would stay here for a while before she went back to bed.

* * *

The sound of a chair being overturned woke Rosalyn. She sat up, startled and blinking in the semi-darkness. Was someone in the room?

She strained her eyes to see, then got to her feet as she heard a muffled curse. 'Who is it?' she said. 'Who is there?'

'Rosalyn?' Relief swept over her as she heard Damian's voice. 'Damnation! Stay where you are—let me light a candle. I thought you long abed and asleep. Why are you sitting in the dark?'

The candle flared to life. The effort to fetch it had almost been too much for Damian. He was wounded! She saw him slump down on a sofa, a grimace of pain on his lips. Blood was seeping through his breeches. She strangled the scream of fright that rose to her lips. Now was not the time to become hysterical. He needed her help.

Oh, the foolish, foolish man—to fight a duel over such a small thing!

'Damian!' She went to him at once, her heart racing. 'What have you done? Have you fought a duel with the *comte*? Have you killed him?' She bent over him, catching the smell of brandy on his breath. 'You have been drinking!'

'Yes…a glass or two,' he muttered, sounding a little slurred. 'It helped to dull the pain when the physician dug Devere's ball out of my leg. Damn him for being a poor shot!'

'If he had not been, he might have killed you!'

Damian gave a snort of laughter. He seemed vastly amused and she wondered if he were drunk.

'Not a chance in hell. He meant to fire into the ground but the pistol misfired, his arm jerked and he hit me by accident.'

'How do you know he did not mean to hit you?'

Damian pulled a wry face. 'It would not have mattered if he had, he could not have done it in his condition; he was three sheets to the wind and could barely stand straight. Damn it! We should never have come to a duel in the first place if he had been sober.'

'You did not force it on him?'

He shook his head. 'Devere insisted. I tried to reason with the fool, but there was no dissuading him. He was adamant we should settle it between us in a gentlemanly fashion—and that it should be immediately.'

Rosalyn was looking at his wound. It had obviously been bound up but the blood had started to seep through the bandages.

'You should be in bed,' she said. 'Your wound has opened again.'

'I had to ride home,' he replied. 'Couldn't stay there all night. Devere wanted to give me a bed for the night, but somehow it didn't seem quite the thing to do in the circumstances.'

She saw a gleam of laughter in his eyes and recognised it: this was the old Damian, the man she had fallen in love with so desperately. He had come back to her. Whatever had happened that night had somehow released him from the shadow of his past.

'No, I would not think so,' she said, a faint smile on her lips. 'You have not killed him, then?'

'If I went round killing every man who wanted you, I should wipe out half the male population of wherever we happened to be,' he said, a wicked look in his eyes. 'I never intended to kill him in the first place. I just wanted to let Devere know he was not at liberty to insult my wife.'

'But you took your pistols with you…didn't you? You meant to challenge him to a duel.'

'Who told you that?' Damian groaned as he tried to stand. 'Was it Nessa? She is forever spying on me. Damn her impudence! She will have to go, Rosalyn. Jared won't like it, but it cannot be helped.'

'Rajib has already decided to leave,' Rosalyn said. 'He told me this evening. He believes Jared has outgrown him and Nessa—and I think he is right.'

'I shall not be sorry to see them go,' Damian replied with a frown. 'Rajib has proved his worth, but they have both resented me from the beginning. It will be better for us all if they leave.'

Rosalyn agreed, though she did not say. Her concern at that moment was for his injury.

'If you were to lean on me, Damian, I might be able to get you upstairs. Then I could change the dressing on your leg.'

'You will do nothing of the kind,' he replied. 'Sit

still and listen to me. In a few minutes you can summon a footman and he will take me up. You have been told to rest. Why are you not in bed?'

'I couldn't rest,' she said. 'I wanted to talk. We must talk, Damian. I do not know why you have been so restless of late, but…'

'Guilt,' he said frankly. 'Freddie was right, Rosalyn. I have taken you away from your home and family. I *have* laid you open to insult from men like Devere. I admit, it was in my mind to challenge him, but by the time I got there I realised it was ridiculous. Can't kill a man for wanting you. I meant to have it out with him. I demanded an apology—to you, not me—and would have knocked him down, but he was drunk. And then he insisted on the duel. I fired into the air, of course—and he meant to do the same. He apologised afterwards, both for wounding me and for insulting you. But the fact remains, I am at fault. I brought you to France. Had I not done so, this would not have happened. '

'I came because I wanted to,' she replied. 'Because I love you.'

'That does not make it right,' Damian said and winced. 'This damned leg is giving me hell. Would you pour me a glass of brandy, please?'

'Yes, of course.' She went over to the decanters on the sideboard and brought him back a glass half-filled with a pale golden liquid. 'You must let me look at your leg, Damian.'

'Later,' he said, gulping some of the brandy down. He gazed up at her as she stood over him, waiting to take the glass. 'Thank you, that was welcome. Have you seen your brother since we left England?'

The sudden change of subject made her stare.

'Yes. He brought me some papers to look over when we were in Paris. Charlotte told him where we were living—apparently he knows Edward. But why do you ask?'

'Why didn't you tell me he had called?'

'I did not think it was important.' She sighed. 'It was not a pleasant interview, Damian. He came only on business—and informed me that there would be no need for us to meet again.'

'Damn him! How dare he treat you so scurvily?' Damian was furious. 'That settles it. I was wrong to run away. I should have stayed and sorted things out. We must go back, Rosalyn—we must face up to the scandal. Only then shall we be free of it.'

'Go back…to England? Why?' The idea appalled her. 'Give up our dreams? What about Jared? How can we go back?'

'Jared will be safe enough now that he is no longer his father's heir. Besides, if we do not, the rumours will follow us,' he said. 'Don't you see, my love? We…I have to face those who would call me a murderer. And I intend that Freddie shall apologise to you.'

'I do not care what Freddie says or does.' Rosalyn was disturbed. He might be in serious trouble if they returned to England. He might even be accused of murder officially. 'No, I do not see why we should go back,' she said. 'We both know you did not kill Bernard Harrington, so…'

'Have you never thought it?' he asked, looking at her intently. 'Never for one moment?'

She could not lie when he looked at her like that.

'I have wondered once or twice,' she confessed. 'I believed it would have been for my sake, because he threatened me…and yet in my heart I knew you would have challenged him to a duel. I have never truly thought you capable of murder, Damian. Besides…'

'You loved me enough to come with me whatever the truth,' Damian said softly. 'You put your faith in me, your life in my hands. And because of your trust, I must go back…please try to understand that, my darling. If I force you to share my exile, I can never live with my conscience. Once before I let a woman down and she died because of it. She died of shame. I could not bear it if that happened to you.'

'Oh, Damian,' she cried, kneeling at his feet and looking up at him. 'How can you think that I…' Tears sparkled on the ends of her lashes and he bent down to brush them away with his fingers. 'I love you. I would follow you anywhere and never regret it for a moment.'

'You asked me why I have been restless,' he said. 'I shall try to tell you, though I hardly know myself. It is all so confused and goes back so many years. I left Helen alone in the garden that day. She begged me to go and I went…because my feelings had been so lacerated by what had been done to her that I could hardly bear to look at her. I did not truly think of her pain. I was so angry, so overcome with disgust, that I did not realise she was contemplating taking her own life. It was my fault she killed herself, Rosalyn. I failed her—'

'No!' She pressed her fingers to his lips, her eyes bright with tears as she felt his pain—the pain he had carried too long alone. 'No, my darling. How could you think that? How could you believe it was your fault? It was Bernard Harrington who shamed her. It was his vile act that drove her to take her own life. Whatever you had done that day, you could not have saved her if she was determined to die.'

'Yet I did nothing to help her,' he said, that haunting sadness in his eyes. 'I left her alone and she took her own life…. I think because I had shown my horror and revulsion too plainly. I fought that duel to ease my conscience, Rosalyn—and an innocent man died.'

'Hardly innocent,' she said. 'Roderick enticed her into that coach. He must share his brother's blame.'

'Did he deserve to die?' Damian looked into her eyes and found his answer there. 'No, my darling, he did not.' He smiled wryly. 'Can you see now why I have felt so frightened of losing you? Why I do not deserve the happiness you have given me?'

'I see that you were badly hurt when your father

called you a murderer and drove you into exile,' she said robustly. 'Roderick brought what happened on himself, Damian. Charlotte told me what happened that day. After his shot missed, you would have let him live. You were walking away when he fired at your back. You killed in self-defence. If there is blame, it is entirely his own.'

'I killed in anger,' he replied, determined that she should have the truth from him. 'The laws of duelling cleared me of murder—but my own conscience will not. I should have thrashed him for what he did, or put a ball in his shoulder—but I took my time and fired deliberately. I meant him to die, because of what he had done to that child—and she was a child, Rosalyn. Roderick deserved his punishment—though later I would have done anything to change what had occurred. I wantonly took a man's life, and it has haunted me all these years.'

'You wrong yourself,' Rosalyn cried. 'You are too hard on yourself.'

She saw what it was: his father had called him a murderer and alone, exiled from everyone he knew, he had come to believe it—but it was not so. Fate had played a cruel trick on him and he had suffered enough.

'Have you not paid for your mistake long since?' she asked. 'Damian, my dearest love. Is it not time to forgive yourself? To put the past behind you and think only of the future—of us?'

'Perhaps…but to do that, I must go back,' he said.

'I must face up to it—to whatever accounting may be demanded of me. Please try to understand, Rosalyn.'

'Yes,' she said. 'I see it now.' There was no denying him. Unless he followed his conscience, he would never be free of this guilt. 'Yes, you must go back, and I shall come with you. And now you must rest.'

'Then ring the bell for the footman and let us go to bed,' Damian said. 'This damned leg of mine is giving me hell!'

'But why should we go back to England?' Jared asked, looking at her angrily as they sat talking in the parlour the next morning. He jumped up, walking away from her, before turning to look at her once more. 'Damian promised we were going to Spain—and you promised we would breed horses.'

'We can still do that in England,' Rosalyn said. 'I am sorry you are disappointed, Jared. I am too—but Damian has to do this, for his own sake.' She could see he was still unconvinced, perhaps because he feared his freedom would be curtailed as it had been before. 'It may only be for a short time…'

'Damian broke his word,' Jared said. 'I'm going to find him—to have this out with him.' He walked off, his back stiff with pride.

'Jared…' Rosalyn was about to go after him when she heard a commotion in the hall. As she hesitated, a maid came in. She was carrying a huge basket of wonderful, exotic blooms: huge lilies, roses, camellias and several strange, new flowers Rosalyn had never seen before. 'This came for you, *madame*—and there are visitors asking to see you.'

'Thank you, Isabel,' Rosalyn said. 'You may leave the flowers. Please show the visitors in.'

She saw a card attached to the flowers and bent to pick it up. The flowers had come from the *comte* and she was still frowning over the message his card bore, when she became aware that two people had entered the room. Glancing up, she was shocked to see her brother and Beatrice standing there, looking hesitant and uncertain of their welcome.

'Beatrice!' she cried, getting to her feet gladly. Then she hesitated, looking at her brother uncertainly. 'Freddie…I do not understand, why have you come?'

'You did not get my letter?' Beatrice gave a little cry of distress. 'I sent it some days ago. It was to tell you that we should be calling today. I hope you do not mind that we have come, Rosalyn? My letter would have explained everything.'

'Of course I do not mind. It is a surprise—but I am pleased to see you, Beatrice. Of course I am,' Rosalyn said. She stood up and Beatrice came rushing to embrace her. She was so emotional that Rosalyn was surprised. 'Is something wrong, my dear? You are not ill?'

'No, not all,' Beatrice said, tears trickling down her cheeks. 'It is just that I have been so upset over this quarrel between you and Freddie. It was so unkind of him to deliberately cut you that night in Paris. I promise you, I have given him no peace over it.'

Rosalyn glanced at her brother. He looked ashamed of himself and was finding it hard to meet her gaze.

'Freddie?'

'It's deuced awkward you haven't had the letter,' he said. 'I suppose you still imagine I killed Harrington?'

'No,' Rosalyn said. 'It seemed to me once that you might have done it, Freddie—but I never believed you capable of such a thing, not truly.'

'You accused me of it!' he cried, indignantly. 'I can tell you, Ros, I was furious. Bea says I should apologise to you for…being so short with you, but I think you have something to apologise for, too.'

'If I accused you of murder, I do so unreservedly,' Rosalyn said, looking into his eyes. 'However, you accused Damian of the same crime. It was you who said you did not wish to be associated with the wife of a murderer. *You* who told me you had no wish to see me again.'

'Oh, Rosalyn!' cried Beatrice, gazing at her in distress. 'It was wicked of Freddie to speak to you like that—and I told him so, even before—' She broke off and looked straight at her husband. 'Tell her, Freddie. Tell your sister what has happened. We know the truth now, Rosalyn. We know who killed Bernard…'

'How can you?' Rosalyn stared at her, an icy chill

moving slowly down her spine. 'Unless…did she tell you herself?'

'You know!' Beatrice was astonished. Her eyes opened wide with distress. 'How can you know if you did not read my letter? We only discovered the truth after she died.'

'Mrs Jenkins is dead? Oh, I am so sorry,' Rosalyn said. 'Was it her illness? She seemed so much better before I left, that I quite thought she would soon be well again.'

'She…she took her own life,' Beatrice said, and began to cry into her handkerchief. 'It has been so awful. When we heard of her death, we had to leave Paris, to go home—and then to discover what she had done!' She ended on a sob.

Rosalyn went to her, putting an arm about her shoulders, leading her to the sofa. She pressed the sobbing girl to sit down. Beatrice turned to her, burying her face against her shoulder. Rosalyn comforted her, looking to Freddie for further clarification.

Freddie cleared his throat. 'Mrs Jenkins took something, laudanum, I think…foolish woman. If she had confided in us, I dare say we could have sorted things out between us. It need not have come to law. A man like that deserved all he got. She left a letter telling us the whole story.'

Rosalyn nodded. 'Yes, I imagine it played on her conscience. She discovered that it was Bernard who raped Helen Renshaw, didn't she? Roderick enticed Helen into his coach, but it was his brother who shamed her so deeply that she was driven to suicide. Damian did not know the whole story at that time. He went after Roderick and killed him in a duel…but it ought to have been Bernard Harrington who died that day, not his younger brother. The truth has haunted Damian for years. His father somehow discovered it, but it seems not to have been generally known.'

'It appears you know the whole story,' Freddie said, somewhat disgruntled at finding she had guessed the whole.

'I should have realised it at the time. Indeed, I did wonder. I know what must have happened. Mrs Jenkins heard me accuse Bernard Harrington of being his brother's true murderer,' Rosalyn said. 'When he attacked me in the garden, she was standing at the window on the landing and she heard everything.'

'Yes, that's about the size of it,' Freddie said, 'but not quite everything. You see, Bernard had been putting something in her powders to make her ill. He was hoping to inherit some of her money…and was prepared to hasten her death to get his hands on it.'

'He was poisoning her?' Rosalyn stared at him in shock. 'And she knew it. Of course, she knew he had been tampering with her powders after the doctor took them away…so when she heard the truth about her younger brother…'

'Who was the only person she ever really loved,' Beatrice said and sat up to dry her eyes on a lace kerchief. 'She took one of your father's pistols, Rosalyn, and she went after him. She killed him…intentionally. It was not an accident. She meant him to die. Her letter made that perfectly clear.'

'Oh, the poor woman,' Rosalyn cried. She had sensed that something was wrong that afternoon, after Bernard had assaulted her, when she'd knocked at Mrs Jenkins's door. It had crossed her mind that Mrs Jenkins might have witnessed the incident—but how could she have guessed what would happen later? 'How distraught she must have been to do such a terrible thing.'

'She said in her letter that she had nothing left to live for now that I was married,' Beatrice said. 'She has left everything to me—except a diamond brooch for you and also a letter confessing her crime, which she says you may do with as you wish. It was to bring you the letter and brooch that we came here today.'

'And to apologise,' Freddie said. 'Damn it, Ros! If you knew all along who had killed Harrington, why did you not say?'

'Because I could not be certain,' she replied. 'Besides, it did not matter so very much…or so I thought at the time. No one could prove anything one way or the other. We were leaving England for good and…I did not want to make more trouble for anyone. Besides—'

'Rosalyn loved me enough not to care what people might think of her,' Damian spoke from the doorway. 'It was only my foolish conscience that made me imagine a little scandal might matter to her. I know now that I was wrong. My wife is made of finer material than the rest of us, Freddie.'

Freddie's neck had gone bright red. He made an embarrassed noise in his throat, his gaze directed at somewhere beyond Damian's head as he apologised.

'I have been a damned idiot,' he said. 'I was furious because Rosalyn seemed to accuse me…and I *did* think it might have been you. If I had met Harrington when Bea first told me what he had tried to do to her, I might have thrashed him. I might even have killed him, if I could manage it, though it would have been with my bare hands, not a pistol. I have an aversion to guns. Nasty things, have a habit of making loud noises.'

'Oh, Freddie…' Beatrice got up and went over to him. She reached up to kiss his cheek, then looked at Damian. 'I hope you will forgive him, Lord Marlowe, because I do miss Rosalyn so very much. I could not bear it if we were never to be friends again.'

'Then I should be a brute to bear a grudge, should I not, Beatrice?' he said and smiled at her. 'Rosalyn, of course, has already forgiven you both, and I could do no less.' He limped across to where his wife was sitting, lowering himself a little awkwardly to lodge beside her.

'Should you be up?' Rosalyn asked, looking at him in concern. 'Your leg is obviously still painful.'

'A mere scratch,' he murmured, a wicked glint in his eyes. Her heart caught as she saw his smile. Damian had come back to her, all the dark clouds were gone. 'And quite my own fault. As any other woman would have pointed out long before this.'

'Had an accident, did you?' Freddie asked.

'Yes, you could say that,' Damian murmured with a glance at Rosalyn. He had noticed the huge basket of flowers. His mouth twisted in a wry smile. 'From an admirer?'

'An ex-admirer,' she replied. 'To apologise…'

'Ah…I see.' He nodded. 'I thought as much.'

'Damian?' Rosalyn looked at him, but the haunted look of the past few days had gone. She could see he was amused by the *comte*'s gift. Relief flooded through her: this was the man she loved, wanted to spend her life with. 'I think I shall keep them.'

'Yes, indeed. Why not?' He looked at Freddie, who was still hovering. 'Won't you sit down, Freddie? Care for some tea—or perhaps you might like to try a rather nice burgundy I have discovered? I bought several cases. You may take a couple back with you if you wish.' He stood up. 'Shall we leave the ladies to talk for a while…settle a few matters between us in my study?'

'Settle…' Freddie looked slightly alarmed, then recalled the papers he had left with his sister. 'Oh, business, I suppose? I gave Ros some papers, but I dare say she hasn't bothered to sign them. Never could get her to take an interest in things like that.'

Rosalyn watched as Damian limped off with her brother, then turned to Beatrice, who had come to sit beside her on the sofa once more.

'It is lovely to see you again,' Beatrice said and kissed her cheek. 'I was so cross with Freddie that night at the theatre, Rosalyn. We quarrelled over it and he went off in a temper the next day.'

'He came to see me—and he was in a terrible mood. I did not realise he had quarrelled with you.'

'Was he awful to you?'

'He was thoughtless, as he sometimes is,' Rosalyn replied carefully. 'I dare say you have not noticed, but…'

'Oh, I am well aware of Freddie's faults,' Beatrice said, a spark in her eyes. 'Do not imagine he can do no wrong in my eyes. He is used to having his own way. I think he has been spoiled, Rosalyn, but he must learn that he cannot always do just as he pleases. He must take more note of other people's feelings.'

Rosalyn smiled inwardly. There were hidden depths to her sister-in-law! She did not think Freddie would be getting quite so much of his own way in the future.

'I am sorry you quarrelled over me,' Rosalyn said. 'But I am glad that you persuaded him to visit us.

It is much preferable that we should all be on friendly terms.'

'He did not need so very much persuading once he had read my aunt's letter,' Beatrice said. 'That was very sad. If I had only guessed what was in her mind, I might have been able to do something…to prevent her taking her own life. I know she could be unpleasant when she chose, but I believe she had led a very unhappy life.'

'Yes, I think perhaps she had—and I dare say she had come to regret what she had done,' Rosalyn said. 'She was hurt and angry when she took Papa's pistol. Bernard said some cruel things that afternoon, things that must have driven her past the point of bearing. What she did was wrong, of course, but understandable in the circumstances.'

'I do not think it was so very wrong,' Beatrice said, a flush in her cheeks. 'He was a horrible man, Rosalyn. He frightened me and I am glad I shall not have to meet him ever again.'

Rosalyn kept her silence, as she had since it had first occurred to her that the most likely person to have killed Bernard Harrington was his own sister. It had been such a terrible thought that she had told herself she must be wrong.

'Well,' she said now. 'It has all been most unpleasant, but I think we should try to forget it and look to the future. Tell me, Beatrice—what did you think of Paris?'

* * *

Rosalyn was sitting, brushing her hair in front of her dressing table that night when Damian came in. She put down the brush and stood up, turning to greet him as he came towards her.

'Are you tired?' he asked. 'It has been quite a day for you, my love. And you ought to be resting.'

'I am perfectly well,' she said, opening her arms to him. 'I know I fainted yesterday, but…'

'Twice,' he reminded her. 'You must take care in your condition, Rosalyn. I do not want to risk your health, or that of our child.'

'Do not scold me,' she said, lifting her face for his kiss. 'It was very warm yesterday and I was feeling the heat. It has been much cooler today. Besides, I have been sitting with Beatrice most of the day.'

Damian kissed her, then released her, retreating to the bed to perch on the edge and watch as she finished brushing her hair. She was so beautiful, so serene. He could still not quite believe he had been lucky enough to find her…to marry her. Fortune had smiled on him at last. He must not let his memories destroy their happiness. It was time to let the past go.

'It was a surprise finding Freddie and Bea here,' he said. 'You had not realised they were coming, had you? I sent up some letters for you last evening—did you not read them?'

'I did not feel like it,' she said, 'and then I forgot.'

'It is not surprising, considering what happened later.' Damian frowned.

'It was quite an eventful evening,' she replied, laughing at him. 'First Rajib's announcement that he and Nessa were returning to India—and then you stumbling in with blood all over you.'

'I should not have disturbed you, had I known you were there.'

'But I am glad you did, my love.' She looked at him anxiously. 'Is your leg truly better?'

'Much. It is merely a scratch, Rosalyn.' Damian said, looking at her thoughtfully. 'I have been thinking. Do you want to be with your own people? Now that Mrs Jenkins has confessed to murdering her brother, we could go home without fear of scandal. We might not be universally welcomed, but I dare say we should soon make a few friends—enough so that you would not feel ostracised.'

'I have no doubt that we should be invited to the houses of all but a few narrow-minded people,' Rosalyn said. She put down her brush and moved towards him, the scent of her stirring his senses, making him aware of a sharp desire. 'And I should not care for them—but I have never cared particularly for mixing in polite society. It was not just the *comte*'s attentions that made me want to leave early the other evening, Damian. To be honest with you, I was bored.'

'As was I,' he admitted with a wry smile. 'I was

ready to go when you first asked me, but I thought you were doing it for my sake—so I was determined we would not leave. Perverse of me, I dare say.'

'You do not care for gambling, then?'

'It ruined my father,' he said, his mouth hard. 'Playing for small sums, for amusement's sake, is one thing—but reckless plays can be so destructive. Men who become addicted ruin themselves and their families. I worked hard for what I have, I see no point in throwing it away on the gaming tables. I can find better uses for it.'

Rosalyn stood before him as he sat on the edge of the bed. He put his hands about her hips, looking up at her.

'Do you still need to go back to England?' she asked. 'Jared was very upset about it—but if you want to go…'

'I do not need to go now that I have nothing to prove,' he said, pulling her down so that she was across his lap and gazing into her eyes. 'It is your choice, my love—we can go back to England or we can go to Spain as we planned…'

'We'll think about that tomorrow,' she whispered, pressing her lips to his neck, her tongue nibbling at his earlobe, teasing him so that he felt desire leap inside him. 'Does your leg hurt very much, Damian?'

He chuckled deep in his throat as he caught her meaning, then laid her back on the bed and bent over her, beginning to kiss and caress her with such tenderness that her body melted with delight.

'Not so much that I cannot make love to my wife,' he murmured throatily. 'You are so lovely…all that I have ever wanted…'

Rosalyn gave herself up to his loving, which was even more tender and sweet than it had ever been. Their bodies fit together perfectly, moving with a slow rhythm which brought them both gradually to a satisfying climax.

Long afterwards, Rosalyn lay with her head against his shoulder, dreaming of the future. She was not yet sure where it would take them, but she knew it would be wonderful.

* * * * *

CP